"Children will rebel against their parents and have them put to death..."

Matthew 10:21 (NASB)

MORE TITLES FROM KRISTOPHER RUFTY!

Hell Departed: Pillowface Vs. The Lurkers
Anathema
Master of Pain
(written with Wrath James White)
Something Violent
Seven Buried Hill
The Vampire of Plainfield
Desolation
Bigfoot Beach
The Lurking Season
Jagger
Proud Parents
The Skin Show
Oak Hollow
Pillowface
The Lurkers
Angel Board

Jackpot
(written with Shane McKenzie, Adam Cesare, & David Bernstein)
Last One Alive
A Dark Autumn

Collections:
Bone Chimes

PRANK NIGHT

Kristopher Rufty

Prank Night
2nd Paperback Edition
Text Copyright © 2013 by Kristopher Rufty
This Edition Copyright © 2021
Cover Art © 2021

ISBN: 9781492938583

For Brian Moreland.

ACKNOWLEDGEMENTS

Books are never the work of just one person, and this novel is no exception. There are so many people to thank on this roller coaster ride called a writing a career. First off, I want to say mega-thanks to Brian Moreland, for your friendship and all the advice you've given to me this last year. You are truly a blessing to the horror genre. I also want to give warm fuzzies to Ronald Malfi. Without Ron I would not be writing novels, end of story. And, very special thanks to my children, my Mom and Dad, Janet, Alan Spencer, Jeff Strand, Erin Sweet-Al Mehairi, Hunter Shea, Heather Graham, Kathleen Pickering, Aleka Nakis, Traci Hall, David Bernstein, Shane McKenzie, Vanelle, Kevin Woods, Jonathan Janz, Paul Synuria II, and so many more.

IT BEGINS

Cali Fortner twisted the dials. The water spraying from the showerhead ceased to a drip. She stood in the stall, shivering as steam billowed from her wet skin. There was a draft in here that never went away, even with the windows closed. Her tawny skin was slick and wet, her hair matted and tangled. She took a handful of the sand-colored mane, pulled it beside her face, and twisted. Heavy nuggets of water slapped the stall's floor.

Her hand was reaching for the curtain when she heard the faint thump of knocking.

Cali froze.

Tilting her head, she listened more attentively. *Did the heat click on?* Usually she could hear a bump when the fan in the unit outside started to spin. The thermostat hovered at seventy, and was constantly clicking on and off. And, it had been a colder than normal October.

She listened a bit longer before deciding she wouldn't hear anything else.

Cali gripped the cold wet curtain, tugging the plastic back on its dowel. A thin wall separated the toilet from the shower stall. A deep garden tub was on the opposite wall across from the shower. She rarely used the tub. It took too long to fill up, and she didn't have the patience to soak in soapy water unless she planned on using the massager attachment for areas it wasn't intended for. Usually she preferred hopping in the shower, washing, and getting out.

She'd left a folded towel on the toilet lid, and she quickly snatched it from the seat, hugging it to her breasts. Goose flesh had pimpled up her arms and sides. Her rigid nipples poked her hands through the thick fabric. She began wiping the water beads off her arms and chest. As her skin started to dry, the trembling slowed. By the time she wrapped the towel around her torso, it had stopped completely.

At the mirror, she wiped the wet fog off the glass, then flicked the excess on her fingers into the sink. She looked at herself in the saturated glass. There were dark crescents under her eyes, and she had frown lines arching down from her nose, trying to touch her chin. She was approaching forty, but thankfully didn't look it. The puffy bags under her eyes had been there since her twenties, and because she was a smoker, she couldn't help the lines around her mouth. She took daily walks and tried to visit the gym at least twice a week. Although she had a pack a day habit that she couldn't break, she took decent care of herself.

Her breasts weren't as perky and springy as they used to be, but still sat high on her chest. They weren't enormous, but she was pleased with their handful size. Her belly was flat, with a wavy, tight line intercepted by her navel. She turned around, stood up on her toes, and examined her rump. Two dimpled, glossy knolls sloped out from under the towel. She'd always wanted a bigger butt. Nothing colossal, but some kind of meat back there would be nice. Whenever she wore pants, it looked as if she had nothing but air in the rear.

Small butt aside, she was still known as Autumn Creek High School's Hot Librarian. She'd never become romantically involved with any of the students—although she suspected at least three teachers currently were—it still felt good knowing teenagers considered her a sexy woman. She wished adult men shared their enthusiasm. Cali was a member of every dating website on the internet, including the Christian ones, even though she was far from a Christian. She'd answered personal ads in magazines, newspapers, and social websites, but so far hadn't met a man worth keeping.

But, I still have Hot Librarian to my credit.

Maybe she should add that to her profiles. Cali Fortner, thirty-eight, slender and blonde, known by most of the male and some of the female students at Autumn Creek High as the *Hot Librarian*.

Smiling, she took the hairbrush from beside the sink and began grooming her gnarled hair. As the knotted pieces started to smooth and compress, she heard the *knocking* again. Standing in this spot, she was able to pinpoint its location:

The front door.

Her hand, maneuvering through her wet nest of hair, slowed its stroke.

What time is it?

She'd been watching a rerun of *Burn Notice,* and had caught herself dozing off, so she'd gotten off the couch, shut off the TV, and headed straight to the shower.

Has to be pushing midnight.

Who would be here at this hour?

A mess of possibilities fluttered through her mind. None of them were good. She kept coming back to the possibility that one of the many internet creeps she'd met online might have tracked her down. She'd encountered several weirdoes in the chat rooms, the kind of people she'd never thought actually existed, including some fetishists, men and women who found the oddest, sometimes most-appalling acts to be erotic.

But, ever since she'd read the novel, *Night Visitor,* by thriller writer Richard Karr, she'd become obsessed with the fear an internet stalker might one day get her information from one of her various profiles and pay her an unforeseen visit. In the book, a serial killer researched would-be victims on dating sites, stalked them, harassed them, and eventually brutally murdered them.

The knocking resonated again, not faster, but the force behind it was stronger—as if whoever was out there was getting annoyed. She stopped brushing her hair, letting the towel drop to the floor around her feet. She stepped out of it, took her robe from the back of the door, threw it on, and was tying it taut at her belly as she made her way through her bedroom.

In the short hallway outside the living room, she heard the squeaky groan of the storm door closing. Whoever had been knocking seemed to be leaving.

Cali entered the living room. The front door was metal with three panes of glass across the top. She saw the shadow of the screen door flickering as it slowly closed.

Just as well…

Cali really didn't want to risk answering the door to some sick-o whose fetish might be hot librarians.

Where she lived was private, but not secluded. At the end of Laurel Lane, a quiet and private street, her modular doublewide home was the last one on the left. The lot across from her was vacant, and she was divided from Mr. Macready's yard to her right by a line of trees and a wooden fence.

Not very secluded.

Secluded enough.

As she approached the front door, something heavy and wet splattered against the glass of her storm door, shattering it. She jumped back, gasping, hand rising to her mouth. Her fingers lightly brushed her lips.

Gloppy goo had spattered the jagged teeth of glass at the top, slowly smearing as it slid down. Footsteps crackled across the concrete of her front porch. She heard them descend the brick stairs, and become raspy when they met the grass. They continued fading until she couldn't hear them at all.

Cali ran to the door, pressing her chest flat against it. She could feel the coldness of the metal on her breasts through the thin robe. Leering through the glass, she couldn't see much thanks to the wax-like smudges.

"You better get the hell out of here before I call the cops!"

What's stopping me?

Her legs felt soft and stringy. She didn't trust them to carry her to the phone. Not just yet. She'd try in a minute. But by then, whoever did this would have gotten away.

Probably some kind of prank anyway…

At least it wasn't one of her windows. That would be much more costly than replacing the storm door. Still, it wasn't like she had tons of spare money available to throw at this.

Cali caught a whiff of something burning, and her already frazzled mood folded in on itself. *Where's that* coming *from?* She pointed her nose into the air, sniffing. It smelled like Thanksgiving. The stuffy scent reminded her of the year her mother had placed a pumpkin pie on the stove and torched it when she'd accidentally turned on the wrong burner.

She wrenched the door open. Grayish smoke stung her eyes. There was a football sized hole in the glass and from there it had spread snaky fissures across it. She heard soft tinkling sounds as the cracks continued to stretch. Carefully, her fingers pinched the clasp and pushed the door open, hopeful the glass wouldn't shatter and shred her skin as it rained down.

Thankfully, the glass held.

Cali's eyes followed the path of smoke to its source: a candle slowly charring its peach-colored inner walls. Shards had splattered the concrete at her feet, gooey and stringy innards surrounded the broken chunks. *A pumpkin.* Not just any old pumpkin, it had once been a jack-o'-lantern. She saw the pointy tips of a broken mouth.

She quickly stomped the flame out, wincing as her bare foot slid across slimy chunks. Lifting her foot, she looked at the smeared mess of pumpkin entrails clinging between her toes.

"Gross," she muttered. As nasty as it felt, she was glad it had soused her foot, shielding her from being burned.

Leaning back into the house, Cali flipped the light-switch next to the door paneling. Expecting her porch light to come on, it remained dark. *What the...?* She tried a couple more times to no avail, and looked up at the fixture.

The bulb was gone.

Her throat tightened. Her scalp went prickly. She always kept a working bulb in there. Someone, whoever smashed her window and the pumpkin no doubt, had taken the bulb. But, why would they do that?

No, she realized, *they hadn't taken it. They'd removed it so I couldn't cut it on and expose them.*

The need to get back behind locked doors and call the police became imperative. She whipped around, her feet sliding on the slippery pumpkin mess. She almost fell, but managed to save herself.

As she was shutting the door, it was suddenly jerked from her grasp.

Two ghosts barged in!

*No...*not actual ghosts—they'd taken old bed sheets and turned them into suits, even going as far to stitch fragments around their hands like mittens. She felt them on her skin, soft and downy, as they tore the robe away, exposing her naked body.

Her feet tangled at the ankles, tripping her. She dropped onto the hardwood floor, her skin squeaking as the floor grated fire across her body. She rolled onto her back. Her hip and thigh stung. She rubbed her hand across the ruddy markings on her skin.

Another figure emerged from outside, closing and locking the door behind him. He was also disguised, but his costume was devised of dark fabrics, a mantle hung around his knees like a cloak. His face was hidden behind black mesh, a hood shrouding his head.

Something popped a flash of bright light, blinding her momentarily. She blinked her eyes against the bursting splotches in front of her. The flash repeated. She looked to her left, and found one of the ghosts snapping pictures from an old Polaroid camera. It popped again, spewing a white and black square from the slit in the front.

"Please...What do you want? Go away..." She shielded her eyes with her hand as the ghost pranced around her excitedly, snapping pictures, the camera discharging the photos through its tight mouth. "*Stop* it!"

The other ghost—the shortest of the three—had a knife in each hand. Two black circles had been colored on the white face for his eyes, and his mouth was an averted gasping oval. Raising both hands, he began raking the knives across the other. The blades screeched, spouting sparks as he rolled his hands this way and that.

Finally the other ghost, whose sheets were plaid and white, stopped taking pictures. He joined the other ghosts, towering over her. None of them spoke. They just gazed at her blankly and motionless.

"What do you want from me?" It was pointless to ask, because she doubted they would answer. And, even if they would, she didn't want to know what they would say. "If you leave right now, I won't call the police. Okay? Just go. Leave." Her voice betrayed her, going thick and squeaky as she whined, "Pleeeaseee…"

The one in black advanced. He leaned over, grabbed her ankles, and heaved. Her buttocks felt as if someone had taken sandpaper to it as she was dragged across the floor. She squirmed, wriggled, and kicked, grabbing at the floor, hoping to catch a grip of something. Finally, she stopped fighting, allowing him to take her where he wanted.

Cali assumed their destination would be the bedroom and was expecting the three intruders would take turns raping her. *Oh God…I'm going to be raped!* She couldn't comprehend how or why this was happening to someone like her. She'd done nothing to deserve this. Mostly she'd lived a good life, done the right things, been nice to all the right people. And, now she was going to be raped…in her own bed.

To go to her bedroom the one in black would have to enter the hallway to his left. Instead, he continued going straight.

To the dining room.

He dropped her feet. Then he scooped her up under her arms and slammed her into the nearest chair. Her teeth clacked together. "Ow!" Before she had the chance to consider an escape, the dark ghost was pulling her arms behind the chair and trussing them with itchy rope. The one who'd been taking pictures began binding her feet to the legs of the chair with rope as well.

While they worked, Cali continued to plead. She hoped if she talked enough, maybe they would actually hear her. "Please…Tell me…What is this about? What are you going to do?" None of them replied, just continued tying her up whereas the third one stood off to the side, watching—his knives still moving.

That sound…the scrape and screech of the blades as they grated together was too much. Although she'd never been a Godly person, she began praying, and when she began to hear her voice over the ruckus she realized she was doing it aloud.

They finished binding her, then returned to the front of her. Standing in a formation, the shortest in the middle, still scraping those damn knives, the taller ones were fixed at each of his shoulders. They tilted their heads as if curious why she was reacting so frenziedly.

"Why are you duh-doing this? I didn't do anything wrong. I didn't do any—"

The bladed one stepped forward, approaching Cali with his right hand back, the piercing tip of a knife brightly reflecting light from a lamp in the corner.

Her pleading stopped. She knew it was useless to bother, and even if she wanted to, she had no voice left to try. Her final moments were here. She'd been a decent person in life, and if there was anyone to meet on the other side, she hoped they realized that.

Cali saw her distorted reflection in the knife as it plunged forward.

The blade punched into her throat.

She thrashed against her bondage, rocking and bucking. Trying to swallow, it felt as if she were choking. The blood streaming out felt like hot soup, deluging her breasts, and splashing her thighs.

With her life draining from her throat, the other two brandished their own knives and joined the shorter one. Together, they began to carve.

Worked at her face... removing her eyes ... slicing off her tongue.

CHAPTER 1

(✝)

"...*thought it was Christmas when I woke up this morning.*" The man's distorted voice penetrated the stillness of the room.

Tabitha Stoner's eyes cracked open. Lying on her side, her head was nuzzled into the pillow. Sometime during the night she'd tugged the blanket over her exposed ear and around her head like a shawl. She smacked her lips. They felt brittle and flaky. Her mouth was dry and consumed by the stale taste of morning breath. Thankfully no one would be rolling over to kiss her this morning and be forced to suffer her rancid breath.

It was dark in her bedroom except for a small spill of light on the floor from a night light. She kept it plugged into the wall underneath the heavy black drapes blocking the window.

"*Did you have presents under your Jack-o'-lantern?*" another voice asked, female, yet deep and raspy.

"*It was so cold my grass was white. I froze my butt off scraping the frost off my windshield.*"

"How do you think I feel? I wore a skirt this morning."

"I bet your lips are chapped."

They laughed.

"Oh nice, real nice. Trying to get us in trouble again?"

"Well, it's a nice skirt. Short and to the point."

The morning DJs continued their throwaway conversation in the background, but Tabitha paid it no attention. She hated this show and found the hosts to be incredibly annoying. Which was why she'd chosen them as her alarm clock—the necessity to shut them off got her out of bed every morning without fail.

She sat up, swinging her legs around the side of the mattress. From the warmth under the blankets, the room felt chilly. She hugged her chest, rubbing the goose bumps on her arms. She'd slept in a tank top and yoga pants. A year ago, she'd vowed to start taking Yoga, so she'd purchased a few pairs of pants for her new hobby. After only three classes, she'd had enough confirmation to decide Yoga was not for her. She'd kept the pants, though. They were the most comfortable clothes she owned.

And she liked the way they shaped her legs and butt.

The DJs were still swapping irritating dialect from her clock radio. She glared at the time displayed in red blocky letters. *5:45 am.* Seeing that configuration of numbers never failed to make her groan. She ran a hand through her mussed hair, reached forward with the other, and flicked the switch on the clock to the off position. The distorted chatter went away, and she was glad to be rid of it.

Sitting back up, her hair hung in front of her face like a veil. She poked out her bottom lip and shot a gust of air into her messy locks. *At least the four-day weekend starts tomorrow.* Technically, it was only a regular weekend, with tomorrow (Friday) and Monday being teacher workdays. However, if she wanted to, she could go in late or leave early, but just being at the school without the children made the work seem not so arduous.

She rubbed her eyes with her fists and stood up. The carpet felt warm and ticklish under her feet. She arched her soles, putting her weight on her toes, and held out her arms at shoulder height. Slowly stretching, she focused on her feet first as she wiggled her teensy digits, letting the tugging sensation travel into her calves, through her thighs, and into her lower back. Then she quavered at the waist, guiding the tingles up into her shoulders, and wiggling her fingers as the stretch seemed to flow out from under her fingernails.

Her body felt much better, and she was even tempted to have a quick jog before taking a shower. *Forget it. Too cold.* It had dropped down into the low forties last night. This kind of weather was common in Wisconsin, where she was raised, but in North Carolina it was rare.

Tabitha had lived in Autumn Creek for almost three years, since accepting a teaching job at the elementary school, and although the leaves usually had altered from dark greens to flamboyant yellows and reds by now, the temperature was usually still crawling toward the eighties. She was no longer accustomed to this kind of weather, but she welcomed the cold. Made it feel like home.

But the nostalgia still couldn't make her jog in it.

Kicking a trail through dirty laundry scattering her floor, she made her way to the dresser. It was Thursday, laundry day. And having the next few days to herself, she planned to wash all of it. Maybe she'd finally go through the boxes of old clothes in the basement she'd neglected to sort after moving in.

Don't get ahead of yourself.

If she just dropped the boxes off with Goodwill, they would sort through them for her, but she didn't want to risk one of her more diaphanous outfits to have been accidentally tossed in with those old rags. She could just hear the residents of Autumn Creek gossiping about the fifth grade English teacher's lingerie.

Can't believe such a sweet girl, such a good teacher, would wear something so slutty.

Even Tabitha couldn't believe she owned them.

Those had been the old days, back when she'd been engaged to Clint Robinson.

Ages ago...

She tugged open the top dresser drawer, grabbing the first pairs of panties and a bra she saw. She couldn't care less if they matched. Then she crossed the room to her closet, opened the door, and went inside. A string of thin metal dangled from the center of the cramped space. She grabbed at the air a moment before her fingers found the pull cord, yanking it down. Dim light pushed the blackness against the clothes.

It was Halloween, and the faculty encouraged its students to dress festively in accordance to whatever holiday. She had nothing to wear with black cats, witches, or goblins flaunting the front of it. *Thank God for that.* She was thirty-four, not sixty-four, and doubted she would ever own anything of the sort. She decided to wear all black, which would match her wavy black hair. Plus, her caramel-colored skin (a unique and lovely shade thanks to her African American father and Asian mother) might look somewhat ashen against the solid black material.

Maybe I'll put some powder on my face to pale it even more.

Forget it.

Too much work for a holiday she didn't really care about. It wasn't that she hated it, but she hadn't really enjoyed Halloween since she was a kid. Which contradicted her moving to a town notorious for its Halloween carnival. Sadly, as much she regretted it, the holiday had become nothing more than a night she sat on the couch with a bowl of popcorn watching bad horror movies on TV. Sometimes trick-or-treaters came by, mostly they did not.

Maybe if she had someone to enjoy Halloween with, or to take trick-or-treating...

She shook her head, stopping those thoughts.

So what if *she* wasn't in the Halloween spirit this year, her students were. She could suffer a little for their sake. The kids would be tickled to see Ms. Stoner dressed up for Halloween.

Tabitha sorted through the clothes. She found her knee-length black skirt, then turned around and examined her blouses and sweaters that hung from the rod on the other side of the closet. It took two searches before she spotted her plain black sweater. She crouched down. Under the clothes on both sides of the closet were shoes: tennis and everyday shoes under the sweaters and blouses, boots and heels under the skirts and pants. She scanned her boots and chose a black knee-high pair that zipped on the sides.

With her outfit selected, she stood up, cut off the light, and exited the closet.

She chucked the clothes onto her unkempt bed on her way out of the bedroom.

Tabitha walked down the hall into the bathroom, shutting and locking the door. She was about to shower and hated doing so in a room without a lock. Maybe it was the movie *Psycho* or the plethora of movies that ripped off its infamous scene, but she had a love/hate relationship with showers. She loved how they made her feel, how they cleansed and revivified her, but she despised how they deafened her to all sounds beyond the bathtub.

She lifted the toilet lid, slid her pants and panties down to her ankles, and stepped out of them. She sat down on the cold porcelain lid and winced. It felt like frozen needles stabbing into her rump. But, just as quickly as it had shocked her, it began to fade. She emptied her bladder, wiped. Then she headed over to the tub and turned on the faucet. The old pipes behind the wall groaned as they began to heat up. Water shot down from the shower nozzle. She adjusted the temperature to the hottest she could stand.

Tabitha stripped of her tank top. Her breasts prickled from the chilly air, so she quickly stepped over the tub and into the streams. Hot water hammered her. At first it stung her skin, but soon it was perfect. She let out a long sigh as she eased her face into it. The pounding pressure against her eyes and mouth hurt a tad, but she didn't care.

Tabitha grabbed the shampoo, squirted a hefty mound in her hand, and massaged it through her hair. A yawn surprised her. As good as the shower was making her feel, she still was exhausted.

Tabitha was up late last night. Again. Grading papers and mapping out her lesson plans for the Christmas quarter. She'd also gotten a jump-start on report cards. It would save her some work this weekend. It was long after midnight before she finally reached a stopping point.

Glancing at her body, she discovered she'd lathered it in a sudsy coat of soap and had yet to wash it off. She stepped under the spray. The soap spilled down her body. When she was finally clear of all the suds, she took some shaving cream and frothed her leg from ankle to hip. Carefully, she went to work. When all the shaving cream was gone, Tabitha rubbed her caramel legs. Smooth and slick and gleaming. She studied the usually spruce band of hair between her thighs. It had grown to a tuft and needed to be trimmed, but she didn't feel like messing with it right now. *Not like anyone will be seeing it anytime soon.* All done, she climbed out, dried her body, and put on her robe. She then wrapped a fresh, dry towel around her wet head.

Tabitha opened the door. Steam coiled into the hallway as if she was stepping out of a portal. From the warmth of the shower, the hallway felt like a freezer. Shivering, she pranced up the hall, through the living room, and hung a left to go for the kitchen.

Her house was a one story, ranch-style abode. The floors were a combination of hardwood and carpet. She'd chosen to paint soft colors over the harsh whites the walls had been when she moved in. On cold nights when she fired up the gas logs, it put off the atmosphere of being in a cabin in the mountains. The exterior was made up of bricks and stones, like a house from Bedrock. She loved it here. Before she'd come along, the house had sat empty for almost a decade.

Tabitha turned on the kitchen light. The kitchen was shaped like an L, a narrow rectangle that branched to the right where a side door led outside. She thought the design was unique and added to the house's charm.

Three years ago, her father was killed in a car accident, and after the arduous paperwork and myriad meetings with lawyers and the Clerk of Court, she'd learned Daddy had left her everything. It wasn't terribly much, but enough that she could live comfortably for a few years to come. Soon after, her mother hired a lawyer, and took her to court, suing her for Daddy's life insurance money and belongings.

Although it was thrown out of court rather quickly, her relationship with her mother had been severed. She decided to put her resume online and hoped for the best. A month later came a blessing, a possible job in North Carolina at Autumn Creek Elementary.

She flew out here, took a tour of the school, and told Superintendent Connor before they were even finished walking the main floor, she would take the job. He gave her his wife's business card (she was in real estate) and told her about the house on Amity Hill Road.

Tabitha made an appointment to meet Jill Connor in front of the school. An hour later she was following the superintendent's wife to Amity Hill Road, to the house located where the road dead-ended.

And the rest, as they say, was history.

Tabitha opened the cabinet, found her coffee container, and scooped a few spoonfuls into the coffeemaker. Then she poured water into its side compartment and clicked it on. As the coffee began to brew, she hurried back to her bedroom, and prepared her *costume.*

When she was finished getting ready, she returned to the kitchen, and found a full pot of coffee waiting for her. She grabbed her thermos from the dish rack and emptied the coffee pot into it. She sat the pot back on the burner, then shut off the machine.

The condiments were kept in a basket on top of the microwave. She opened three packs of sugar and dumped them in. Then she walked over to the fridge, retrieved the hazelnut creamer from inside, and added it. The dark black liquid turned creamy brown. She capped the thermos with the lid and shook it for nearly a full minute to mix it all together.

In the living room, she grabbed her shoulder bag and purse. She stuffed her arms into the sleeves, threw her bag over her shoulder, and carried her coffee and purse with her to the door. She fetched her keys from the mantle on her way outside.

The cold air slapped her. She hunkered over, scrunching her shoulders up to her ears to block the chilly wind as she used her key to lock both the knob and deadbolt. She hurried down the porch steps and onto the gravel driveway.

And froze at the front left tire of her Nissan Altima.

The rubber was flat on the rocks. She checked the rear tire. It was the same. *What the hell?* She crossed the frontend, finding both tires on the passenger side matched the others.

Gashes were in the sidewalls. All four of her tires had been slashed.

(11)

Sheriff Ben Holly parked his Jeep at the mouth of the driveway, gazing into Cali Fortner's front yard. He counted four deputy cars on the lawn since he'd sent two officers out to investigate the slew of vandalism reports. Apparently, several tires had been slashed during the night.

Ben moved his eyes to the driveway, finding a white van behind Cali's car. He recognized the van and had expected it to be here. *Dr. Warner.* Other than what he'd already spotted, there were no other cars.

The press hadn't shown up.

He snorted.

The press.

That was an exaggeration. The local *press* consisted of four of Autumn Creek's eldest residents, and their journalism expertise ranged from local sports to farming. The more mainstream affairs were either read online or in the *Charlotte Observer*. What made Autumn Creek prominent, when it wasn't the Halloween season, were the farms: dairy, pig, chicken, and produce farms made up the majority of Webster County.

Yet still…Once those old kooks caught wind of this, they'd be here to obtain all the information they could get.

Ben's eyes landed back on the house. He shook his head.

Cali Fortner.

Two years ago, they'd dated for a brief but wonderful stint of four months. She was still his favorite of the countless ex-girlfriends he'd accumulated over the years. She'd challenged him, had a great sense of humor, and was great to be around. Plus, she was the most dynamic lover he'd shared a bed with—enthusiastic and charming, the perfect partner.

What had gone wrong?

Me.

He'd started screwing around with Patti Thompson, a waitress from Quigley's Diner in Hollyleaf. It had been a foolish affair that, he was certain, had also wounded Cali's self-esteem because of Patti being ten years younger.

He had never been able to forget the hurt in Cali's eyes when she'd found out.

The affair with Patti ended shortly after Cali broke things off with him. Again, no fault of Patti's, all of it was Ben's. She hadn't dated anyone since Ben yet had somehow gained a two-year-old daughter with Ben's eyes who she'd named Christian. He supposed he was the father, but Patti wouldn't admit it. She'd made it clear that she wanted nothing else to do with him, even if it was just child support. Most of the time, he felt a selfish relief knowing that, but sometimes there were those lonely nights when he'd like to know for sure. If he *was* the girl's father, maybe a relationship with her wouldn't be a bad thing. A father influence in her life could steer her away from guys who might take advantage of her—guys like Ben.

Sighing, he reached over the seat, grabbed his hat, and climbed out into a damp cloud of bitter cold air. He clenched his teeth against the sharp embrace. The sun was rising in the east, disgorging orange into the gunmetal grey sky, and hopefully bringing some warmer temperatures with it. He wasn't sure what the high for the day was supposed to be, but he remembered the forecast calling for record-breaking lows through the weekend.

On his way to the front door, he put his round-brimmed hat on. The bow pushed his hair, making the twenty minutes of styling and gel this morning purposeless. He reached behind his padded coat to the chest pocket of his uniform shirt where he kept his cigarettes. Fishing one out, he placed it between his cold-dry lips, lighting it.

Ben was good at his job and the residents of Autumn Creek, plus the other four towns populating Webster County respected him for it. But his reputation of being a womanizer hampered his appeal. He never feared he'd lose at re-election, but his *loving* repute most likely left a sour taste in the voters' mouths. How some of the women smugly communicated with him made him think they secretly thought he wanted to bed them. And some of them, he probably wouldn't mind.

One day they might not reelect me when someone younger and stronger comes along.

He'd vowed to focus even more on his constabulary duties, leaving the women alone, but he was only fooling himself if he truly thought he could. He was a good-looking man, with a strong jaw and hairline. He was tall, lean, and always kept just a brush of stubble on his cheeks. Single women—and a lot of married women—ate it up.

"Sheriff!"

Puffing on the cigarette, Ben looked through discolored smoke toward the front door. Deputy Carla Jenson had exited the house and was galloping down the porch steps. Her dark hair was slicked straight back on her head and tied in a tight knot in the back, so it didn't sway with the movements of her body. Like Ben, she wore her padded coat. Her breasts rocked tightly behind her badge.

"Good morning, Deputy Jenson."

"Hardly a good morning, Sheriff." She joined him in the yard. "Got an extra one of those?"

"For you? Always."

Either she was blushing, or the cold had turned her cheeks red. Ben figured it might have been a little of both. He and Carla had never had sex, though they'd shared everything leading up to the actual act. She was aware of his experienced status and had successfully eluded his efforts of taking her to bed. He doubted she would hold out forever and hated himself for knowing he would take advantage of it.

He passed her a cigarette, then fired his Zippo lighter, holding up the flame so she could lean over and ignite the end. She stood up straight, puffing the filter until the fire took hold. She inhaled a heavy drag, sighing as she let it fan out through her nostrils.

"You don't look like you feel too well, Carla."

She shook her head. "I don't. And when you see inside, you'll understand why."

Ben's stomach tingled. "That bad?"

She huffed out a deriding laugh with a puff of smoke. "I wanted to catch you on your way in."

"What do you...?"

Carla cut him off. "I know you two used to have something going on, so I wanted to give you a heads up before you saw her."

"Is it *really* that bad?"

"Ben, it's so brutal it doesn't seem real. Like it's some kind of awful scene in a horror movie."

He studied her. The natural dark complexion of her skin was pale and sickly. True fear was in her eyes. "Okay...thanks..." He turned toward the house. His legs suddenly felt so weak he doubted they could carry him up the porch steps. "Do me a favor and a keep an eye out for the press."

"Want me to keep them back?"

"Yeah. For now. Tell them the investigation is ongoing and I'll make an official statement later."

"If they come."

"*Big* if for now, but eventually they'll be all over us. If not here, at the station later."

Carla nodded. "Will do." She studied him a moment. "Are you going to be okay?"

He felt her hand slip under his coat and wave circles on his back. It felt good to have her touching him, assuring. "I don't know yet, Carla. I don't know." He glanced back at her. She flashed a quick grin at him that wasn't convincing. He gave one back to her that was probably even less. "Hang around out here for as long as you need. Get some air."

"Thank you, Ben."

He watched her walk toward her cruiser, a sway in her step. Still dazed from what she'd seen. As much as he didn't want to go in the house, he knew they were waiting for him inside. He took a deep breath, letting it out slowly.

Ben took the steps up to the porch, carefully, one at time with a hand on the guard rail. Nails were loose, so it wobbled in his grip as he approached the front door. He saw the shattered glass, the carpet of jagged shards on the porch, and the mushed rotted pumpkin among it. Grimacing, he looked away. From where he was on the porch, he could hear indistinct voices barking back and forth from inside. Quick flashes registered from the living room, then went dark again.

Probably Deputy Rileson taking pictures of the scene.

Ben took a deep breath, flicked the cigarette into the yard, and entered the home of Cali Fortner for the first time in two years, which had turned into the scene of a homicide during the night.

As soon as he'd crossed the threshold, he could tell he was in the house of a dead person. It was a feeling he could never explain, but it was the same every time—a familiar place abandoned by the person who used to reside there. Even the house seemed to be in mourning, an emptiness that Ben could feel to the marrow in his bones. It seemed even worse this time, like losing a spouse, although he hadn't spoken to Cali in a very long time.

"Guys, it's Ben," he called from the living room.

"We're in here," answered Deputy Carpenter, entering from the dining room. Carpenter, his youngest and freshest deputy, had only been on the force for a few months. He was just eighteen, tall and wiry, and wore glasses that looked more like side view mirrors from a classic Mustang. Appearances aside, he was a good kid and, so far, had been a good deputy.

"I heard it's bad," said Ben.

Carpenter's already pasty face would be translucent if it got any whiter. "It is sir...I'm not sure if you want to go in just yet..."

"Save it. I appreciate your concern, but it's my job."

"Right."

"No offense meant."

"None taken."

"Good." Ben crossed the living room and joined his young deputy. "What am I going to see when I get in there?"

Carpenter opened his mouth to speak, but no words came forth.

Ben nodded once. "That's all the confirmation I need." He stepped past Carpenter, and into the dining room, just as the room popped from the high-quality flash bulb adorning the top of their crime scene camera. When he saw what remained of Cali in the blinding burst, his breakfast belched up from his stomach and shot out of his mouth. Thick froth splashed the floor at her bare feet.

Ben looked away, coughing as the bile singed the back of his throat. Carpenter was there in a hurry with an antibiotic wipe. Ben took it, swabbing the gooey strings of phlegm dangling from his lips.

He took several deep breaths, then forced himself to take a second look.

Cali was tied to a chair, her arms pulled taut behind her back. She was naked and the color of her skin had turned an unnatural blue around the areas of blood and black bruises.

Ben gagged again, raising the back of his hand to his mouth. Such abhorring exhibitions of murder, early stages of decay, usually had little effect on Ben, and that was true in this situation as well. Sure, he had known the victim, intimately, and even though it had caused him great pain seeing her this way, it wasn't what had made him throw up once already and threatened a repeat. What had caused his abnormal reaction wasn't just the shape her body had been left in. Not entirely. It was awful, no doubt the most brutal he'd ever seen.

But her head...

The once lovely face had been mangled, produced to what could only be described as a flesh-colored jack-o'-lantern on top of a naked woman's torso. Her hair dressed her cheeks and touched the tops of her shoulders in straw-like strands. A stick candle flickered orange swashes behind her hollowed triangle eyes and crooked mouth. The candle had melted down to a quarter's height. Where her once grassy green eyes had been were now two triangle-shaped cavities. Her lower jaw looked as if it had been removed completely, along with her upper row of teeth, to make the zigzagged mouth even bigger.

"Jesus H. Christ..."

Dr. Warner quickly approached Ben, took him by the arm, and led him back into the living room.

Carpenter followed.

The coroner, who was also the county doctor as well as the local undertaker, spoke in a hushed voice. "God Almighty, Ben, what did you think you were doing?"

Ben shook his head. He tried to shrug his shoulders, but it caused his stomach to flex which in return made him heave again.

Warner frowned. He removed the latex gloves from his hands and stuffed them down into the pocket of his white lab coat.

Dr. Russell Warner had been the county's one-man pathology team for over thirty years. At sixty-seven he was still good at his job, possessing the momentum of a person two times younger. He used a finger to push his black, plastic glasses back on the smooth bridge of his nose. What hair he had left on his head was cotton-white and outlined the base of his skull. His face was younger than his age and matched his personality: kind and pleasant. "I know you have to examine the scene, but damn it, there had to have been a better way."

"It's okay," said Ben. "It's my own fault. Carpenter and Jenson warned me, but I underestimated the severity of it." Ben moved out of Warner's support and stood with his hands on his hips. "Why was the damn candle still burning?"

Warner looked at Carpenter.

Ben took a deep, quivery breath. "The damn candle in her mouth. Why was it still burning?"

The young deputy's eyes rose like a child about to be scolded. "Well, no one wanted to…uh…get close…"

"Carpenter will you kindly go tell either Rileson or Duggins to blow that fucking candle out that's in her mouth?"

He nodded once. "Yes sir." Then he hurried back into the dining room.

Ben could hear him quietly relaying the message to his other deputies.

Dr. Warner leaned against the couch, resting his butt on the back of it. "This is bad."

"You think?" He looked up at the old man who suddenly looked his age.

"Are you going to be okay?"

He waved a hand. "I'll be fine."

"Sure?"

"Not really." He took a deep breath, held it a moment before slowly letting it out. "What can you tell me so far?"

Dr. Warner removed his glasses and began wiping the lenses with his thumb. "She was already dead before this was done to her."

"Well…that's reassuring."

Warner sighed again. "Come on, Ben. Snap out of this kick in the teeth and get your head back into your job."

Nodding, Ben straightened his shoulders, trying to steel himself. The air came into his lungs like icy pin pricks, making his chest and back ache. "You're right…I'm sorry."

"No need for apologies. I just need you to be Sheriff Holly right now and not Ben, Cali Fortner's friend."

"Absolutely." Ben pursed his lips and puffed out a quick blow of air. "I'm all right now." He took another deep breath. "What else do you know?"

"Your deputies will have to inform you on how they think the murderers got in. I can only give you my initial approximation of her death. Judging postmortem, I estimate that she's been deceased for about two days…"

"Two days?" Warner nodded. "But the candle—that would mean someone has been coming in and swapping out the candle?"

"Or relighting it."

Ben couldn't grasp the morbidity of the notion. "Jesus…"

Warner continued. "But, after the autopsy I can give you more concrete information of course."

"Of course." Ben paused. "Murderers? Plural?"

Warner put his glasses back on and nodded. "Yes. There were multiple knives used on her and, now I'm only guessing, but I believe they were used simultaneously. From the numerous points of penetration, it looks as if there were at least five different knives…used by different hands. This is just an assumption, but I believe there were two, maybe more, killers."

"Shit."

"It's hard to know for sure, not until I can examine her better."

"Right. I'll get this moving quicker so we can release the body into your care."

"No rush, Ben. I'm going to go out to my van and get a body bag ready. Will one of your deputies assist me with the stretcher?"

"Absolutely." Ben stared at Warner, seeing something in the cultivated old man's face he never had before. Worry, distress, and maybe even some fear. "Are *you* okay, Russell?"

Warner smiled without merit. "Sure, Ben, sure." His expression suggested otherwise.

"Are you sure?"

"For now."

Ben narrowed his eyes, considering Warner a moment before he faced the dining room. "Duggins? Come here once, huh?"

The quick approach of boots on hardwood increased as Deputy John Duggins appeared in the doorway. "Yeah, Ben."

Duggins was the Deputy Sheriff, not a Sheriff's Deputy. Two years younger than Ben, he sported a clipped beard, reddish-blonde hair that was slightly thinning. He was married to Jill Duggins, and together they were the parents of twin eight-year-old girls: Lisa and Lane.

Duggins was also the closest, and perhaps the only friend Ben had.

"Would you go outside with Dr. Warner and assist him for a minute?"

"Yeah, of course." Duggins approached Ben, patting him on the shoulder as he walked by. "Let me know if you need to talk."

"I'm sure I will once this slows down."

"No problem."

Warner nodded once in greeting, then led Duggins outside.

Now that he was alone, Ben could feel an urge to weep reeling inside. He took several deep breaths to settle himself. The last thing he needed to do at this moment was break down in front of his deputies, but he supposed the first thing he *should* do, personally, was question the neighbor and find out if he heard or saw anything suspicious. *Like someone returning to the scene of the crime to set a candle in her mouth.* Ben doubted he had, or they probably would have heard about it sooner.

It had been the high school principal who'd phoned in a request for Cali's house to be checked out since she had failed to show up for work. This morning marked two days in a row without calling. He'd been trying to reach her to no avail and couldn't visit her himself on account of school regulations.

Guess I better head over there.

Anything to get him out of here for a few minutes, far away from the...corpse.

Ben put a cigarette in his mouth, gnawing at the cotton filter.

His gut was telling him as bad as this situation was, it was about to get a lot worse. And Ben was rarely wrong when it came to his gut feelings.

(III)

Jackie Farrell had Joey's lunch packed and sitting on the counter. She looked at the personal cooler with Minecraft printed across the front, smiling. She wondered what the kids would think was cool next year, and which childish visual element Joey would pick to have exhibited across his lunchbox.

If we allow him to go back next year.

Jackie had home-schooled Joey until this year. After they'd moved to Autumn Creek so her husband Allen could take over pastoral duties for the Blessed Waters Community Church, Joey had become friends with the local kids at church. And the desire to go to their school had started almost immediately. She'd managed to convince him that being home-schooled was what he really wanted last semester, but he couldn't be swayed this year. Joey was determined to go to Autumn Creek Elementary this year. So far, he seemed to be enjoying the fifth grade, and liked his teacher Ms. Stoner. Jackie even suspected he had a crush on the cherished educator. She was very pretty, but since she never attended church, Jackie's conversations with her had been strictly school related. She'd like to get to know her. They were around the same age and finding friends in this small town her age who weren't raffishly out of control had been nearly impossible.

The soft taps of feet on linoleum called Jackie's attention. Turning around, she saw her ten-year-old son running into the kitchen. He was dressed like a character from Minecraft, his favorite game and one of the few that was allowed in the house. He had it on their IPad tablet and the Xbox and played it devotedly everyday—if his parents allowed it. Jackie didn't mind the game and even sat down to play it herself on occasion.

Smiling, she was surprised how well the costume had turned out;

being that she'd made it for him. The large cardboard box that with its splotchy face colored on the front, the clothes and fake sword, all put together he looked like a live-action version of his character, Steve.

"Lookin' good, Joey."

"Thanks, Mom!"

Her smile faltered some. Since starting public school, he'd stopped calling her Mommy and Allen Daddy. Now it was just the simple Mom and Dad unless he was excited or wanting something.

"The bus should be here in a minute. You ready to head outside and wait for it?"

"The bus?" asked Joey. He grabbed his lunchbox, shaking his head.

"Yes. You know the big orange vehicle that transports kids to and from school?" Smiling, she went to ruffle his hair, but forgot she couldn't get to it from the box on his head.

Joey reached up and tilted the box back from his face, making him look as if he had a cube of hair. He looked so much like a shrunken down Allen right now that she wondered if Joey had acquired *any* of her traits. Maybe it was the lines in his face from the confused frown.

Jackie was about to ask what had him so bothered, but the phone rang.

Its chirping chime seemed to relax him some.

Jackie was tempted to ignore it since they needed to get to the end of the driveway before the bus. It was an endless guess as to what time the bus would actually roll by. It was never the same time each morning. But Joey had already headed for the cradle where the cordless phone sat. Snatching it from the base, he read the screen. "It's the school."

"What?" She walked around the island, passing Joey's lunchbox on her way to where Joey stood with the phone held out to her. Taking the phone, she read the screen herself.

Autumn Elementary: 716-525-5013

"Are you going to answer it?" asked Joey.

"Hmm?" She looked at Joey, momentarily forgetting the phone.

"Oh, right." She pressed the *Talk* button and raised it to her ear.

A pre-recorded voice of Mr. Horton, the principal, came on.

Good Morning. Principal Horton calling. There will no bus transportation this morning due to vandalism of our buses. We've reached out to the middle and high school for assistance but have since learned they are also victims of vandals. If your child will be coming to school today, you will have to provide their transportation yourself. I apologize for the nuisance this will cause. We hope to have this problem resolved by the time students return to school next Tuesday after the four-day break. Have a good day and Happy Halloween. Seems the pranksters are going to be out in full force tonight.

A robotic woman's voice came on afterward: *If you'd like to repeat this message press one, if not, you may hang up.*

Jackie pressed one and listened to Horton's announcement in full one more time. When it ended, she cut the phone off and stared at it as if she might be able to figure out why she was so…

So what?

Spooked.

A cold prickly sensation scattered up her spine.

"Are you okay, Mom?"

Jackie stared at the phone, her thumb rubbing the little grid of holes covering the transmitter. How could the buses at all three schools have been vandalized during the night? And *how* were they vandalized? Horton hadn't said, but she suspected it was something pretty severe if it couldn't have been repaired in an orderly manner. And what he'd said at the end had really bothered her, the part about pranksters.

"*Mom?*"

Gasping, Jackie nearly dropped the phone, but managed to catch it against her belly. "Don't shout, Joey!"

"I didn't. You're shouting."

Jackie closed her eyes, took a deep breath. Her heart slammed inside, making her throat cluck. She felt a migraine trying to come on. Putting the phone down, she walked over to the fridge and took down the basket from the top. Inside they stored over-the-counter medicines, bandages, and gauze. She popped two Tylenols and dry-gulped them. When she turned around Joey was standing at the backdoor that led outside, the sword held out, his lunchbox dangling by his thigh. The light above the doorway wasn't on, so he was bathed in shadow. Her sweat turned frigid seeing him like that. He looked nothing at all cute or imaginative like he had in the light. Now he looked like some kind of…intruder.

Stop. You're bothered by the phone call, that's all.

"We're going to be late," Joey said, his voice muffled and flat behind the cardboard helmet.

Jackie gave him a smile that felt awkward on her face. "Right. Since when are you so eager to get to school."

"Mommm."

"Okay, okay. Forget I asked. Let's go."

She headed for the backdoor, grabbing her keys from the rack on the wall. The spot for Allen's was empty. The mower and shed key were all that remained, twinkling in the shadowy space like fireflies.

They headed outside. The cool air was a frosty slap on her warm skin. She wished she'd have thought to grab her jacket. She decided to leave it, not wanting to risk another groan from her son for having to go back inside.

And because of the phone call, for the first time since moving to Autumn Creek she locked the door.

(iv)

With the windows up in his car and knowing there was no way anyone could hear him, Pastor Allen Farrell felt completely secure in his singing abilities. As Chris Tomlin blared from the radio, he sang along loud enough to make his chest hurt. He was halfway through the second chorus when Jackie called to inform him what had been done to the buses. She'd seemed very upset, though she kept promising she was okay. He'd told her he'd ask around and see if he could find out what had happened. She was on her way to the school with Joey as he pulled into the parking lot of the Blessed Waters Community Church.

"Let me call you back in a little while, okay honey?"

"Is everything all right?" she asked, the alarm returning to her voice.

"Well…" He'd never once lied to her a day in his life, even so much as editing the truth for her benefit. "I don't know. I'm a few cars short this morning."

Actually, he was *every* car short of his ration, and withholding even something so small to her made him feel guilty.

"You mean they're not there?"

"Right. I'll call you later, okay?"

She sighed. "Okay. Love you."

"Love you, too."

He hung up the phone and set it in his lap as he steered toward his parking space. To keep the main parking lot empty, the staff—from the salaried to the volunteers—always parked in the back, even during the week. He hadn't told her about his other calls during his drive to the church, but he would later. She already seemed concerned enough as it was.

I should've said something, at least.

He wasn't sure he agreed with that. When she was at home and could sit down, he'd tell her about the calls from *some* of his staff to tell him their tires had been slashed in the night and were trying to get replacements so they could come to work. Judging the empty lot, he assumed the damage was more prevalent than he was aware of. Thankfully, their cars had been spared, probably because they were locked up in the garage. He wished he could say the same for the others.

He parked in his designated space and shut off the engine.

Allen was the lead pastor and loved his job. At thirty-six, he was the youngest to not only be voted into the Blessed Waters Ministry, but by far the youngest ever to lead it. But times were changing, and the deacons understood this, so they'd allowed him to take over, granting him the freedom to run the church as if they didn't exist, by his own methods and ideas.

So, he'd done just that, and so far, it had been a successful transition.

He'd brought in two more pastors no older than himself from other churches and, together, they'd completely turned the church from a crumbling eyesore the town only glanced at sullenly in passing, into a fun and exciting place to be. It'd become so popular that he was thinking of opening another campus on the western side of the county where his other pastors lived.

One of the reasons, he assumed, they continuously attracted so many people to the church was because of the building's renovation from a traditional church into a unique worship center. They'd avoided putting a new steeple on the roof when the old one had been taken down due to weather damage and opted for a large sign that only stated the name of the building. It wasn't conventional by any means, but everyone seemed to prefer it.

As he climbed out of his car, he heard the sighs of tires on asphalt taking a turn too sharply. He spotted Judith's car swerving into the lot's entrance, plumes of dust being thrown up behind her like a jet stream. She was later than normal, but he was gracious she'd made it in at all. Judith was already on staff when Allen took over, and she'd welcomed him on board compassionately. On any other day she would have been the first one inside with the day mapped out for the rest of them, and a fresh pot of coffee brewing in the kitchen by the time the rest staggered in.

Her car squealed to a halt in her parking spot. She already had the door open before the engine had completely shut off. Springing from the car, she slammed two large white boxes onto the roof in one swift motion as the engine puttered to silence. Allen recognized the boxes from Alice's Bakery.

Judith turned to face Allen in a rush that swung her lemon-colored hair out in wave.

"Slow down, Judith, you're going to make *me* sweat." He smiled and waved. One of the many things Jackie always complimented him on was his smile. He always good-humoredly retorted by giving all the credit to God because he had ugly parents with hideous smiles. "I see you got some tires." He took the box down from her car. The sweet doughy aroma of pastries emanated from the box, carrying into his nostrils.

Judith slammed her door. She had her pocketbook over her shoulder, and her carry bag in front of her. "Yeah, barely. Tom couldn't find anyone with Jeep tires in stock, so he got stranded at home and I had to take the kids to school. I thought I would run by Alice's and get us some treats, but I was *not* expecting that kind of line."

"Busy?"

"It was like she was going out of business or something. The line was out the door by the time I left. So many people had their tires slashed last night, Allen, that it's a little scary. It's all they were talking about at the bakery."

"I bet so. But you're here, so it's okay. Thankfully, you got some replacements for yours."

Judith nodded. "True. I was trying to call you on my way in to let you know I'd be here, but for some reason I couldn't keep a signal." She exhaled a heavy breath.

Allen frowned, adjusting the boxes to one arm. "Odd." Checking his phone, he saw his regular four bars had dropped to one. He'd just had full-service minutes ago when he was talking to Jackie. Putting the phone away, he decided not to give it much thought. Cell towers weren't too reliable anywhere, but out here in the sticks they seemed to be particularly temperamental. "Looks like it's just us for the time being," he said, leading their trek for the backdoor. "Hopefully, more will start rolling in before too long."

"I doubt it. Apparently, this whole tire thing is pretty serious."

"No worries." He unlocked the backdoor and held it open for Judith. "I guess once we get inside, I'll start making calls to see who all needs a ride and go pick them up."

"You'll be driving all morning."

"I hope not."

"You might want to take the church bus."

By bus, she was referring to their remodeled service van. He'd purchased it from the school system and had four rows of seats installed. They'd only used it a handful of times, for transporting the youth mostly, to and from events.

"Good idea," he said.

Turning his head, he saw the van sitting at the edge of the yard beyond the parking lot. Even from this great distance he could tell it sat lower to the ground than normal.

"Great," he said.

"What?" said Judith, poking her head out. She stared at the van, eyes squinted. "Oh, no. Are the...?"

"Yes," he finished for her. "The tires are flat."

CHAPTER 2

(I)

Tabitha had finished the coffee in her thermos by the time she saw the old truck zipping around the bend in her driveway. A block of woods was to the right of the driveway and an open field to left that led to more woods on the other side. It was a nice change from the residential street she lived on in Wisconsin, where she could reach through her bathroom window and tap fingers across the siding of the house next door.

She stood up on the steps, brushed off the back of her skirt, and waved. Two quick beeps fired back from the rusting Toyota as it squeaked to a halt. The engine was loud and rackety, coughing exhaust, obviously protesting being out in the cold today.

She could relate.

Tabitha gathered up her things and sauntered to the truck. On the side wall of the truck's bed, she noticed several lines of black duct tape covering a copious number of rusted holes and gashes in the metal.

Hope the truck can even get to the school.

She opened the door and was greeted by Becky Loflin's smiling grille of white teeth. A head band with black cat ears protruding from the top of her head pushed spiral curls away from her rotund but pretty face. Shorter than Tabitha, she had a narrow waist that slanted down to ample hips and muscular legs. She wore a purple buttoned-down shirt on top of a white tee with a black skirt and fishnets. Other than ears and hose, she didn't look to be dressed up for the holiday. Becky taught third grade and was adored by *all* her students. Outside of the office staff, she was the first member of the faculty Tabitha had met, and they'd become instant friends. Within a few minutes of chitchat with Becky, Tabitha felt as if she'd known the petite third grade teacher all her life.

"Like my ride?"

"Thankfully, I recognized this old beater from you helping me move in or I might have called the cops."

Becky coughed a laugh. "Well, after I got off the phone with you, I went to crank the car so it could warm up and found my tires had been slashed also."

Tabitha settled in the seat. "You're kidding." She shut the door.

"Wish I was."

"*Your* tires?"

"Yep. Thankfully, Tom had taken the Ram with him out of town, because if he'd left that for me to drive, it would have been parked where I usually park the car. I guess the bastards that did the slashing didn't see the beater behind the house."

Becky was right about the Ram. They'd have slashed its oversized tires as well since the only thing the Loflin's used their garage for was storage. Becky's husband Tom was an antique dealer and collector. He made decent money doing it, too. In fact, the reason why he was out of town was because he was in Georgia acquiring several crates of things that were old and valuable.

Shifting the gear into reverse, Becky backed onto the grass to turn around. She stopped, her eyes staring at the house.

"What is it?" asked Tabitha.

"How can you live out here all by yourself? It's so creepy."

"No, it's not!"

Becky laughed. "The hell it isn't!" She shoved the gear into first and started to pull away. "I'd be scared of a maniac hiding in the woods."

"Gee, thanks. Put that idea in my head."

"Sorry, sorry."

"You talk like I'm shut off from the rest of the world. I have neighbors." Just then, they drove past a house on the other side of the woods. "See?"

"I guess you're not *completely* a recluse, but close enough."

Tabitha laughed.

Amity Hill Road was a private dirt road that branched off from Cedar Drive. The houses located here had been built and scattered all over the woodland. Tabitha enjoyed the isolated privacy. She liked not being able to see or hear any of her neighbors. But Becky was right, even though she would never verbally admit it. It was creepy out here, especially at night.

"So," Becky began, "who do you think got knife happy with our tires?"

"Who knows…could've been anybody I guess."

"Pissed off any students lately?" Becky laughed.

"Come on, my students aren't capable of anything like that, and even if they were, their parents should be keeping them inside after dark."

"True. That's not always the case, though."

"I suppose not."

"So, did you call Sully's about new tires?"

"No, I'm going to call from the school."

"Don't expect them to have anything in stock. I called and apparently, we're not the only ones that woke up with slashed tires this morning. He was out of stock on everything. And he said his backorder list is several pages long already. They should have a shipment in a few days."

"Great." Tabitha sighed. "That's Halloween for you."

"The pranks?"

Tabitha nodded. "Always jerks out there taking things too far."

"Not here. This is new to me."

They entered the downtown district of Autumn Creek: rows of historic buildings on both sides of the street that were local businesses, Sheriff's station, courthouse, post office and one lawyer office. No popular fast-food chains to be seen, only Mom and Pop establishments with some of the best food Tabitha had ever tasted. She wished they had time to stop by Alice's Bakery so she could refill her thermos with coffee and grab a bagel, but there was no time. It was heartbreaking to smell the wonderful aromas of pastries only to zip by without stopping.

"Mmm, smells good," said Becky, apparently thinking the same thing.

Tabitha stared at the bakery through the glass. The customer line trailed out the door, and as the truck puttered past, heads turned to watch them with irritated grim expressions.

Probably wondering how this truck got so lucky.

They braked at the four-way intersection of the town square. Not one car was coming from any direction, so Becky signaled, turning right onto Warrington Avenue. The school was at the end of this road and could already be seen from here, cresting the hill.

Built in 1957, the elementary school was two stories high and still bricked by the same aboriginal bricks it had been built with. There had never been any renovations other than adding central heat and air, and a plethora of interior paint jobs. Another building branched off behind the main one that housed the gym and auditorium. The parking lots were too small, and the playground areas too big. They had more land than school, but the kids didn't seem to mind.

"It's really cold this morning," said Becky, trying to kill the silence.

"I know. If you wouldn't have come and picked me up, I would've had to walk to school."

"Malarkey my dear."

Tabitha smiled, shook her head. "Thanks for coming to my rescue."

Becky shrugged. "Eh, I had nothing else to do this morning."

They both laughed, but their lighthearted banter died when they noticed the parking lot.

"Oh my God," Becky muttered.

"What the hell happened here?"

Becky stopped the car where the buses were parked. From the looks of it, none of them had been able to move since being parked yesterday afternoon. Three maintenance vans were parked near the buses, workers scurrying back and forth, removing the flattened tires off the buses, and hurriedly replacing them with good ones.

From what Tabitha could tell, there weren't nearly enough new tires to replace all the damaged ones. Becky eased the truck past the buses, avoiding the frenetic working men, but neither of the women could tear their eyes away from the hectic scene transpiring outside the truck. The truck rolled across the connecting path to the faculty parking lot on the other side of the school, slowing as Becky steered into her space. The lot was almost entirely deserted, save six or so cars. It looked as if the vandals hadn't nailed *every* teacher's car but judging the numbers they did get; it hardly felt like a victory in the staff's favor.

"What the hell is going on?" asked Becky.

"I...don't know."

Both sat in silence. Tabitha assumed she and Becky were sharing the same apprehensive thoughts. At first, what she thought was possibly a few sporadic acts of vandalism looked to be shaping into a widespread operation.

"Looks like we're a few short today," said Becky, insinuating the lack of cars occupying the faculty lot.

"Do you see anyone from the cafeteria?"

"No."

"Great. What are the kids going to eat?"

"How many kids will be here, do you think?"

Tabitha shrugged. "Not many, probably."

"Well…let's get inside and find out how bad the damage is."

They exited the truck. Tabitha left her thermos behind. Outside, she bumped her door shut with a hip, throwing her bag on her shoulder. She walked around to the front and waited for Becky at the headlights. Looking across the field to where the middle school was located, she could see at least two service vans parked by their buses as well. "They got the middle school, too."

Becky dropped her keys in her purse. "And the high school." She pointed her thumb over her shoulder.

Tabitha looked past Becky. Across the street was the high school. Its parking lot looked eerie and abandoned, except for a short expanse of orange that were the buses parked in formation on the right side of the building. Service vans sat in front of them as an army of workers attended to the tires.

This is out of control.

"Come on," said Becky.

"Yuh-yeah…" Tabitha took a few steps backward, not taking her eyes away from the high school. Finally, she turned around, and followed Becky to the side entrance of Autumn Elementary.

(11)

Tabitha and Becky stood with Principal Horton in the teacher's lounge. He peevishly tugged at the tie under his sweater vest. His forehead was shiny with sweat, and his jet-black hair was oiled straight back on his head to cover the bald spot at the back of his skull.

"Eggs all over the damn place…" He shook his head and took a careful sip of coffee from his *An A for an Ass-kisser* mug.

For the past ten minutes, he'd been sharing the story with Tabitha and Becky about how he'd wakened this morning to discover busted eggs across the siding of his house and smeared glops of yolk across the windows. His and his wife's cars had been locked up safely in the garage, and he figured that the vandals were angry about that, so they'd egged his house.

Tabitha agreed.

"So, what's the plan for today?" asked Becky.

For as long as they'd been slumming around in the teacher's lounge, drinking coffee, no one else other than Principal Horton had come in. Students weren't due in for another ten minutes, but Tabitha doubted she'd have much of a homeroom to tend to.

"We'll have to play it by ear. More of the staff will be coming in, but they'll be late, or at least I think they're coming. Some were able to find rides, but so far, the majority has called out. Same goes for the students. I say we do a final role call in an hour or so and just go from there. If there's not that many here, or if there are more students than teachers, I'm just going to cancel the rest of the classes and send everyone home. Unless I can think of anything else before then."

They all settled on that idea.

Tabitha and Becky excused themselves and left the lounge. They walked through the halls shoulder to elbow since Tabitha was much taller.

"I'm telling you, Tab, this is some weird junk."

"It's scary."

"That too. I mean—I can't *believe* this. What's going on here?"

"I don't know. My tires, your tires, the other teachers and staff…"

"The buses."

"Yeah, the buses."

"It's so weird."

Tabitha scratched her head. Her scalp felt sticky from the hairspray holding her wavy hair in place. "It's more than weird…" She stopped talking.

Becky put a hand on her arm. They ceased their march. "What are you saying?"

"I don't know." She sighed. "I mean…it just seems like the whole thing was calculated. Doesn't it seem like there's a method behind it or something?"

Becky made a face. "What do you mean?"

What do I mean?

Tabitha shrugged. "I have no idea. I don't think I mean anything."

"You were scaring me..." Becky playfully swatted Tabitha's shoulder.

I'm scaring myself, but this does seem like it's part of a strategy.

They started walking again. She wanted to kick herself for allowing such nonsense to even ripen in her brain.

Part of what?

Nothing. It wasn't part of anything.

Tabitha could see the blue sign above the doorway marking Becky's classroom by the white numbers stamped on the front. The door was bedecked in Halloween illustrations created by her students and a large paper decoration of a hissing black cat. "Well, here I am," Becky stated. "See you at lunch."

"Bye."

Tabitha left Becky at the door. She could hear the rattle and snap of her unlocking the door behind her. She approached a set of blue doors. Usually, they would have been propped open already by one of the janitors, but this morning they were nevertheless closed.

Looks like Mike and Abigail didn't make it in.

She pushed the doors open and kicked the pegs down on each one to keep them braced open.

She avoided the science hall on her way to the stairs. At the end of the hallway, hunched in the corner as if hidden from the rest of the building was a stairwell. It led to a flat landing, then another set of stairs took off to the upper floor.

The fourth and fifth grade hall.

She slunk past unoccupied classrooms, their doors closed, lights off. It was quiet up here, too much for Tabitha's liking. She could feel the stillness pressing against her ear drums. *Feels like I'm walking through a sauna.* The silence around her was unsettling. She picked up speed, nearly jogging the rest of the way to her room. She fished the keys out of her bag. Her hands trembled as she tried to fit the key into the lock.

Knock it off! she ordered herself.

She stopped, closed her eyes, and took a deep breath to calm herself. She hated getting worked up like this and wasn't going to allow it to happen now.

Finally, she attempted the lock again, and this time succeeded.

Entering the classroom, Tabitha quickly turned on the lights. The long cylinder bulbs ticked, then began to hum as yellowish fluorescent light spilled through the empty room. Being in here didn't feel any better. *Like a damn funeral home.* She remembered her father's viewing, and right away she regretted thinking about it. She shivered. Her arms were bumpy with goose flesh, and a trickle of sweat slid down her side. She hung her jacket on the rack behind the door, went to her desk, and sat down.

Tabitha unpacked her bag. With the lesson plan for the day open on her desk, she turned the chair to face the doorway.

And waited for her students to arrive.

(III)

Katie Carpenter was the first student to saunter in. She wasn't wearing a costume, nor had Tabitha anticipated her to. She was a good kid, extremely smart, but she isolated herself from the other students as well as any kind of activity that might be considered fun.

Or that might help her make friends.

Her older brother had just graduated high school last year and took a summer course for law enforcement. He was now a deputy, and still attending Webster County's community college. Tabitha had heard nothing but good things about him. There was even talk that in a few years he could be sheriff.

"Good morning, Katie."

"Morning, Miss Stoner." She heaved her backpack off her shoulders, sat in her assigned chair, and placed her backpack at her feet. Her lava-colored hair was pulled back in a ponytail. She was taller than most of the other students, and very thin. A pretty girl, with eyes so blue they looked as if they were chiseled from sapphires. "Anyone else coming in today?"

"I don't know," said Tabitha. "I guess we'll see, huh?"

Katie nodded. She sat there, obviously uncomfortable, and nervous to be the only student in the classroom.

Tabitha smiled. "If you want, you can pick a book off my special shelf over there to read."

Smiling, Katie slid out of her desk, and trotted over to the bookcase. It was a half size case that Tabitha kept stocked full of books. She called it her *special* shelf because the students were amazed by some of the titles she carried. The books were all age appropriate, but the school's library didn't shelve any of them.

Katie chose a voodoo story written by a popular YA author. Tabitha hadn't read that one personally to approve it, but the age range on the spine ended at eleven, and Katie was ten so it should be fine.

As Katie returned to her seat, Nicole Henderson came bounding in. Her pale cheeks were pink from the cold air. Her yellow-white hair jutted up straight from her head. "Hey, Ms. Stoner."

"Hey, Nicole. You made it, huh?"

"Yeah." There was disappointment in her voice.

"What are you supposed to be?"

Nicole patted her wild hair with a smile. "I stuck my finger in a power outlet!"

Tabitha laughed. "That's great. How'd you get your hair to stand up like that?"

"Mama used Daddy's hair gel."

"Ah." Tabitha laughed again. "Have a seat, and we'll see who else shows up this morning."

"Okay." She walked to her seat, her bright hair spiked behind her, and sat.

44

Another student rushed in. This one had a bulky block for a head, wore a green shirt and jeans, and clutched a cardboard sword in one hand and a lunchbox with an identical-looking character across the front in the other. She recognized the book bag and lunchbox as belonging to Joey Farrell. She adored him. He was one of her favorite students.

"Well, I see we have a new student joining us today," Tabitha said.

The girls giggled as Joey found his desk and began to sit down.

"I wouldn't sit there," said Tabitha. "That's Joey Farrell's desk and he won't take too kindly to anyone messing with it."

Joey reached up, putting a hand on each side of his cubed head. Lifting off the helmet, she saw Joey's sweet face underneath, albeit with sweaty hair and red cheeks. "It's me, Ms. Stoner!" He spoke in a way that suggested Tabitha was incompetent of understanding even the simplest of ideas.

Putting her hand to her chest, Tabitha exaggerated a gasp. "Joey? My *goodness*! I had no idea."

Joey beamed with pride as he set the helmet/mask on his desk. "Like it?"

"It's a *great* costume."

His cheeks darkened even more. "Thanks."

Thirty minutes passed and she'd acquired two more of her students: Eric Brady who was dressed like a football player, and Maggie Barnes donning a witch's outfit. Tabitha waited another fifteen minutes. When no one else had made their way in, she assumed that was all she'd get for the day.

Five students. Really packing the seats.

Tabitha sighed. She had to come up with something quick to keep the few unlucky ones busy and in good spirits. She'd decided not to continue with her originally planned lesson since so many would miss it. Glancing at her special bookcase, her eyes immediately found the *Scary Stories to Tell in the Dark* series on the bottom shelf. She smiled, doubting that any of the students would object to her reading to them some creepy—yet somehow child appropriate—stories.

CHAPTER 3

(1)

Officer Karen Albright swung open the door to Alice's Bakery, throwing a splash of light onto the several customers waiting at the booth. A dozen or more heads turned in her direction, frowns and aggravated expressions masking their usual cheerful faces. When they saw her, their frustrations seemed to lift slightly, and she was greeted enthusiastically.

"Hey there!"

"What brings you in today?"

"Good seeing such a pretty face on such a dreary morning!"

Albright smiled. "Good morning, everyone. I see some of you are getting around on your own accord."

Herman Dobson shook his head. He was tall, with a block for a head, and dark hair. His bangs hung in an even strip across his forehead. He'd been the caretaker of Shady Elms Cemetery ever since Albright was a little girl. A kind man, gentle spoken with a deeply loud voice, and a pair of crystal-like eyes. But, because of his ogre-like appearance, it was no wonder he'd acquired the unfortunate nickname—*Herman Munster.*

"I've been hearing about all over town," said Herman. "Lots of tires been popped."

Albright nodded. "Yeah, it's been a mess all morning. Hodges and I have been pretty much going door-to-door to get statements. It's all over town."

Winston Chambers, the postmaster, waddled away from the front counter. A pink box, probably packed full of glazed doughnuts, was tucked under his arm. He was a plump man with a sagging corpulent gut and a bushy moustache over his top lip. He had on his thick, postal service coat, and a cap with fluffy muffs covering his ears. The postman was never in a good mood, and today looked to be no different. "What's that Ben Holly planning on doing about it?"

"Everything he can," answered Albright, taking her place at the back of the line. "Everything he can."

"I hardly believe that." He turned around, bumping the door open with his behind. More light poured in. "What's he going to do about what I told him about?"

At first Albright wasn't sure what Chambers meant, but the memory came to her. Two months ago, he'd reported spotting a bunch of kids congregating in one of the fields behind Patterson's farm, and the next day he'd seen even younger kids out there playing. Since it was private property, he thought children of any age shouldn't be anywhere near it. Albright had to agree.

I wonder if Ben ever did anything to stop the trespassing.

To save face, Albright shrugged. "He's on it."

"Sure he is." Sighing, Chambers shook his head as if he was what held this tiny community together. "He only does what he can to get by."

"That's your opinion and you're entitled to it."

"Winston, it's too early for your mess," said Herman.

"Just stating facts," Winston claimed before stepping outside. The door slowly swayed shut, engulfing them once again in shadowy dimness.

With Winston Chambers no longer consuming the room with his complaints, Albright could detect the faint sounds of music coming from the old-fashioned jukebox in the corner. It took her a moment to recognize the song.

I'm Your Boogie Man.

Though it wasn't necessarily a Halloween tune, it somehow seemed to fit the holiday. Albright smiled. She enjoyed coming here, and she didn't mind the ridicule she got for it. Sure, it was common practice to tease cops about doughnut shops, but if all of them were this good, she could understand why. The bakery gave off a good mood, peaceful, relaxing; a place you could come and sit while you drank your coffee and enjoyed your soup or delicious pastries.

Betty Wetzel was the owner. She'd bought it from Alice Griswold ten years ago after a stroke had left her incapable of conserving the bakery any longer. Albright had also known Betty since she was a little girl. Saw her every Sunday at church as well, and on holidays, sometimes even cookouts and get-togethers.

Betty was her aunt, and she could see her scurrying behind the counter from where she stood, running back and forth from the racks to the register. No one acted bothered that it was taking her longer than normal. Maybe it was Albright's presence that made them remember their manners.

Betty glanced up and saw Albright. A smile curved her lips. "Hey, Karen."

"Good Morning, Aunt Betty."

"Getting the usual for you and Greg?"

"You know it."

"Okay. I'll put it on your tab. It'll be ready in a few." She flung back her head, getting the bangs that had slipped out from under her hairnet away from her eyes.

And by putting it on her tab, Betty really meant it was free as usual. "No hurry."

"Please. I know you're in a hurry with all that's going on."

That was true. Albright couldn't deny how crazy her morning had been. The Fortner murder that thankfully hadn't leaked out into town yet, plus the vandalisms that kept her and Hodges driving all over town all morning gathering statements. So far, all the accounts had pretty much been the same. The vehicle's owners had come outside to leave for work, take kids to school, or to run an errand and had discovered all four of their tires ripped open and flat. She'd lost count of how many they'd already talked to, and the list they hadn't even touched on yet continued to grow.

She sighed. Whenever she thought about how much work they had to do today, she began to sweat. *Don't let it get to you.*

Oh, sure.

It was the victim's anger that she hated dealing with. How they always expected her to have it figured out and the problem resolved before leaving the residence. Just like Mr. Chambers. They assume because you wear a badge, then you have all the answers. But the reality was, she was just as confused as the rest of them.

Even her tires had been slashed, but she hadn't told anyone. Not even Hodges.

(11)

Jackie carried the dirty laundry into the washroom with both arms. She felt a few pieces drop off along the way. She'd go back and pick them up, then add them with the others.

The laundry room was down the hall and to the left where another shorter hall branched off. There was only one light, which was above the washer and dryer, so she had to walk the short distance shrouded in darkness. She felt the light hairs on her arms stand along with those on the back of her neck. Her scalp went crawly and tingly.

What is wrong with me?

Shaking her head, Jackie stopped in front of the washer and dumped the laundry inside while simultaneously leaning to the side and flipping the light on with her elbow. She spread the clothing out around the agitator to prevent the machine from locking up. It was a large load inside an old machine, and she wasn't taking any chances. Once the clothes were all inside the tub, she leaned forward, resting her elbows on the brim.

And sighed.

"Get it together, Jackie."

She'd been home from dropping off Joey at school for more than twenty minutes and she was already almost crazy with dread. She could feel it in her chest and stomach, a cold squeeze in her back. It was the buses that had started it, but when she'd talked to Allen and he'd mentioned the staff had also been vandalized, she hadn't been able to shake this icky feeling inside.

Maybe it was the holiday. It was the time of year for people to be scared, so it was possible she was just really into the holiday spirit. Slightly smirking at herself, she poured detergent into the washer and pushed the start button. She then hurried out of the laundry room, leaving the light on.

I should call Allen back now that I'm home.

She'd tried during the drive back but had been unable to keep a signal long enough for the call to connect. There had never been a problem before with her cell service. But, for whatever reason, it seemed to not exist on the way home.

Her phone sat on the coffee table in the living room. As she walked by, ignoring her panties that she'd dropped from the laundry load, she snatched the phone up and checked the screen. No bars with *Searching for Service* in red over the picture of Joey and Allen she'd chosen as her background. Frowning, she set the phone on the arm of the couch and headed for the kitchen.

The cordless phone was on the counter where she'd left it this morning. Picking it up, she thumbed the button. The sound of the dial tone brought a relieved sigh out of her. It took her two tries to dial the church because of her jittery fingers.

As the other line rang in her ear, she took two deep breaths.

"Blessed Waters Community Church," said Judith, on the fifth ring.

"Hey Judith, it's Jackie."

"Good morning! How are things?"

"Well, not *too* bad out here, but I've heard it's not so good everywhere else."

"Oh my *gosh*, you have no idea."

Judith told her about her morning, the visit to the bakery, adding her own theories and nonexclusive gossip.

"That's awful," said Jackie. "I bet Sheriff Holly's going to have his hands full today."

"I bet so. As if he didn't need even more flak from some of the citizens, this happens. I hope he handles it right or he might be in trouble come reelection time."

Jackie doubted that. Sure, she'd only known the man about a year, but he seemed to be the local hero to most of the town. She'd also heard about his loose preferences when it came to women. Hopefully one day that would change, but he seemed set in his ways. "So, is my husband free to talk?"

"Oh, no, he's out playing taxi."

"What?"

"He managed to convince a couple of the staff to come in and get some kind of work done. Have you tried calling him on his cell?"

Jackie resisted the groan that wanted to come out. "I can't even get a signal to try."

"You too?"

"Pardon?"

"I don't have a signal, either. It comes and goes."

"That's weird."

"It is, isn't it? Maybe something's wrong with the tower or something?"

"Maybe." Jackie heard Judith take a breath in before speaking to keep the conversation going, so she used the momentary break to quickly say, "Well, I better get back to things around here."

"Aw, all right."

Jackie felt bad for rushing off the phone. She understood Judith was probably a little bored, possibly even spooked as well and would love to talk herself out of the mood she was in. So would Jackie, for that matter. But she really did have things around the house to do. "I know. Will you have Allen call me when he gets back?"

"I sure will. Call if you get bored or anything. Not much going on here."

"I'll do that."

They said their byes and Jackie returned the phone to its cradle. She scratched her head and felt the oily texture of hair that needed to be washed. She hadn't showered yet this morning, plus she and Allen had made love last night, so her skin felt a little tacky with old sweat. They'd had a lot of sex lately since they were trying to have another child before Joey got too much older. So far, Jackie hadn't become pregnant. Dr. Elwood in Springston promised her nothing was wrong with either her or Allen to prevent impregnation, but from how long they'd been unsuccessfully trying, she was thinking of getting another opinion.

So, a shower sounded great. Sniffing herself, she detected a slightly musky odor of sex on her skin. Yes, she needed to wash herself. The warm shower might also sooth the chill in her bones.

Jackie headed for the stairs. Though their house was two stories, it was still small and cramped. All that was on the top floor were bedrooms and a half bath in the hall. In the master bedroom was a compacted full bathroom. Downstairs had its own full bath between the dining room and kitchen, which Joey used.

The house's features sounded more spacious and elegant than what they really were, but it was a great home on private land, so she was very happy with it.

Climbing the stairs, it felt as if the house's silence grew even more astringent. Harder to breathe, the rushing sounds of blood in her ears made her feel slightly off balance. She reached the top and kept moving to their bedroom at the end of the hall. Usually she'd leave the door open, but this time she closed it, popping the lock button into the knob.

Inside her bedroom, she stood on the other side of the door. Strained morning light seeped into the room through the curtains. Taking a deep breath, she ran her hand through her hair, ruffling it as she reached the tips.

Get a hold of yourself.

Good advice.

Jackie nodded her head once, and headed toward the bathroom, removing her shirt as she walked. The clothes hamper was against the wall beside the vanity mirror. On her way to toss the shirt in, she caught herself in the glass, walking closer. Wearing nothing but lounge pants, she studied the reflected version of herself. She noted the decently sized breasts, small nipples from not breast-feeding Joey. An argument that her mother liked to revisit whenever Joey acted up.

The bond between a mother and son is stronger if she breast feeds him!

Jackie would disagree. Her bond with Joey seemed just fine, though it couldn't compare to the bond he had with Allen. There were times she caught herself feeling envious of their relationship. But right now, standing half-naked in front of the mirror was not the time to think about it.

She gave herself another look and nodded with approval. Her body was still holding up nicely. Their closest gym was an hour drive from the house, so for exercise, she and Allen would take walks with Joey through the woods and around town. They all enjoyed it and it gave them quality time together where they could talk about anything.

Rubbing her semi-flat belly, Jackie wondered if another baby would one day be growing inside. She hoped so, but also understood it was out of her hands.

Jackie put her back to the mirror and walked into the bathroom. The carpet under her bare feet felt squishy and soft. The texture changed to cold and slick when she entered the bathroom. Closing the door, she made sure to lock the knob in here as well.

She walked over to the tub and turned the faucet on and pulled the diverter up to launch the shower. As the water heated up, she stripped out of her pants and panties, visiting the toilet to empty her bladder before getting into the tub.

Heavy torrents of hot water tapped the top of her head, soaking her hair and plastering it to her face. She could feel those icy feelings of consternation washing away and swirling down the drain. When she started to wash her hair, they'd vanished completely.

Taking her time, she relished the heated spray, the feel of the soap suds sloughing down her slippery skin. It was nice. She didn't know why she never slowed down long enough to truly enjoy the shower.

Not enough time in the day.

Today she was making time. And she was glad she had.

How cold is it supposed to be tonight? she wondered. She wasn't sure, but if last night was any indication, then tonight would be freezing. Maybe they should take some hot chocolate with them when Joey goes trick-or-treating. In Georgia, where they'd lived before moving to Autumn Creek, they'd never needed anything more than a light jacket. This kind of weather so early in the season was alien to her, and apparently for the community as well.

A blazing summer and cold and wet autumn. What will the winter be like?

Jackie paused, head under the spray, water dribbling down the back of her neck. She listened.

The phone! It's probably Allen calling me back!

Groaning, Jackie quickly shut off the water, stepped out of the tub. She snatched a fresh towel from the rack and hurried through the bathroom, wrapping the towel around her torso. She tucked the tip between her breasts and flung the door open.

The ringing intensified without the muffle of the door. Running for the bed, she dove when her knees bumped the edge. She landed on her stomach and jerked the phone off the nightstand in one motion.

"Allen?"

Principal Horton here. Due to lack of faculty and students, school will be closing at ten a.m. Please arrange for your child to be picked up no later than fifteen after. Again, I am terribly sorry for any inconvenience this day has caused you. Let us be hopeful all these issues are resolved in a timely manner. Happy Halloween.

If you'd like to hear this message again, press one.

Jackie hung up the phone and rolled onto her back. The towel parted, rolling back at her sides. She hardly noticed the cool air stippling goosebumps on her breasts and belly. She turned her head to see the alarm clock. The red digits told her it was nearing 8:30.

Not much time to do a whole lot before having to leave. So, she decided not to do much other than get dressed and put the clothes in the washer into the dryer.

(‡‡‡)

Officer Greg Hodges was late getting back to the bakery where he'd left Albright. She'd gone in to pick up some coffee and a box of assorted pastries after his wife Ann had called and told him about her tires.

"Can you take the kids to school?" Ann had asked.

"Oh…Ann…I don't know…" They had two boys in elementary school, Luke and Jacob. "Albright and I have been tied up all morning…" He sighed. "Is there not *anyone* else who can?"

"No one. I called Mom and her tires were gotten, too. Everyone I've called either aren't home or are stranded there." Her voice began to thicken. She was about to cry.

If only I would have checked when Albright picked me up this morning, I could have taken care of it then.

Albright, sitting in the seat beside him, was leaning halfway out of the car, about to go in and place their order. "What's up?"

"Got our tires, too. Ann can't get the kids to school."

"Is she asking you to do it?"

He nodded.

"Is that Karen?" asked Ann.

Greg didn't like referring to his partner as Karen. He felt that if he associated her by her first name then he would also be acknowledging that she was female, and he might start to acknowledge that she was beautiful, which would eventually progress to him realizing he was attracted to her. He didn't want or *need* that. So far, Ann didn't act as if she worried over him spending so much alone time with Albright.

And he wanted it to remain that way.

"Yes, that's Albright."

"Tell her I said hi."

"Tell Ann I said it back."

Thankfully, they could hear each other, which saved him from having to relay the messages.

Albright was about to get out but leaned back into the car. "If you have to get them to school, then by all means, run and do it. I'll be in this line at least twenty minutes."

"You sure you don't mind me leaving you here?"

"I can take care of myself."

Greg smiled. She wasn't lying. She wasn't one to mess with. "All right."

Ann exhaled heavily in the phone. He could hear the relief in it. "Tell her thank you so much."

"She heard you."

"I did," Albright confirmed. "It's no problem. See you when you get back."

Then she was out of the car and heading into the Alice's Bakery to wait in a line that looked to be on the verge of leading out the door. He drove away from the bakery, watching her enter through the rearview mirror.

When he'd arrived at the elementary school with his boys singing songs from the backseat, he'd stumbled upon a nightmare. All the buses at all three schools had been vandalized as well.

Slashed tires.

He'd gone into the front office just to sign the boys in and get their tardy slips but was kept there much longer filling out complaint forms for Principal Horton, one for the school and another for the eggs that were thrown at his residence. He'd promised to go visit Mrs. Horton at home later today and get all the details from her and to see the *ruin* his house had been reduced to.

As he drove back to the bakery, six more calls came down about more damaged tires. How was it possible this many people had been hit in one night? Didn't make sense. He tried coming up with a realistic way so much damage had been done but came up with nothing.

Greg slowed the car, clicking the signal as he steered into the bakery's parking lot. It was void of cars, but through the windows he could see a horde of people inside.

A lot of people walking to work today...

Albright was waiting for him at the side of the building, leaning back, a leg bent, and foot propped against the wall. She had a pink box with two cups of coffee on top balanced against her breasts. He could see their firm peaks over the top of the box. Her tan uniform clung to her as if it were her skin. She looked lovely standing there. She waved as he braked in front of her.

He leaned over the seat and opened her door. "Been waiting long?"

Albright leaned in, holding out the box. He took the two Styrofoam cups from the top.

"Not really. Maybe five minutes." She climbed in, keeping the box of pastries on her lap when she shut the door. Her cheeks were flushed from the cold. "What took so long?"

"Forgetting something?"

Albright smirked. Grabbing the buckle of the safety harness, she pulled it down and snapped it. "Better?"

"Much."

"As I was *saying*—what took so long?"

He told her about the buses, and the principal's report.

"This is really serious," she said.

Greg nodded. He sat his coffee in the cup holder closest to him, peeling the lid from the top. Flavored steam seeped out. It smelled delicious.

"All three schools were hit?"

"Yeah," he said. "I took the report for the elementary school but left afterward so I could come pick you up. Six more calls came in on my way. Two of them were for the middle and high school."

"Oh my God."

"While I was out there, I should have gotten statements but didn't want to leave you waiting for me all day."

"Glad you did. The customers were starting to get a little riled up. Most of them were hit too, and they were looking at me like I should already have the person responsible in cuffs."

"Well, you should have. What kind of cop are you?"

"Hey," said Albright, feigning a scowl. "Watch it buddy."

"Just saying…"

"I know. The joys of being a cop."

"Joys?"

She laughed. "Don't act like you hate this job."

He shrugged. Truth was he was beginning to despise it, especially in a town like this, where your every move was watched by all.

Albright, holding her cup before her, stared through the windshield. She pursed her lips and lightly blew into the small hole on the plastic lid. "We should call Holly and ask him what he wants us to do."

"I figured we'd head back to the schools, then from there go hit all the houses on the list, starting with the closest and work our way back into town."

"Sounds good to me."

"Maybe eat lunch in the park?"

She eyed him coyly. "Oh?"

"Yeah. The blanket's in the back. Spread it out and take half an hour to not do anything but eat and enjoy the cool weather."

"I might be up for that. What did you have in mind for food?"

"I don't know yet, but right now, I'd like a cream-filled doughnut."

Smirking, she said, "And what makes you think I got you one?"

"You always do."

"Well, today I didn't."

He mocked a startled surprise. "How could you?"

"Today I got you two."

"You big sweetheart."

"For you I am, just don't tell anyone."

They laughed, but it quickly fell apart when they both realized they were having a much deeper, personal moment. Greg cleared his throat, keeping his eyes on the road. He could hear the whistling sounds of the box being opened. The sugary-sweet scent of baked goods began to fill the car. His stomach grumbled, ready for a doughnut.

"Here," she said, carefully passing him one.

"Thanks." The doughnut was sticky and soft against his fingers. He took a bite. "Mmmm." He felt the cream swish into his mouth.

"Good?"

"As always." He chewed. "Your aunt can really bake, you know that?"

"Yep, I do. And so does my mother, which is why she's always trying to top her."

Greg chuckled. "Really? A rivalry going on?"

"Yep."

"You're a good cook, too."

"Yeah?"

Greg nodded, mouthful of doughnut.

"Don't tell my mom that. She thinks I can barely handle a box of macaroni and cheese."

Albright often brought food to Greg that she'd cooked herself. Usually, he ate it in the breakroom at the station, not wanting to take it home and have Ann ask about it. Albright would sit with him, studying his every reaction as he ate. Not once had he been disappointed by the cuisine.

If she was my wife, I'd be a fat slob.

Greg hated he'd thought that. It was unfair to Ann to even joke about it.

Albright laughed, though neither of them had said anything funny. Looking at Albright next to him, he saw her staring out the window. "It's strange seeing the roads without any cars on them. Like driving around after the big bomb hits, you know?"

Greg nodded. "Yep. And it doesn't look like many of them will be getting back on the road today, buses and all." He stuffed the rest of his doughnut into his mouth and chewed.

"Why not?"

Mouth full he said, "Not enough tires to replace the slashed ones. I talked to the service manager for the schools, and he said they only had enough tires to fully replace two buses. Nowhere near enough for all the bus riders. Said the driver would be driving until lunch time to get them all."

"This is insane."

"Tell me about it." Greg drank from his cup. The coffee singed his upper lip, but it tasted so good he didn't care. His chest warmed as the coffee passed through.

There was no traffic as he approached Hemingway Road, so he didn't bother using his turn signal. As he straightened the car, Albright's sudden gasp nearly made him drop his coffee in his lap. He whipped his head toward her. The pale look of shock on her face made him shiver.

"Stop the car," she demanded.

"Wha—?"

"*Stop the car!*"

He stomped the brake pedal with both feet. The tires screamed as the car skidded sideways across the asphalt. When it finally came to a stop, smoke from the burnt rubber was coasting up from under the cruiser.

Greg slung his seatbelt behind him. "Are you all right?" He put his hand on Albright's shoulder. It felt warm through her shirt.

Her lips were pulled back, baring her teeth. She nodded toward the road.

Greg faced the front. His stomach twisted when he gazed through the windshield. Somebody stood on the yellow line with a foot planted on each side of the blacktop. His shoulders were hiked up, neck slanted forward. He wore checkered sheets roughly stitched up the front and both sides into a mock-suit. A crudely fashioned hood covered his head, and for a face, black ovals had been painted for eyes and a mouth.

As disturbing as the attire was, it wasn't what bothered Greg the most. What had him nervous, had his back feeling as if it were being scraped with an icy fork were the knives. One was clasped in each hand, gummy spatters of blood blemishing their surfaces.

"Is this some kind of joke?" Greg knew he'd asked it, but the voice that spoke it was too shaky and higher in pitch than his own.

"Well…It *is* Halloween. Maybe they're trying to show off their costume."

"I'm not impressed."

"Me either."

Greg studied the figure another moment, noticing something swaying in the mild breeze from its chest. It looked like an envelope. "Something's on his chest…"

Albright leaned closer to the windshield, still clutching her coffee in her shaky hands. "I see it."

Greg opened his door.

"What are you doing?" asked Albright.

"I'm going out there to either get him out of the way or arrest him for disturbing the peace."

"Disturbing the peace?"

"Jaywalking?"

She smiled. It made his knees rattle just as it usually did.

"I'm coming with you." She opened her door, tossed her coffee into the street, and dropped the empty cup in its holder.

Together, they walked to the front of the car, their guard raised, hands hovering above their guns.

Greg flicked the hammer lock out of place just in case he needed to grab his gun. "You're blocking the road." The figure didn't move. Greg began to wonder if an actual person was underneath the sheets and rags or if it was some kind of dummy. "I'm only going to ask you one time to move to the side. We have some questions for you."

"Move!" shouted Albright.

Her sudden command startled him. Greg shot her a sour look. Nibbling on her bottom lip, she shrugged bashfully.

The ghost man suddenly relaxed his hands. The knives fell, clamoring when they hit the road. Greg grabbed him by the arm, jerked him toward the cruiser, and let go. His thighs slammed against the car, folding him at the waist. Albright was quick to meet him and hold the ghost man down on the hood.

There was no resistance.

Approaching, Greg asked, "So, what were you trying to accomplish just now?" He snatched the handcuffs from the back of his belt. As Albright pinned the ghost's arms behind his back, Greg latched the curved steel around his wrists. Then he clicked them in place.

"Now, turn around..." Grabbing the ghost by the shoulders, he spun him around, and slammed his back down on the cruiser's hood. "And take this damn mask off!" He jerked the hood off the ghost's head, then jumped back. What was underneath was not what he'd expected to find.

The ghost wasn't a man at all. It was Annette Carter, a senior at Autumn Creek High. Pretty enough to be a cheerleader, but instead she devoted her time to studying and maintaining her perpetual honor roll status. "Annette?" Her brown eyes seemed darker than usual. She stared at Greg, but it felt as if she were looking straight through him, to something beyond him. A chill scuttled up his spine. "What are you doing out here?"

He looked at Albright. She was gaping at the teenage girl.

"I killed her..." Annette's voice was raspy and quiet, but its meaning exploded on the still street.

"Killed...who?"

"Cali Fortner. I killed her. My confession is in here." She jiggled her shoulders, flapping the envelope stapled to her costume. "And so are the pictures..."

Greg turned to Albright. "Get on the horn and notify Holly. Tell him we're bringing someone in."

Albright bolted for the cruiser.

Greg watched her climb into the car. As she radioed Marge, he turned back to Annette. The bags under her eyes were so puffy and dark they could almost be bruises. And she smelled bad. As if she hadn't showered in several days of swimming through swamps.

What the hell is going on?

CHAPTER 4

(1)

Herman Dobson was making his morning rounds through the cemetery when he found the disturbed grave. "What the shitstorm is this?" he muttered, adjusting the orange beanie on his head.

Someone had been digging. Where there was supposed to be neatly trimmed, albeit faintly browning grass, was a shallow depression of loose soil. Looked like it was about three feet deep. Not far enough to reach the coffin, but someone had definitely been trying.

Footprints trampled through the rim of dirt strewn around the hole. Smaller-sized sneakers that odds-on belonged to a kid. What would make them think something like this was fun? He could think of countless better means of entertainment.

"Son of a bastard witch."

Shaking his head, Herman turned away, heading for the shed where he kept his tools. He'd have to get a shovel and fix this. More work on his already full day. Hopefully he could get it done quickly. Filling in this damn hole would take time away from the flowers.

Every Thursday he plucked the old, wilted buds left by mourners and emptied the vases. Weekends usually saw a lot of traffic in the cemetery, so he liked to have the graves ready for them just in case they wanted to leave something for the departed.

That was what people liked most about him, he cared. It showed in his work—his attention to detail, the little bit extra that he always put into the overall appearance of the cemetery. He wanted people to feel comfortable being in here, like him. He generally relished the amicable consent he felt while plodding around the graves and welcomed the substantial hush in the air. Aspects of his job that he loved, just not today though. There was a foreboding murmur biding under the cold, sharpened drifts of wind. He pulled his coat taut in the front, holding it shut with a gloved hand. This kind of weather made him long for a bowl of hot soup.

He turned right at a bench, taking the gravel path along the back boundary. The entire cemetery was enclosed by a brick wall. It would do nothing to keep anyone out after hours, but before today it had never been a problem. On the rare occasions he forgot to lock up when he left at night, he never fretted someone might come in and sully a grave. However, last night he had *remembered* to put the lock on, and the damage had been done regardless.

Herman cut across the grass, descending a small hill. The ground leveled out and he moved back onto the pathway. Stone-gray headstones were lined rigid on all sides of him like the dentures in his mouth. This back area was full. There was no more room to add anymore coffins.

Seems to be filling up fast out here.

No matter to him. His plot was already accounted for and had been since before his pappy passed on. He was the last of the Dobson clan and would be buried with the others on the south side.

The wind picked up, brushing his face with cold tendrils. Dark clouds waved over the sun. The shadowed replica of himself that had been stretched across the grass in front of him vanished. He looked up. The sky threatened rain, but he doubted it would. Most fall mornings were like this, gunmetal gray skies and nippy winds that eventually broke apart to unveil a honey-gold sun underneath. But, when the rain would come, it usually stayed for days.

Nearing the shed, he spotted a woman to his left, standing by a grave. Her back faced him, and there was long, curly hair lightly swaying in the breeze against her back. She looked to be dressed in old, dirty clothes.

Herman stopped. She shouldn't be here. He hadn't taken the lock off the front gate yet. Checking his watch, he confirmed there was still another twenty minutes before it was time to open up.

How'd she get in here?

He took a step towards her but stopped. Something about her wasn't right. He studied her, trying to figure out what it was. The way she was standing, so rigid and motionless.

Like a damn statue.

Whenever the wind pitched her way, her body seemed to rustle with it. His bowels felt like crushed ice as he took another vigilant step.

"Ma'am?" His voice sounded craggy and thick. He cleared his throat. "Excuse me?" She gave no indication he'd said anything at all. He continued to approach, brittle leaves scampering over the grass and his boots as he walked with the breeze. "If you don't mind me asking, how'd you get in? We don't normally open the gate until after nine."

Another couple steps and he noticed the smell. Putrid and old, like something that had been stored in a damp basement. A combined odor of mold and something else. Something rotten.

Decaying teeth. A leaking septic tank. That was what it reminded him of.

Herman was now close enough to her that if he reached his hand out, he could tap her shoulder. He didn't dare. He was wary to touch anything that smelled so bad.

His foot snagged something. Looking down, he noticed a strip of rope running across the toe of his boot.

"What the…?"

He slowly raised his foot. There was tension in the rope. As he pulled against it, the rope seemed to pull back. He kept at it, drawing the rope taut. His eyes followed it around the headstone where it was looped around a plastic stake with a coiled head.

Who put that there?

He twisted his foot from side to side. The stake slowly rotated in the ground.

There was click.

Then the woman whirled around, crashing into Herman.

"Jumpin' Jesus Butterscotch!" Staggering back, he threw his arms up, catching her under the armpits. Her added weight shoved him backwards. The rope still had his foot, so when he tried to maintain his balance, his leg was jerked out from under him. He fell on his back. Hard. Air blasted from his lungs in a wheezy gust.

The woman landed on top of him. Herman felt dry hair brush his cheek. He looked up and nearly kissed a gnarled mouth. The lips were curled back, showing a full set of yellowed teeth. Her rotted skin was dry and leathery, the color of driftwood. Where there had once been eyes were hollow sockets chockfull of darkness.

A corpse! A damned corpse!

Screaming, Herman threw the cadaver off him and rolled away. He could still feel it on top of him, the unbending weight like an artificial Christmas tree. He slapped at his shoulders, his chest, stirring up a small cloud of death dust. Flecks went into his mouth, adhering to his tongue.

As much as he wished it were a prop, he knew it wasn't. The smell made it obvious he'd just been lying with a corpse. Herman got to his knees, out of breath. Pulling air into his lungs was like trying to breathe through a coffee stirrer. His chest made asthmatic rasping sounds. He could feel the thudding of his heart in his throat.

The woman lay on her side. Her arms were tightly folded across her chest. The ragged dress had slipped down, revealing shriveled bladders for breasts. A white strip of collar bone showed through thinning skin.

Herman tore his eyes away from the hideous cadaver and screwed them shut. He bit down on his lip hard enough to taste blood. Taking slow breaths, he let them hiss out through his nose. He repeated this several times until he felt brave enough to open his eyes.

He raised his head, avoiding the corpse's empty stare. He put his hand on the tombstone beside him and used it as a brace to hold him up. The name chiseled in the rounded wedge marking the desecrated grave was Henrietta Paulsen. Across from the rectangular-shaped chasm was a pile of dirt, with a shovel protruding from the top like the sword in the stone.

"What in the world is going on?" he said to the air around him. He glanced at the rotted woman as if she might answer. If she did, he knew her deathly voice would stop his heart.

Herman got to his feet, keeping his hands fixed on the tombstone for assistance. There was a dull pain in his lower back that twisted tighter as he stood up straight.

He looked over the lip of the hole. Six feet down was an opened coffin, the lid resting against the packed dirt wall. Flakes like coffee grounds had rained into the coffin, dusting the white interior in brown.

They'd gotten two graves. The job here was completed, but for whatever reason, they were unable to finish the first one he saw. He wondered why.

I probably interrupted them.

As he turned his back to the unearthed grave, he spotted another gaunt sentry. This one was three rows over, and male. Herman determined the sex by the tatty suit he was dressed in. He was mounted above a headstone, just as the woman had been, like a scarecrow defending a garden of the dead.

Herman shivered. His back felt like it was being gouged with icy nails. He hiked up his shoulders as if shrugging, stepped forward, and slowly looked around. He spotted three more corpses spread through the cemetery, all standing tall and rigid, displayed like menacing Halloween decorations.

Then he realized that was exactly what they were supposed to be. Decorations.

"A goddamned joke…"

Snickering drew his attention behind him. He spun around. Four little demons were perched atop the small hill of dirt.

"Ahhh!" Herman jumped back, thrusting out his hands. The demons watched him, four heads tilting in synchronicity.

Not demons, he comprehended, only dressed like them. Their ghastly demonic faces were just matching masks, painted a mixture of lumpy purples and greens. Horns trailed up from the bridge of the nose into the hairline. He could see the fine white strings attached at the ears leading back into bushels of hair. *Wigs!* No real hair could look like that. Their clothes were crudely assembled by either old rags or towels…maybe even blankets. Whatever they'd been concocted from, the craftsmanship was shoddy at best.

"So, you're the little bastards been terrorizing my graveyard. I think it's best you all just got your little asses out of here before I call the cops." He doubted he could move without fainting, but he was going to keep the bluff going.

They raised their arms. Poking out from their hands were three long silver spikes, thin like pencils. Herman had seen some superhero comic books in the drug store with weapons like that, but he couldn't remember the name. Some kind of animal, but Herman was clueless as to which one.

"What do you want?" He'd tried to keep his tone stern but failed. His voice was way too shrill and had a whine to it. Seeing the weapons had put an end to his sham.

Slowly, they scaled down the dirt pile. Herman noticed their size. Much smaller than he was.

Kids. I knew it. One of these bastards belongs to the footprints I found!

"Just keep moving. Get out of here." He pointed towards the gate. "You know the way out. *Get!*"

The demons split up. Two went one direction while the other two went another. They quickly surrounded him.

"Stay back," he ordered. "Just get out of here. Go on now!"

They didn't listen. Continuing to move in, they slowly started closing the small space between Herman and them.

Closer and closer, they were on each side of him, the one to his rear stood on the opposite side, the hole separating him from Herman. All had their spikes wielded.

Unable to think of anything else to do, Herman raised his fists. It'd been so long since he'd been in a fight that it felt strange balling his hands into clubs.

"You little shits are making a mistake."

The one to his right lunged. Herman stepped to the side, easily dodging the sharp tip. He swung his fist and felt flimsy rubber caving against bone when his hand struck the demon's face. It dropped and didn't move.

His attention diverted, it allowed one of the others to slice him across the stomach. The blade slit through his coat, shirt, and the skin underneath. The wound burned with a frosty sting as the deep gash percolated with blood. He clutched his stomach, hot blood leaching through the cracks between his fingers.

Herman stepped back. The ground under his boot broke away. His arms pin-wheeled open space as if there was something to keep him up. Nothing was there. He careened backwards into the open grave.

His leg struck the coffin's lid, snapping his foot at the ankle before his body crashed into the bed. Pain jolted up his leg. It felt as if his ankle was being broken on a continuous loop of agonizing bursts. Herman pulled his leg up by the knee. When he saw his foot dangling awkwardly to the side, he howled.

Dirt smacked his chest. He shook his head, coming back from the far away region his pain was trying to take him. Another pack of dirt knocked him on the shoulder. It took another moment before he grasped that he was being hit from above. Looking up, he saw three of the four demons standing over the hole, gazing down at him with their painted, dagger-like grins. They looked to be holding staffs by their sides. One of them turned away, momentarily vanishing from Herman's sight, before reemerging. He titled the staff towards Herman.

Dirt dropped into his lap.

Herman was wrong. They weren't holding staffs, but shovels, and they were using them to dump the dirt back into the hole.

They're burying me alive!

He tried to get up, but pain in his hip knocked him back down. He quickly shifted his body, then felt another wave of pain from his broken ankle. Broken hip, broken foot. He was in bad shape.

More dirt slapped his face, dumping into his eyes and mouth. Blinded, he choked on the dirt in his throat. His hands slipped in the specks sprinkled over the velvet lining of the coffin's interior wall. He fell, cracking the back of his skull on the lip of the casket. His vision went splotchy as fuzzy tingles rushed through his head.

Herman shouted, screamed—begged. The dirt kept coming. It rained down on him much heavier now, swallowing him up to his knees. His thighs disappeared under the brown, flakey loam, then his hips.

They shoveled even quicker, dumping in more and more dirt. Laughing like toddlers who've just heard a fart for the first time. Dirt continued to entomb his torso. He could no longer see his stomach, and his chest was well on its way to obscurity.

Herman was exhausted. Too tired to struggle anymore, too tired to fight. He looked up at the grave diggers. The fourth one had rejoined them and was ardently piling in his share. He blinked, and when he opened his eyes, again, all he saw was darkness, like trying to look through the glass in an ant farm.

He sucked in breath for a scream, and his lungs filled with dirt.

(11)

Leaning back in her chair, Tabitha thumbed her cell phone off, groaning. She tossed the phone onto her desk. It spun away from her. Running her hands through her hairspray-stiff hair, she wanted to scream.

"Bad news I take it."

At the sudden sound of the voice, she did scream. *"Shit!"*

Becky stood in the doorway, grimacing. "Sorry. Didn't mean to scare you."

Tabitha rubbed her eyes. "It's okay. I didn't mean to snap. It's just that this day keeps getting better and better."

She'd been reading the final pages of *Scary Stories 3* when the intercom buzzed. It was followed by Principal Horton announcing classes had been canceled for the remainder of the day. The five students stuck in her class were ecstatic that they were being released early. As they charged out of her classroom, practically leaving smoke silhouettes in their places, she realized she could have stayed home and it wouldn't have mattered.

That's the teacher in you talking. But she couldn't help feeling that way. Unlike most teachers her age, and even some older, she actually cared about making an impact in her students' lives. She wanted to give them something they could carry with them for the rest of their lives.

Now, that's the hippy in you talking.

After the students were cleared out, she'd taken her phone out of her purse, sat at the desk, and began calling auto shops looking for tires. None of them had any in stock, and there was a two-day backorder, just as Becky had told her there would be.

And that was when her perky friend snuck up on her and scared her so badly, she now had to pee.

She let Becky in on what she'd learned about the tires.

"At least I've got the beater to hold me over."

"For now."

"That's for sure. I better make sure it stays behind the garage when I'm not using it."

"Just for tonight. After Halloween has passed, I doubt we have to worry about it."

"Until next year."

"That's true too."

Becky wrinkled her nose. "And, you know the little mischief-makers will probably try to surpass this year's mayhem."

"God, I hope not. Hopefully the police will be better prepared next year."

"We can only hope. I mean…it *is* the *local* police we're talking about." She laughed. "We have two cafeteria workers preparing lunch for what little faculty actually made it in today. I was going to go grab a tray, want to come along?"

Tabitha sighed. She *was* hungry but didn't really feel up to mingling with the other unfortunate faculty members who'd come into work. "I'll pass."

"Want me to bring it up to you?"

"Would you?"

Becky smiled. "Only if I can join you."

"Sounds like a plan."

"Great. I'll be back shortly."

"Hold on." Tabitha stood up. "I'll walk with you as far as the little girl's room."

"Scared you *that* bad?"

"Yes."

Becky shook her head. "Sorry."

"No worries. If I would have shot pee out of my skirt, then we would be having a different conversation entirely."

Laughter erupted from Becky's wide mouth. "The stuff you say floors me sometimes."

Together, they left the classroom and ventured up the desolate hall. The hollow clacks of their footfalls resounded off the lockers and walls.

"You know," Tabitha began, "I've always thought empty schools were creepy."

"You mean like today?"

"Exactly like today."

They walked in silence for a minute.

Becky nodded. "I know what you mean. It feels…barren. Abandoned."

"Like being in an office building when everyone's already gone home for the day."

Becky wrinkled her nose. "Yeah."

"I don't like it."

"You prefer having kids invading the place with their loud babble, fights, and all of the disruption?"

"Better than *not* having it."

Shrugging, Becky said, "I guess you've got a point."

At the bathroom, they said their byes, and parted. Tabitha turned left, but Becky forged ahead for the cafeteria. Tabitha stood at the head of the girl's restroom. There were five stalls, all of them unoccupied, with the doors slightly agape. She could practically hear her heart beating. She took a few steps. Each one bounced off the walls as if she were hearing it with reverb.

A large, empty bathroom was something else that Tabitha found creepy. So many stalls, so many places for someone to be hiding, *lurking*. It was all those urban legends she'd heard growing up about young women entering supposed empty restrooms, only to be jumped and raped from someone lying in wait inside. Sometimes those hapless women were killed, others were mutilated horribly. It'd left a lasting impression on her throughout the years. But the teacher's lounge was two halls over and she didn't feel like walking all the way over there just to pee.

Just pick a toilet, do your business, and get out.

Tabitha chose the closest one. She threw the bolt into the catch once she was inside the stall. Above the toilet was an empty box that usually held sanitary covers for the toilet seats. Since Abigail was unable to make it in today, the empty box hadn't been replaced. So, she tore two trails of toilet paper and placed them over the seat's rim, and then she placed a smaller line along the back. Finally, with something keeping her bare rump from touching the cold plastic lid that probably hadn't been cleaned since yesterday, she reached under her skirt, slid her panties down to her knees, and sat.

Her business was done in record time.

At the sink, she washed her hands. The sound of running water resonated off the walls as if she were standing in a cave. She studied herself in the mirror. Under her eyes were purple half-moons made even more perceptible by the white powder she'd put on her face. She wished she'd stuck to her original decision of not wearing any, but she'd wanted to be festive. It was time to wash the crap off.

She cupped her hands together under the faucet and let them fill with water. Then she leaned over, splashed her face. She repeated this process a few times, rubbing her face good and hard to loosen the makeup. When she stood up, she was slightly dizzy. There were caramel streaks cutting through the powder down her forehead and cheeks. She wetted a paper towel and scrubbed her face with it.

The skin on her face felt as if it could finally breathe. Droplets of water dripped off her chin. She used another paper towel to dry. On her way out, she dropped her trash in the waste basket.

The hall felt just as forlorn as it had earlier, worse now that she was alone. Tabitha looked toward the cafeteria but didn't see Becky heading back.

Maybe she's waiting for me in the classroom.

She headed back to her room, feeling slightly rejuvenated now that her face was clean.

Walking through the open door, she could tell right away that something wasn't right. She stopped. Letting the room's strange vibe seep into her, she stood there, slowly turning her head from side to side.

Someone's been in here.

Tabitha could feel her furtive visitor's aftertaste violating the usually pure air of her classroom. She took a couple more steps in, noticing her desk. Something had been placed on top.

A green apple.

Who'd leave me an apple?

Tabitha walked slow and stilted toward her desk. She reached for the apple but snatched her hand back as if were hot.

Is this some kind of gag?

She stared at it a moment longer before daring to try again. Her fingers curved around the apple's shiny green rind. As they clamped on its backside, her fingertips sunk into a mushy surface. Grimacing, she turned the apple around. The other side was black with rot. An infestation of mealworms slurped and wriggled inside the dark squishiness.

She gasped, flinging the apple into the air. It landed somewhere behind her. On her desk she kept cleaning wipes for her hands after using the chalkboard. Snatching one from the glossy packet, she viciously rubbed the moist towel over her fingers.

As she was about to drop the dirty wipe into the waste basket beside her desk, she noticed her purse in the bottom of it. Kneeling down, she reached inside the can and grabbed her purse. It was lighter than normal. She tilted it over, and nothing sprinkled out. The contents had already been dumped out into the trash can, Tabitha guessed, during its fall. She found her wallet right away. Her license showed through the plastic display on the front. The edge of her debit card poked up from behind it.

She rummaged through the waste basket. So far, everything appeared to be there. As she put the belongings back into her purse, she realized she was wrong.

Her keys were missing.

Shit!

She dropped down on all fours, searching under her chair. *Nope.* She crawled under her desk, not finding them there either. *Damn it.*

She turned around, crawling back around to the side of the desk. Her knees were starting to hurt from the hard floor, so she stood up.

Maybe I left them on the desk.

Although she knew she hadn't, she checked anyway.

Of course, she didn't find them, but during the hunt, she realized that her cell phone had also vanished.

What the hell?

She hadn't noticed it on the floor or in the trash can, but she hadn't been looking either. She did a quick recheck, but just as her keys, the phone wasn't there to be found.

Winded, standing with her hands on her hips, she slowly turned around. Her eyes immediately locked on the chalkboard.

A breath of fright tickled her throat.

"Oh…Christ…"

Her chalkboard was two navy-green rectangles on the wall. Every morning she would write down the day's activities and lessons in different colors of chalk. She hadn't written anything this morning, so it should have been blank.

But it wasn't.

Written in red chalk in a spooky scrawl were two words.

PRANK NIGHT.

"Got your food order right here!"

Tabitha shrieked one continuous squeal as she spun around. Becky was gaping at her with two rounded eyes, and a yawning mouth. Her lips formed words that weren't being spoken. The two Styrofoam trays of processed food trembled in her hands.

Becky took a deep, shaky breath. "Did I miss something?"

(ɪɪɪ)

Sheriff Ben Holly threw open the door and stormed into the Sheriff's department. He was interviewing Cali's neighbor, Stan Macready, when Carla had come running across the lawn to notify him of

Officers Hodges's and Albright's arrest.

Apparently, Annette Carter was taking credit for Cali's murder and had surrendered into their custody. Before leaving Rileson and Carpenter to wrap things up at Cali's home, he'd sent Deputy Duggins to the Carter residence to confirm or debunk Annette's story. She'd told Albright that her parents were out of town and couldn't be reached until they were back after the fifth. Ben was doubtful the story was true.

Annette Carter.

A good kid with a clean record and faultless reputation. She wasn't one of the regulars he often caught in random backseats with their legs spread and a different cock being rammed inside of her. She never got into trouble, sung in the band at church, and even volunteered there. He'd asked Hodges twice for confirmation that the person who was admitting to the slaying of Cali Fortner was indeed the *same* Annette Carter, and each time he'd replied *yes.*

Ben marched to Marge's desk. She had the phone pressed against her ear, probably listening to another vandalism casualty. The lights on the switchboard were lit up like a Lite Brite sheet. A plastic jack-o'-lantern sat at the front of her desk, dimly lit by a low wattage bulb. His stomach clenched, remembering Cali's crooked mouth and triangle eyes, the flickering candle where her tongue used to be...

"Sherriff?"

He looked towards the voice. Hodges stood at the back of the station, waving him to the interrogation room. Being a small station, the interrogation room doubled as the record room. They kept file boxes stacked in alphabetical order against the far wall, and a small table and some folding chairs were used when they were questioning a potential suspect. But normally the table was covered with pizza boxes, or some other kind of takeout food.

Must have her waiting for me.

Ben gave Hodges a brisk nod. He waited for Marge to finish with the call, avoiding a glance at the plastic Halloween decoration.

"What's been coming in, Marge?"

She groaned. Marge was sixty-four and today she looked it in a black sweater that had pumpkins embellishing the front with goofy grins on their orange faces. Ghosts with curling tails hovered above them. Her hair was feathery and dyed, trying to conceal the fact that it was thinning. She had a mole above her lip and a red ink pen nestled behind her ear. "More slashed tires. Seem to be coming in every couple minutes. There've been some reports of missing property, but nothing major."

"What kind of property?"

"Mostly tools. Pitchforks, axes, along those lines."

"Any break-ins?"

"Not yet. The tools have been taken from some of the farms. Usually, they were just lying around or pinned up in a shed without doors. But I wouldn't be surprised if there were some before the night was over."

"Me either." He huffed. "All right, just make sure when they call that you tell them we are seriously under-staffed for the amount of calls we're getting, and we're doing our best to remedy the situation."

"I already have, Ben. Should we reach out to the state police, see if they can spare a few to come out here and help us?"

It would probably be the wise thing to do, especially now with the Annette Carter development. But Ben wanted to wait. The state boys loved to throw it in his face whenever he asked for their help, poking fun that he couldn't handle business. Yes, it was his pride influencing his decision, but he would wait until there was no other choice before radioing in backup.

"Not right now," he answered. "I think we should hold out for the time being."

Though Marge nodded, the frown on her face showed she didn't agree. "Sure, Ben."

"Just let the residents know we're doing the best we can."

"I will do that."

"Also, check in with Rileson, find out where he's at. Tell him to keep close to his radio in case we need him."

"What about Carpenter? He's still out there too."

He debated sending Carpenter to question the owners about their tires now that Hodges and Albright were here but decided not to. He wanted as many people around the station, or as close to it as possible. "Get him back here."

"You got it."

He left Marge alone as she tugged the microphone to her mouth. It was attached to a small stand, and to make an outgoing call to any of the cruisers, all she had to do was push a button on the board. And she was doing that as Ben crossed the room.

Ben joined Hodges in front of a pinboard that hung on the wall next to the interrogation room's doorway. "Annette Carter in there?"

"Yeah."

Ben stepped around Hodges and peered through the observation glass. Annette Carter sat on the left side of the table, hands cuffed, elbows resting on top. She was dressed in a costume of sorts—bed sheets of different patterns that had been sewn together to make a complete suit. She stared beyond Albright, who sat across the table, with vacant eyes.

"What's she been saying?" asked Ben, his voice losing momentum and coming out as a whisper.

"Not much since I last talked to you. I was afraid to delve too much, with her only being seventeen and her parents not here."

"Didn't she give up the right to have them here?" Hodges nodded. "So, what's the hold up?"

"Honestly? She hasn't spoken a word since then and I haven't even tried to get her to. All she's been doing is just sitting there…staring."

"At what?"

Hodges swallowed. It made a wet clucking sound as it went down. This was the first time Ben had ever seen fear in the young man's eyes. "It feels like she's looking straight into my soul."

Ben resisted the urge to shiver. "Is Albright having any luck?"

He shook his head. "She brought Annette some water and a pack of Ball Cakes hoping she could get her talking."

Ben saw the paper cup and fluffy pink cocoanut balls on the table. "Ball Cakes?"

"It was all I had in my desk. My last pack, too."

"I'll replace them." Ben patted Hodges on the back. "You did really good today."

"I don't know, feels like I just stepped in knee-deep shit."

Smiling, Ben squeezed Hodges's shoulder. "Why don't you hit the coffee pot? Pour yourself some cheap coffee."

"I think I'll have a smoke, if you don't mind."

"I don't mind." He reached into his coat pocket and pulled out his cigarettes. He handed the pack to Hodges. "Have one for me too."

Although Hodges's expression didn't falter from a confused blank, he nodded. Ben waited until his deputy was out of sight before entering the interrogation room.

If Annette had noticed his entrance, she gave no indication.

Albright stood up. "Here to take over?"

Her pretty face displayed her disturbance. Both she and Hodges were extremely spooked. Ben didn't blame them for it. "Yeah, I'm just going to sit and see if she has anything she wants to tell me."

"Want to read the confession letter?" She crossed the room to the file boxes and grabbed a clear plastic bag off the top. She returned to Ben, handing him the envelope in a sealed evidence bag. "I made copies. They're on your desk. The Polaroids are in there too."

Ben raised his eyebrows. This was the first he'd heard about there being pictures. "What Polaroids?"

"Of the body. She took the pictures."

Ben stared down at the bag. He slowly rubbed his fingers, feeling the stiff bulk of photos behind the paper. Knowing there were pictures of Cali in the bag made him want to toss it.

Annette must be the one who kept lighting the candle.

Albright frowned. "Want me to hang around?"

"You don't have to stay in here but stick close by."

"Okay." She walked past him, patting his shoulder on her way out of the room.

He looked down at the crinkled piece of paper inside the evidence bag. It was a thicker weight, a lot like drawing paper. The *confession* was scribbled in a hasty scrawl. Some of the letters had smeared from spatters of blood.

The note was brief, but it told all he needed to know.

I, Annette Carter, killed Cali Fortner for Prank Night.

His hand started to tremble. He dropped the letter onto the table. There was a numbing sensation tracking through his hand now, as if the meaning of the letter had somehow contaminated him. Rubbing his fingers, he looked up at Annette. She hadn't moved. She almost didn't even look real.

Ben felt helpless and vulnerable with Annette. He regretted sending Albright out.

At least she's nearby if I need her.

But why would he? Certainly, if it came down to it, he could subdue a teenaged, handcuffed girl with little effort.

He studied her. Annette no longer appeared to be the same immaculate kid he'd watched grow up over the years. Not anymore. The blank expression on her face, the cold emptiness in her eyes made her look like some strange feral woman they'd trapped in the woods and brought into civilization to try and domesticate.

Ben's stomach felt as if it was coiling like rope. He tried to hide his jitters as he sat across from Annette. Cold sweat beaded on his forehead. A dab trickled down his side.

He cleared his throat. "Annette…" His voice was a raspy whisper. He cleared his throat once more and tried again. "Is there something you want to tell me?"

Her eyes flicked towards him.

Ben nearly shouted.

CHAPTER 5

(1)

"I wish you were home," said Jackie. She sat at the dining room table, the phone cradled between her ear and shoulder as she thumbed through the newspaper. Wasn't much going on, other than an article about the lack of a carnival this year due to budget cuts.

"Me too," said Allen from the other side. "I'm basically on my own now. Jeremiah left early, and I had to let Judith leave since the schools dismissed early."

"Yeah. I was barely home half an hour when Mr. Horton's automated message called telling me school was being let out."

"It's a mess out there. I drove to Rick's Barbeque for some hot dogs and decided to eat there and work on some notes for my message on Sunday, but I couldn't handle it."

"What was wrong?"

"So many people in there talking about what happened last night and acting like it's a big conspiracy. Some people had some very rotten things to say about Sheriff Holly. There were even a few whispers of a possible murder."

"A *what?*"

"Yeah, the high school principal was in there eating as well, and he was saying something about calling the sheriff to report his librarian…"

"Cali Fortner?"

"Yeah, that's her. He called to say she hadn't reported to work in a couple days, and he was worried. Next thing he heard was there was a swarm of cop cars at her house all day, and a white van showed up and left a couple hours later. Now the whole area is blocked off with yellow tape."

"Oh…no…It *does* sound like a murder, doesn't it?"

"Could be, but I'm not one to gossip, so until I hear for sure that it is, then I'm not assuming anything. I just pray that it's not that."

"Me too, and you're right. I shouldn't assume anything either. What time will you be getting home?"

"Later than normal. I'm manning the ship solo."

"Don't forget, we need to get going no later than six, or Joey will miss out on all the good stuff."

"Where are we going?"

"Allen, it's Halloween. Trick-or-treating?"

"Oh, right! I forgot what day it was with all the crazy excitement. Then I should probably just leave the candy at the front of the church since no one will be here to hand it out. Pastor Steve was supposed to, but he didn't make it in."

"Won't someone just take it all?"

"I've got a fantastic plan for that."

"Oh?" Jackie felt a smile forming on her face. "What's your masterful plan?"

"I'm going to put a sign on it that says stealing is a sin, please don't take more than two pieces."

Jackie laughed. "If that works, I'll eat my socks."

"Better get some ketchup ready."

"Ewww, gross."

"Where's Joey now?"

"Upstairs in his room. I've been trying to get some cleaning done but I can't get focused enough to do it."

"Don't worry about it. It'll be there tomorrow. I'll handle it then."

"You've got to work."

"Are you kidding? After today, I'm taking a personal day tomorrow."

Jackie felt an excited tremor inside. Allen usually took Fridays off, but if he was taking a personal day tomorrow, then that meant they'd have two days in a row to spend together as a family. Other than vacations, she never had her husband at home for more than a day. "That's wonderful! We need to take advantage of it."

"We will, after I finish the laundry."

Jackie laughed. "All right. I'll let you get back to work. Will you be home around five?"

"Why don't you just come pick me up when you're ready to head out? That way you won't be waiting on me to get home."

"What about your car?"

"You can drop me off when we're done, and I'll follow you home."

That did sound easier. "All right. I'll be there around five-thirty."

"Sounds good. I love you."

"I love you, too."

She listened to the rustling of Allen taking the phone away from his ear, followed by the click of him hanging it up. A deep silence filled the earpiece. Before her line started its annoying chirp to alert her of the phone being off the hook, she cut it off.

Her mouth felt strange. Putting her fingers to her lips, she realized she was still smiling. Allen's news about taking a day off had definitely helped her feel better. However, remembering what he'd overheard at Rick's seemed to sap out what smile she had.

A murder. Here?

Jackie couldn't even fathom such a morbid possibility, not in Autumn Creek. Where they'd lived in Georgia, yes, it was—sadly—easy to accept. People were killed out there all the time, so much so that there was hardly ever that startled shock when you heard about it. But here? No…she hoped not.

Jackie turned the pages in the newspaper, eyes skimming words but not reading them. When she reached the end, she had no recollection of what she'd seen. Maybe she'd try again later. Folding the area news section, she set it on top with the few other sections. Then she leaned back in the chair, folding her arms over her breasts.

It was too quiet in here, especially with Joey home. She wondered what he was doing. Most likely he was playing Minecraft, but still, she thought she would have at least heard him moving around up there. Far as she knew, he hadn't moved an inch since going to his room.

Checking the time on the microwave timer, she saw the lunch hour had nearly passed. *Wonder what Joey would like.* She could be that mother who makes him eat the lunch she'd already packed, but she wouldn't force him. If he wanted to, that was different. Going and asking him what he wanted to eat would be a great excuse for checking up on him.

Standing outside his door, she put her ear close, listening. Seemed awfully silent and still on the other side.

"Joey?"

No response.

Could he be taking a nap?

Knocking, she repeated his name. The same lack of sound came back at her.

Her hand went for the knob, but she paused. What if he was…doing something in there? Somewhere along the way, she assumed, an experimental friend had explained to Joey the concept of masturbation. There was a time when she'd walked into his bedroom without knocking and had found him under his blankets, lying on his back, and sweaty. He'd seemed a tad flustered and very irritable for being disturbed.

But what about now?

They had a block on their internet so nobody could explore websites they weren't supposed to, so he couldn't be watching a video he shouldn't be.

Plus, if he was in there...doing *that*...then he would at least hear her knocking.

Either he was napping, or playing a game on his tablet with his earbuds in.

Feeling a smidgeon of relief, she twisted the knob and opened the door.

The bed was made. Joey's book bag and costume had been tossed on top, but after a quick search of the room, she didn't find *him*.

"Joey?"

Her voice sounded on the verge of panic. His room was small, so there weren't many places he could be if he wasn't on the bed.

"*Joey?*" Her voice had succumbed to panic, shrieking her son's name.

Rustling outside called her attention to the window. It was open, and the screen had been raised.

With a squeal, she ran over to the window. Putting both hands flat on the sill, she ducked out and scanned the yard. Leaves carpeted the grass in an assortment of faded colors. Beyond the yard was a block of trees that ran behind the property. She caught a flicker of movement to the right.

Joey ran into the trees. He seemed to be wearing old dark clothing, nothing that she recalled buying him.

"Joey?" She called. "What are you doing?"

It was hard for Jackie to comprehend what she'd seen. To her, it appeared her son was running away from home. Somehow, he'd managed to sneak out of his room and was now on his way to who knew where.

Her knees trembled. Tears trickled down her cheeks in cold streaks from the crisp air drifting across her face. The leaves rustled like wrapping paper on the trees, raining down in crinkled, flimsy blades.

"Joey..." His name blubbered into sobs.

Wiping her eyes with the back of her hand, she stepped away from the window. She needed to go after him. If she hurried, she could probably catch up to him.

She turned around.

Joey's closet door flung open. Someone rushed out, hands extended in front of them. Dressed like a phantom, his ragged costume fluttered behind him as he ran.

Ran at Jackie.

She skittered back, screaming, throwing her arms in front of her to shield the impact that was coming. It did nothing to soften the collision. The intruder's weight crashed into her, throwing her back. Her head cracked the bottom of the window as her rump slipped over the sill. Folding up, she fell through the block of space, her hands touching her toes as she tumbled out.

Jackie saw the faded blue of the sky spinning above her, the trees zipped by, then she could see the leaves covering the grass when she flipped over. She was falling, stomach down.

And the ground came up fast to meet her.

(11)

There were two ways into the school's main office. Through the commonly used front entrance that was located just past the school's main doors. And there was the back way which was accessible from the science hall.

The front entrance was locked, the blinds on the door and windows drawn. Tabitha, with her purse and shoulder bag, waited for either Becky or Mr. Horton to come let her in. Becky had gone around to the back entrance to see if it was unlocked. They were leaving for the day and wanted to let Mr. Horton know, plus they wanted to report their missing phones.

After Becky had arrived with their lunch, Tabitha had shown her the apple. Becky seemed as bothered by the rotten fruit as Tabitha. She'd volunteered to clean up the mess so Tabitha could keep hunting for her keys and phone.

She never found them. Not that they had ever been lost, because she was convinced someone had taken them.

But why?

There was no reason, and no one to suspect. Maybe she *had* lost them, sat them down somewhere and walked away. Hopefully someone had turned them in to lost and found.

"How are you going to get in your house?" Becky had asked.

"I'm not worried about that. I have a hidden key at home. It's in a good, secret spot."

"Underneath the porcelain turtle?"

"Well, maybe it's not such a good spot, but yeah, I have one."

"Aren't you worried that whoever took them might use them?"

Tabitha hadn't once considered that. "Well, I am *now*."

"This isn't good."

"No. I guess it isn't."

"Why don't we go check lost and found?"

"Why would someone take my keys and cell phone out of my classroom, only to turn them in to lost and found?"

"Maybe you misplaced them?" She raised her eyebrows.

Tabitha shrugged. "I doubt it. Anything's possible, I suppose." She groaned.

Becky pulled the headband of cat ears off her head. There was a crease in her hair where the band had reached across. She shook her hand through the curls until it was gone. "Do you think someone's trying to tell you something?"

"Yeah. *Prank Night.* Whatever that is."

"Let's erase that, it's bothering me."

"How do you think *I* feel?" Tabitha said.

"Probably not so good."

"That's right."

They walked over to the chalkboard. Tabitha grabbed the dusty eraser and was about to wipe away the words when Becky suddenly stopped her.

"Do you think we should leave it here?" she said.

Tabitha groaned. "It was your idea to erase it in the first place!"

"Maybe we shouldn't though."

"Why?"

"I don't know. Evidence?"

"Evidence of what? That someone's jerking me off?" She scrubbed the board until the words had vanished.

Becky looked at her sympathetically. "Why don't you stay with me tonight?" She spoke as someone would to a child who'd had a bad dream.

It had been a caring offer, but Tabitha liked to avoid Becky's house whenever possible. It wasn't anything that her friend was responsible for, nor was it a hideous house. The blame was all on Becky's husband. He kept their house arranged like an antique store. There was a wall covered from floor to ceiling with clocks. Just clocks. And all of them were set to the same time, and all of them either buzzed, chimed, or coo-cooed at the top of the hour, every hour.

In every corner was some form of trinket or fragile object that was worth money, and Tabitha couldn't handle trying to traipse around in there without destroying something valuable.

"Thanks. I appreciate the offer, but I'm not going to let this scare me out of my home. Plus, if someone *does* try to use them, I'd rather be there to catch them."

It wasn't a complete lie, only forty percent.

Becky frowned. "If you think that's best."

"I *should* call the cops though and report it. Maybe they can have someone patrol by every now and then."

"That wouldn't be a bad idea. We can go down to my room and I'll let you use my cell phone."

"Sounds good."

"Want to call it a day? I mean, there's not much else we can do here."

Tabitha thought it over. She'd planned to work on the report cards some more to make one of her workdays shorter, but Becky's suggestion was just too tempting not to take. "Yeah, let's kick rocks."

Tabitha then gathered up her things, followed Becky out. She made sure the door was shut and locked this time. When they made it to Becky's classroom, they discovered that her cell phone had also disappeared. Luckily, her keys had been safely clipped to a belt loop on her skirt.

The same ominous two words had been scribbled on her chalkboard.

"This joke just went too far," Becky had said.

"*Way* too far."

"Doesn't it, though? Don't you feel like someone's trying to be funny?"

"I'm not laughing."

Becky looked flabbergasted and defeated. "It just doesn't seem real. I mean—what's the point in all this?"

Tabitha put her arm around her. "Come on, champ, let's get you home." She led Becky away.

Ten minutes later, Tabitha stood alone at the front of the school, waiting for Becky, who had gone to check lost and found.

What if she doesn't come back?

Her chest tightened.

Way to go. Get that thought going.

Tabitha looked to the narrow hall and felt a cold squirm in her bowels. The mouth and esophagus of the malevolent vestibule had swallowed Becky and was still hungry, with a taste for Tabitha.

Footsteps clapped up ahead. She imagined a hideous ghoul looming around the corner, skulking toward her, its arms outstretched, long strings of foamy drool draggling from its mouth.

Tabitha held her breath as the footsteps grew louder. She was ready to run if it was anyone other than Becky who was revealed.

A short frame of a woman teetered around the side of the office, curly hair bouncy and springy with each step.

Thank you, God.

Becky held her arms out to her sides and shrugged.

"Nothing?" asked Tabitha.

She shook her head. "No one's here. I knocked and knocked. No one answered."

"Not even Ms. Vanderson?"

"Nope. Of all people, she should still be here."

"And no Horton?"

Becky shook her head.

"That's impossible. Horton's creeping around here somewhere."

Becky shivered. "Don't say that. I told you about the time…"

"Yes, a thousand times actually. You thought Horton was spying on you in the bathroom."

"He *was*." Becky closed her eyes as if she were watching the memory projected against her eyelids. "It was the last day of school before spring break last year…"

"Oh, jeez."

"And I really had to do a number one."

Tabitha had never heard Becky refer to her bathroom ventures as *peeing, pissing, or taking a leak,* nor had she ever heard her say, *dump, shit, or squat.* But Tabitha was raised where that kind of talk was common. Maybe Becky's parents were more delicate with their wordings.

"I heard someone come in right after I had sat down. I just thought it was…"

"Another teacher or possibly a student staying after school, I know. Then you peeked through the small gap by the door and saw Horton trying to leer in at you."

"Exactly!"

"You should have confronted him about it."

"How could I have? When I got enough nerve to charge out of the stall and slap him one good time, he wasn't there. I have no proof that he was in there at all."

"Because he never was."

"He was too."

"Horton's a lot of things, but I don't buy him as a perv."

"You'd be surprised at who the *real* perverts are."

Changing the subject, Tabitha said, "So, that's that huh? No way to check the lost and found for our stuff?"

"Not today I guess."

"Well, we'll be back in the morning. We'll look then."

"Yeah…" There was a hint of circumspection in her voice.

Ignoring it, Tabitha pushed open one of the main doors. Then she looked over her shoulder to Becky. "Maybe it was Horton who took our stuff." She laughed like a maniacal specter.

"Oh, stop it. You'll never stop picking on me about that will you?"

"Nope."

Tabitha leaned against the door, holding it open for Becky. She started forward but stopped and turned toward the office.

Frowning, Tabitha looked too. "What is it?"

"Thought I heard something."

"What?"

"I don't know. Sounded like a bump."

"A bump?"

"Yeah, like someone dropped something in there."

＊＊＊

Horton dragged himself across the floor. The knife jutted up from his back like a weird growth between his shoulder blades. Jagged rents covered his back, oozing blood that trickled down his sides as his fingers gripped the carpet and pulled. He moved another inch. He was almost to the door when someone landed low on his back. Blood shot from Horton's mouth, spattering red blots across the beige hairs of the floor.

He'd heard Becky Loflin outside, knocking, calling for him. Trying to cry out for her to hear, all he could do was gargle the blood filling his throat.

He'd been stabbed so many times! How could he still be alive? Horton wished he wasn't, wished he was like Ms. Vanderson, who was already dead when he'd returned to the office. She was leaned back in her chair behind her desk, gutted, chest ripped open. Her blondish hair hung in tangles around her face, snarled with blood.

Then he was assaulted from behind.

And he was still alive. If only he would die, the pain would be done with him. How'd this happen? Who was doing this?

Too many questions.

So close to the door now. He wasn't going to let the added weight of his attacker prevent him from reaching it.

Almost there!

Fingers brushed the door...

The knife was wrenched from his back.

Horton's palm slapped the door.

He saw the flash of the blade as it moved in front of his eyes, lowering. He felt coldness against his Adam's apple.

Then the knife was yanked across, slitting his throat.

✳✳✳

Becky shrugged. "Maybe I'm just hearing things."

"Must be. I didn't hear it."

Becky walked past Tabitha to go outside. Tabitha followed. A chilly breeze wafted over them. It pushed Tabitha's skirt against her legs, forming around her thighs. Leaves scampered over their feet as they walked across the concrete of the entranceway, sounding like wadded paper as it pranced across the parking lot. Other blades crunched under their feet.

Looking to where the buses were parked, Tabitha saw the maintenance men had left, but their jobs were incomplete. It appeared that only a couple buses had been totally repaired.

Circling around the building to the side parking area, Tabitha half-expected to find the truck with its tires slashed. Though, old and balding in spots, the tires weren't flat.

Strike one for the good guys.

They drove along carless streets. It was negated of life other than a few early bird trick-or-treaters scurrying along the sidewalks. Tabitha noted there were no adults supervising them as they ran in front of the buildings.

Strange costume choices.

Old-fashioned and homemade. Nothing she recognized. No Transformers, superheroes. No Barbies or Beauty Queens.

The small pack ducked between two buildings, out of sight.

Becky tried to keep some form of conversation going. Tabitha could tell it was hard for her. Plus, she wasn't being very responsive since she wasn't much in the mood for talking herself. Tabitha wondered if Becky was as bothered about her missing phone and the two words on her chalkboard as much as she was.

When the truck's tires left the black top and slapped the gravel of Amity Hill Road, Tabitha started to feel better. Then she remembered her keys had been stolen and felt the heavy poke of dread return to her chest. *What if someone does show up?* She pictured her front door opening, and Horton walking into her living room while she sat on the couch watching a black and white horror movie during the Halloween marathon on TV.

"Hey Miss *Stoner*. Care to grade me on this *boner*?"

She snickered.

Becky glanced at her. "What'd you say?"

"Oh, nothing. I was just thinking."

Becky steered the truck into Tabitha's driveway and drove up to the house. She shifted the gear into park but left the engine idling. "Are you sure you wouldn't rather stay at my place?"

"Yeah…I just want to hang around the house. Watch some bad movies on TV tonight. Maybe read a little."

"I see. Okay." Becky lowered her head, keeping her eyes focused on the steering wheel.

Tabitha doubted there was anything interesting printed across the horn, so she assumed Becky's feelings had been hurt.

Way to go, bitch. She's just trying to be helpful.

Tabitha felt lousy. "Why don't you stay here instead?"

Becky's head whipped around. "Really?"

Though she didn't feel like having company, Tabitha nodded. "Yes."

"Here?"

"*Yes.*"

"I mean, I will...if you really don't mind."

She was looking forward to being alone tonight, but figured she'd done that enough every other night she'd been living here. Plus, it might be safer for the both of them if they stuck together, at least for the night. "No, I don't mind at all."

Becky's smile nearly reached the tips of her ears. Genuine relief was displayed on her lovely face. "Thank you. I was *not* looking forward to spending the night alone."

"Honestly, I wasn't either."

"Well, I need to run home and get some things."

"Clothes? I've got plenty you can borrow."

"Well, that and my toothbrush, shampoo, and all that stuff. Plus, my meds." She winked at her. "You know. My anxiety medicine."

Tabitha couldn't recall Becky ever mentioning being on any kind of anxiety medicine before.

Becky tilted her head as if to say: *Come on!* "You know. The kind you smoke. Wrapped in thin white paper."

"Ah," said Tabitha, finally understanding what she meant. "You smoke?"

"Please. It's what keeps me sane. You don't mind, do you?"

"Not at all. In fact, I might need some anxiety medicine tonight as well, if you don't mind sharing. I am a trifle stressed."

"I shall bring a *trifle* amount for the both of us."

They laughed. Tabitha gathered up her things and opened the door.

Becky leaned across the seat. "Give me an hour or two to get back. Want me to bring anything specific?"

"Just plenty of medicine."

"No worries there. Anything else?"

Standing outside of the truck, Tabitha propped her elbow on the door. "Maybe some munchies? I don't have much here that doesn't require cooking."

"Deal. Do you have coffee?"

"I *do* have plenty of that."

"All right, sounds like a plan. I'll be back in a flash."

"Can't wait." And she was telling the truth. She honestly couldn't wait for Becky to get back. It was going to be sort of like a girls' night, something Tabitha hadn't experienced since college. Plus, she was going to be spending time with Becky and partaking in some excellent anxiety therapy. She was excited.

"I'll hang around and make sure you get inside safe."

"Thanks."

Tabitha shut the door, waved, then walked to the front of her house. There was a small flower garden to the left of the front stoop that she'd allowed to dwindle and die. For her first year in this house, she'd maintained it very well, but then she'd eventually lost interest. Now it was just a bay of weeds. And scattered throughout were fake rocks, washed out painted gnomes chipped on the hats and faces, and the porcelain turtle where she kept a key under its shell, hidden in the weeds like Easter eggs.

What if that key's gone too?

The way this day had been going, she wouldn't have been surprised to find it wasn't there. Leaning over, she opened one of the squares on the turtle's back. She spotted a twinkle of metal. Tabitha breathed with relief as she removed the key from its housing. Standing up straight, she waved again, then walked up the steps as the truck began backing up. She could hear its tires popping and crunching the gravel as she unlocked the door.

Maybe you should have Becky come in with you just to make sure you are alone.

She turned around, waving her hand above her head to signal Becky's attention. The truck was already well on its way down the driveway. It vanished behind trees when it took a curve. If Becky had seen her trying to catch her attention, she had ignored her. Tabitha dug through her pocketbook for her cell phone to call her, then remembered it was gone.

"Damn it!" She groaned. "Guess I'm on my own."

She wondered if it might have been better to ride with Becky back to her house, made sure it was okay there, then she could have waited for her the few minutes it would have taken her to pack up.

Good plan. Just a few minutes late. Genius.

She turned around, approached the door. Putting the key to the lock, she began to fear it wouldn't open.

What? You think they'd snuck over and changed your locks while you were gone?

Tabitha smirked. Then she twisted the key without any trouble. Now the task of actually going inside awaited her. She was tempted to stretch that duty out until Becky came back.

You're being stupid. Just go inside. There's no real danger. Someone took your keys and phone to be funny.

Still, she wasn't thrilled to be going in there alone.

Do a quick look around and make sure everything is where it needs to be, triple-check that you don't have any unwelcomed visitors, then call the cops and report your phone and keys have been stolen.

Tabitha put her hand on the doorknob. It felt cold and smooth in her palm. She would have to change the locks whether she found her keys or not. Money she didn't want to spend, and a chore she didn't want to do, but it would need to be done.

She turned the knob. There was a loud pop of air when the door pulled away from the rubber shield inside the frame. She let the door sway open. With the sun behind her, there was a Tabitha-sized profile cast across the hardwood of living room floor. She looked from right to left. The living room seemed okay. No one was hanging out on any of the furniture. The TV was still there. Nothing seemed to be missing.

So, she went inside.

The silence inside the house was heavy on her, making it difficult to lift her feet to walk. Her heart hammered her chest like heavy punches. Keeping the door open in case she needed to make a quick exit, she rambled through the house and into the kitchen. All looked fine on her way. She went to the knife rack on the counter, found one with the biggest blade, and took it. Now that she was armed, she felt a little braver.

Still have to check the rest of the house.

Tabitha came out of the kitchen, crossed the den, and made her way to the hallway. It seemed darker back here than usual, like a tunnel with crushing walls, closing tighter on each side of her as she slowly crept towards the bathroom. The door was open. She peeked in. Nothing looked out of the ordinary, but the shower curtain was closed. It was dark purple in color, and too thick for her to make out if anyone was standing behind it. She held the knife in front of her as she approached the curtain. She wanted to start stabbing through the plastic, making whoever might be hiding back there regret they had ever attempted getting the jump on her, but she didn't. Grabbing the curtain with her left hand, she kept the knife prone in the right.

Then she jerked back the flimsy curtain, thrusting the knife forward.

The blade punched through the hanging basket, imbedding halfway into her shampoo bottle.

Terrific.

She'd murdered her shampoo, shanked the plastic bottle all the way through. A wedge of blade protruded through the directions and ingredients label on the back. Maybe she could claim self-defense? Tabitha tugged the knife out. Pink liquid bled out of the gash in the bottle's front. She took it to the sink, laying it flat so it could seep down the drain.

Good thing I have a wide selection of shampoos.

This one had been for color treatment. Since she hadn't had highlights in her hair in over a year, she figured she no longer needed this bottle. Tabitha left the bathroom to the burbling sounds of shampoo draining out.

She checked the rest of the house, ending the manhunt with a quick stroll through the basement. No one was hiding behind the storage boxes, and the aluminum track door that led to the outside was lowered. Whenever she needed to mow the yard, she simply raised the door and drove the mower out. She walked over to the door, leaned over, and took the handle. Then she tugged upward, making sure the door wouldn't open. It didn't budge. Locked. She might want to go check the outside and make sure the padlock was still in place but decided against it. If the door wasn't opening, then it most likely was how it should be.

Tabitha stood up straight, exhaling a long sigh of relief.

All looked to be in order everywhere in the house.

She returned to the front door. As she was about to close it, she glanced outside and froze. At the bend in her driveway, she spotted someone in a costume standing there. He was between the trees and the field that surrounded the property on the other side.

He wore all black, a hooded jacket zipped in the front, with matching black pants, boots, and gloves. A black beanie was on top of his head, and a cheap vampire mask hid his face. Even from this distance she recognized the mask. She'd seen an entire collection of them at the drugstore, consisting of different masks of several different monsters—mummies, Frankenstein's monster, a witch, a skull, and more.

This one was the vampire.

A cold draft flowed through the doorway, nudging at the door. She put her hand on the edge to hold it open and looked outside. Motionless, he stared at the house, at *her*. He was so stiff he didn't look real. But she knew he was because she could feel his eyes, feel their cold stare through the light breeze.

Tabitha slammed the door, locked it, and when she peeked through the windowpane at the top of the door, she couldn't find him.

The vampire was gone.

CHAPTER 6

(1)

Becky closed the door behind her and twisted the deadbolt. When it clicked home, she put her back against the door, and exhaled the deep breath she'd been holding all the way inside. It felt good to be home. Driving through town had been spooky, and as excited as she was to spend the night at Tabitha's, she dreaded the drive back. It was a ghost town out there from the way cars sat, abandoned, left where they'd been parked, tires slashed. Some businesses had remained closed for the day, probably because the owners and employees had no way of getting there to operate them. Whoever was responsible for this folly had sure pulled a good one over on just about everyone in Autumn Creek.

She willed herself to leave the refuge of the locked door. She needed to make some calls, starting with the Sheriff's office to report her missing phone and what was written on her chalkboard. Probably should go on and call the cell phone company. And she needed to call Tim and inform him of her phone, also give him Tabitha's number just in case he needed to reach her tonight. She would neglect to inform him of the chalkboard.

Prank Night.

What did it mean?

Wind picked up outside, slightly howling. She heard the scraping of leaves as they glided across her windows. The house popped as if it was just getting up from a nap and stretching.

Thump.

Becky stopped walking and looked up at the ceiling.

What was that?

She waited a moment to see if it repeated. It didn't. Probably just the house settling, doing those creak and pop resonances that old houses do for no good reason other than to frighten a woman home alone. She stepped around the side of a wall and looked beyond the living room to the back door. Becky could see the sliding glass doors that led onto the back deck. Vertical blinds hung in front of them like thick vinyl hair. Two of them were swaying slightly.

Entering the living room, she dropped her pocketbook on the couch. She thought about cutting on the stereo and blasting some Adele but decided to make this trip a quick one. If she cut on Adele, she'd be dancing around the house singing for an hour.

She needed to make those calls.

Becky glanced at the glass doors again on her way to the kitchen. This time something clicked in her head, stopping her, making her take a moment to focus on the doors. The blinds were making light whispering sounds as they rubbed together. She could smell dry leaves, and one of her neighbors must have been burning something from the subtle scent of smoke. She'd smelled it outside earlier, either burning leaves or wood. A smell she actually enjoyed, especially when it was cold outside. Maybe someone had gone ahead and opened their chimneys and gotten a fire going.

Then Becky realized something else, and her chest felt as if it dropped into her stomach. The blinds would only be moving if wind were hitting them, and wind wouldn't be hitting them unless the doors were opened. There were no vents over there, so the heat couldn't be what was causing them to move. And, she always kept the doors locked, unless she was at home, and even then she was nervous of leaving them open.

She headed for the doors.

How *could* air be hitting them?

She stepped off the carpet and onto a crescent shape of tile. Her foot came down on broken glass that crunched under her shoe.

There was a hole in the glass beside the latch.

And it was unlocked.

"Shit," she whispered.

Thump.

There was that sound again, but now it had moved, sounding as if it had relocated to her bedroom.

Someone's up there.

There was a slight shift in the sound, an audible creak in the boards followed by a sly shuffle as something slid to another position, then stopped. She waited another moment, but no other sounds came.

Becky knew her house, even standing here she could tell the layout of the floor above her. The sounds had resonated from her bedroom, and more importantly the sounds had come to a halt where her bed was.

Someone just hid under my bed.

Whoever was up there hadn't heard her yet. She was pretty certain of that. They would already be down here to confront her had they known she was here. At least she had that to her advantage. She'd come home undetected.

Jogging on her tiptoes to her left, hoping the carpet would conceal her movements, she moved toward the landline she and Tim kept on the wall in the kitchen in case of power outages. Then she delicately removed it from the base, putting it to her ear.

Nothing.

What the…?

She tapped the button several more times, acknowledging she was doing what they did in the movies, but she didn't care. After several pats there was still nothing on the other end.

It's dead.

Becky's plan had been to call 911, but someone had thought enough ahead to make sure that couldn't happen. Her cell phone was taken, now her home phone wasn't working, and someone had smashed their way inside.

She needed to get out of here. Fast.

No longer concerned with being quiet, she dropped the phone on the kitchen tile. Its plastic shell was like a blast on the linoleum. Then she dashed through the kitchen. Using the entrance from the far side, she came out, and spun on her heels to make a hard right.

And rushed for the front door.

Her shoulder rammed it, bouncing her back. Her hands fidgeted with the knob. They finally gripped it, and she twisted. The door flung open, slipping from her grasp, and smashing against the wall.

A scarecrow waited for her on the stoop. She glimpsed a straw hat and a burlap sack for a head with stitched X's for eyes and a mouth. Old flannel shirt, hay dangling out of the collar and cuffs, overalls for its clothes.

Becky sucked in a breath to scream. Then a sharp pinch of coldness struck her stomach, killing the scream in her throat. Her eyes went wide, mouth becoming a gasping ring as she slowly looked down.

A scythe had punctured her stomach. A burlap hand clasped its handle, straw obtruding from the wrist. She felt behind her and found a curved blade protruding from her back, tacky with her blood.

Becky stumbled back, keeping her eyes locked on the scarecrow. He released the handle, tilting his head to watch her as she attempted moving on legs that seemed not to be in the mood for moving.

Her knees gave way, and she dropped.

Becky lay on her side, not in a lot of pain, but feeling awfully light, as if there was no weight in her body. She could feel her blood, warm as it secreted from her, but swiftly dropping in temperature as it pooled around her.

Footsteps resonated from the stairs. She looked over and spotted someone taking his time on the way down, dropping one foot on a step, pausing, then bringing down the other one. A black-gloved hand glided down the railing.

I…wasn't…crazy…

She *had* heard someone up there. He was masked as well, a green demonic-like face.

A witch.

Everything suddenly made sense to her now, the realization hailing down on her so quickly that she would kick herself for not comprehending it sooner if she could feel anything from the hips down.

Her phone, the chalkboard, the tires.

She lost the thought. Before she could try finding it again, she was barely cognizant.

And as the rest of her life spilled out of her, she prayed for Tabitha, prayed that she would be okay, because Becky assumed, whoever these people were, would be after her too.

(11)

Ben wished Annette would stop staring at him. He would swear she hadn't blinked once in the last half hour. He'd tried questioning her, had even shouted at her once, but she had given him nothing in return, not even a flinch.

"Cat got your tongue?" he'd finally asked before giving up.

He wondered what was going on behind her vacant gaze, but at the same time was terrified of learning.

Someone lightly rapped a hand on the door frame. Ben looked over his shoulder. It was Carla. "Can I come in?" she asked.

"By all means."

Carla walked in, cautiously, keeping her eyes on Annette as if she were an animal that might strike. Ben thought Carla wasn't far off in her assumption. He'd never been so intimidated by anyone he'd questioned in this room. And he shouldn't be now. Especially by a kid.

Carla leaned over, putting her lips close to Ben's ear. Chills pimpled up his neck.

"Just wanted to let you know that the blood on the knives was a perfect match for Cali Fortner's."

Ben figured as much.

"And Carpenter's here. Just got in."

Annette's eyes twitched. She glanced at Carla a moment, then pointed her eyes back at Ben.

"He is?" asked Ben.

She nodded. "Yes. And Duggins is on his way."

"Great. Any word on the parents?"

She shook her head. "No luck contacting them. We reached Annette's grandparents in Maryland. They won't be here until the morning, but they did confirm her parents were going out of town. But they can't confirm if they actually have. They haven't heard from them in three days."

"Their cell phones?"

"Just getting the outgoing messages."

"Contact where they work, the airport, the…"

"We did…and they didn't make their flight."

"What?"

"Duggins checked the residence but found nothing to suspect foul play. But, as of right now, we don't know where her parents are and neither do the grandparents."

"Jesus."

"Rileson is on patrol just as you requested."

"Okay, good. Tell Albright and Hodges they're on call tonight. Even if their shifts end at seven, they need to keep their phones on. I'm planning on staying all night. We have to be ready for anything."

"You think it's going to get worse?"

Before Ben could answer, Annette did it for him.

"It is." Although her voice wasn't higher than a whisper, Ben and Carla started as if she'd shouted.

"What'd you say?" asked Ben.

Annette looked down at her handcuffed wrists. Carla parked her rump in the chair beside Ben as if she'd been commanded to.

He leaned forward. "You better start talking. Where's your parents?"

The corner of her mouth curved up. "Where they belong. Where you all belong."

"What's that mean?"

She didn't answer.

"We know you didn't act alone in Cali Fortner's murder. It's not possible. So, who helped you?"

Nothing.

"Why did you kill her?"

Nothing still.

"What is going to happen tonight?"

She looked at him. "It's already happening."

"*What's* been happening?"

"Prank Night."

"Prank...what?" He shook his head, grimacing as if he'd eaten something fetid.

"And you're too late to stop it." Suddenly she looked away, revolving back to the blank, mannequin-like persona she had been as if her batteries had died.

Ben knew that was all he was going to get out of her for now and didn't hassle with trying to make her talk. "Keep her here," he told Carla, and stood up. His legs were wobbly, his head dizzy. "I need some air."

"Okay, Ben."

Ben left the interrogation room and bumped into Carpenter on his way out. He jumped back, hollering. On reflex, he grabbed Carpenter's shoulder.

Carpenter's eyes behind the overly large glasses were worried. "Sorry, Sheriff, I didn't mean to..."

"It's fine."

"Are you okay?"

He released his young deputy's shoulder. "I've been better. I need you to do something for me."

"Name it…"

"Find out what you can about Prank Night."

"Prank Night?"

"Yes. Annette Carter hasn't said much, but she did say *that*. It was also in her confession note. I want to know what it is. Maybe we can figure out what she means."

"Okay."

"Find out anything you can."

"You got it." Carpenter slowly looked past Ben's shoulder to the interrogation room. "She's in there?"

"Annette? Yeah."

Carpenter gulped, throat bulged. "Okay."

Squinting, Ben studied the deputy's bland tone, the thick sweat on his forehead. "Are *you* okay, Carpenter?"

"There's probably something you should know."

Oh, boy.

Whenever someone said that, usually what followed was awful news. "Come with me."

Grabbing Carpenter's arm, Ben pulled the young officer down the hallway. When they were close to the breakroom, he stopped. "What do you have to say?"

Carpenter lowered his head. He picked his index fingernail with the nail of his thumb. It made thin clicking sounds as he nervously flicked. "It's about Annette…and *me*."

"Jesus, Carpenter. Are you about to tell me what I think you're going to?"

A slight shrug of a shoulder, Carpenter seemed to shrink even more. "We've been seeing each other."

"Jesus H. Christ, Carpenter. She's a *minor*." Ben made sure to keep his voice down, but even in a whisper, his point was loud.

"She just turned seventeen," said Carpenter. "I'm still eighteen."

"In the eyes of the town, she's a minor. She's still in high school."

"Graduating this year."

Ben opened his mouth to argue more but stopped. Taking a deep breath, he closed his eyes to compose himself. It wasn't like he had much of a right for dispute when he would have done the same thing at Carpenter's age. If Annette was eighteen, truth be told, he might have tried for her himself. He put a hand on Carpenter's shoulder. "Thanks for telling me."

Carpenter nodded. "Maybe I should go talk to her."

"Not yet. Find out about this Prank Night stuff first. I might let you go in there later."

"Okay."

Ben patted Carpenter's shoulder and turned around, heading back into the main area. He saw Hodges sitting at his desk, filling out the required paperwork for the arrest.

"Hodges. Got my cigarettes?"

The pack launched at him. He caught it with one hand without stopping. Ben took the back hall to the emergency exit. He shoved the door open with his shoulder. Cool air brushed his face. It felt good. He was feeling less lightheaded already as he put a cigarette in his mouth and flamed it. His hands were shaking. Before today, he couldn't remember the last time he'd ever felt like this.

Prank Night.

He took a deep drag from the cigarette.

What in God's name is Prank Night?

A dull poke inside, hardly noticeable, told him he'd know before the day was over.

Deputy Ken Rileson sat in his cruiser under Miller's Bridge, parked in the shadows where no one could see him until they were right on top of him. By then it would be too late for them to back off their speed. He'd taken the graveled off-ramp and backed the car under the bridge, its front end facing the ramp for a quick departure if needed. It was his favorite spot, and even on some days he wasn't in his cruiser, he would come out here and spend some time enjoying the view of the plains and pastures in the distance, appreciating the solitude and the quiet. It was also an ideal spot to interrupt fornicating teenagers, or secret lovers. He'd busted several cheating spouses in this out-of-the-way section of town.

The bridge was at the end of Miller Road where it crossed over to Patterson Farms. Even from here, he could see the orange bulbs of pumpkins in the patches. Passing trains got a nice view during the fall of colorful trees, dairy cattle, and acres of pumpkins. The summer offered something of a different variety, but to Rileson, it couldn't beat what you saw in the autumn.

The bridge was built for the railroad in the early 1900s, but over the subsequent decades it was eventually condemned. The trains kept to the newer tracks in town that were laid in the 70's. Miller's Bridge was overgrown with tall weeds and forgotten, and where Rileson was parked looked more like a cave burrowed into the hillside than an actual underpass. No one ever came back here anymore unless to participate in something they didn't want anyone to see, and Rileson was just happy to be the one who busted them.

He loved it here. This was the place where he used to go to goof off as kid, bring his dates as a teenager to make out with, and eventually, where he'd lost his virginity. Even these days he would accompany a date or two out here for some fun of his own. Sure, it sounded like the usual fare of anyone growing up or living in Autumn Creek, except Rileson's difference to the norm was he brought men out here. Yes, Rileson was a discreet gay man living in a terribly small town. He'd been hiding it all his life, and though there were some who suspected him of being a homosexual, he'd never been exposed.

Rileson checked the time on his phone. He'd been parked under the bridge for an hour, eating a bag of beef jerky, and drinking Dr. Pepper. The hectic morning caused him to miss lunch, but he also hadn't had much of an appetite. He tried to eat beef jerky whenever possible because it was high in protein and helped him from getting hunger headaches. Those were the worst, making him irritable, and often plain mean. And being that he was on a necessary diet, it was one of the few things that he could eat which actually tasted good.

Not a vegetable person, he despised salads, and had a wilting waistline that proved it. He'd switched from whole milk to 2% and nearly cried when he drank his first glass of it. It was so thin and runny, like chalky water. He took a swig of his soda and sighed. He'd earned this Dr. Pepper after the day he'd had, a small reward he'd granted himself after all his eyes had lamentably endured today.

Cali Fortner's jack-o'-lantern face, her mangled body.

He shivered.

How long did it take to carve her up like that?

Just guessing, he would say that whoever had killed her had spent the rest of the night doing that to her. He'd heard on the horn that Annette Carter had turned herself in, claiming she'd done it.

No way in hell.

He wouldn't believe it. He knew Annette quite well and knew her parents even better. They were good people, and Annette was a peach if he'd ever met one. Just didn't make sense.

But he also knew all about her exploits with Carpenter. Probably was the only one who knew. Carpenter trusted him, and Rileson trusted the kid back. They knew where the other hid the skeletons in the closets.

A sound like a wet bomb hitting his car made him jump.

Rileson flinched, sucked in a quick gust of breath. The Dr. Pepper flew from his hand and into the floorboard, fizzing as cola chugged out from the bottle's mouth. The windshield was dark with mushy strings spreading in thick glops. Broken chunks were entwined in the viscous tan-colored filaments. He saw teardrop-shaped seeds and realized what had splattered across the glass.

A pumpkin.

Someone had thrown it from above, on the bridge.

He threw his door open, climbed out, and drew his Colt. He aimed it up. The sun was a yellow blur over the horizon, and its rays were peeking over the bridge. He squinted against their brightness, using his free hand as a visor above his eyes.

"Who's up there?" he shouted.

No response, nor did he expect one.

"If I have to walk up this hill to get you, I'm going to be even more pissed than I am now." He waited another moment. "*Really* pissed. So come on down here. Now!"

Something whisked by the front of his eyes. He saw it only for a second before he felt a scratchy texture around his throat. It tightened, severing his air. He couldn't breathe. He tugged at it with his empty hand.

A rope!

Someone had noosed him.

It heaved.

Rileson staggered back, shifting his weight to the foot behind him so he wouldn't fall. He was pitched again. This time his foot couldn't stop him, and he flew back on his ass, losing his gun in the fall. He heard it clatter across the ground somewhere behind him. He felt useless without his weapon. Using both hands now, he tried to slip his fingers behind the rope so he could pull it away from his throat.

It was much too tight.

He was jerked onto his back. Looking up, he ascertained the rope was trailing up along the bridge and over the lip of the stone side-rail. He wasn't a complete fatass, but he weighed in the vicinity of two-thirty. So, for his height, he was a heavy guy. Hauling him like this wouldn't be an easy feat.

Must be more than one person up there.

He felt the ground go out from under him and his body lift into the air.

Then he was dangling, feet kicking as he ascended higher.

The engine of his cruiser roared to life. The gears clunked when it was put into reverse. He heard the tires crackling over gravel as someone took his car.

How many are there?

He scaled upward another foot, then stopped. The rope constricted around his neck so tightly he feared his head was going to be pulled clean off. He could feel the pressure in his head pushing against his eyes, making them bulge. His tongue darted out of his mouth, dry and useless, desperately trying to lick air.

Then he began to hear an awful tearing sound, began to feel wet heat drizzling down his chest.

He realized that his head *was* being pulled off.

Then something cracked and ripped.

His body plunged back to the ground, but his head remained in the rope.

(iv)

Ben had lighted a second cigarette off the cherry end of the previous one and was smoking it when Carpenter found him behind the station. He opened the door, poking his head around the edge to spot Ben leaning against the wall. It was early afternoon, and the temperatures were already dropping. They were in for a cold night.

"There you are," said Carpenter. "I've been looking for you."

"I guess so, since you're out here."

Carpenter stepped out, letting the door close. A single piece of copy paper waved in his hand. "Want to be alone?"

Ben shook his head. "Find something already?"

"Yeah, it wasn't hard. Just typed Prank Night into a search engine and it brought up several pages of information."

Ben thrust himself off the wall, turned to face Carpenter. "Spill it."

"Prank Night is relative to Halloween. It starts on the nights leading up to Halloween, the pranks getting worse and worse until finally they hit a peak on the actual night of."

"*Pranks?*"

"Yeah, that's how it began back in the day. Harmless pranks that got more intense each year."

"Cali Fornter's brutal murder is a *prank?*"

"I'm not saying that, but it fits the mold, doesn't it?"

"Maybe, maybe not. To me, it's a senseless crime. I don't know anything about this Prank Night business."

"I read a brief history about it on the Halloween Facts website and apparently this was something that started shortly after the Irish settlers came to America. It spread to the American natives' villages and sort of escalated—for the worse—from there. Kids were throwing rocks through windows, eggs at houses, then they started vandalizing wagons and barns, before long they were mobbing people on the streets, beating them within inches of their lives."

"And you think Annette and some friends are taking it to the next level?"

"I don't know, could be."

It made sense in an unconditional outlandish kind of way. "Thanks. We can bring it up when we talk to her again."

"There's something else, Ben. Something that I noticed when I was doing the web searches."

"Yeah?"

"I typed in Prank Night, Autumn Creek, Halloween, and some other tags to see what all it pulled up and I found this…" He apprehensively passed the paper to Ben. The breeze blew it back, folding it around his hand. "It's something you should definitely see," Carpenter added.

Ben flicked the cigarette into the parking lot, then held the paper with both hands. The golden spray of sunlight reflected off the white surface in blinding gleams. Ben had to angle the sheet to kill the glare so he could actually read what was printed. An old newspaper article, and seeing the date in the right-hand corner, he saw it was from the Webster Journal on November 1st, 1948.

"Webster Journal?" said Ben.

"You really need to learn the town history," said Carpenter. "That was the county's local newspaper until the late sixties, then it became the Webster Herald."

Ben's eyes read and reread the headline. His blood pressure dropped.

Seven murders on Halloween! Prank Night to blame!

"Holy shit," he said.

"I know."

"You've never heard of this before?"

Carpenter shook his head. "No."

"Looks like I'm not the only one who needs to catch up on their history."

"Sorry. I didn't mean anything…"

Ben held up his hand. "Can't read the article, though."

"I know. It's a low-resolution scan of an old newspaper, so the font is far from legible."

"Damn. I'd really like to know what it says."

"I thought you might. That's why I put in a call to Kathy Morgan over at the public library. She's pulling together all the information she has on the micro-fiche."

Ben lowered the paper, looking at Carpenter with a small, but proud grin forming. "Good job. Do you mind heading over there and picking it up?"

"Even better. She's going to run it by here in an hour, two at the most, on her way home. Apparently, her tires were missed in the massive strike last night. Since I was able to give her an exact series of dates, she said it wouldn't take too long to pull together something for you. She doesn't mind."

Ben figured so. He'd taken Kathy on a few dates a couple years ago. Every now and then she inquired for more, but he always declined. She was married to Pat Morgan now, who worked for the power company. And Ben did not need home-wrecker added to the deleterious list of negatives the town already had against him.

"Great job, Carpenter. You did good."

"Thanks."

"I mean it." Folding the paper, he tucked it into the back pocket of his pants. "If Kathy finds anything helpful, and my gut tells me that she will, I believe a phone call to the mayor may be in order. If anyone can teach us some unknown history, it's him."

"Uh, Marge said he's already on his way in. Apparently, word got to him about Annette, and he's coming to find out what's going on."

"Great," said Ben, not happy. "Think it's spreading through town yet?"

"Probably."

"I might need to make an announcement soon."

"Probably wouldn't hurt."

"Yeah." Ben sighed. "I'll hold off a while longer, though. I want to see what Kathy manages to round up."

CHAPTER 7

(1)

AMC had been showing horror movies all week, and sadly Tabitha had missed nearly all of them. Today, however, she had the TV on, and was lying on the couch, still in her school clothes and finishing a strawberry cereal bar while watching AIP's black and white classic, *Earth vs. the Spider*. She'd rented it on VHS as a teenager, and still had a soft spot for it. Not that it was fantastic filmmaking, but she could enjoy it for what it was.

She reached for her mug sitting on the coffee table. When she lifted it, she noticed it was much lighter than it had been. She raised her head enough to look inside. Empty.

Damn.

She looked at the screen. The spider's supposed carcass was locked up in a school gymnasium because of its size, and the rock band that revived it was just starting to rehearse.

Sorry guys. I'll be right back.

Tabitha rose with a groan.

On her way to the kitchen, she glimpsed at her phone on the small end table in the den. It was one of those sets with an answering machine built in, and the message light was blinking in a succession of three blinks.

Three messages?

Usually she had zip, so she rarely checked the machine, but today there were three.

Aren't I the popular one?

She pressed the *Play* button and waited.

The first was from a man with a deep, but pleasant voice, sounding embarrassed and apologetic about having the wrong number. Tabitha smiled. "Don't you have a sexy voice, Mr. Wrong Number?" She was almost sad when it beeped again, signaling the end of his message.

I wonder if his number's on Caller ID.

Oh, that would be rich, calling a complete stranger like that. What would she say to him?

Hi, I heard you on my answering machine and you sounded setsy...

He'd take her for a loon.

Hell, *he* might be the loon, and enjoy that kind of cold call.

The robotic voice announced the second message.

A pause. Then a click of the caller hanging up.

She wondered if the hang up was the man trying a second time, feeling too silly when he got the same number to leave a cute message.

Third message.

Another pause.

Great. Three times? Maybe I should see if his number's on Caller ID and give him a call. Sounds like fate's trying to tell us something.

When the voice spoke, her playful banter died. It was not the deep, sexy voice of the man, but a voice so scratchy and shrill it hurt Tabitha's ears, distorting the one-inch speaker built into the base.

"Tonight is Prank Night. Tonight, you meet God."

Click. Beep.

Tabitha's hand trembled so badly she almost dropped her coffee mug. She rubbed her bumpy, goose-fleshed arms. "What the hell *is* this?" She slammed her mug down on the end table, snatched the phone off its base, and pushed the ID button. She scrolled back to the last call.

Unknown Caller.

Of course it is.

She dialed the operator, demanding the Sherriff's department from the flat, uninterested voice that had answered. After a short wait, an automated message played back: *Due to the heavy volume of calls, this number is unavailable, please try again later.*

"Son of a *bitch*." She thumbed the *off* button. Lightly tapping the phone against her chin, she stood there, not really thinking of anything, but consuming her mind with everything. She hit the TALK button. Then she dialed Becky's number.

Your call cannot be completed as dialed. Please check the number and try your call again.

What the hell?

She looked at the phone in her hand as if it had the answer.

It didn't say it had been disconnected. Just that it couldn't be completed.

What the hell did that mean? She wanted to keep the phone nearby, just in case, so she clutched it tightly in her hand as she grabbed her mug. Then she made her way into the kitchen. She checked the time on the microwave clock. The small green numbers told her it was nearing four. Becky had had plenty of time to get to her house, pack, and come back. *Plenty* of time.

Tabitha sighed. The coffee pot was almost empty. Two more cups and she'd have to make more. She probably shouldn't make more, though. Usually when she had too much coffee, she'd get the jitters.

Too late.

Maybe she'd already had enough coffee for the day.

Or maybe more coffee would balance out the unease she felt thanks to the message on her machine. She was tempted to listen to it a second time but didn't want to hear that voice again. It had done enough damage. One more time would be too much.

Tabitha mixed her preferred blend in her mug, then took a sip, careful not to burn her lips. It tasted fine and sweet. She carried the mug and phone with her through the den and back to the living room. She glanced at the TV. It was on a commercial. She went to the front door, peering through its small pane of glass.

And gasped.

The vampire was back. And now he wasn't alone. He'd brought along a friend.

A devil.

His clothing resembled the vampire's, but instead of a pale white mask, his was red. Yellow triangles for horns lined its forehead, and there was a black smear across its face that Tabitha assumed was a poorly painted beard. Both were motionless as they monitored her house.

Enough!

She sat her mug on the mantle above the fireplace, jerked the door open, and stepped out onto the stoop. She was barefoot and the concrete was cold under her feet. From the coziness she'd enjoyed inside, the air outside was chilly and caused her to hug herself. "Get the hell off my property!"

Now I sound like a bitter old lady.

Tabitha didn't care. If it meant making these assholes leave, she'd start heaving cats at them. She gaped at them a moment longer.

"Go!" She shooed them with her hand. "Go!" They remained frozen like statues. "Just great," she muttered. She waved the phone at them. "I'm calling the cops! See?" She dialed the operator again and got the same bored person. She requested the Sheriff's department.

It began to ring.

"Yes!" She jumped in celebration. "Got through, jerks! Last chance to leave!"

The wind rustling their clothing was all that moved.

Tabitha hated how frightened she was, absolutely despised it. She should take her knife, march down there, and demand them to leave.

Where is my knife?

Although she knew she hadn't brought it outside with her, she looked around on the stoop as if it might be out here.

She'd left it inside.

Smart, Tabitha. Real smart.

"Webster County Sheriff's Department, this is Marge, how may I assist you?"

"Yes...thank God...I've been calling for a while now..."

"I apologize. It's been crazy here."

"Two people in masks are stalking me!"

"Whoa, please repeat that, ma'am. Slower."

"Sorry." She took a deep breath and tried again. "There are two people standing about halfway up my driveway. They're wearing masks and just..."

"Just what?"

"*Staring* at me." As the words left her mouth, she realized how silly they sounded.

"What's your name, ma'am, and where are you?"

"I'm Tabitha Stoner. I live at..."

"Oh, Miss Stoner from the Elementary school!"

"Yes."

"Out on Amity Hill Road, right?"

"Yes, that's right."

"Okay. I know who you are. Now, these two people, what are they doing?"

"I told you. They're just *staring* at me."

"Have they tried to make contact?"

"Well..." Tabitha already knew where this was going, but she couldn't lie. "No."

"Have they threatened you in anyway?"

"Nuh-no...I mean...not *yet*."

"But they are on *your* property. Correct?"

"Yes!"

"Have you asked them to leave?"

She wanted to shout *"Duh!"* into the phone, but instead she opted for another response. "Yes. I've told them to several times."

"And I take it they're not listening."

"No, they're still right th..." Tabitha's voice trailed off. The vampire was gone. But the devil remained in the same spot, the same stance.

"Ma'am? Are you there?"

"Yuh-yes...I'm here."

"Is everything okay?"

"The vampire's gone."

"The what?"

Tabitha sighed. "The one in the vampire mask. He's gone, but the devil hasn't left yet."

"Is *he* trying to contact you?"

"No! He's still just standing there, but he's on my goddamn property and he shouldn't be."

"Calm down, Tabitha. I'm trying to help you."

"Are you sure?"

Marge harrumphed. "Please keep in mind that it *is* Halloween. Maybe they're just trick-or-treaters."

"Well..." Tabitha hadn't considered that, but she doubted their arrival was anything so innocent. "Then they should come up here and get their candy and leave." She had a green bowl in the kitchen, skulls and ghosts garnishing its thin plastic, with two bags of Snickers and two bags of Twix bars in the cabinet that she planned to dump in. She was more than prepared for candy beggars and to snack on them herself while waiting.

"I will make a note of this and send it out. I can't guarantee we'll be able to spare the manpower for loiterers, but if they *do* attempt contact with you, or seem to threaten you in any way, call us immediately."

"You're not going to help me?"

"Tabitha..." She paused before speaking again. "On any other day we'd be able to send an officer out there right away, especially since our office is local to you. But with everything that's happened in Autumn Creek over the last twenty-four hours, we just don't have anyone available who can. And, honestly, it doesn't sound to me like you're in any kind of danger."

Tabitha closed her eyes, scrunching her face into a scowl. She nearly bit her tongue to keep herself from shouting at this woman. When she opened her eyes again, the devil had vanished. She assumed he'd joined the vampire behind the trees. *Her* trees.

"But if that looks as if it might change," Marge continued, "please, call us, and I'll dispatch someone right away."

"Do you know how hard it was for me to get through? Just so you can tell me you can't help me."

"I understand, Tabitha, and I'm sorry." There was a short pause. "Let me give you my cell phone number. If you can't get through our main line, call me directly."

"Oh—I'd almost forgotten!"

"Yes?"

"At the school today, someone stole my house keys and my cell phone…and something had been written on my chalkboard."

"By keys, I assume you mean *house* keys."

"Yes, absolutely."

"Okay. This changes things." Marge's voice showed its first sign of genuine concern. "What was on your chalkboard?"

"Prank Night. It was written in red chalk. And…someone left a rotten apple on my desk too." She was certain there was probably more she should report but couldn't come up with anything as she racked her brain.

"Oh my…" Marge huffed with frustration in the phone. "Okay. I'm going to pass this over to one of the deputies, and I'll get you moved up the list and see if we can't get someone out there soon."

Tabitha nearly cried she was so happy. "Thank you!"

"It will still take some time. We have just been…swamped…to say the least."

"I understand."

"Got a pen?"

"I'm sorry?"

"In case you need to reach me again?"

"Oh right, your cell phone number." She gazed out at her *private* property. Right now, it felt *too* private. As if she was alone at the edge of the earth. She went inside, locking the door and dead bolt. Then she walked over to the couch, sat, and got her pen and pad ready. "Go ahead."

Marge gave her the number. "I'm going to trust you with that. Please don't be one of those to call over every little gust of wind."

"I won't. It's very windy out there."

"Right," said Marge with a soft chuckle. "And if you are one of those people, my phone will be ringing every thirty seconds."

Tabitha smiled. Marge was a nice woman. Just stressed and overworked today. "I'll refrain from doing that."

"Thank you."

They exchanged good-byes and hung up. Tabitha dropped the phone on the coffee table and sat back against the couch. She looked at her mug sitting atop the mantle.

Damn.

She felt tired. Drained. Much too exhausted to get back up and walk across the room to fetch her coffee.

She groaned.

Earth vs. the Spider had returned from its commercial break, but she no longer felt like watching it. She wouldn't mind reading some more of the Dean Koontz book on her Kindle, but that was even farther away on the nightstand in her bedroom.

Forget it.

She lay on her side, resting her head on the fluffy arm cushion, curling her legs up to her stomach, and draping her arm over her thighs.

She could already feel a nap coming to greet her.

(11)

Jackie's back hurt. Soreness, but also something hard underneath seemed to be jabbing into her kidneys. She tried to move, but an even heavier firmness on top of her prevented the freedom to even wiggle.

Where am I?

Were her eyes open? Blinking, she confirmed they were, but the simple act sent jarring blasts of pain through her skull. Her scalp felt tight and stretched to its capacity. There was something soft and dark blinding her. It felt like fabric. Too thin to be a blanket. Maybe a shirt.

And what was under her? A hump that hurt from its pushing into her back, prodding.

There was a whistle of splitting air, like someone swinging a golf club, then a punching splat. A moment later she heard a wet thud.

"Get another one," said a voice. It was young in pitch, not adolescent, but definitely not belonging to an adult.

Footfalls crunched dried leaves, growing louder as they neared Jackie. She froze, listening. Soft smacks, like fingers snapping, then the mass on top of her began to move away. Jackie quickly shut her eyes just as the blindfold vanished from her face.

The heavy mass pounded the ground. More crunches came and a whispering crinkle of something being dragged away. Jackie continued to lay there, unmoving, holding her breath. She wasn't sure why she was doing this, but something told her it needed to be done. As she listened to the harsh shuffling to her right, she searched her mind.

Why was she here? How had she gotten here? And where was here?

Joey...

Yes, she remembered seeing Joey fleeing into the woods. Then what?

The window.

That was the missing piece. She'd been knocked through the

window. She'd hit her head, which was why it felt so swollen and enlarged right now. Probably a mild concussion on top of the pain.

And now she was…where, exactly?

Jackie could no longer hold her breath, so she carefully exhaled through her nostrils. Pinching her chest, she kept her outward gust slow and gentle. When she dared to breathe in, the sweet-smelling scents of autumn filled her nostrils: leaves and pine, an odorous hint of wildlife.

I'm in the woods.

Behind their house?

Only one way to know for sure would require her to open her eyes. So, she did, slowly. Harsh light poured in, triggering a cramping lug in her skull. She snapped her eyes shut. Fresh tears dotted the corners of her eyes and trickled down the sides of her head, into her hair. Cracking her lids again, the light didn't seem as severe as before. She could see a faded dark blue sky, small purple blemishes of clouds moving across in swift swirls. It was late in the day, nearing sunset. Brightly colored, contorted branches curled on each side like leafy hands trying to clasp together.

Pausing, she listened. She could still hear movements to her right. Nothing had changed. So far, no one had noticed she was awake.

"Step back," said the same voice.

Jackie looked. Her lips trembled as her mouth stretched, seeming to strain the corners of her mouth. She saw the ax come down, severing the head of John Peterson, her nearest neighbor. The head dropped off the tree stump, struck the ground, and rolled over to the few others that had already been decapitated. A jagged stick of bone poked out from the pulpy neck stub. No blood sprayed, so that meant John was already dead before the beheading.

Jackie could hear shrill squeaks and when the heads of the two costumed people spun around, she realized the noises were coming from her throat.

"She's alive!" shouted the one with the ax, pointing. He wore a dark hooded cloak. A white cardboard mask with a sloppily smeared face painted on the front disguised his face, the straps reaching around his head and holding the hood in place.

The other was dressed like a ghost from an old cartoon in a long, tattered poncho cut from bed sheets, a white hood that fit snugly over the head, a face bereft of emotion—black eyes and an oval-shaped mouth—colored onto the front. As the ghost ran for her, arms outstretched, a machete clutched tightly in one hand, she recalled this being the one who'd pushed her through the window.

And she also comprehended she wasn't running away from him.

Screaming, Jackie launched herself off the uncomfortable bedding beneath her. She looked over and saw both were now coming. As she turned back around, her eyes caught a quick glimpse of the body pile. Bodies arranged in jumbled disarray, and she'd been the next one on top. Her hands gripped her hair as she scanned the dead, recognizing many familiar faces of those belonging to residents in her neighborhood.

"N…No!"

The padding of rushing footsteps snapped her out of the shock trying to overtake her. Shaking her head, she glanced back. Saw the two murderers were just feet away.

And started to run.

Each pounding step caused her head to scream. It felt as if her skull was splitting open. Reaching up, she dabbed her forehead with a finger and felt the swollen split in her skin. Definitely a concussion, possibly even worse.

Muscles fired up with pain, she kept going. No matter how much her body protested, she wouldn't stop.

Find Joey. Got to find Joey!

As she moved deeper into the woods, the trees choked out what little remained of sunlight. With Daylight Savings Time, the days had become much shorter. Dusk was already on the verge of swallowing the day.

Darkness would be here within minutes.

CHAPTER 8

(1)

Ben had Albright move Annette to a holding cell at the back of the station. He was tired of seeing her each time he walked past the interrogation room. It was his fault, suffering from the rubberneck complex. Just like a grisly car accident, riding past he *had* to look. Didn't want to do it, but for some reason he couldn't resist.

And knowing Annette wasn't in there when he walked by this time, he had no desire to look. Marge had buzzed him to say Mayor Vincent Cobblestone was here, but when he entered the main room, he saw Kelly Morgan had also arrived. Her homely frame stood in front of Marge's station. She had on glasses that seemed to swallow her face, and to her chest she hugged a large hardbound book that resembled a dictionary, with a worn spine and aged covers. She wore a sweater over her long dress.

Through the windows, daylight had all but vanished, and what he saw instead of the town through the barred glass were black reflectors displaying the room before him from another angle.

What time is it? Has to at least be half past five.

Pacing in his expensive suit, Cobblestone neglected the waiting bench to Marge's left. He looked every bit Italian in his dark skin and the thin dark hair on his head. He'd been born here, but his grandparents had come here a long time ago, claiming citizenship and building a wealthy life in their small town that was made even wealthier when Vincent's Italian mother married Mel Cobblestone from Cobblestone Industries, the biggest novelty supplier in the south. The fact that he was the *only* novelty supplier, and his company still was, did nothing to retract the claim that was printed boldly on all their packaging. They provided decorations, souvenirs, props, and more for the respected holidays—Halloween included.

Approaching, Ben noticed Cobblestone was struggling to feign patience. He looked up, spotted Ben, and the strained politeness dropped off entirely. "Sheriff Holly, a murder happens in our small town and you fail to tell me you have someone in custody confessing to it?"

"We're still investigating," said Ben. "Just because she confessed, doesn't make it true."

Though all evidence accurately supported Annette's confession. Even the pictures Ben still hadn't worked up the stomach to look at.

"Is it true your suspect is Annette Carter?"

Ben lowered his head, nodded. "It's true."

"Jesus," said Cobblestone, putting his fist to his mouth as if he wanted to bite it. "I play golf with her daddy." Cobblestone's head snapped up. "Has he been contacted?"

Ben explained how Duggins was trying to confirm where exactly they were, and how he wasn't having any luck.

"Jesus," Cobblestone repeated. "This is a mess."

"You're telling me? I'm trying to make it work with the limited number of staff that I have."

"Have you called for any reinforcements?"

This was where he knew he'd have Cobblestone's support. "No. I will if it gets much worse."

"Good. Best not to rush into anything, not unless we absolutely know we can't handle it on our own."

"Agreed."

"So, what have you figured out?"

"Honestly, not much."

Cobblestone's face hardened. "Ben, I don't like hearing that."

"I'm sorry, but it's all I have at the moment."

"Which is nothing."

"It is what it is."

"And what do you plan on doing about it?"

"Well," said Ben, looking to where Kathy stood, still clutching the book close. She noticed him looking and smiled bashfully. "I'm hoping Mrs. Morgan can shed some light on some things."

Cobblestone turned around, seeing her. "How the hell can *she* possibly help? She's just the damn librarian for Christ's sake."

"That's what I'm going to find out." He motioned for her to head over. "Will you be sticking around?"

"You better believe it. If it's in regard to my town, I should know as much as you."

Ben had figured as much. "Fine. But keep your mouth shut. Your town or not, this is my station, and I call the shots in here."

Cobblestone nodded in respect. "Of course."

(ʇʇ)

Ben made Cobblestone take the uncomfortable bench against the wall, allowing Kathy to sit in the comfortable chair at the front of Ben's desk. Once his guests were seated, he shut the door, heading for his desk. He sat down, the chair popping in protest of its age.

"Thank you for coming in, Kathy. I can't even begin to tell you how much it means to me."

"It's no problem," said Kathy, her pale cheeks reddening slightly. "I don't mind. I drive right past here on my way home, so it was no trouble."

"You're helping me out a great deal, thank you."

"I bet it's been a…trying day. It's just completely scary out there."

"Scary?" said Cobblestone. "How so?"

"Oh," said Kathy, obviously having forgotten he was back there. "From how…desolate it seems. No one was really out trick-or-treating, yet. Usually on my way home on past Halloweens, the sidewalks are congested with kids and parents by now. I hardly saw anyone. Alice usually gives out cookies, but even she looked to be closed already. The lights were off, and no one seemed to be hanging around."

"Desperate times right now," said Ben. "No cars to get around, and probably a lot of people are too scared to."

"I can understand," said Kathy.

Ben looked at the book again. "What's that you brought with you?"

Sitting it on his desk, Ben saw the golden embroidered lettering that matched the font on the paper Carpenter had showed him. *Webster Journal*. The date gate stated: *1947-1948*. Kathy opened the book and sitting inside the cover was a single sheet of paper. She passed it Ben. "I brought everything I could find in the short amount of time I had to look. I'm sure I can find more tomorrow with the whole day ahead of me."

Ben studied the paper. It was a much more legible copy of the article Carpenter had found. "This is great."

"I printed it right off the micro-fiche, but it's also in the annual." Kathy tapped the book. "There're some other articles that follow up that initial story you have in your hand."

"Have you read it?"

Kathy nodded. Her face seemed to lose its flush.

"What is it?" asked Cobblestone.

"A brief account from our town's history," said Ben.

Cobblestone scowled. "What history?"

"Have you heard of this?" Ben turned the paper around.

Leaning forward, Cobblestone reached inside his suit pocket and removed a pair of thick glasses. He put them on, but still squinted as he read the headline. "Of course I have. I'm the damn mayor. It's my duty to know everything that's ever happened here."

"Seven murders in one night? Prank Night? Don't you think I should have been educated in this as well? It certainly would have helped me when Annette Carter mentioned Prank Night earlier."

Gasping, Cobblestone snatched off his glasses. "What'd she say?"

"She did it for Prank Night."

"Jesus…"

"So, you want to save me the headache of reading this small print and tell me about it?"

Cobblestone looked at Kathy as if wary of talking in front of her. Realizing this, Ben held up his hand to calm him.

"Don't worry about her. Whatever you tell me, I'm sure she could find out on her own. So, get to talking."

Ben leaned back in the chair, fished out a cigarette, and lighted it.

Frowning, Cobblestone said, "You know there's no smoking in government buildings."

"Sue me."

Kathy smiled. Cobblestone couldn't see it from where he was sitting. A private little smile shared between her and Ben.

"Fine," said Cobblestone. "What's heard in this room, stays in this room."

"We'll see."

"The Halloween of forty-seven was the worst yet, from all accounts. Vandalism was huge, so many homes and businesses, personal properties, destroyed. Wagons overturned. Pasture gates opened so the livestock could wander out. Some of the livestock was slaughtered and strewn across houses as if they were throwing eggs. Innards hung from the trees like toilet paper. People attacked and beaten…"

"Okay," said Ben. "Save the gory details and just state the facts. I think Kathy could do without hearing all that."

Me too, for that matter.

"Fine. So, my father, joined with the public committee and mayor and judge, all decided it would be in the town's best interest if

Halloween was canceled the next year."

"In forty-eight?"

"Right."

"I see. And is this when Prank Night started?"

"What? No. That didn't come from here, it came *to* here. Spread through stories around the campfires all summer long. The kids looked forward to Prank Night as much—if not more—than Christmas."

"The kids?"

"Yes. Kids are behind Prank Night. That's how it's always been."

"*Kids* did this? They slashed all the tires?"

"Most likely, yes."

"Why didn't you tell me that sooner?"

"I figured it would be an isolated incident and nothing more would happen. I had no idea it was connected to Prank Night. But I should have known after the Fortner killing…"

Kathy gasped. "Killing?"

"It hasn't been made public knowledge," said Ben. "But Cali Fortner was murdered in her home."

"Oh my God."

"I know," said Ben. He shrugged, not knowing what else to say.

"Anyway," said Cobblestone. "The Fortner killing complicates things."

"You think?"

"Hey, get off my ass, Holly. I'm only telling you what I know."

"You're right. Sorry." Ben puffed on the cigarette. "So, your father, King of Novelties, agreed to cancel Halloween? Wouldn't he be out of a boatload of money if his product wasn't in the stores?"

"He wasn't selling Halloween merchandise then. Halloween didn't become an advertising goldmine until the fifties."

Ben nodded at the useless vat of knowledge.

"So, Halloween was canceled, but it wasn't announced until the end of summer. Right away, they knew they'd made a mistake."

"How?"

"Something in the air."

Ben was confused, and he was certain the expression on his face showed it. How did Vincent know so much about something that happened a decade or more before he was born? Curious, he asked him.

"You don't know the whole story of my dad's illness," said Cobblestone. "When the dementia set in, it was only the small things at first. He'd tell us the same stories multiple times a day without any recollection he'd already shared it. We got used to it, and even found it funny sometimes. Harmless. Then it got so bad he couldn't remember anything short term. He could tell you stories about me as a kid, the time I swiped a Mister Goodbar from the drugstore, or one of the many times I got into a fight at school. But he couldn't tell you what he ate for breakfast, couldn't repeat what you'd told him five minutes before. Then he started forgetting to eat and nearly killed himself from malnutrition." Cobblestone sighed. His eyes had become red and watery. Obviously, the memory still hurt, even now. "He didn't remember much by the end, but one of the things he never forgot was Halloween of forty-eight."

Cold sprinkled down Ben's spine.

Cobblestone took a deep breath, then began. "A pack of kids brutally slayed seven adults, painting Prank Night on the walls in blood. They used their skulls as jack-o'-lanterns, perching them on top of scarecrow bodies. It was a bloodbath. Barns were burned to the ground, livestock slaughtered and strewn across the farmland. Houses raided and demolished. A complete nightmare..."

"How did they know it was the kids?"

"Because the kids did nothing to hide that it was them. The next morning, they hardly acted as if they'd done anything wrong. Their actions were more celebratory, like a baseball team after a victory, you get it?"

Ben nodded. He sucked in a swirl of smoke from the cigarette. It tasted stale and sour, hitting his throat like a finger gagging him.

"Now, it wasn't *all* the kids in town, only a group of them.

Around fifteen, I think. But only five of them were convicted of murder. And they were sent away, locked up forever and eventually forgotten about."

"What about the others?"

"They served some time in detention centers and were eventually released and sent home. But out of fear of a repeated attack the next year, Pastor Mallory came up with the idea of the carnival. If the kids were…distracted…by this carnival, then they couldn't assemble and come after the adults again. It worked. And every year since we've had the carnival."

"Until this year."

Cobblestone's eyes gazed at the wall behind Ben, though they showed no recognition.

"Whose idea was it to cancel the carnival?"

"It was voted by the town during a meeting in August."

"Why?"

"To save money, Ben. In case you haven't noticed, times are hard."

"And now…we have another murder with our suspect talking about Prank Night."

"If you're saying they're doing this because we canceled the carnival, then you're out of your ever-loving mind, Holly."

Ben wanted it to be that simple. Darkness was spreading through his town, and he needed to know why. "That's not what I'm saying at all."

"We're being punished," said Kathy.

Ben started at the sound of her soft voice that was like a book being slammed in the quiet office. He'd nearly forgotten she was even in here. "Repeat that, Kathy."

"Don't you read the Bible?"

"You of all people should know I've never read the Bible."

"Horseshit," said Cobblestone. "No offense, Mrs. Morgan."

Kathy shook her head. "There are several stories in the Bible about retribution, sins of the father, children turning against their parents. Most of it revolves around a great collective sin. We've done something to warrant this."

Ben stared at Kathy a moment, then put his hands together. "Thanks for coming by, Kathy. I really appreciate all your help." He stood up, walking around the side of his desk.

"Wha…? You're sending me out?"

"Yes. You should get home. I'm sure your husband's wondering where you're at."

"I suppose he is." She stood. "I'll pick this up tomorrow sometime." She patted the book.

"It's fine. I'll make some copies of what I find useful inside and return it to you myself."

Kathy's eyes showed excitement. "Really? Great. I'll see you then."

As she talked, Ben escorted her to the door. He had it open and was gently shooing her out when she told him she would see him tomorrow. Cobblestone waved at her. As it looked like she was about to say something more, Ben closed the door. Turning around, he stood in front of the door, exhaling a deep breath that puffed out his cheeks.

"Wow," said Cobblestone. "And you used to run around with her?"

"A lifetime ago."

"That husband of hers has always been a Bible thumper. Guess it's rubbed off."

Ben felt drained. He could feel increments of a headache on its way. "Maybe." He walked back to his desk, sitting in his chair that welcomed him like a padded hug. "Maybe there's some truth to what she'd said. Not so much the Wrath of God stuff, but…something. Done any great sins lately, Vincent?"

The mayor seemed to squirm uncomfortably in his seat.

"Holy shit," said Ben. "What have you done?"

"Nothing."

"No, you did something that you're not telling me. Let's be honest in here."

"I plan on announcing at the first of the year, *after* the holidays."

Ben frowned. "What did you do?"

"I sold the factory to a group out of Arizona."

"Jesus, Vincent..."

"I thought they were going to keep it open and let us continue to assemble the product, but they're going to have it done at their main factory in Arizona. Which means..."

"The plant will be closing next year. Hundreds of people will be out of a job."

"I thought it was best if I sold the company to people who could manage it full-time. And, honestly, I'm happy to wash my hands of it."

"Your father wanted you to keep the company in the family."

"I'm all the family that's left. I don't have any kids. My brother's kids are nothing to be proud of, so who would I have left it to?"

"Someone local."

"Oh, please," said Cobblestone, standing.

"So, you cancel the carnival, and now you're sending the factory out of here. Got something against Halloween?"

Cobblestone strained a smile. "If you had to hear my dad tell that story as many times as I did, you'd be glad to get Halloween as far from here as possible too."

Ben had nothing to say to that. He supposed Vincent might be right.

The mayor headed for the door. He had his hand on the knob when Ben stopped him. "You said the other kids back in forty-eight, the ones who didn't do any of the killings were sent away to detention centers."

"Right."

"What happened to them after that?"

"They came home."

"And?"

"Lived out their lives."

"So, they're residents now?"

"Only a couple of them are still alive. Remember, not *all* the kids participated, just a handful."

"Who's still living?"

"Well, Herman Dobson is one of them."

"The caretaker at the cemetery?"

Cobblestone nodded. "That's the one."

"And who else?"

"Russell Warner."

Ben's chest felt as if it was locking up. A sensation like spider legs tickled the back of his neck.

Warner.

A man he'd come to know quite well during his years as sheriff. Someone he considered a friend. Someone who he'd spoken to this very morning at Cali Fortner's.

No wonder he'd looked so out of it. He knew. Even this morning, he knew what it was.

"Something wrong, Holly?"

"I don't know yet."

"Well, I'm sure you'll tell me once you figure it out."

"I'm sure I will."

Cobblestone opened the door and gasped. Ben's eyes snapped at the door.

Deputy Duggins was on his way in. "Sorry I scared you, Mayor."

Cobblestone waved his hand. "It's no problem. I was on my way out. Goodnight." He stepped past Duggins as the deputy entered.

"Got any updates for me?" asked Ben.

"Some. Not many."

Ben nodded. "Shut the door."

Judith had taken the boys trick-or-treating, so that left Tom home alone to maintain the candy duties. He didn't mind, because it also meant he would get to enjoy ogling the teenaged trick-or-treaters, the girls wearing slutty clothes passed off as costumes. It was the one night of the year he was actually allowed to gawk at them without the risk of going to jail.

Ah, to be a teenager again.

Plus, it wasn't like he could go anywhere. Luckily, they'd been able to get replacement tires for Judith's car, but he would have to wait for some to come in for his Jeep. That was okay, because the kids were out of school tomorrow, and since Judith was staying home with them, he could use her car. And they both had the weekend off, so there were no worries there.

He stood in the kitchen, mixing himself a Bloody Mary. His third. Not wanting to be plastered when Judith and the kids got home, it would be his last for the night. His vision was already starting to get a little fuzzy, and his head felt pretty light on his shoulders.

As he was dropping a piece of celery into the tomato and vodka concoction, the doorbell chimed throughout the house.

Please be someone dressed like a cheerleader or a sexy nun.

He carried his drink with him to the front door. Beside the door they kept a small table, usually a place to sit the mail or newspaper on, but tonight it supported a large candy bowl filled to the brim with goodies.

He picked it up, putting his drink in its place. Then he opened the door.

And frowned.

No one was there.

He stepped outside, looked from right to left, and didn't see anything other than his neighbor's houses. It was approaching six, and because of the recent time change, the sun had already vanished behind the trees and dusk had made the sky look as if it was burning and someone was trying to extinguish the flames with puffy purple paint. It would make a nice picture, he realized, and was tempted to break out his camera for some shots.

Freelance photographer was the job he'd wanted since he was fourteen and sneaking his Dad's old flashbulb camera outside to take pictures of the woods behind his parents' house. Sadly, all these years later, he hadn't advanced very far. His business came from the local paper which left little room for creativity. It wasn't the glamorous, exciting career he'd hoped for, but it was a living.

Where're the models? The sexy shoots?

Tomorrow morning, he was supposed to accompany one of the reporters to take pictures of vandalized cars while the reporter questioned the owners. It was a town-wide thing, so the day would be a long one.

He stood on the stoop in front of his house a moment longer before the chilly air sent him back inside. The door bumped shut. He grabbed his drink and chugged. It was cool when it touched his lips, yet warm as it sloshed down. When the drink hit his stomach, it spread a cloud of tingling warmth through him. He set the candy bowl back on the table and was on his way to get his camera before dusk had completely vanished when the doorbell chimed once again.

He turned around, grabbed the candy, and opened the door.

No one was there. Again.

Am I really hearing this?

He checked the stoop once more and found no one.

This is only my second drink, right?

Tom wasn't the best at math, but he figured he could at least count to two. Then he remembered it was actually his third. Maybe it had been one too many.

"Hello?" he called.

He heard a short whistle. There was a fragile smack on his chest. Something cracked, spewing thick goo across his shirt. He looked down at himself and saw the spatter dribbling down his abdomen. He ran his finger through it.

Egg yolk.

"Yuck," he muttered.

Nice. He'd been egged.

"Very funny," he said. "I congratulate you for catching me totally by surprise." Another one glanced off his shoulder, making him drop the candy bowl, spilling candy all over the porch. Now he was getting mad. "You think that's going to send me running?" He shook his head. "Nope. Why don't I go and get my paint gun and start firing randomly into the yard? I might not hit *all* of you, but I'll definitely get some of you."

He saw the next one coming and dodged it. It splattered against his house. Cussing himself, he realized he should have just let the egg hit him.

Better me than the house!

It was going to be hell trying to get the stains off the siding.

The trample of footsteps above him pulled his attention upward. He saw two small figures dressed in rags darting across the roof where it slanted above the stoop. They wore mostly white, but other colors looked to have been stitched in as well.

When they got into position above him, he noticed what was in their hands.

Buckets.

Here comes the tar and feathers.

He was laughing at himself for being taken by such an old trick as they tilted the buckets. What came out wasn't black or feathery, but greenish yellow. When it doused his upturned face, it immediately burned like fire. The fluid flooded his opened mouth, ripping him up with sweltering blasts of heat. It felt as if he was melting from the inside out. Then he felt his skin starting to bubble and realized that he was.

He tried to scream. Couldn't. His tongue and throat had been soused and was dissolving. Skin sloughed off his arms, neck, and face in a doughy glop.

He couldn't see. His eyes had liquefied. What he was able to smell was atrocious, absolutely unbearable, like a corpse soaking in heated raw sewage.

Tom collapsed on the stoop, twitching as the horrendous pain began to shut his body down piece by piece. He heard more human traffic coming from all sides, slowly surrounding him.

Then his eardrums popped, and he couldn't hear anything at all.

CHAPTER 9

(1)

Ben sat in his office, leaning back in his favorite chair with his boots propped on the corner of his desk. His head was tilted back, his eyes closed, and both forefingers rubbing the soft spot at his temples. He was fighting a migraine. His eyes felt as if they were swelling, and his neck was stiffening up.

He glanced at Duggins. His deputy's head was down, eyes moving back and forth as he read the article Kathy had printed. While he read, Ben opened the top drawer on his desk and was happy to find the bottle of aspirin was where it should be. Taking the bottle, he popped the cap, and shook out two pills. He tossed them in his mouth, grabbed the coffee mug from his desk, and washed the pills down with cold coffee. Grimacing, he put the mug back on his desk.

Duggins set the sheet on top of the annual. "Wow."

"I feel the same way."

"You think it's connected?"

"Has to be. Somehow."

Duggins nodded, his eyes staring off.

"How's it looking out there?" he asked Duggins.

"There's not many kids out tonight."

Ben glanced at the clock on the wall. It was just after six. Usually, the sidewalks were packed with a variety of ghosts and goblins by now. "That's what Kathy Morgan said earlier. I thought maybe they'd be out there now."

"There're *some*. But not many."

"Maybe there's just no way of getting the kids out tonight."

"Could be. Maybe the parents are playing it safe and keeping them in."

"We can only hope."

"Should we bring some of the kids in?"

Ben considered it. "We could."

"Maybe state some B.S. about there being a curfew or saying they're not allowed to be on the street alone? Bring them to the station, ask some questions while we wait for their parents to come pick them up?"

"That can work. As much as I need you guys here at the station, I think I'll have to send you out there, at least for a little while. I know our county's just a dot on the map, but with some of the cops in the other towns being volunteers, it might be best to have actual trained law enforcement out there."

"I agree." Duggins was silent a moment before saying, "I still can't believe it."

Ben sighed. "It's almost *too* unbelievable."

"I've known the Carters all my life. I can remember when she was born."

"Something's not right about this, even more than Annette Carter being one of the killers."

"What are *you* thinking?"

From Duggins' tone, Ben recognized his good friend had been thinking something along the same lines he'd been tightrope walking himself. Especially after reading the article. "I have no idea," admitted Ben.

"Me neither."

They sat in silence for a moment. Duggins spoke first.

"Seems like we're missing something."

"Something obvious," added Ben.

"Very obvious. Like it's being rubbed in our face by someone silently laughing at us."

Ben pointed at him. "Exactly. That's exactly it. Whoever is behind this knows we have no clue what's going on and they're getting off on it."

Duggins groaned. Ben noted how pale he looked. There were dark crescents under his eyes from zero sleep. He admired his deputy's eagerness and loyalty, but he also knew when someone needed rest.

"Why don't you head out, bud? I'm sure the wife and kids will appreciate you being home."

Duggins shook his head. "Can't."

"Come on. You work the night shift. You've put in your time and then some."

"It's night."

Ben laughed. "Yeah, it is. But you're at least entitled to a day off in between. Go on and get out of here, I'll be here all night anyway. I'll catch you up on things in the morning."

"No thanks. Jill understands a lot's going on. Plus, I feel like if I leave, I'll miss something."

Ben felt a cold chill work its way through him. He agreed with Duggins, though he wouldn't admit it. Thankfully, he was staying on. Ben needed his help. Needed him out there patrolling.

There was a soft knock on the door.

"Come in," said Ben.

Marge opened the door. She had a small stack of Post-it notes in her wrinkled, blue-spotted hand.

Duggins smiled. "Hey Marge, how's it going up front?"

"The damnedest thing. The phone suddenly stopped ringing. No one's calling in anymore."

"Strange. Are the phones working?"

"I checked. We have a dial tone." She turned to Ben. "I brought a few messages I thought might need some urgent attention."

"Okay."

She walked past Duggins and handed Ben the papers. "They've been coming in regularly for the last three hours, but since no one's called in the past five minutes—a damn miracle—I thought I'd bring them to you."

Ben smiled. "Thanks Marge. Go take a break, grab some coffee."

"I think I'll do that, Sheriff." She walked back to the door but stopped before leaving. "Are you sure you don't want me to radio the state police?"

Ben sighed.

"I'm sorry, Ben, but there's just too much going on out there for the few of us to handle."

"Marge," he began but Duggins interrupted.

"She's right, Ben."

Marge looked heartbroken for even having to suggest it. Ben felt bad knowing she had probably torn her nerves to shreds working up the courage to tell him this.

"Ask Albright to watch the front while you get some coffee."

She nodded. "I will. Thank you." She shut the door.

Duggins took a heavy, wary-sounding breath. "Ben, I know how you feel about the state guys, and I'm the same way, but just think about it for a minute."

"I've been thinking about it for several minutes."

"The town needs available police protection tonight, not just a few guys and gals who are holed up in a police station promising they'll get around to their requests eventually. Plus, you said yourself that you don't want the volunteers out there alone. We need the state police here to help us patrol."

Duggins was right and Ben knew it as he thumbed through the yellow squares of paper Marge had given him. Some reported trespassers, and Ben agreed with Marge that those needed to be looked into. There were reports of pranks: eggings, toilet paper, the usual fare. A few reports of stolen property, farming tools mostly. Then he stopped on one when he saw *Prank Night* written in Marge's backhand scribble. His hand jerked as if it had been stung.

Duggins noticed his reaction. "What's up?"

"Prank Night..."

"What?"

Ben read the rest of the note. Tabitha Stoner on Amity Hill Road reported two costumed trespassers on her property, and her keys had been stolen sometime at the school along with her cell phone. Prank Night had been written on the chalkboard.

Prank Night.

"Holy shit."

"What is it?"

Ben rolled his chair away from his desk to where he kept the coat rack. "You're in charge while I'm gone."

"You're leaving? Ben, you're freaking me out. Want to tell me what the hell's going on?"

"I'm going to pay a visit to Tabitha Stoner out on Amity Hill Road. Someone wrote Prank Night on her chalkboard."

"Damn..."

"Get the state police on the horn, posthaste." Ben stood up, put on his coat, and patted his pocket to make sure his cigarettes were in there. He felt the familiar square of cardboard through the heavy fabric. "I'll probably just pick up Stoner and bring her here, screw the questioning."

"Do you think she's in danger?"

"She very well might be."

(11)

Tabitha was with Clint Robinson at their favorite restaurant back in Wisconsin: Skip's 50's Grill. So, it wasn't a five-star place, but they enjoyed eating there. The food was affordable, greasy, and Clint served his plates teeming with heavy portions.

It was also where Clint had proposed to her.

Tabitha sipped her raspberry tea. They were waiting on their hot dogs and chili-fries to be brought to the table. She was so happy, albeit confused, that Clint was dining with her.

He'd been deceased even longer than her father.

One night, assuming he wasn't home, someone had broken into his house, and when Clint surprised them, he'd been shot and killed. The burglar was so distraught over what he'd done he killed himself right there on the spot.

Tabitha hadn't dated anyone exclusively since. She'd gone to a few bars, taken some men home for a couple hours of fun to get a release, but then she'd sent them away, only to wallow in guilt for weeks after, hating herself.

But that didn't matter now, because Clint was here and they were at Skip's Grill. Together. The way it should be.

"It's been so long since I've been here," said Clint, smiling. His short brown hair was perfectly styled. He still had a brush of whiskers on his cheeks, just like he usually would no matter how often he shaved. And he was just as handsome.

"I'm glad you're here. It's so hard still."

His smile faltered. "I'm sorry about that."

"It's not your fault."

"If only I would have gone to bed like you told me to. I might not have even heard the guy. But instead, I stayed up grading papers."

Clint had also been a teacher. That was where they'd met, at the elementary school in Wisconsin where they both worked. The click was instant. It was her first day on the job, and she'd been having a bad one. The kids hadn't adapted to her teaching style at all, and the other teachers treated her as if she had some kind of disease they could catch just by acknowledging her. But not Clint. When they were introduced by Principal Poplar in the teacher's lounge during class break, she was immediately drawn to him. There was something about his eyes. And how whenever he spoke to her it felt like he was looking into her, not just *at* her.

She might even say she loved him the exact moment he first spoke to her.

"Please don't blame yourself," she said, taking a nip of raspberry tea. It tasted sweet, but was also a little tart, giving her a slight chill in her back.

He smiled again. "I'm not meaning to ruin this."

She grabbed his hand. It was warm and soft, just as she remembered it to be. "You're *not* ruining anything."

"I have to tell you something."

"What?"

"Tonight. You need to know…"

The waitress appeared as if out of the air. "Sir, we don't want to spoil her meal, do we?"

Clint shrugged. "I guess not."

"What were you going to say?" asked Tabitha.

Clint shook his head. "Don't worry about it."

The waitress put a hand on Tabitha's shoulder. "Oh, if he said too much, it would have ruined your appetite."

Tabitha was confused. As the waitress began setting down their food, Clint began to jot something on a napkin.

What's he doing?

The waitress asked if that was all for now, and Tabitha nodded. When she was gone, Clint slid the napkin across the table. She looked at him, aware how her face was probably scrunched into a confused scowl.

He mouthed the words: *Read it.*

Tabitha picked up the napkin. There was a short message scribbled in a black Sharpie.

Prank Night.

Then she was jolted awake by the brutal clamor of her phone ringing.

She looked around, jumbled over where she was and why it was dark. Slowly, she began to comprehend she'd dozed off on the couch. She looked over to the front door and saw a dark sky through the pane glass. Little twinkling dots were sprinkled across the black. She'd slept through sunset.

Sighing, she sat up and rubbed her eyes as the phone chimed from the coffee table.

Where the hell's Becky?

She grabbed the phone and thumbed it on without looking at the call screen. "Huh-hello?"

Before she'd finished mumbling the greeting, the phone was clicking in her ear.

They'd hung up.

She pressed the *Off* button and tossed it back on the table, then stood up and walked over to the lamp. She clicked it on. A sheaf of dim light spread through the living room.

It was chilly in here. Rubbing her cold arms, she walked over to the fireplace. The pilot light sputtered from underneath the artificial wood. She twisted the dial. Fire whooshed to life, licking the logs as if thirsty. The heat smelled strong like bleach at first, but as it warmed her, the smell diminished.

She stood in front of the fire, her hands hovering palms down. She was tempted to park her rump right here on the floor so the heat could spread all over her cold body.

Becky should have been back by now.

Tabitha couldn't produce any casual explanations for her tardiness. She turned away from the fireplace and was on her way to the den when the phone chimed again.

This better be Becky telling me she stopped to get pizza or something.

She walked back to the couch, grabbed the phone, and sat down. The caller ID was illuminated in green. Tiny letters spelled out: *Rebecca Loflin.*

"Finally." She pushed the *Talk* button. "Hello?"

There was a pause. She could hear someone's raspy breath through the crackling pops of static. Wherever she was calling from, the signal was weak.

"Becky?"

"T'was Halloween night *(crackle)* and you were home alone, but outside creatures are stirring, surrounding your house *(crackle)* nobody will survive the night, not even a mouse..."

Her bowels felt heavy, and her back was cold as if ice cubes were being slowly melted on her skin. This wasn't Becky. This wasn't her friend pulling some kind of joke. This was someone else. She checked the phone, rereading the name on the screen. The number etched underneath began with *Cell.*

They were using Becky's missing cell phone to call.

"Who the *fuck* is this?"

The throaty voice spoke again. "*(crackle)* Prank Night has come." *Click.*

Tabitha remained rigid, the phone clutched to her ear until it began to annoyingly pulsate. She thumbed the button, killing the beep. A strong bout of the shakes began in her legs and traveled to her jaw. She gritted her teeth to keep them from clattering and forced her hands to settle enough so that she could dial. Grabbing the paper she'd written Marge's number on, she pressed the *Talk* button. There was a delay, then the phone beeped three times and shut off. She tried again only to have the same result. She looked at the ID screen and saw *No Service* written inside.

What the hell does that mean?

She pressed the button again and put her ear to it.

There was no dial tone.

Her phone was dead.

Judith took the alley and came out at the rear of the houses. The boys had gone this way to catch up with one of their friends but hadn't come back. When she found them, she was going to call it a night, go home, and share a Bloody Mary with her husband Tom.

As long as he hadn't hogged it all.

The street behind the houses lacked wandering children, the asphalt slick with dew. She could smell a hint of burning wood or leaves in the air. Fingers of smoke reached over the roofs of nearby houses, curling around the streetlights. It smelled good. She'd enjoyed the smell of brush smoke since she was a little girl helping her father rake piles of leaves in the driveway and burn them. Sometimes they even roasted marshmallows around the blaze.

She took another whiff, enjoying the sweetly warm aromas.

As consoling as the smell was, it did nothing to alleviate the escalating dread in her belly. It had been a weird day, so many tires slashed. What if those delinquents were slinking around tonight? What if they did something to the boys?

Don't think like that. They can take care of themselves.

And they really could. With TJ being thirteen and Donavan nearing ten, they were more than capable of avoiding strangers. It had confused her at first how they were so eager to go trick-or-treating this year, but she didn't mind taking them because she enjoyed it as much, if not more, than they did. It also granted her another year of them still being kids at heart. Wouldn't be long before TJ started rebelling, then to mimic his older brother, Donovan would start doing the same.

All Judith wanted was to get them all home at a decent hour. She didn't care that she was off work tomorrow and the schools were closed.

And that was where the problem had stemmed from. They'd wanted to go trick-or-treating without her. Sure, they were old enough to stay away from strangers, to be able to tell the good guys from the perverted ones, but she was not ready to let them parade around town at night without adult supervision. With all the freaks out there? No way. She would be chaperoning them whether they liked it or not, especially with the strange activities the town had suffered in the last twenty-four hours.

"What kind of parent would I be if I let you go out on your own?" she'd asked them.

"A totally *cool* one!" TJ had said.

Donavan had agreed with an enthusiastic nod.

Laughing, Judith told them just how much she disagreed. "How about I just trail you guys from a distance? That way I can still see you, but your friends can't see me?"

They hadn't liked that idea either, but still agreed, probably just so they could go out. It was either submitting and allowing Mama to come along or stay home pouting. But the tricky little turds had seen one of their friends ahead of them on Ginger Avenue, and with Judith wanting to be a nice mom, she'd allowed them to go on so they could catch up. When they'd reached the friend, *all* of them took off through the alley, leaving Judith behind.

The worst part of it was how they were laughing the whole time, mocking her. As if they'd planned on ditching their mom all along.

She was upset, angry, and absolutely heartbroken.

The longer she walked along this residential street, the heavier the fog became. It drifted across the road like a thin, whirling wall of cotton. Every house she passed was dark. The windows were tar-black squares inside pale gray structures. The only light she had was from the street bulbs. She wanted to kick herself for not carrying a flashlight of her own. She'd given one to each the boys but hadn't thought enough of herself to bring a third.

As she took slow, heedful steps, she also noticed there were no barking dogs. In fact, she couldn't recall hearing any all night. Surely, she had but just hadn't paid enough attention to detect them. But there definitely hadn't been any since she'd gotten on this back street. It was quiet here. Even her footfalls were silent, their echoes dying in the soundless air.

Judith came to the next alley. The burning smell was much stronger here, making her eyes water. She'd arrived at Sixth Avenue which was actually a connecting street that would take her right back to where she had been previously on Ginger.

Maybe they circled around and are heading back the way we came.

She decided to try it, hoping she would intercept them.

Judith hugged herself as she slowly made her way onward. The houses on either side seemed to be pressing in on her, as dark as the others she'd already passed. The fog was trapped in the narrow gaps between the residences.

Then she spotted human shapes standing like guards at the end of Sixth. She counted four heads. There was a tall one in the middle, and three shorter ones around him.

She stopped walking.

Oh…no…

They were dressed up in old costumes or something. It was hard to tell really, but she could see enough to decipher they hadn't bought their disguises at a store. There was a staccato sequence of cracking plastic, then four short belts of light slowly faded to life. Red, green, purple, and orange. They became brighter as those holding them began shaking their hands, sloshing the liquid inside the tiny tubes.

Judith recognized the floating slits of light for what they were— glow sticks. She remembered them from when she was a kid. Back then, she'd loved them, and would buy multiple packs so she could keep them throughout the year. But they were never the same as they were on Halloween. Tonight, she didn't find much joy in the neon beams. Tonight, they terrified her.

Judith turned around, putting her back to the assemblage. She tried to keep her pace casual, to come across like they weren't bothering her when, in truth, she was more scared than she ever had been. If she heard one of them following her, just one, she was going to run like hell.

Where are you kids?

She prayed they hadn't run across the same pack.

Nearing the opposite end of Sixth Avenue, she was met by an additional, albeit larger, array of glow sticks and costumes. She stopped counting at six. Turning around, she could see that the other group had inched in closer, although it looked as if their bodies hadn't faltered from their formation. Her heart pounded.

Judith spun around, trying to determine some options. There was a house to her left and right, but both were pitch black inside, and a fence in front of her and behind. That was it. There was nowhere else to go.

She was alone out here.

The two bands suddenly swarmed her.

Shrieking, Judith swatted and slapped and pushed, fighting them off the best she could. She ran at the house to her left. There was a chain-linked fence surrounding the property. It didn't stop her. Gripping the top rail, she jumped, swinging her legs over. She landed flat on her feet, thanking God her parents had allowed her to take gymnastics as a kid.

Sprinting across the wet grass, she headed for the back door. The dew soaked through the tops of her shoes, dampening her socks, saturating the bottoms of her pants legs.

Not wasting the time to climb the three concrete steps, she hurdled to the top, fists wailing on the door before her body had slammed against it. "Hello? Help me! I'm being chased! They're after me!" She stole a flustered glance over her shoulder. They were climbing over the fence, dropping one after another into the yard. They wore pillow sacks on their heads, holes crudely cut in the front.

She made a noise like a shrilly gasp. Then she commenced pounding on the door. "Anyone! Please, help me!"

They were closing in, the safe barrier between them shortening with every step they made.

Judith banged the door with everything she had. It shook violently on its hinges. The faint clicks of tumblers resonated from the other side of the door. She looked at the knob, saw it turning, and screeched with delight. When the door opened and she saw who was standing there, her glee turned to confusion.

When she saw the large knife grasped in his hands, she began to sob. Not so much in fear this time, but betrayal and defeat.

"Wuh-why?"

Those behind her shoved her into the house.

And TJ brought the knife down.

CHAPTER 10

(1)

Sheriff Ben Holly left the station through the rear exit. It led him to the back parking lot where they kept the cruisers. A tall, chain-linked fence wrapped around, barricading the vehicles away from the rest of town like quarantined animals at the shelter. He hurried past the cruisers to his SUV. Nearing the driver-side door, he began to detect a faint hiss. He stopped, looked around with his ear cocked to the sound. Sounded like a balloon slowly losing air. He removed the flashlight from his belt, thumbed it on, and shined it this way and that.

A funnel of light slit the dark, its disc highlighting the areas around him. He didn't find anything out of the ordinary, but the hiss hadn't dissipated. He continued walking. The hiss grew steadily louder as he neared his SUV. He skulked even closer, aiming the light at the vehicle, already knowing what he would find.

Son of a bitch.

The front tire had been slashed, deflated to a narrow bar of rubber on the grass. He shined the light over the rear tire. Its rim was already on the pavement, the rubber of the tire the density of a belt. Checking the other side, he wasn't surprised they'd been slashed as

156

well.

He did a quick scan of the cruisers. Also slashed. The personal vehicles belonging to himself and his team had identical damage. His old personal Silverado looked much smaller without its bulky wheels raising it high like a small building.

Ben ran to the service garage that was connected to the rear of the station. The aluminum door was usually kept closed with a thick chain and massive padlock securing it. He found the chain on the ground, the padlock opened. It sat on the pavement, the clasp out of the hole.

Unlocked. Not busted.

Someone with a key...

He lifted the door, heaving it above his head. It rattled thunderously across the tracks as the wheels slipped into the grooves and held open. Inside, he saw the car lift, unoccupied since there weren't any cars being serviced. He scanned the walls on the other side. Everything *seemed* okay. He tugged his gun out of the holster as he moved toward the tire racks.

Nearing the racks, he realized that everything was *not* okay.

The tires on the racks had all been punctured. Ten tires and not one of them had been spared. There were slits in the sidewalls from a large-bladed knife.

"Fuck me," he muttered.

His mind scrolled through the events of the day like he was rewinding an old tape, trying to find a section that he'd missed, like rerunning a movie for a particular scene. Something had been tugging at his gut all day, something that just didn't feel right. He could feel it beginning to come together, to make sense, but not entirely. It was a large jigsaw puzzle, and he was missing a few crucial pieces.

We've been stranded.

Why?

Prank Night.

All of it revolved around those words. The answers, the methods behind the mayhem. Was tonight a repeat of what happened in 1948? He ran out of the garage, his boots applauding across the pavement as he rushed to the station's back door.

He turned the knob. The door opened an inch before bumping against something unmoving. He tried again with force, but the door would not budge beyond the slim gap. He looked through the strip of mesh-glass and could see the heavy wooden bench they kept in the break room had been moved against the door with each end poking through a doorway as a bar latch.

He pounded his fists against the cold metal of the door. "Hey! It's Ben! Let me in!" It was doubtful anyone could hear him through the two sets of closed doors separating him from the heart of the station.

"Shit. Shit. *Shit!*" He almost kicked the door but luckily stopped himself before doing something so foolish. All an act like that would accomplish was a busted ankle or pulled knee.

He left the door, running around the backside of the brick building. He expected to find the chain that secured the gate to be unlocked as well, but it was still tightly coiled around the aluminum posts.

He froze as the concept truly sank in.

Whoever opened the garage had come from inside *the station.*

Annette.

He didn't take a moment to ponder any further. Flipping through the keys on the ring, he located the one for the padlock. He put key to hole. Then he opened the gate and ran up the sidewalk alongside the station.

He entered through the front.

Marge sat behind the desk, a *Reader's Digest* magazine open in front of her. She was rubbing her sleepy eyes, unaware of his entrance. Ben observed the station. He felt hot and squirmy inside as he gazed from one side of the room to the other. He scanned vacant desks, closed doors, and a complete absence of sound, like he was peeping through a soundproof window. Everything looked normal but nothing felt it.

He approached Marge's desk, keeping his eyes trained around him. "Where's Duggins?"

Marge jumped, lowering the magazine in a laughing gasp. "I didn't even realize you were standing there. Did you say something, Sheriff?"

He realized he'd been whispering. This time he spoke louder. "Duggins. Where is he?"

"In your office."

"Has he made the call?"

She shook her head. "Our phone's not working. He's trying to find a line out."

"He hasn't reached the state police?"

"He's working on it." She paused. "Everything okay, Ben?"

"Where's Carpenter?"

"He went to visit with Annette Carter. He said he could probably get her to talk."

Something like glass shattering hit him in his bowels. He suddenly felt the urge to shit come on.

Marge must have seen the gravity in his eyes because she dropped two shades in color. "Should he not have gone back there?"

"Probably not." As Ben moved through the station, heading towards the interrogation room, Marge was turning the chair to watch him.

"Keep an eye on things for me," he said.

"O-okay…"

His walk turned to a sprint. Then it became a run as he headed for the holding area. He shoved through the door and ran for the cells.

He saw the pooling blood on the floor first. Then he noticed a pair of police-issued boots in the puddle. Ben stopped running. He followed the boots to a pair of legs. His eyes kept going until he saw Carpenter's lifeless face gazing back at him. The eyes were gone.

Not gone.

Shoved back.

He could see the mushed peripherals had been pushed far back into his skull.

"Damn, Carpenter. What'd you do?"

He noticed the empty gun holster at his side, the clip where keys should be dangling from was vacant.

And the door to Annette's cell hung open.

The scene that flashed in his mind was quick, simple enough. He'd gone in to talk to Annette, thinking because of their relationship she would trust him enough to share what she knew. Instead, she'd killed him. Most likely, their relationship was just a ruse for this very night.

No way. No way she could know how things would play out from the beginning.

"No way," said Ben. He slammed his fist against the bars of Annette's empty cell, then turned around. He ran out of the room.

Returning to the station's main room, about to announce the girl had escaped, he saw Annette had emerged from behind Marge as if materializing from the air around her. Marge's back was to the teenager, nose wrinkled as she studied Ben.

"What's happened?" she asked him.

"Look out, Marge!"

Marge barely had time to acknowledge Ben's warning before Annette had gripped a handful of her hair and snapped Marge's head back. The wrinkled slant of Marge's throat was exposed. Annette punched a knife-like letter opener into the side of Marge's neck, twisted it one way and back, then yanked it through the front.

"No!" screamed Ben.

Marge's throat opened like a plunging gulley, jetting blood across the radio board and microphone. She pawed at her throat, gargling blood, her mouth yawning open, mewing sounds coming from her lips.

Her head dropped forward on the desk with a thud.

"Drop the knife!" Someone shouted.

Ben glanced to the right and spotted Hodges on the opposite side with his gun drawn. The shock that had been trying to freeze Ben subsided. He drew his gun also, aiming it at Annette as well.

The teenage girl looked from Ben to Hodges as if trying to decide who she wanted to lunge at first. Her glassy eyes were wide and darting.

"Annette?" Ben cocked the pistol ready to fire. "Drop it!"

A wicked smile curled the corners of her mouth. But she dropped the letter opener anyway. It hit the floor with a sharp clang.

"Cover me," said Ben.

Hodges nodded, keeping his gun trained forward.

Ben took a step in Annette's direction. Laughing, she ducked down behind Marge's desk.

"Annette!"

Then he remembered Carpenter's gun.

But it was too late.

A shot blasted the small room. Its boom reverberated all around Ben, making it impossible for him to decipher where it had come from. Another one popped like a small explosion.

Hodges's chest was slapped both times, his body jerking with each hit. Swashes of red spurted from his tan uniform before he hit the wall. Slowly, he slid down, leaving two smeared trails of red on the paint. His face was pale with shock and surprise, as if he couldn't comprehend he'd been shot.

Ben spun around, leering at Annette as she rose from behind the desk, pulling her hood down over her face. Its black, egg-shaped eyes cut daggers straight through Ben. He spotted Carpenter's gun clutched in her gloved hand.

Looks like she got into the evidence bags. Got her mask, her gloves.

He heard movement behind him, the gasping cries of Albright and Carla as they entered the room from the restroom. He didn't turn around to acknowledge them. His eyes remained on Annette.

She raised the gun.

Ben didn't hesitate. He dropped to his knee, leveled the barrel, and popped off three rounds. Two of the bullets each picked an eye. Two blossoms of red tracked out the back of her head. The third got her in the chest. More shots rang out, tearing holes through Annette's body. The force of the bullets threw her back several feet. She hit the floor with a ruffled thud.

Ben turned, finding the ladies poised, their guns held out. Smoke curled from the barrels.

"What happened?" asked Carla.

"Carpenter's dead. I think Annette tricked him, got his keys and gun. Hodges was hit."

Albright was already on her way to check on her partner. There was no need. Ben could tell he was dead before she got to him.

"Our vehicles have been sabotaged too. We're not going anywhere."

"The radio?"

"Dead. Phones too."

A noise bumped from Ben's office. He looked to the doorway and saw Duggins leaning against the frame, crouched over and peering out. Color was absent from his face. His skin looked pasty, dough-like and insipid, eyes pink and bloodshot. He held his hand against his chest. It was saturated in the blood sheeting down from the four narrow slits in his chest.

He'd been stabbed, multiple times.

"Buh-Ben...?"

"Stay where you are, Duggins!"

Duggins tried to raise his gun. For a brief, terrifying moment Ben thought he was going to turn the gun at him. The barrel pointed past him, toward the door. "They're coming..."

"What?"

"She called them...from your phone before killing the line. They're already here."

The front door burst open.

One after another, costumed assailants charged in—armed with axes, machetes, pickaxes, knives, and pitchforks. Ben stopped counting at seven and started firing his gun at eight.

The eighth one dropped.

Albright and Carla stood together, back-to-back, rapidly firing at the intruders as they entered and spread out. But they just kept coming, piling in one after the other. Bullets hit some, but nowhere as many as they needed to accurately stop the invasion.

Ben stopped firing and turned to his two remaining deputies. He shouted over the gunfire. "I'll cover you! We need to huddle in the center!"

The ladies nodded. Ben started firing as even more barged in. The ones that hadn't already been shot found cover. At first, he thought they were Klansmen by their white cloaks and hoods, then others entered who weren't dressed the same way. Some had plastic, dollar store masks on; others bore mesh to blackout their faces—Halloween costumes, mostly homemade, matching the style of Annette's rough-hewn wardrobe.

Ben rolled to Hodges's desk in the middle of the room.

Carla slid in next to him. Albright kept to a squat behind them. She was putting another clip in her gun when she said, "Hodges is dead."

Ben nodded. "I'm sorry, Albright."

She bit down on her bottom lip and looked away for several moments. Ben saw how her shoulders bounced a few times, crying with her back turned so nobody could see. When she faced him again, her eyes were moist, her cheeks puffy and red.

She sniffled. "I'll tell his wife…and kids…"

"If we don't get out of here, someone will be telling *all* of our families."

The front entrance was slammed shut followed by the earsplitting clang of hammers against nails.

Ben peeked around the corner of the desk. The invaders were nailing boards against the door, like bars to keep anybody else from entering.

And to keep anybody from exiting.

(11)

Jackie was late. Which was odd for her considering she was never late. And that she was well past thirty minutes of her estimated time arrival had Allen a little concerned. He stood on the steps of the front entrance of Blessed Waters Community Church, hands buried in the pockets of his heavy coat. The comfortable temperatures of the day had been conquered by the cold. Winter was imminent, but that was okay, he loved cold weather, and loved the snow. Also, he loved Christmas, and not just for the biblical meanings behind it. He adored the colorful lights, the smell of apple cinnamon and the sound wrapping paper made as it was being torn away from the presents. Yes…winter could come on.

If only Jackie would come on, he'd feel better.

He had been hanging out front for the better part of an hour now and the number of trick-or-treaters he'd had could be counted without using his hands. *Zero.* He'd been prepared for *some* of the parents not to expect the church would participate in Halloween, though he'd hung fliers, even making announcements during the last couple services. He not only endorsed Halloween, he encouraged trick-or-treating. To him, celebrating it for the fun it was meant to be was good for kids, and good for the town.

If only the kids would show up.

Where's everyone at? Are they hanging out with Jackie at a party I'm not invited to?

Smirking, Allen raised his arms, but kept his hands in the pockets, so he could adjust the coat's weight on his shoulders. The collar was pulling heavily on the back of his neck. He hated how it felt when the fabric rubbed his neck, like sandpaper scratching his skin.

Maybe the majority decided to stay in tonight. He couldn't blame them if they were.

I'll give them five more minutes, then I'm driving myself home. Please don't let anything be wrong.

What would be wrong, though? If something had happened, certainly he would have heard about it by now.

Nothing's happened. Don't even think that way.

The smell of burning wood was heavy in the air. When he looked up at the sodium arcs rising over the parking lot, he could see a light haze of smoke curling around the bulbs. He wondered what might be producing so much smoke—fireplaces, or maybe a bonfire was going somewhere. The blended sweet scents made him crave a hot dog, or maybe three. If only he had some chilly (no beans) heating in a crock pot and a fire going to roast some wieners from the edge of a sharp stick.

He looked at his watch, and even though five minutes hadn't quite past yet, he decided to head back inside. Putting the card over the plastic cauldron that instructed honest children to take only one piece, dishonest kids need not apply, he entered the church.

Jackie, where are you guys?

(↓↓↓)

Jackie was up in a tree, hugging a thick limb that reached over the woods below. Her feet were crossed at the ankles around the bendy limb, face pressed firmly against the jagged scales of bark. She'd been up here a few minutes and, beginning to think she'd lost her hunters, was about to climb down.

Then she'd heard the soft scuttles of their feet on dried leaves, doing nothing to mask their approach. It was doubtful the leaves carpeting the woods' floor would have allowed it had they been trying. Taking a deep breath, she angled her body so she could look over the edge of the limb. It was dark down below, but not so dark that she couldn't see the pale smudges of their costumes scurrying about. They were directly under her. If she were to dangle herself down from the branch, she could touch the tops of their heads with her toes.

What are they doing?

From what she could tell, just standing there. Their backs pressed together, each scanned a different section of the woods.

"Wish we had a flashlight," one said.

"And tell her exactly where we are? Brilliant."

The second voice was female. A tad raspy in tone, fluctuating with age. A girl just reaching sexual maturity.

Jackie had no idea what was happening, but she was certain these two weren't working by themselves. No way could only two people their age had killed the lot that was in that body pile. There were definitely more, somewhere. Were they out here? If she managed to lose these two, would she run right into more?

No matter what the possibilities were, she knew she had to keep trying. Joey was out here somewhere, too. He must have seen the one in his room and climbed out his window to escape. That was the only explanation she could come up with as to why he ran away.

But why didn't he warn me? Why didn't he call for help?

Plenty of reasons. He might have thought she was already dead, or maybe he was too scared to. He's only ten. She couldn't expect him to think like an action hero.

"Come on," said the girl.

"I know I saw her come this way."

"Well, she's not here, so she's probably still heading that way." The girl pointed beyond the tree. "Let's go."

She ran. The other lingered a moment longer before following her.

Jackie exhaled a breath of relief. In the movies, the victim would climb right down, expecting all to be fine. Though she didn't watch many now, she'd seen plenty of horror movies to know they'd be waiting for her if she were to try. She'd give it a few more minutes before getting down from the tree.

Jackie had no idea what time it was but being dark out meant it was definitely past six. Allen was expecting her a half hour ago. Surely he'd realize something wasn't right. He was probably calling the house, trying to reach her at this moment. He'd come. When he got home, everything would be all right again.

Allen would save them.

(IV)

Throughout most of her life, Tabitha had been afflicted with the horrible practice of chewing her fingernails down to the skin. It had taken her years to break the addiction, and she hadn't missed it. Nor had she missed the horrible stinging pains in her fingertips, the bleeding. Or the burning she felt when sticking her fingers into a batch of French Fries. This was the first time she'd been tempted to clamp her teeth on a nail and gnaw until there was nothing left. She'd been sitting on the couch, rubbing her fingertips over her lips as if daring herself to.

I can't call anyone. I can't go outside. I'm trapped.

Trapped!

Becky will be here soon.

Becky isn't coming. They got her.

Tabitha needed such thoughts to stay away.

It's true.

And she knew it was. Becky wasn't coming because they'd already made sure it couldn't happen. She knew this with unconfirmed certainty.

Becky's dead.

What had they done to deserve this? Who would want to kill two teachers that had done nothing wrong to anyone?

I need to get out of here.

How? If she attempted to leave by foot, not only would she have to secretly patrol through the cold, but she also ran the risk of bumping into the vampire, devil, or both.

But they took off, didn't they?

Although it *looked* as if her two peepers from earlier had left, she doubted they'd actually gone very far. Probably returned and were trying to look in her windows.

I bet they are!

She jerked her head back and forth. The blinds over the living room windows were closed. And she never acknowledged the windows in the dining area, so the blinds there were never open. The bathroom only had a frost-stained porthole in the shower, and she hadn't opened the set in her bedroom this morning.

So everything was covered.

The kitchen!

Tabitha sprung to her feet, rushed through the den. She checked the two windows in here as she passed by, determining they were fine, as she'd assumed. Entering the kitchen, she saw a sheaf of bluish light on the floor. She left the light off as she jogged to the sink. Then she peered through the small window above it.

Through the smudgy glass she saw into the backyard. It looked washed out from the safety light crowning the power pole. The wind stirred the trees, and she could just vaguely hear the sighs of the branches as they rubbed together, the rustle of leaves as they sprinkled across the grass.

No one was out there.

Tabitha gripped the drawstring and pulled it, dropping the blinds. They smacked the windowsill. She could no longer see outside and more importantly, no one could see in. She felt a little more relaxed, but not much.

Poom! Poom!

Tabitha cried out at the pounding. Her heart felt as if it had leaped into her throat.

The front door.

She slowly turned around. Her teeth pressed down on a manicured fingernail. She tasted nail polish and quickly pulled it out of her mouth. The knocking repeated with two heavy strikes.

Tabitha, arms rigid by her sides, walked out of the kitchen. Her teeth needed something to chew on, so she sucked in her bottom lip and began to gnaw.

From the den, she could see the front door. Inside the small pane of glass was an even smaller, condensed version of herself.

"Who's th-there?"

No one announced who they were.

Tabitha cautiously stepped into the living room. It seemed like such a foreign area to her. Not the usual inviting atmosphere she'd grown to love. The ambiance had been despicably violated.

Poom!

She jumped, hugged her arms tight over her breasts.

"I asked...who's there?"

Nothing. Venturing forward, she kept her pace careful.

At the door, she leaned forward, squishing her breasts against the thick wood, and looked outside. She couldn't see much thanks to the lamp beside the couch generating the window into a mirror. She needed to add some light outside for balance, so she reached out to her left, feeling around for the porch switch. Finding the light switch, she flipped it upward.

Nothing happened. She tried a few more times before concluding it wasn't going to work. "Who's there?"

Someone stepped into view, standing directly where the moonlight was swishing across the face of the house. Tabitha jerked with a shuddering gasp.

A witch stood in the brush of whitish light.

Just like the vampire and devil, her face was a cheap foam mask, dark green with a black wart on its mushed nose and a black hat painted on top. A gold-painted square for a buckle was cheaply portrayed on the hat's rubbery brim. The mouth was an oblique, gap-toothed grin.

There was one main difference between the witch and the other two. Her size. She was a lot smaller than the other two.

"What do you want?" Tabitha asked.

The witch slowly raised her arms. Hanging from both of her tiny hands was a plastic trick-or-treat sack with cartoon jack-o'-lanterns on the front of it.

A trick-or-treater.

Tabitha closed her eyes, releasing the breath she'd been holding. A trail of fog spread across the glass. She curled her fingers over the cuff of her sleeve and used it to wipe the glass.

"Give me just a minute. I totally forgot about the candy."

The witch slowly shook her head. Tabitha frowned. Next, the witch shook the bag. Something heavier and more solid than an assortment of candy was inside. Tabitha could see its shape pressing against the plastic.

Tabitha tilted her head. Her body was tense. She felt a ridge creasing between her eyebrows. The witch shook the bag again. Whatever was inside tugged at the plastic handles as if they might tear. The witch bent at the waist, setting the bag between her feet.

Tabitha spoke through the glass. "You're giving that to me?" She cringed at her voice booming back at her.

The witch nodded.

"Why?"

The witch slowly ambled backwards, becoming decapitated by the darkness. She kept going until it had swallowed all of her. Tabitha couldn't quite identify the wardrobe, but she looked as if she was dressed in the same fashion of dark clothing as the other two.

Tabitha lowered her eyes to the bag. It was on the porch, slightly crinkled as the wind nudged it. She could hear the indistinct rattle of plastic. She checked for the witch one more time before opening the door. The wind swooshed through the gap, fluttering her skirt as cold air gushed between her legs, sharp like pinches. She took the plastic handles in her hand and lifted. The bag was much heavier than she'd anticipated it to be. Felt like bricks were inside. A handle ripped away. Tabitha quickly set it back down before she could drop it. No way was she getting the bag inside without ruining it. Squatting, she pushed the handles to each side.

Filaments peeked out, pirouetting in the breeze. They looked like nylon strips, floss, or something. She couldn't tell exactly.

Against her better judgment, Tabitha reached inside the bag.

Her fingers scoured over something soft, yet also dry and brittle. Stringy. Using her pinky to feel around, it became tangled. It felt like the hair on a baby doll that had been stowed away in a closet for years.

Hair.

She intertwined her fingers with the hair, then pulled the item out of the bag.

Becky's inert face stared back at her with enormous bulging eyes. Her jaw yawned wide and stiff. The curls of her hair were matted into sticky clumps from dried blood. Tracks of congealed blood trailed over her face like a roadmap, and the jagged points of her spine stemming from a fleshy neck stump.

Tabitha loosed a scream, flinging the head away from her. There was a juicy *thunk* when it hit the concrete. The head trundled towards the steps, then disappeared over the edge. There were more *thunks* as the head bounced down.

Tabitha looked at her hand. It was tacky and looked as if she'd poked her fingers into strawberry jam. Knowing it was actually her dear friend's blood, she screamed again.

Scuttling to her feet, she staggered back until her rump banged the door. It shot open, spilling her into the house. She landed hard on her buttocks and didn't stop screaming even as she scampered backwards on her elbows. When she had cleared the door, she kicked it shut, got to her knees, and twisted the deadbolt.

The solid click of the lock's tongue hitting the inner cladding silenced her. She leaned against the door, resting her sweaty forehead against its cool, slick surface. Her breath came in rapid spurts. She looked the room over, wanting to do something, and not having a clue as to what it should be.

Then something heavy banged against the door.

CHAPTER 11

(1)

Screaming, Tabitha flung herself away from the door as if it was hot. Her feet slipped out from under her, throwing her on the floor. She didn't slow down. Crawling on all fours, she made it around the wall, snuggling into the crease of a nook, her back flush against the wall.

Tremors continued all around her.

Boom!

The chairs in the dining room slightly vibrated on their legs. An object splattered against the house, scattering down and dropping off.

What the hell were they throwing at her house?

Rocks?

Another wet explosion outside the living room triggered a squeal from her. Cupping her hand over her mouth, she took quick breaths through her nose.

After a couple more of the heavy bursts, the assault ceased.

Tabitha sat there a few moments, still feeling the effects pulsating under her skin. She was shaking all over. Now, she let the tears come. Burying her face into her hands, she sobbed against her palms, making wet slurping sounds. She allowed this to transpire for a bit then forced herself to stop, to think. She couldn't afford to break down like this.

Think Tabitha...

She looked around the corner, her eyes landing on the coffee table. She could see the phone sitting on top. It might as well have been an oversized plastic child's toy. It would do her no good since they'd killed the line.

The thought froze her.

The phone.

There was a rational explanation for how they had taken control of her phone line.

They must have access to the link under the house.

Not only were they outside the house, but they were *under* it as well. Either clambering through the crawlspace or they'd busted the aluminum lifting door and were making their way through the basement.

Tabitha wasn't taking any chances on either.

She got up, using her sleeve to wipe her tears. She ran to the basement door in the kitchen across from the backdoor. The lock was a hook and eye combination on the door and paneling. She pushed the point into the hole.

And still didn't feel any safer.

So, she ran back to the den, taking a chair from the dining table. Dragging the chair behind her, the legs grated over the kitchen tile as she returned to the basement door. She tilted the chair, wedging the backrest under the doorknob.

Better.

Not entirely secure, but it would definitely hold. She jiggled the chair to check its stability. It was fine.

Tabitha went over to the drawers above her cabinets under the sink. She found the junk drawer and opened it. Inside were old bills she'd never opened but had been promising herself she'd get to eventually, batteries, and other junk that needed to be sorted through. She knew there was a flashlight buried in here somewhere.

She found it—a small plastic tube that operated on AA batteries. She pushed the button. A weak warren of light funneled through the kitchen's darkness.

It would do.

She checked the sink for the knife she'd accidentally used to slaughter the shampoo bottle. It was there, tilting into the drain. She grabbed it. The blade screeched across the acrylic surface, making her teeth hurt.

With the flashlight in one hand and the knife in the other, she ran for the hallway. Her bedroom was to the right, and her office to the left. In her office was a small trapdoor that led to the crawlspace behind the walls.

She decided to check there first. She hurried out of the kitchen and through the den. The living room was much warmer than the rest of the house. She could hear the faint hiss of the flames in the fireplace. She'd much rather be on the couch, cozy under a blanket with the gas logs going nearby, and a cheesy horror flick on the TV. Her night had *almost* turned out that way. She sank inside knowing it wasn't going to be and probably never would be again.

Keeping the lights off, she scrabbled her way through the office, bumping her hip on her desk, stumbling over jutting mounds in the carpet as she waved her arms ahead of her for balance. To her astonishment she managed to make her way across the room without accidentally stabbing herself, a magnificent accomplishment. She clicked the flashlight on, briefly, long enough to find the trap door in the wall.

She went to it, got on all fours, and gripped the bronze handle. Then she pulled it towards her. The door opened like the lid to a laundry chute. Leaning inside, she shined the flashlight here and there as musty damp air wafted into her nostrils. Except for some dust bunnies and strands of insulation, it looked empty. She wasn't going to tempt fate and crawl inside to check the rest of it. Especially since she was confident they'd already infiltrated this area. And if someone was where the phone line ran under the floorboards then they had probably concealed themselves somewhere behind the walls of her bedroom.

Tabitha crawled back out, shutting the closure. She stood, crossed around to the opposite side of her desk. Putting the flashlight in her mouth, she sat the knife on the desk to free up both hands. Then she placed them on the lip of the desk and shoved with all her might. The desk skated over the carpet. She steered it to the trapdoor. It bumped the wall, knocking her forward a few inches. Her college diploma jiggled on the wall in its frame for a moment, then dropped. It hit the desk. Glass shattered.

Damn it.

She grabbed the knife and took the flashlight out of her mouth. The plastic handle was awash in her drool.

Gross.

She wiped it on her shirt, then left the room.

Tabitha returned to the den, found the spot on the wall where she'd huddled earlier, and nestled herself there once again. She slid down to the floor, keeping her back flat against the wall and her legs pulled up to her chest. She draped her arms over her knees, then peeked her head around the corner to see into the living room. The front door seemed okay. Nothing looked any different than when she left it. She couldn't sense anyone out there, but there was no way of knowing for sure with the lamp on. It needed to be shut off, that way she could look out without them seeing her doing it.

As if reading her mind, the power went out, shrouding her in darkness.

(11)

Ben had never been so scared in all his life. And he couldn't stop feeling his shoulders were weighted down with the duty of protecting Albright and Carla. It was chauvinist to think in such a way, and he knew this, but that was how he'd been raised. His father had told him all his life it was the man's responsibility to take care of his own. And, damn it, he considered these lovely ladies huddling with him behind a desk while several masked assailants trapped them inside the police station as his own.

They were *his* deputies, *his* partners, and he cared about them greatly. He would take the duty, and the honor, of defending them; doing all he could to ensure their safety, even if by doing so meant jeopardizing his own.

Ben peeked around the desk.

Two phantom-dressed figures stood guard with axes while a small pack of them tended to the hammering.

Now would be a good time to strike back.

Most of them were occupied, and the others wouldn't expect them to fight back right now. "All right, listen." The girls leaned in. "I'm going to try and peg those two off to the side."

"The ones with the axes?" asked Albright.

He nodded. "Yes. Be ready for *anything*."

Ben turned around, getting positioned in a squat.

They had already seen him. And charged.

He raised his gun quickly and fired four rounds. His index finger was beginning to cramp. The phantom on the left took two hits in the chest and spun like a top before dropping, the other ducked behind Marge's desk. Ben took cover once again.

Carla looked to her right and gasped. "My God, they're spreading out, surrounding us."

Ben watched as four of the intruders, dressed in crudely fashioned sheets and rags, separated throughout the station. The way they were dressed reminded Ben of an old photograph he'd seen of his dad with his aunts and uncles dressed for a Halloween bash. *Back then*, his dad had told him, *you couldn't just go into any store and buy a costume; you had to make your own.* And that was exactly how these people looked. As if they'd designed their Halloween garb out of whatever was lying around the house.

Home-produced costumes weren't what bothered him. Not at all. What bothered him were the assault rifles they brandished. Police-issued assault rifles.

"Son of a bitch," he said. "Carpenter's keys!"

"What?" said Carla.

"They got into the gun safe!"

Larger police stations had gun rooms, this one only had a single safe of the variety hunters or gun collectors kept in their homes. Inside were four AR-15s, a riot gun that shot massive cannon-like rounds, and a small assortment of pistols. Plus, plenty of ammo.

For people lacking proper police training, the four popped clips in the rifles with ease, then cocked them ready to fire. Though these three were small framed, they were the biggest so far of the group.

And they were raising the rifles. Ben spun around. "Take cover!"

Carla and Albright dipped down next to Ben. He put his arms around them, holding them close as a drum roll of blasts ripped through the station. Holes knocked into the walls. Frames exploded. Glass shattered. Debris sailed all over as the room filled with gun smoke, heavy like a fog coming from the ocean. The hot smog singed his eyes, filling them with water.

The gunfire came to a popping close. Ben spun around, keeping the edge of the desk blocking his chest. He aimed his gun in the vicinity of the shots.

And fired several rounds toward the ruckus.

He turned back to face Albright. "I wonder if I hit any of them."

"It's hard to tell," said Albright. "I can't see a damn thing."

"No!"

Ben paused. Looking at the women, he saw both of their faces were wide with confusion as well.

"Who…?" started Carla, stopping when another plead cried out.

"Stop! Please, let me go!"

Ben leaned forward. "Vincent?"

Albright gasped. "Cobblestone?"

"Where the hell he'd come from?" said Ben. He hadn't seen him come in during the onslaught, but he also hadn't been looking the whole time.

"Ohhhh, Sheriiiif?"

The voice was deliberately squeaky, altered to sound daunting. And it worked. The shrill tone ran caustic tingles through Ben's stomach. "Who is that talking?" he called back.

"We are the destroyers of worlds. Now, stand up."

Ben rubbed his thumb on the edge of the gun to confirm the safety was still turned off. It was. Then he slowly stood up. The smoke was thinning and through its hazy curtain Ben could see Vincent Cobblestone, tensed, his head pulled back to expose his throat. His arms were behind his back, most likely bound in some way. Behind him was a darkled figure, a ragged burlap hood over his head that was haphazardly constructed, clothes darned from old plaid sheets and rags. It looked as if whoever had assembled the costume couldn't sew a straight line. But the face on the hood was the creepiest part—two ragged holes for eyes, the mouth a toothy crooked line. Like something from a nightmare.

"Let him go," said Ben.

"He's…he's…" stammered Vincent. "He's got a gun against my back!"

Ben raised his pistol, aiming it at Spooky's head. Vincent twitched, his head intercepting Ben's target.

If he doesn't be still, I'm going to shoot him by mistake.

"Drop your gun!" said Spooky.

"Not a chance!"

"Shoot him!" said Vincent.

"I…"

I don't have a shot was what he'd planned to say, but his words were cut off by the loud burst of Vincent's stomach exploding. Innards flew out in viscera chunks with splashes of blood.

"Oh my god!" screamed Carla from somewhere behind Ben.

Ben blinked to erase the image of his friend's insides spraying out and dropping at his feet in red and brown glops. He focused on Spooky, stepping out from behind Vincent's lifeless dropping body. Before the old mayor landed, Spooky jacked another round into the riot gun he'd taken from the gun cabinet.

The scene seemed to slow down: Spooky raising the gun. Ben cocking his head, closing one eye to center his target, which was between the goon's haunting eyes. Movement behind him of Albright and Carla getting into position to back him up.

Ben had the shot.

He pulled the trigger. And—

Click.

Expecting to feel the pistol buck in his hand, a loud pop following, all Ben got was a hollowed click. The gun was out of bullets.

"Shit..."

Spooky pulled the riot gun's trigger. *He* wasn't out of bullets. A flash from the muzzle came a split second before the blast. Then Ben felt a mule kick to his chest that lifted him off his feet and threw him onto his back.

(↓↓↓)

Tabitha stood in the darkness, the knife clutched to her breasts, the flashlight down by her side.

Great... They cut the power.

The refrigerator no longer hummed, and other than her own rapping heartbeat, all she could hear was the lapping flames of the gas logs. The living room was swathed in a glint of orange. Since the fireplace was directly tied to propane tanks outside, it didn't require a power source.

A whisper of footsteps in grass came from outside the den windows. She tiptoed to them, and slowly lowered herself. Her knees popped as she worked her legs under her. Setting the flashlight on the floor beside her, she kept the knife clutched firmly in her hand.

Tabitha decided not to tug the blinds down to see out. They might be watching, trying to pinpoint where she was, and spot the dip suddenly appearing between the slats. So, she leaned her head against the wall. It was cold against her ear, sending short twinges of pain into her head as she reached for the blinds, slowly angling them away from the glass just enough that she could see out.

The devil was looking in. His mask squished and deformed against the window.

Shrieking, she fell backwards. The blinds smacked the window as her back hit the floor. On her back, she tried to catch her breath. She scrunched her eyes shut, breathing through her mouth. Her throat made a light wheezing sound as it filled with saliva.

There was a light tap on the window. She opened her eyes. The tap repeated. It was quiet for a few seconds before repeating another time.

The devil was requesting her attention.

Fine.

She sat up.

If he wants my attention…then he's got it!

She crawled back to the window, grabbed the dangling cord, and yanked down. The blinds volleyed up, exposing the devil down to his shoulders. "What do you want?"

He stepped back from the window, keeping his gaze directed at her through the darkened eyeholes of his mask.

"Huh? What the hell do you want?"

His head tilted as if he couldn't understand what she was asking.

"Can't you hear? Are you deaf *and* ugly? You must either be ugly or…or just completely chicken shit to hide…to hide behind a mask!" She'd started losing her momentum, the gallantry behind her words taking a hike. She wanted to drop down on the floor, shrivel up, and hug her knees to her chest. Maybe if she stayed like that long enough, they would eventually get bored and leave.

But she didn't. She forced herself to remain where she was, conveying a bogus stare of confidence.

The devil raised his hand. Something was clutched between his fingers. He slapped it against the glass. Leaning forward, she strained her eyes to see what it was. Rectangle in shape, small and plastic. Knowing she was having difficulty deciphering what he was holding, his thumb pushed against the side. The square light of a display screen became visible in the darkness. She recognized the picture inside the glow. A shot of the earth was showcased in the small square.

Her cell phone.

He waved the phone from side to side.

Tabitha drew in a trembling breath. A scream lodged in her throat that wanted to be released. It was *his* voice on the phone. He'd been the one calling her, the one speaking to her in that scratchy voice. Now that she had a visual to go with the voice, she began to shiver. It was even worse knowing which one it had been making the calls.

His head suddenly ducked down, footfalls squishy as he retreated through the grass.

Wanting to see where he was going, she got to her feet, and leered through the window. She couldn't find him. It was as if the darkness outside opened its mouth and gobbled him up. She scurried to get up, then ran for the back. The chair leaning against the basement door didn't allot her much room, so she pulled it away, and swung the backdoor open.

And was met by the vampire.

Tabitha jumped back, screaming, nearly stabbing her face with the knife. She felt the wind of the blade just miss her, and a slight coolness against her cheek. Another half an inch closer and she would have a wound matching the one in her shampoo bottle.

He stood on the other side of the storm door. As he advanced for the latch, she slammed the wooden door in his face, and locked it. Then she twirled around, ramming her rump against the firm form of the door to hold it there.

"Just go away! Go away!"

A light tap on glass came from behind her. She bawled harder. It tapped again. Slowly turning around, she put her eye to the peephole. In the fish-eye lens she saw the contorted image of the vampire, shrunken and expanded. He was staring directly at her. She knew he couldn't *actually* see her, but she could still feel his amorphous eyes ogling all over her skin like a slimy caress.

Tears discharged down her cheeks. "Go away!"

The vampire lowered his head, as if he was trying to peak through the peephole back at her. His mask was so pale that it looked as if it was a glowing face in the night. He raised his head, only an inch, but from how dark his clothes were his body appeared as if it weren't there at all.

A floating head.

What if it was?

She saw movement at his waist, determining that he was not a floating head, but she didn't feel any better.

"Why are you doing this to *meeeee?*" Tabitha whined like a kid being bullied. She *was* being bullied. By at least three masked prowlers, and there could be even more traipsing around out there for all she knew.

He knocked again.

He wants me to open the door.

She wasn't that stupid. She'd already opened it once without thinking, and she didn't plan on doing so a second time. He could keep on wanting for all she cared.

Oh, you want me to open up? Sure! Let me make it as easy as possible for you to cut off my head like you did Becky's.

He knocked once more, but this time, there was more force behind it.

He was growing annoyed with her.

She thrust herself away from the door with her elbows, and slowly turned around. She noticed a trembling hand reaching for the knob and bawled when she realized it was her own.

What am I doing?

Her hand curled around the brass circle.

Stop this! Don't open the fucking door!

The knob felt clammy in her sweaty grip. It turned.

I'm ordering you to stop!

Then she pulled the door open. There was a sucking pop of air as

182

she slowly tugged it away from the panel.

The vampire hadn't moved.

She was certain the storm door was locked, but she felt no comfort because the glass was so thin that the vampire could smash through without effort. But it was better than nothing being between them.

"Tell me what you want from me." She strained to keep the fear out of her voice.

The vampire leaned his head so far to the side it looked as if he was trying to touch his ear to his shoulder.

"If you go right now, if you get your friends and leave, I won't say anything. Okay? Can we make that deal?"

He shook his head.

She whined in her throat. "Please?"

He shook his head again.

"Wuh-why not?"

He raised his right arm. She quailed back, holding the knife in front of her. Her other hand was ready to shut the door if he made any sudden lunges. His hand was balled into a fist. He opened it one finger at a time. Something dangled from his pinched thumb and forefinger. He jiggled it. The object clinked and rattled.

Oh, my God.

Her keys. She'd forgotten all about them. Again.

Tabitha's face stretched as her eyes rose and her mouth parted. The vampire's shoulders bopped up and down, his head twitching. At first Tabitha wondered if he was having a spasm of some kind, but it wasn't hard to figure out what he was really doing.

Laughing.

Laughing at her.

Groaning, she slammed the door, locked it, and instead of putting the chair against the basement door, she wedged it under the backdoor.

The sound of the vampire's feet scuffing down the steps resonated through the door. For a moment she was relieved he was gone, but then a fresh worry knocked her back.

He's going to the front!

She darted into the den, grabbing a chair from the dining table in passing. She dragged it behind her, the wooden legs bouncing and scraping marks into the hardwood floor. She was almost to the door when she heard the click of the deadbolt disengaging.

Oh shit!

She picked up speed. The door was cracking open as four gloved fingers began peeking through like wiggling worms.

Tabitha rammed the door with her shoulder, the thick wood crushing the fingers. She heard whoever they belonged to cry out.

A guy.

She pushed against the door with all her might, mashing the fingers between the door and the paneling around the frame. The audible sounds of metacarpals and phalanges cracking like breaking pencils brought a smile to Tabitha's face. She lifted off the door but slammed back again before he could pull his hand out. A deep, splintery chomp that sounded like taking a bite from an apple drowned out the muffled screams coming from the other side of the door.

The hand tugged and tugged until finally pulling the fingers back. The door slammed shut. Tabitha relocked it, putting the chair under the knob. Then she hurried to look through the pane of glass. The vampire stood on the porch, bent at the waist, and holding his crooked fingers while moaning in agony.

Tabitha felt lousy for hurting him, but it had been rightfully deserved. He was trying to come into her home to do God knew what, and she had to defend herself. It *had* to be done. But when she noticed his moans had turned to sobs, it didn't matter how justified her actions had been. She'd made him cry, and now felt like a bitch for it.

"I'm sorry," she said.

His head whipped towards the door.

She continued. "If you would have just left like I said, this wouldn't have happened." She realized she was speaking to him in the same regretful authoritative tone she used on her students when they did something they shouldn't have.

Bowed at the hip, he slunk to the door, snatching the keys from the lock with the hand Tabitha hadn't ruined. Even behind the mask she could tell he was fuming. And his humiliation had been made even more apparent by crying. She'd gotten him good. Definitely all four of the fingers on that hand had been broken.

He turned away from her, and disappeared down the steps, the night outside engulfing him like a body of black water.

A fleeting victory, she knew that, but it was all she had, and no matter how rotten she felt she would relish in this moment.

CHAPTER 12

(1)

Ben sucked in a thin gust of air. It was difficult to breathe, like trying to inhale threw a flattened tube. His chest felt as if a boulder was slowly crushing him, compressing his front into his spine. Glancing down at his chest, Ben found his shirt had been split and torn. And instead of an opened chest cavity, he saw only metal. The riot shard was lodged in it, flattened against the chest plate. He smiled, although it still hurt as if he hadn't been wearing any kind of protective gear.

Definitely some cracked ribs, maybe worse.

Ben glanced over and saw Spooky taking aim again. Ben guessed he'd only been swimmy for a couple seconds. Though even such a short time could mean the end for them all.

Carla was already training her pistol on Spooky. She fired. A pop of red appeared on the spook's chest before he spun around and dropped.

She got you, bastard!

Albright fired two shots at the other gunmen, but they were already moving, and she only managed to peg one in the back as he hurried for cover.

Carla went to Ben, crouching next to him. "Had your armor on, huh?"

"Yeah…"

"This doesn't look so bad."

"Could've fooled me."

She smirked. "Stop being such a baby."

He gritted his teeth as she attempted to sit him up. Ben's torso stung as if fire-ants were crawling around inside. "Ow!" He couldn't find air. "Stop. I'm hurt."

"I have to move you. You're out in the open."

Ben looked around. He was lying on the floor, away from desks that could offer minimal protection from the gunfire and the several others swarming inside. He wondered what they were doing now, since the hammering had stopped.

Probably finding a way to attack.

"Okay," he said.

Carla slid her hands under his arms and started to pull. He kicked with his feet, assisting her. Finally, she got him behind Hodges's desk once again.

"See?" she said, panting. Half her mouth curved upward into a semi-smile. "That wasn't so bad, was it?" A chunk of her skull blew away, leaving a curvilinear crater where her right eye had been. She seemed to act as if she hadn't noticed from the way her head turned to the side, confused. When she looked back to Ben, lumpy matter was spilling out of the wound. Then she slumped forward, remaining in the sitting position, her chin resting on her chest. More lumpy fluid oozed from her head.

"No!" cried Ben.

Albright squatted, holding the gun close to her head. She looked at Carla's dead body with frustrated remorse. Ben recognized it as what he was also feeling. The yearning to help, but knowing there was nothing that could be done, and knowing there was nothing that could help her now.

Looking over his shoulder, Ben found the spook Carla had shot was not killed. He'd gotten Carla. Now he stood, slouched and bleeding, with the riot gun pointing in front of him. His finger twitched, triggering Ben to roll into the nook of space under the desk.

A corner of the desk exploded, spraying splintery slivers of wood.

"Get down," he said, pulling Albright under the desk. Another explosion ripped a massive hole through Carla's chest, toppling her onto her side.

"Dammit!" shouted Ben, causing his chest to feel as if he'd been kicked.

"What are we going to do?" said Albright.

"We've got to make our way to the back."

"That's impossible…"

Ben looked around. The station was starting to look like an overcrowded nightclub. "How many rounds do you have left?"

"Five in here. And another full magazine on my belt."

He reached for his ankle, pulling his pants leg up, and revealing the .32 at his boot. "I have this." He tugged it out of its holster.

Albright crawled over to Carla's body as another staccato chain of gunfire tore through the station. None of the bullets seemed to be a threat of actually hitting her. Ben wondered what they were shooting at and decided it didn't matter to them, as long as they were shooting.

Just wanting to destroy whatever they can.

Albright returned with Carla's gun and another magazine. She thumbed the switch, releasing the clip from Carla's weapon. Then she slid the fresh magazine inside, slamming it in place with the palm of her hand. She offered it to Ben.

He took it.

"Even if we make it…" Albright choked back tears. "What are we going to do? We don't have enough rounds …"

"We'll worry about that later."

A tumult of uninterrupted war ruckus shook the floor under them. Then, bit by bit, the noise faded. The tinkering sounds of them trying to reload told Ben their turn had come. He held both guns up. "Ready?" She nodded. "Let's go!"

They stood up, aimed their guns at the throng of goons, and opened fire. Bullets punched into chests; a few heads spurted red clouds before they dropped. Even with the pressure of pain in his chest, Ben tugged at Albright's arm, wanting to be between her and the others. She was a good deputy. All of them were. He couldn't have asked for a better team. Now they were dead because of their loyalty. If he wouldn't have made them all hang around the station, then they would still be alive, out there on patrol.

The dying stopped now. His plan had never been for both of them to get out. His concern was for Albright.

"Listen," said Ben, as they took cover by the hall. "Under the backseat of my car is my .12 gauge. There's a box of shells out there also."

"Why are you telling me this?"

The goons were reassembling, Spooky at the helm of the assembly.

"There's no way both of us will make it. They'll catch up to us outside. I'll keep them off of you the best I can. But you have to move fast."

Albright's eyes swelled. Her lip quivered. Tears spilled out of her eyes. "Don't do this. If you're staying behind, then so am I."

"I'm still your superior, and I'm telling you to go."

She sniffed back a sob. Nodded.

He put a hand on her shoulder. "Let's not do this farewell stuff, okay?"

"Yes, sir."

He raised his guns. "Here it goes…" He took a deep breath. "Take care of yourself, kid."

She smiled. She looked as if she wanted to hug him but held it back. Ben was glad she did. If she would have hugged him, he probably wouldn't have let go.

"Go!" He shoved her. As she ran to the back, gunfire resumed in the station. The edge of the wall crackled and popped into dusty sprays. Ben *could* follow her out. He knew they'd at least make it outside.

But then what?

No. I have to do this. She'll make it if I can keep them off her.

Ben took a deep breath, waiting for a break in the gunfire.

It came.

Charging around the corner of the station, he raised both guns and started squeezing the triggers. Bullets launched. Tore through goons.

Spooky dropped to his knees. He fired.

The round blasted Ben in the stomach, almost directly below the first hit. The impact twirled him in the air. His ass hit the floor hard enough to jar his teeth. He looked up the hall just in time to see the back door closing.

Albright made it.

Thank you, God.

Ben faced Spooky as he approached. He pointed his gun at the masked goon, only to realize his hand was empty. He looked at it dumbfounded.

I must have dropped it.

Then he remembered his other gun. He checked that hand. It was empty as well.

Son of a bitch.

He let his hands drop onto the floor by his thighs.

Spooky nodded his head toward the backdoor. Two took off after Albright. *No!* Then he clucked his tongue, bringing his attention back to Ben. "Got protection on, huh?" He still spoke in the womanly voice.

Ben shrugged. "Not much left of it…" Talking brought agony, so he stopped. His torso felt as if he'd been beaten with spiked clubs.

Spooky jacked another round into the chamber. He pointed the gun directly at Ben's skull. "As hardheaded as you are, I doubt it can stop a slug. What do you think?"

Ben coughed. "Going to shoot a man whose down and unarmed?"

"I've done worse. Like pulled the head off one of your deputies. Rileson."

The fuzz behind Ben's eyes cleared. "What? You?"

"Oh, yeah." He took a deep, savoring breath as if he'd just tasted prime rib. "It was gooooood."

Ben shot his foot out, planting it against Spooky's shin, then quickly rolled to the side just as the gun went off. A softball-sized hole appeared in the floor where his skull had been.

Spooky stumbled back, cussing.

Ben couldn't hear much from the ringing in his ears, but he saw his .32 on the floor where he'd been standing before getting shot. He rolled forward, ignoring the hurt in his chest and gut, grabbed it, and pointed it to fire at an approaching goon. Then he felt the ring of heat of the riot gun's barrel pressing against his temple.

Cha-Chink!

He slowly lowered his pistol.

"That hurt, asshole,' said Spooky. "Didn't break it though, but I'm sure you were trying."

He had been trying to crack his shin in half, and ten years ago he probably would have. Over the years, he'd let himself go, hadn't kept up his proper training. Now, he was sloppier than he wanted to admit.

"Grab his gun," ordered Spooky.

A goon dressed like some kind of low budget clown took the pistol. He had a mop head for hair that had been shoddily painted red. A white sheet fabricated with pink cheeks, a yawning red mouth, blue eyebrows, and black grape-shaped eyes shrouded his face. It was probably the scariest thing Ben had ever seen in all his life. Like something straight from one of his nightmares. He'd never liked clowns, but hadn't ever had a phobia of them, until now. He doubted that if he survived this ordeal, he could never look at a clown again.

Spooky looked at Ben. "I should shoot you. But now I want you to suffer."

Ben shrugged. "Whatever…"

Go for it, Albright.

Ben prayed she was okay.

(11)

Albright flipped through the keys on the ring, unsure which one fit Ben's truck. She didn't have the time to guess. Two assailants, armed with pitchforks, had already exited the back door, and were heading her way.

She didn't know how many bullets she had left, but aimed the pistol anyway, and squeezed off two shots.

The goon in front, wearing an old, stained sundress with a hood wrapped around her head like a lollipop wrapper dropped to the pavement and slid to a stop. She pointed the gun at the one dressed like a scarecrow in old overalls, flannel and straw, as he changed his position to come up on the other side of the truck.

He was perfectly aligned in the gun's sight.

She pulled the trigger.

Click.

The sound of the empty magazine seemed as loud as the gunshots. "Oh…shit," she muttered.

She spotted the scarecrow in pursuit through the glass on the other side of the truck. He was coming around the backside. She jerked the baton from her belt. As he appeared at the back of the truck, she spun around and clubbed him in the throat. A painful throb vibrated up the length of her arm and into her shoulder. His feet went up in front of him when his body suddenly stopped. Air blasted from his mouth when he hit the ground.

Not bothering with the keys, she used the nightstick to smash the back window, knocking away the jagged shards still clinging in the frame. Then she reached through the improvised opening and unlocked the door. She checked on the scarecrow. He still lay at her feet, grasping at his throat, rolling from side to side. He made wet gargling sounds.

Flinging the door open, she leaned into truck. Shards of glass sprinkled the seat and floorboard. Carefully, she felt around under the backseat. Her fingers brushed something cold. Realizing it was Ben's shotgun, she exhaled a triumphant reprieve.

Thank God.

She curled her fingers around the wooden stock, pulled it out.

Then she reached under again. Her fingers found an old drink bottle, a plastic wrapper of some kind, and finally a cardboard box. The shells. She grabbed the box, sliding it out from under the seat. It was a green and yellow packaging with *Winchester* printed across the top.

She smiled.

Arms hugged her legs, pressing them together as if she were being tackled.

Her balance shifted and down she went. Her rump struck the pavement. Hard. Her neck popped, and her vision jarred. The shotgun hit the pavement, sliding out of reach. She still held the small box of shells in her hand.

The scarecrow was up on his hands and knees. The pitchfork lay between them. Both of them noticed instantaneously and reached for it at the same time. He shoved her hand away as it neared the handle. She tried again, but this time he swatted it. Her hand stung from the slap of straw. He dove on top of the pitchfork, blocking her from it. She could go for the shotgun, but figured about the time she grabbed it, four thin spikes would tear into her back and out the front of her stomach. No, she would have to fight him for it.

She scooted back as he got to his knees and began to trail her. He used the pitchfork as a cane, the pointed tips scraping the pavement. Sparks sprayed as the metal screeched.

Albright looked at the shotgun. It was probably three feet away but could have been a hundred. There was no way she could make a grab for it without being spiked.

Her stomach made a lurch when the scarecrow threw himself at her, the pitchfork poised to kill. As he came forward, she dropped onto her back and spread her legs. Then she pivoted with her hips, catching him. She threw her legs around his head, her thighs crushing against his ears, and began to squeeze.

The box of shells flew out of her hand as he crashed down on her.

The scarecrow used his feet to push against the pavement, and since it was slick with dew, they only slid out from under him, allowing her legs to constrict even tighter around his neck. She heard him choking behind the burlap face. He swung the pitchfork blindly. It came close to puncturing her. She managed to grab the base of the handle and hold it away from her chest.

She growled as she crossed her ankles behind his head. She had him trapped. There was no way he could break free. He swung his free hand madly, latching onto the collar of her shirt, ripping it open. Thankfully, she had on a white tank top underneath to conceal her breasts from his view. Sweat beaded the round patch of exposed skin, trickling down the tight line between her breasts.

Albright put all her force into her legs, gritting her teeth as she slowly crushed his throat. She heard a sound like a tire slowly rolling over a plastic bottle. Then he went limp. His wilted burden was heavy between her legs. She pulled the pitchfork away from him and rolled onto her side. He plopped onto the pavement, motionless.

Sitting up, Albright pulled her shirt taut at the front. She went to refasten it and discovered the buttons had been ripped out.

Hell with it.

She decided to leave it as it was. She slid out from under the scarecrow, half expecting him to return to life one more time. He didn't, of course, but that didn't keep her attention from faltering.

Albright got to her feet and tossed the pitchfork. It clamored when it landed several feet away. She scooped up the box of shells, walked to where the gun lay, and picked it up. Then she hurried to Ben's truck, sitting the box of shells on the hood. She quickly loaded five shells, jacking the final one into the chamber. Other than the safety being on, it was ready to fire.

She climbed into the truck, sitting the shotgun between her legs, the stock on the floor and the barrel pointed at the ceiling. Then she snatched the CB off its base from the dashboard.

Holding the mouthpiece in her left hand, she used the right to spin the dial. She found a channel and squeezed the button to talk.

"Mayday, mayday, this is Deputy Albright from the Webster County Sheriff's Department in Autumn Creek, can anyone hear me? Over."

She waited. Static crackled from the bottle cap-sized speaker on the unit.

"Mayday, Officer Albright of the Webster Country Sheriff's Department is seeking any kind of assistance, over."

Nothing from Rileson. She'd expected him to respond, but so far hadn't. This wasn't good. She decided to try the volunteer officers in the neighboring cities. "Meaker and Banks, are you out there? Got your ears on? This is Albright. We need backup at the station, over."

Static.

Albright groaned. She felt as if she might cry. Pushing back those defeated emotions, she twisted the dial to another working channel. It hummed and whistled.

"Mayday, Mayday, anyone out there? Over."

No response. Just more noises that sounded like an old radio from the fifties.

"Fuck!"

She flung the mouthpiece away from her. The coiled chord expanded, then snapped back, whacking her in the knee. It stung like being hit by a baseball. Being the final straw, she finally did cry.

Tears poured out of her eyes. Her nose leaked. The top of her lip was a moustache of moisture that she wiped with the back of her hand.

"You're okay. You're okay." Her voice was shaky and thick. She sniffled a wet breath and let it slowly out. "You're okay. You're fine." The tears subsided, but she was still shaky with a case of the splutters. Another deep breath lessened that. "You can do this. You're amazing, you're powerful. Hodges has told you this. He would not like you breaking down like this."

Hodges was dead.

Another fit almost took her, but she intercepted it.

"Another reason to make these assholes pay…"

Albright took another deep breath and held it as if trying to rid herself of the hiccups. Her chest tightened. Her lungs began to ache. Then she released it in a heavy rush.

Ben had wanted her to get reinforcements. She could probably find a pay phone and call 911, inform them of what was going on, have them dispatch some state boys out their way. Sure, she *could* do that, but she wasn't. Her senior officer was trapped inside the station with a mass of costumed maniacs, and she didn't plan on leaving him behind.

She'd lost her partner, quite possibly the man she was in love with. She wasn't about to let Ben die, a guy she looked at as an older brother. Other than her aunt, she didn't much have anyone she considered family. Her fellow officers were her family.

Ben will be pissed, but he'll just have to get over it.

She took the rest of the shells out of the box and stuffed them in her pockets. She didn't count them but guessed there were at least fifteen more rounds.

Then she stepped out of the truck, searching the pavement for Ben's keys. She found them near the dead scarecrow and picked them up. The tires were slashed, yes, but if the engine worked it would be all she needed.

Climbing into the SUV, she pulled the door shut behind her. She put the keys in the ignition and twisted the key. The engine rumbled as it awakened.

Squealing, Albright patted the steering wheel. Finally, something in her favor. Looking down in the floorboard, she saw a lever for the four-wheel drive. She pulled down, hearing the click of the wheels being unlocked.

Albright stomped the gas.

When the engine was revved to its peak, she yanked the gear to D.

The wheels spun, slapping the undercarriage with flattened streaks of rubber. The truck jerked forward. Sparks showered up around the windows as the tireless wheels carried Ben's vehicle toward the station. In the heavy haze of smoke and fog, it was a malevolent place, a dwelling for madness.

And Albright, along with the shotgun, was the end to it all.

The potent odor of gasoline singed Ben's eyes. It made his struggle to breathe that much harder. From the chair Spooky had cuffed him to, he watched as goons moved about the station with gasoline cans, sloshing the walls, floor, and desks in flammable liquid. He knew what would come next.

Spooky was obviously the ringleader of this pack. He stood before Ben, his back turned, watching his minions work. He hugged the riot gun to chest, rolling his hands together like a mad genius.

"So, Annette was the distraction," said Ben.

Spooky gave no acknowledgement to Ben's statement. He didn't need to. Ben already knew she was. He'd been putting pieces together in his mind and even if Spooky never responded to any of it, he was going to speak it aloud, so his thoughts had merit.

"The tires were a way to strand everybody, to keep the residents distracted. Cali's murder would keep *us* busy, and Annette's surrender would get her into the station." Something else clicked in his head. "And Carpenter was the love-struck idiot with jailbird fever, so he'd obviously go see her. She could influence him into opening the cell, and that was when she struck. Right?"

Spooky continued to observe the gas being thrown around.

And Ben continued to talk. "While we were researching Prank Night, trying to assemble any kind of plan, she was sneaking around the station, unlocking the gun safe, getting everything ready for your attack. Am I getting warmer?"

Nothing.

"And with the authorities out of the picture, that gives you the freedom to…" And that was where his notions ended. He had nothing beyond this moment. "The freedom to what, exactly?"

Now Spooky turned around. His wicked mask seemed to smile with sinister knowledge. "The freedom for anarchy."

Ben felt a flutter of tingles course through him.

There's no way out of this.

The goons approached, hands clutching handles, gasoline cans hanging by their thighs. They were ready to douse the remaining piece of the station that had been missed.

Ben.

As they moved forward, angling the cans at Ben, he closed his eyes. Holding his breath, he prepared himself for the splash of gas.

The station quaking as if a missile had struck the building shocked Ben's eyes open. He saw the goons scramble, shoulders hitched high, ducking as they ran. Spooky jumped back, aiming the riot gun towards Ben's office. The wall exploded as the front of Ben's Suburban came barreling through. The front end plowed through Spooky.

Before Ben could comprehend what he'd just witnessed, Albright had already flung herself from the cab. She fired. Ben's shotgun flashed with the accompanied blast. A goon's gas can exploded in his hand. Flames launched from the can, hitting the gas-sodden walls and igniting. Flames scattered across the far wall as they grew in size.

Albright didn't hesitate. She jacked another round into the pipe. Fired. The head of a ghost exploded into a chunky red mass. His body continued to run several feet before dropping.

The rest didn't hang around to fight, they charged for the massive hole in the wall as fire licked around its edges like a flaming hoop in a circus act. The old walls and paint were going up fast, making for great tinder to the hungry fire.

A mysterious figure zipped through the smoke. By this point, Ben couldn't see much beyond an inch from his face. The flames were spreading in haste, nipping at his shoes. His toes felt as if he'd dipped them in hot water. Another minute or so and he'd be on fire.

He felt hands on his shoulders, then they slid down his arms to the cuffs snapped around his wrists.

"Where's the key?" shouted Albright.

Relief flowed through Ben. He'd never been so appreciative someone had deliberately disobeyed him. But it quickly squandered when he remembered Spooky had the keys. He looked to where the cloaked body had landed, finding Spooky had become fodder for the fire. His body was being consumed by flames. "Gone."

"Let me try my keys!"

"No! There's no time. You need to get out of here!" As if to solidify his point, pieces of the ceiling crashed down in front of them, showering them in red hot ash.

Albright slapped at Ben's shoulders and back, putting out baby sparks trying to mature into flames. Then she worked on her own clothes.

"Go!" shouted Ben.

"I didn't fight my fucking way back in here just to turn around and leave you again, asshole!"

The chair suddenly jerked back, balancing on two legs. Ben's feet pointed toward the collapsing ceiling. "What are you doing?"

"I'm dragging your ass out of here!"

And Ben took off, sliding away from the flames. In his retreat, he saw the spot where he'd just been become devoured by the fire. He could almost feel the searing heat melting his skin.

They reached the hallway where it wasn't as smoky. Albright let the chair drop, then began searching her keys. He could feel her trying different ones. As he was starting to think she wouldn't have a match, he heard a soft click and the clasped ring fell away from his wrist.

Yes!

She unlocked the other one, freeing him entirely.

CHAPTER 13

(1)

Allen slammed the phone down. Dead. Leaning back in his chair, he exhaled a breath of frustration. He glanced down at the message he was preparing to preach on Sunday and pushed it away. How mad he was right now, seeing words he'd written about feelings of forgiveness made him feel disappointed in himself. Like he was somehow cheating. What was wrong with the phones? His cell phone kept dropping its signal, and now the landline was dead. He'd tried every phone in the building, even returning to his office to give his phone another chance to work.

His plan had been to call Jackie and find out why she was late.

Now, he was done with waiting. Concern had given way to worry. He wasn't going to hang around any longer. Something was wrong. It was the only reason why she wouldn't have shown up by now. He hoped it was nothing major but could not come up with anything minor that would have prevented her from picking him up.

Allen checked the wall clock. *6:35pm.*

That was the last straw. He was going home.

He stood up, stretched his tired muscles. Then he leaned over the desk to click off the lamp.

It went dark before his hand reached it.

Allen snatched back his hand as if something had nipped at it. He looked through his door and into the foyer. It was dark out there as well. There was a clack of the generator turning on, then the safety lights came on, throwing dim orange glows in the foyer. His lamp came back on as well.

Other than hunger making his stomach cramp, he also felt an appending dread beginning to bubble like bad indigestion. He left his office. Standing in the assembly room, he looked from left to right. The restrooms were to his right, and the Kid's Club was to his left. During the service, children could hang out in there for fun and games, learning about the Bible in ways appeasing to them while their parents went to worship.

He turned around.

Then he froze, his eyes gaping at what he saw. Painted in black screwy letters on the wall was *PRANK NIGHT.*

Had that been there when he'd come inside? He didn't think so. But, if it hadn't, how had it gotten there while he was in the office without him noticing?

Someone else is in here.

Allen tested the phone once more. Still dead. He was going to be smart about this and not go strolling through the darkened worship center alone.

I'll just drive to the police station later and report it.

First, he was going home to check on his family.

He marched out of the office, patting his leg where his keys should be. He wouldn't have been surprised to find he'd forgotten them, but they jingled inside his pants pocket.

Cautiously, he walked through the lobby, bypassing the worship center on his way to the rear exit. He opened the door. The burning wood smell was heavier now, drifting inside through the opened space. His eyes scanned the parking lot. He could make out the faint blotch of his car through the whirling wall of smoke. Blankets of gray fog smothered the sodium arcs, swirling around the lights like vaporous vines.

Allen was *almost* too scared to step outside.

Stop freaking yourself out.

He couldn't help it. The smoke and fog was so thick, he wouldn't be able to see anyone until they were right on top of him.

But staying in the church was also a bad idea.

He felt trapped.

Allen decided to chance going to his car.

The door slammed shut, automatically locking behind him. Smoke churned on either side of him, swimming over his body like a swirling opaque flood. It dried out his eyes as he walked, parting a path through the smolder. Nearing his car, the haze thinned some and he was thankful.

Then his gratitude died when he saw his tires had been slashed.

(11)

Tabitha was in the den, back at her spot on the floor by the window. She slowly raised the blinds, just enough to see out. The witch stood at the center of her backyard like a little troll, the safety light atop the power pole illuminating her. Her feet vanished in the high grass.

The vampire approached her from the left. He still clutched his hand to his chest. She watched as the witch turned her head toward the vampire. His head was bobbing from side to side, obviously saying something. The witch listened a moment longer, then slapped him across the face. She had to stand up on her tiptoes to do it.

Tabitha snickered. That had been a nice treat to see.

The devil joined them from the right.

Where's he been?

The devil's head moved as he was telling the witch something. Tabitha hoped she would smack him too and was disappointed when she didn't.

Then the witch focused her attention on the den.

Tabitha froze. She stifled a scream. It was doubtful the witch could see her, but she could feel that the witch knew she was there. Then, as if to prove her right, the witch raised her arm and pointed directly at Tabitha. She sucked in a startled gasp that made her ears clog up.

The vampire and devil also turned toward her.

Her eyes widened. "Oh…God…"

The three quickly disbanded. Tabitha tried to see which way they went, but it was impossible. They'd chosen different directions. She got up, bracing herself against one of the dining table chairs, and ran a hand through her sweat-damp hair. It felt sticky and muddled from the hairspray she'd put on this morning.

She entered the living room. The flames from the fireplace danced orange and black streaks across her body. The blade of her knife glimmered in the muddy light. She walked through the room as if the floor were ice and she might slip. Looking around, she could tell something was about to happen. She could feel it deep in the marrow of her bones. Any moment, one of them would—

Something heavy splattered against her living room window. Glass cracked. It startled her enough to trigger a sharp cry. Just like earlier, the same pounding on her house. She darted for the window. Raising the blinds, she found gluey strings and seeds smearing down the cracking glass.

Pumpkin guts.

In the corner of her eye, she caught a glint of light. She looked and screamed at a face of triangles floating toward her. As it neared the window in a hasty speed, she realized it actually wasn't floating, but had been thrown.

A jack-o'-lantern.

The book *Sleepy Hollow* flashed through her mind less than a second before Tabitha hurled away from the glass just before the window blasted inward.

The pumpkin hit the floor and exploded, spilling innards across the hardwood. Keeping low, she crawled to the fireplace, safely away from all her windows.

Tabitha looked at the goopy mess on her floor. A single brick had been shoved into the pumpkin, and the candle was festooned into one of its holes.

Cheating bastards. Using bricks and jack-o'-lanterns.

There was a small fraction stuffed into the other hole in the brick—a small roll of paper. At first glance, Tabitha wondered if it might be a cigarette. When she removed it, she realized the coiled stick was actually a note. Unfurling the paper, she found a message written in shaky scrawl on Halloween stationary. The letters were slightly smudged from the pumpkin grease.

IT'S THE TRICK FOR YOU, SO WE CAN GET OUR TREAT. TO GET YOU TO COME OUT, WE'LL JUST HAVE TO BURN THE WHOLE HOUSE DOWN.

She could smell something, a strong smell that stung her eyes, like rubbing alcohol, but not. Tabitha dropped the note. The smell was becoming stronger. And now she could recognize what it was.

Gasoline.

She stood up, gripping the mantle as she rose. She looked at the lapping flames in the fireplace.

Shit!

She quickly leaned over and twisted the dial until the fire went out with a poof.

Now, she was in complete darkness.

They're going to set my house on fire!

Panic seized Tabitha in a constricted embrace. She looked at the shattered window, figuring they'd intentionally broken that one, probably wanting her to come out that way. She wasn't going to do that. She had to get out of here, but she wouldn't make it so obvious for them on how she planned to do it.

The crawlspace?

She thought it over. No. If she crawled around in there, she might become trapped, and that would be an even worse situation than the one she was already in. She pictured herself stuck in the tight space as the house crumbled on top of her in flaming portions.

They'd be expecting her to try for the windows, even the back door. She wouldn't be surprised if they had spread out to scope the doors and windows. Could she go out through the ceiling? She looked up as if expecting to see an escape route that she hadn't noticed there before.

Of course, she didn't find squat.

As she stood there, she could hear the faint sounds of sloshing, gas splashing against the house and trickling down the siding. The smell was becoming more prominent each second. She moved into the den. She could still smell it in here, but it wasn't as strong.

Think Tabitha, damn it. This is your house; you know it better than them!

The basement.

She sucked in a breath. That was it. She could go out through the aluminum track door in the basement. Maybe they hadn't even noticed it yet. The way her house sat on the hill, the aluminum door was practically hidden in a small cove. There was a good possibility they hadn't seen it.

Fuck possibilities. I'm going to try.

She ran through the den, keeping as quiet as possible as she traveled through the kitchen. At the basement door, she removed the hook from the eye, and slowly turned the knob. There was suction in the frame, so she had to put some strength behind it to open the door. It popped when it came free.

Tabitha peered down into the basement. There was absolutely no light down there. She shined the small flashlight down the stairs. The furrow of light barely penetrated the dense blackness.

The stairs leading down were wooden, and no matter how hard she tried, she couldn't stop lime from building on the planks of wood. So every time she had to go downstairs and do her laundry, she feared her feet would slip, and she'd either fall to her death, or break both legs and be stranded down there on the cold concrete while the spiders and granddaddy long-legs scurried all over her.

Tabitha put a foot on the top step. It nearly slid out from under her. She shined the light at her feet, taking each step slowly and carefully. Surprisingly, she didn't take a tumble. At the bottom, her feet settled on the dry concrete. She shined the light from one side of the basement to the other. Everything looked as if it hadn't changed since her last visit. The door was still closed, and that meant the padlock was probably still clicked on the outside. They either hadn't noticed it yet, or hadn't tried to get in. She was thankful for this.

But that still left the obstacle of getting out though the door was locked from the outside.

Tabitha felt disappointment pour through her like sludge. She was on the verge of giving up when an idea struck her.

Crawl under.

Tabitha smiled. Yes. Squirm her way under the small gap when she lifted the door. There were probably a couple inches of space at least before the padlock terminated the door's raising. If she hadn't put on any extra weight in her ass, she should be able to shimmy out. It would be tight, but doable.

I can do this.

Then, as if to destroy every bit of her secured ambiance, something slammed against the aluminum door, violently rattling it on its track. She nearly screeched but covered her mouth to prevent it.

Another bam, then something tinny clinked and dropped.

Bye-bye, padlock.

The door groaned. She pointed the light at the bottom and could see two gloved hands reaching underneath. Whoever it was had to be squatting on the other side. She quickly killed the light and tucked it back in her skirt. Hopefully they hadn't noticed it.

Tabitha understood her time was limited. She could go back upstairs, barricade herself up there, but how long would she last before being burned alive?

Not long, she figured, so the best bet, although she hated it, would be to make a stand down here.

She looked around. The nearest place to hide was the stairs. Duck behind them where there were plenty of shadows to conceal her, plus it was near enough that she shouldn't break her neck trying to get there. She hurried for the stairs, hiding on the other side of them. She watched the aluminum door through a space between the steps.

A beat passed before the door groaned again on its track, the rusted hinges probably nearing extinction. As the door rose, two dark legs, silhouetted in the gray light from outside, came into view.

A J-shaped tool dangled by the right leg.

A hook?

There were two squares at its edge, and a dip in between. Not a hook, a crowbar. A massive one, the biggest Tabitha had ever seen.

The devil ducked under the door and entered. The door rolled back down and smacked the concrete. It vibrated explosively in the small space. Methodically, he walked through the basement, giving it a good look over as he moved through.

Tabitha slowly breathed through her mouth, hoping to keep the hiss out of her nostrils. She could hear other heavy breaths that sounded like someone breathing through a tube resounding from the dark. It was the mask making the devil sound like he was sucking air through a snorkel.

The devil was at the stairs. He looked around once more, then started to climb. He hadn't noticed Tabitha hiding behind them. Her heart quickened its already hasty pace. The dark smears of his shins were right in front of her eyes. She was almost giddy with the need to slash her knife across the front of them.

He lifted his right leg, about to take the next step up, but stopped. "Hmm?"

Tabitha flinched at the devil's muffled reaction. His foot stepped back down where it was.

He's probably noticed the door's opened...

The pair of boots stood stock-still for another a beat before turning around and coming back down. He must know she was down here. The door was still locked from the outside when he'd broken in, so he was probably smart enough to guess that she hadn't gone out that way.

He knew she'd come down here, but he didn't know with certainty that she was *still* down here.

And that meant she needed to act.

But he was already on the floor before she could reach between the steps to cut his leg. Something cracked, then he shook his hand, sloshing juice back and forth. Neon green leaked through the darkness, illuminating him in a halo of the goblin light. He held the light above his head.

A glowstick. The kind Tabitha used to take with her when she went trick-or-treating as a little girl.

He raised the crowbar into an attack position as he crept toward her. She doubted he could see her, yet, but was ready just in case he did. Another few steps and her hiding place would be revealed. She stepped around the other side of the stairs, keeping to a crouch as she dodged the green cloak that highlighted him.

Now, she was at his back.

Tabitha raised the knife.

But she couldn't stab anyone from behind, probably didn't have the valor to stab anyone from the front either, even a psycho such as this guy.

If only he'd turn around…

He didn't.

As he looked behind the stairs, she decided to get his attention. That way, if he came at her, she could defend herself. Stabbing someone trying to kill her with a crowbar seemed justified.

But what if I screw up?

Then she would be dead, simple as that.

Keeping that in mind, she reached out, and tapped him on the shoulder.

He stopped walking. Slowly, he turned around. They faced each other, but he still he didn't strike. Probably because he was so damn confused as to why she'd just nonchalantly tapped him on the shoulder.

She gnashed her teeth as if growling. He tilted his head.

Then he ran.

What the hell!?!

She found herself chasing him in a circle around the stairs. He only stopped every couple of steps to blindly swing at her. The crowbar didn't even come close. He stumbled over boxes, nearly slipped on lime deposits by the washing machine, while trying to make his way to the aluminum track-door. He jumped over another unpacked box, and then bumped into a stilt coming from the ceiling down to the concrete floor like a wedge holding up the house.

It stopped him flat, but Tabitha didn't have the chance to stop. She accidentally slammed into him from behind. He grunted as the knife punched into him up to the hilt where his kidney should be. She stepped back, cupping her mouth with both hands. The glowstick dropped to the floor, sliming the both of them in sickly green light. She could see the handle poking out of him from above his pants.

"Oh…shit," whispered Tabitha. She didn't mean to stab him. Sure, she'd planned on doing it if she needed to, but didn't mean to *actually* do it just then.

The crowbar clamored on the concrete when he dropped it.

Pawing behind his back at the knife, it was out of reach no matter which way he approached it. He began to sob, muffled snuffles from behind the mask. He slipped two fingers in each eyehole and tugged the mask off his head.

Tabitha couldn't see his face all too well, but what she could make out, was that he looked young.

A teenager no older than fourteen.

Clean-faced, smooth skin, short sweaty hair.

He coughed up a gob of blood. It drooped from his bottom lip, stringy and viscid.

"I'm so sorry…," said Tabitha. "I didn't mean to…"

"You killed me!" He was crying. Lines of tears streamed down his face. "My God…you killed me…" He fell forward, bracing himself up on his hands and knees.

Although he and his friends had been trying to kill *her*, she still felt awful over what she'd done. She'd expected it to have been a more valiant slaying, but watching him slowly die, bawling as he did so, made her wish that she was the one dying.

"I'm sorry," she whispered.

His palms gave way. He fell on his face and didn't move.

Dead.

(III)

Jackie was moving again. Almost convinced she'd lost her hunters, she still moved as quietly as possible, just in case. But it was pointless trying to be quiet. Leaves were all over the forest floor, crinkling and crackling under her feet as if she were walking on a terrain of bubble wrap. She wasn't sure where she was in the woods, but she didn't stop. Eventually the woods would run out, where she would be when that happened, she had an idea.

Out in the open.

That could be good or bad. Good if she could find help. Bad if it was only a field with nothing but a wide range of flatland that offered her zero concealment.

The woods were shrouded in heavy darkness with only nets of moonlight getting through the leafy canopy. Even without the small strains of light, her night vision was clear. She could move about the woods without fear of running into a tree or cracking her head on a low-hanging limb. Did nothing for the ground, though, as it looked like she was treading through a lake of shadow. As if to prove her point, her foot snagged a root, causing her to stumble. Dull pain throbbed in her toes. She kept walking, though, ignoring it as much as she could.

Jackie neared a grove of pine trees that stood in formation like soldiers. Fog clung to the green needles on the branches like vaporous webbing. She stopped walking. No way was she going in there. Way too dark. Plus, there were plenty of places for someone to be lurking. She read a book once about these little creatures in the woods and cornfields of this tiny town. For all she knew, those things could be waiting for her in that shadowy cluster.

No thanks. I'll go around.

A mild breeze drifted across her, hardening her skin with goosebumps. She hugged herself, rubbing her forearms. Leaves stirred, slightly trembling in the gentle wind.

Wish I had my jacket.

Better yet, her heavy coat. The chilly weather hadn't bothered her when she was running, but since she'd slowed down, her blood wasn't pumping as heavily as it had been. And from the damp veneer of gelid sweat clinging to her body, she was freezing.

The pine trees were now to her right. As she walked past them, she surveyed their thickness, the impenetrable darkness beyond. It looked as if she were to reach through the limbs, she'd dip her hand into oil.

Plumes of spiraling fog rose from the black gaps between the dark green.

Limbs rustled.

Jackie stopped. She leaned slightly forward, narrowing her eyes as she looked at the pine barrier. At first, she couldn't find it, but then she saw a slight rocking between the needle-lined stems.

Something's in there!

Before she could put much thought into it, a pale shape lunged straight at her face. Screaming, Jackie jumped back, swatting her hands. Her feet tangled, throwing her to the damp ground. She felt moist coldness seeping through her clothes.

And watched the squirrel that had jumped out from the pine tree scurry away, his bushy tail sticking straight up. Feeling like a complete idiot, Jackie groaned. She would have laughed at herself if she didn't realize how much she'd just screwed up.

"Over there!" she heard a voice call from not too far off.

"Oh, no…" Jackie gasped. Rolling onto her stomach, she gazed to the woods. Trees, black twisting shapes against a washed-out wall of swirling vapors was all she could see. But she could faintly hear them, growing louder with each hastening footfall.

They're coming!

"Jackie, you stupid little…" She stopped herself from going any farther. Now wasn't the time for personal chastising. She needed to get up. And run.

Sprinting through the woods, her clothes felt like dampened weights against her skin. Uncomfortable and cold. Joggling her head like this brought the ache from her welt back. She didn't care. It wouldn't keep her from getting away from here.

Limbs whipped her, leaving lines of heat across her exposed skin. A hand of leaves slapped her face. The stinging pop brought tears to her eyes.

Stupid! I'm so stupid! If I wouldn't have screamed…

Jackie continued to run. Above the trees she noticed the subtle hint of glowing underneath the whirling dome of fog and smoke. It looked like grayish water flowing across the sky. She could smell wood burning, like from a fireplace. The light bouncing off the smoke was what aroused her curiosity. Couldn't be the moon. Not this low to the ground. The moon would be throwing light down, not casting it up against the smoke.

She was getting close. To where, she wasn't sure. But something was definitely up there. Hopefully whatever it was meant help.

The woods began to thin out, the spaces between the trees growing. She could make out something beyond the trees that sat like a capitol T, lit by whatever was causing the light.

She kept going, heading for the T. As she got closer, she realized what she was looking at was one end to a clothesline. In every case she'd ever known, if there was a clothesline, it should be planted in a backyard. And if there was a backyard, then she had no doubt there was a house up ahead.

A house!

The last wall of trees was spread so far apart, the leaves barely brushed her shoulders when she exited. She stopped long enough to do a quick scan of what lay before her: A private backyard, clothesline, well house, and a shed. She spotted a picnic table to the right where the yard ended. The backside of a one-level house was on the far side of the clothesline. No lights were on, the sole source of illumination provided by the safety light on top of the power pole.

Her eyes returned to the shed. Nothing but a tin frame shaped like a tall doghouse, it was all she had to hide behind. The wellhouse was farther up, so she might as well forget it.

Get behind the shed, scope out the area.

A plan was forming in her mind that would require her to knock on the door. Hopefully someone was home and wouldn't mind letting her use the phone to call the police and Allen. And maybe— *please God*—maybe Joey had made it to the house and was inside with the owner.

As much as she wanted that to be true, she knew it wasn't. If a child wandered up to someone's house needing help, there would be police swarming the area. No one was here. The house was silent. And dark.

Most likely, no one was home.

I'll break the door down to get to their phone.

She was surprised, and a little ashamed, that she felt no remorse about breaking and entering. It was a dire situation and surely the homeowner would understand. She'd pay for the damage, definitely. That should help smooth things over.

Bent at the waist, Jackie trotted across the yard. Her feet made whispering sounds in the grass as she hurried to the shed. She reached it, putting her back against the tinny surface. Cold leached through her shirt, making her spine feel tight and numb. She took several short breaths. Sweat trickled down her forehead.

Don't dawdle. Keep going.

Jackie eased her way to the edge of the shed as if she were walking the ledge around a high rise. Reaching the end, she turned, and slowly peered around the corner.

And saw someone in a mask hurry past.

Jackie quickly ducked back around, holding her breath. She listened to the soft sounds of shoes in wet grass fading as they ran away from the shed.

Thank you, God!

She slowly exhaled. That was close. She could have been spotted right then, but thankfully nobody noticed her.

It was the mask the girl was wearing that had most likely blocked Jackie from her peripheral vision. Her face was pointed forward, the tiny body hurrying to get somewhere. She wasn't sure how old the girl was, but she doubted much older than ten from her height.

Maybe it wasn't a girl.

Most likely it was. She didn't think most boys would choose to wear a witch's mask.

(IV)

Tabitha could barely see through the narrow holes. She adjusted the mask for the tenth time, but it still didn't help. It felt like she was wearing blinders on each side like a racing horse. Regardless of how it barely seemed to fit, it would have to do.

She tugged on the pants. They were tight enough and felt like they wouldn't drop to her ankles anytime soon. The crowbar lay on the floor where the kid had dropped it. She picked it up on her way to the aluminum door, glancing back at him one more time. He lay on his side, stripped to his boxers and socks, with a bloody rent in his lower back.

Tabitha was the one who'd put it in the pale flesh.

God, she hated wearing his clothes. Fortunately, there wasn't any blood inside the mask, but it was still damp from his sweat and saliva. She also tried to ignore the cold stickiness against her back from his coagulating blood. Reaching back to adjust the coat, a finger slipped through the hole the knife had made. When she brought her hand back, the finger was capped in the kid's blood.

She took a deep breath, then raised the aluminum door on its tracks. Chilly air licked her. She felt cold and achy outside from being inside the stuffy basement. The sickle-moon looked low enough to stab into the earth. It was red, burning red. A breeze drifted over her, wafting through the orifices of the mask. Even through the foam she could still smell the leaves, and on top of that scent was the smell of burning wood.

Tabitha stood between the valley-like slants of her yard, trying to decide which way she should go first. She looked to the right, which led around to the front of the house. That was probably as good a choice as any. Her plan stunk no matter which direction she proceeded.

Back in the basement and after the deplorable show of the kid's slow death, she realized that she would have to either kill, or seriously injure the other two if it meant saving her own life, her house, or both. And if the one in the basement had been a teenager—a *kid*— then it was probably safe to assume the other two were as well.

Tabitha mounted the hill.

At the corner of her house, she could see the front yard. It was dark, but the grinning curve of moon gave her enough carroty light to see by.

She looked toward the front of her house. The vampire was lowering an open flame to the torn rag dangling from the mouth of an old beer bottle at his feet. He had his mashed hand against his chest.

Oh shit.

He glanced at her and stopped. She froze. Her heart felt as if it was beating in her throat.

"Did you find her?" asked the vampire, his voice muffled behind the mask. It was no longer scratchy and throaty, but deep and stern.

For a moment, Tabitha had forgotten she was masquerading in the devil's clothes. She shook her head to answer him.

"Oh well," he said. Then he lit the rag, lifted the bottle off the ground, and underhand tossed it through the shattered window of her living room. There was a crash, then a gush of light as the flames spread. "Guess she'll burn in there."

Tabitha gawped at her house. Tears misted her eyes as the flames molested the windowsill from inside the house. She could picture the flames engulfing her coffee table, spreading their licking heat onto the couch. She heard a tinny click. Looking at the vampire, she saw he had lighted a Zippo and was about to set fire to another flaming cocktail.

No...you're not.

She lifted the crowbar, holding it in both hands.

You're not going to torch my house!

She charged. The vampire raised the flaring bottle, turning to her as she revved the crowbar above her head.

He didn't have time to react.

She swung.

The curled tip of the crowbar smashed through the bottle's glass, spraying the combustible liquid inside across the lighter's flame. A surge of fire clouted the vampire's body. His clothes went up. The mask's cheap foam immediately began to bubble. The blaze rapidly traveled up his neck, under the mask, and out from the eyeholes. His screams were excruciating.

Tabitha dropped the crowbar. She backed away from him, putting her hands on each side of the beanie that covered her head.

What did I do? What did I do?

She screamed, but it was barely audible under his.

The vampire danced around, flailing his arms as spikes of fire crackled across them. He ran away, slapping the flames with his hands. Finally, he dropped and began to roll, but by this time the fire was too uncontainable to be extinguished so easily. After a few seconds that painfully drudged by, he went still, but the flames continued to live.

Tabitha ran to him. On her way, she removed the jacket. Though she wore the devil's long-sleeved shirt underneath, the cold stung her as if she were bare-chested. She stopped at his feet and began whacking him with it, making sure she hit every lingering ration of fire. With some time, she managed to put it out. He lay on his stomach, groaning, as smoke curled from his scorched-black body. Tabitha couldn't tell which part of him was his clothes, and which was his skin. It had all melted together into blistering, gummy ash.

"I'm sorry," she whispered. "You shouldn't have done it. It's your own fault!"

He groaned in response, then went silent.

Tabitha crouched, lifting the crowbar. The metal was slick in her hands. Standing, she gaped at him another moment, then clutched the weapon tightly.

It was time to find the witch.

CHAPTER 14

(1)

Allen walked along Goodhill Road, his head tucked against the chilly wind, and his hands burrowed deep into the pockets of his pants. The smoke smell had grown stronger the further he'd walked, its haze thicker. His eyes felt dehydrated. There was a lump in his chest from his aching lungs.

He still had a few miles to go until he reached town. After finding the words *Prank Night* on the wall in the church, and discovering his tires had been slashed, he chose not to go back into the building out of fear he'd run into someone who shouldn't be there. So, he'd started walking.

Should have at least gone back in for my coat.

He shivered, then raised his frozen hands to his mouth, and huffed hot foggy breath into them. It warmed his palms, but they were cold again the moment he took his mouth away.

He was still irked someone had marred the church. Not that he was an Old Testament kind of guy, someone who believed people didn't do such things, but it was just weird that someone had done it to *his* church. It was hard to accept someone from town, probably people he knew, had done such a thing to not only the church, but the rest of town.

His worry returned to his family. And the possibility that the two were connected shot a powerful beam through his mind. Shaking his head, he hoped to jar those thoughts. He'd make himself sick with distress if he kept dwelling on it, and that would only cause him more harm.

Allen gazed at the darkened pastures as he walked. Sometimes, he would drive the entire length of Goodhill Road, park his car at the lookout, and enjoy the view. He remembered last summer being surprised with a babysitter for Joey. Jackie had wanted an evening for the two of them, so she'd arranged for Annette Carter to watch their son. Allen drove Jackie to the lookout for a picnic. Much more than eating happened that evening, and it was still one of his favorite memories.

Looks so peaceful out there.

The pale shapes of undulating hills and meadows, the dairy cows grazing naturally and undisturbed by the rest of the world. But he'd learned tonight that he absolutely despised walking so close to it in the dark.

It's creepy.

There were odd sounds in the woods to his left and even odder sounds coming from the fields to his right. He heard what he guessed was a cow, although it sounded like it was trying to imitate a donkey. As he came off an arc in the road, he spotted the wan shape of a mailbox ahead on his left. If he remembered correctly, that should belong to the Henderson's abode. They attended church every Sunday, the first service, and would probably let him use the phone to call Jackie and the police.

But if their phone doesn't work, either?

Maybe they'd *drive* him home.

I'll give them money for gas, plus a tip.

They'd probably be willing to accommodate if they weren't out trick-or-treating with their daughter, Nicole.

Please God, let them be home.

He took the driveway. Gravel crunched under his feet as the path led him uphill. As he reached the top, the smoky fumes became heavier, and he couldn't see as well. Not only was the red moon being blocked by the awning of trees bordering the property, but the smoke had also gotten so thick it was hard to distinguish.

It reminded him of college, before he became a pastor, when he was a partier visiting club after endless club. Their smoke-filled dance floors, the bars that reeked of stale sweat and cigarette smoke. He didn't miss those days and was thankful God had gotten him out of there. But the part he hated the most about being in clubs was the day after, how his chest would feel pinched and his lungs ached from the smoke.

His chest felt like that now.

Are they burning leaves or something?

He covered his mouth and nose with the sleeve of his shirt. Why would they be burning leaves at night? The fear something was wrong made it feel as if his tongue dropped into his gut.

A scream pierced him like a knife.

He ducked down as if he were about to hit his head on something. Looking around, he tiptoed to the nearest tree and slipped against it. He poked his head around the side. Through the thinning spaces between the trees ahead of him, he could see the contour of the Henderson house. There didn't appear to be any lights on, but he could see it gaudily swathed in a flickering orange smolder.

Something's definitely burning.

He got on his hands and knees, crawled to the bushes, and peeked over the top. There was a wrenching twist in his chest as his eyes locked on what was occurring on the Henderson's front yard.

The screaming must have been Faith Henderson, mother of Nicole and wife of Jack. A masked person, wearing a black mask with oddly shaped horns of the same color protruding from the front, had a handful of her hair, and was dragging her bucking body over to where Jack and Nicole had been arranged on their knees. Jack's back was straight, hands crossed behind his head while Nicole seemed to be standing with him, but she didn't look to have her hands up.

Faith was trying to keep up, but her feet kept slipping out from under her.

Two more people in masks guarded Nicole and Jack. From where Allen was hiding behind the bush, their matching masks looked to have been cut out of paper plates, rectangle eyes and mouths colored with crayon. One had an axe and the other one, the shortest of the bunch, held a machete to Nicole's throat.

Dear Lord. What am I seeing?

The horned man slung Faith to the ground in front of her family.

Glass shattered. Flames reached through a broken window to the left. The house was consumed by fire, an inferno that wasn't reserved just for their home. Allen traced flames to the cars, which were parked to the right of the house.

Everything was burning.

The ax man nudged Faith with his boot. She cried out. It didn't look as if it had hurt her, but she was so hysterical that it probably didn't matter. Her light yellow hair looked almost white in the ginger glow. There were a few dark splotches on her night gown that could have been blood.

"Please..." she begged. "Please, stop!"

The horned one walked over to where something protruded from a lump in the yard. He gripped the handle and yanked. A long handle with a large, curved blade emerged. As Allen stared harder, he began to decipher the shape the weapon had come from was furry.

Their dog.

The hound lay on its side, dead by the apparent stabbing from the horned one's scythe. He planted its wooden end into the ground, the bowed blade veering off to the side.

Like the Angel of Death...

The invader pointed at Jack, then mimicked a slicing motion across his neck with a thumb.

They were going to kill the Hendersons. Something needed to be done, but Allen had no idea what he could do to help. If he ran in there trying to be a hero, he'd be killed before getting a chance to do anything. However, that might give the family a chance to escape. Maybe if he caused a good enough distraction.

He would need a weapon, though, something that could hold them off for a little while. Allen felt around the slimy leaves sprinkling the ground. He didn't feel anything hard enough to be useful.

Allen wasn't thrilled to use his fists. He hadn't fought anybody since he was in college, and he'd lost that one. Actually, he'd lost every fight he'd ever been in—all two of them. Even a track record like that wasn't going to keep him from trying.

He stood up, took a deep breath, not giving himself a chance to think about it, and dashed through the bushes.

Going for the shorter one first was probably his best option. Not only was he much smaller, he was also the closest one to Allen. His advance was covered by the crackling noises of wood being eaten by fire. Extending his elbow, he slammed it in the back of the short one's head. The paper mask shot off as the body went down.

The taller one whipped his head around, too stunned to react right away. He looked back at the horned one, then at Allen. There wasn't enough space for him to get a good swing with the ax. Allen was thankful for that, but he needed to dispatch him quickly so he could focus on the one with the much larger weapon already running towards him.

The ax man charged. Allen backed up, wrapping his hands around the wooden handle as its blade lunged at his face. He held it back. They struggled with the weapon.

He could see the horned one was almost right on top of them.

Jack intersected him, planting his fist squarely on the black-mesh jaw. He spun around, his feet soaring over his head, then he landed on the back of his neck. His body crashed down on him in a heap. Jack snatched up the scythe and ran towards Allen while Faith shouted her thanks and praises behind him.

The ax guy detected Jack's approach. Allen tried to hold him back, but the man shot his knee up. It smashed Allen's testicles, blasting the air out of his lungs. He fell, and since he hadn't eaten anything recently to vomit, he dry heaved so hard he felt a tight pull in his back.

Then the guy turned and ran at Jack, the ax wielded above his head. They circled one another, not taking their eyes away from the other. Allen was useless to help.

Nicole crawled over to Allen in her pink pajamas and placed a delicate hand to the side of his face. It was cold against his skin. She smiled at him. It made Allen feel better just seeing it.

The little girl leaned over, putting her lips to his ear. "You stupid son of a bitch. Do you realize you almost ruined *everything*?"

Allen's eyes widened when he noticed the knife clasped in Nicole's hand. It shot for his stomach, but he rolled over, and the blade punched him in the ribs. It hurt, but it didn't feel like it had stabbed him deep. Nicole yanked the knife out, and thrust the blade at it him again, this time higher.

He caught her wrist. She jerked from side to side, trying to break free, but even with his smashed testicles, he was still much stronger than her. Snarling, her teeth were bared like an animal.

Jack shouted at his daughter. "Nicole! Leave him alone!"

She looked at her father, giving Allen the moment he needed. Already regretting what he was about to do, he balled his hand into a fist, and landed an uppercut to the pretty, lemon-haired girl. Her head shot back. The force of her thrusts diminished, and when she raised her head again her eyes were glazed and dopey.

Allen punched her one more time for safety.

She collapsed onto the ground beside him.

Allen felt terrible, but also knew he would quickly get over it.

The bad guy that Allen had ambushed sat up, pushing the hood of his jacket off his head. A thirteen-year-old face was underneath.

Alex Bolden.

Allen recognized him from church as well. The kid was being raised by a single father who worked long hours but was a great dad who loved his son very much. The situation, awful as it already was, was becoming incredibly confusing.

Allen struggled to his feet. He looked at Jack. Down on his knees, the man's opponent stood over him, hand clasped around his throat. Any moment now he'd use the ax to finish him off.

Ignoring the nauseating pain in his stomach as much as he could, he sprinted for the fight, kicking Alex Bolden in the side of the head along the way, and pouncing the one with the ax from behind before the blunt edge was imbedded into Jack's skull.

(II)

Jackie gasped when she heard the screams. Such agony and pain. They seemed to carry on endlessly. After what felt like several awful hours, the screams abated. A few moments later, she heard someone else screaming. These, no doubt, belonged to a woman and she was chastising whoever had produced the first set.

"I'm sorry! You shouldn't have done that!"

Apologizing? Jackie was confused by this. What was going on here?

Jackie carefully left the sanction of the shed and headed for the wellhouse. Reaching the cinderblock structure, she sank to a crouch. The dank scent of mold and mildew was heavy here. The shingles on the wellhouse's roof were rotting and broken. Some had already fallen and littered the ground around the wellhouse, resembling hardened fertilizer.

She looked around. No signs of the witch. Checking the woods behind her, she didn't see the two chasing her. Hopefully she'd lost them again.

Jackie snuck around the side of the well house, hurrying to the house. She veered to the left, being careful as she descended a hill. She came to a small swath of gravel that led towards the house. A risen door opened on what looked like a basement. Inside, she could vaguely make out the insipid form of a body. She couldn't see the face, but from the bare legs she guessed the person was either naked or part of the way.

Should she check on them?

As much as she wanted to keep going, forgetting what she'd just seen, she knew she couldn't. And, more importantly, she knew she *wouldn't*.

Jackie entered the pitch-black basement. She didn't take the time to be cautious as she rushed to the motionless body. From the dying glow of a neon stick on the floor, she could see his back. A quick inspection showed her a gaping wound and a dead boy. Older than Joey, but not by much, his face was frozen in an expression of terrified sadness. It broke Jackie's heart seeing it.

Turning away from the boy, the toe of Jackie's shoe nudged something. The object made a soft scraping sound on the concrete floor. Crouching, Jackie felt around the dark. Fingers brushed tacky coldness.

Her hand curled around the wooden handle of a knife.

$$(\text{III})$$

Tabitha didn't find the witch behind the house, so she returned to the front. The fire inside the living room had almost died out. Luckily, it hadn't ignited the gasoline on the outside. So far it looked as if the rest of her house might be spared.

Find Witchy and I can end this.

She searched around the yard a few more minutes before giving up.

Tabitha decided to walk to The Dalton's house. They were her nearest neighbor, though she hadn't had many conversations with them in the past, they knew each other well enough. They should trust her enough to let her come inside. It was a mile long journey up Amity Hill Road. Since she couldn't call the police from her house, she hoped she could from there. She was briefly tempted to crawl around under the house and reconnect her phone line but decided against it. She had no idea how long that would actually take, and it also came down to the fact that she was too scared to try.

With the crowbar clutched firmly in her hand, she began walking up her driveway. It was quiet out here, bizarrely quiet. Not that it was usually booming with noise, but she expected there to at least be some kind of soundtrack from the wildlife.

Tonight there was nothing.

Maybe they're hiding.

Not a bad idea. She should probably do the same instead of trekking around in the open like this.

Go into the woods?

Probably not the best decision. No telling who she might run into.

Tabitha neared the bend in her driveway, the same spot she'd first noticed the vampire earlier today.

Must've been scoping out the house.

She wondered why they hadn't been in the house waiting for her when she'd gotten home.

"Guess that wasn't part of the plan," she muttered to herself.

Ahead of her and parked in the grass along the verge of her driveway was a truck.

Becky's truck.

She recognized the old beater right away. The holes patched with duct tape gave it away. They must have taken the truck from Becky's, driven it over here.

Weren't they already here right after Becky left?

Unable to recall for sure, Tabitha neared the vehicle, keeping the crowbar close in case she needed to use it. Tabitha prayed she wouldn't have to. She'd already killed two kids tonight and didn't want to make it three unless absolutely necessary.

At the rear of the truck now, there was no doubt it was Becky's. Not that there had been any reservations before. So, how'd it get over here?

Somebody had to have driven the damn thing! It didn't just drive over on its own.

The passenger door clacked open, killing her curious thoughts. There was rustling from the other side of the truck. She could see the dome of a little head bopping up and down as the witch walked around the tailgate. She didn't look to be on alert, or the least bit scared of Tabitha.

You're still wearing the costume, you idiot.

She'd grown so used to it that she'd completely forgotten she even had it on.

"Where's Eric?" the adolescent voice asked. Not a little girl's voice, though the tone was definitely high. The pitch was vaguely familiar, but hard to interpret through the mask. "Did you guys get her?"

Tabitha kept staring at the teensy witch as she moved closer. Her fingers clutched the crowbar, making her rubber gloves crackle.

The witch crossed her arms over her chest. "*Did* you?" There was pure annoyance in the voice. "Did you kill her?"

Tabitha didn't know how to respond to that. She shook her head, then pointed toward her house.

"Eric did?" Nod. "Well, it's *his* ass then. We've got to get moving. He can walk back. Still got the keys?"

Slapping the pockets of the stolen jeans, she felt the jutting edges of keys. They jangled as she removed them from the pants.

"Good. Let's get going."

The witch turned her back to Tabitha. She had the perfect opportunity to whack her one good time but balked and missed the opportunity. The witch was already on her way back to the passenger side of the truck, out of reach.

The witch glanced back over her shoulder. "Now!"

Tabitha marched to the truck and opened the driver side door. She climbed in, leaving the door open in case she needed to perform a quick hop out. She was farther back from the pedals than she needed to be, so without hesitation, she pulled the lever and slid the seat upward. As she was about to put the keys in the ignition, the witch grabbed her forearm.

"What was that?"

Tabitha looked around. Shrugged.

"Not out there. Right *here*." She pointed at the seat. "Why did you just do that?"

Tabitha wasn't sure what she was talking about, but as she thought about it, the witch's question began to make since.

I had the keys in my pocket. That meant the devil was the one who drove.

As the realization began to clear, the witch finished the statement for her.

"Why did you have to slide the seat up? You drove."

Not hassling herself with trying to reply, she took the crowbar and jabbed it at the witch. She ducked, and the end crashed through the window. The witch fell into the floorboard, contorting her body so she could keep her eyes on Tabitha.

"Who are you?" the witch shouted. "What did you do with Jason?"

If Jason was the one she'd undressed, then he was in her basement. Dead. Tabitha was about to strike the witch, but stopped herself, and instead slammed the crowbar against the passenger door, bracing it over the witch. The bar was on level with the witch's chest. She couldn't move from the floorboard.

Then Tabitha removed the mask, tossing it on the seat.

The witch gasped. "Ms. Stoner?"

Tabitha's blood chilled. Now she recognized the voice from having heard it so many times this year, spoken from the kid's mouth. "Take off your mask." The witch quickly shook *his* head. "Do it or I'll do to you what I did to the others."

"What'd you do to them?" There was fear in his voice.

"Burned Eric alive. Stabbed Jason to death." Neither one had been done intentionally, but the witch didn't need to know that. "So, take off *your fucking mask!*" She thought losing it at the end of the sentence was a nice a touch, profanity never hurt to emphasize a point, either.

It worked. The witch raised his trembling hands to the foam mask, lifting it over his head. Tabitha's breath hurdled in her chest. Though she'd already known the face she was going to see when the mask came off, it still crushed her when it happened.

"Joey…"

There he was, a defenseless, frightened child, in the floorboard of the truck.

Joey Farrell.

Her favorite student. The same Joey whose father was the pastor at the local church and whose mother sometimes sent baked cookies with Joey to give to Tabitha. He looked so much like a helpless kid, sniffling, tears filling his eyes. But this little boy wasn't defenseless. He was deadly. Tabitha had the severed head in her living room to prove it.

"My God, Joey. What have you done?"

The ten-year-old buried his face against his palms, bawling. His short brown hair was hidden under the beanie. Even after all he'd done, it was still hard seeing him cry. Tabitha reached her hand down to him, placing it gently on the boy's shoulder. She felt his tiny body bouncing under her hand. When he raised his head, Tabitha saw that he hadn't been crying, but laughing. The tears in his eyes weren't from sadness.

"You stupid bitch," said Joey. Holding his stomach, he snorted with wild laughter. "You actually felt *sorry* for me?" Joey's laughter stopped cold. "And I'm the one that sawed off Mrs. Loflin's head. How could you feel sorry for *me?* It was hard work too. My wittle arms just weren't strong ee-nuff."

Tabitha was so absorbed by the shock of what Joey was saying, the detached intelligence in his words, she hadn't noticed his miniscule hand reaching under the seat. When he pulled it out, a pistol about the size of his head was clutched in his little fingers.

Tabitha realized she was about to be shot just as Joey's fingers squeezed the trigger. She ducked her head, banging her forehead on the steering wheel. The honk of the horn was hidden behind the cannon-like blast. The back windshield exploded behind Tabitha's head. Her ears screamed. Her vision had been jarred, and everything that used to be one now had matching blurry replicas.

Disoriented, Tabitha leaned to the side. Without the solidity of a closed door, she fell through the opening and landed hard on the ground beside the truck.

Joey's screams were muffled through the drone in Tabitha's ears. She looked up to find Joey struggling to get out through her side of the truck. Even through the haze in her mind, she ascertained the gun's recoil had injured his wrist. It dangled uselessly in the wrong direction. The boy held it close to his stomach. This time, his tears were sincere.

But it hardly seemed to matter since what was gripped in his working hand was the crowbar. The elongated tool looked to be as long as his small body when he dropped out of the truck.

"You made me hurt my hand!" screamed Joey.

Tabitha was dazed. She felt nauseous. She could hardly move, could barely hear, and couldn't focus at all. So when Joey raised the crowbar, Tabitha let her head drop back on the ground. Maybe in her jumbled confusion, the pain of the blow wouldn't be so bad.

Joey swung.

Tabitha closed her eyes.

There was a dull thump of something blunt striking soft flesh, accompanied by a groan and scuffle of something landing on the earth.

Tabitha felt herself smile. The pain wasn't bad at all. In fact, she'd felt nothing.

The realization that she could still smell the sweet aromas of wood burning brought a frown from her. And she could still feel the cold dampness of the ground beneath her. The jabbing points of rocks pushed into back. She squirmed slightly and heard the scraping of her clothes on the gravel.

Tabitha slowly opened one eye.

Joey was gone. Standing in his place was a blonde woman, still pretty though a small hill had swollen on her forehead and her face was spattered in blood. The yellow locks were mussed and tangled.

"Um..." was all Tabitha managed to get out.

She opened her other eye and looked the woman down. In one hand was the knife Tabitha had left in the basement, and in the other was a baseball-sized rock that had probably been taken from the side of the road. A small dark patch of wetness was on its tip.

The woman gaped at Joey as what little color she had drained from her face. The rock slipped from her hand, hitting the ground with a soft thud. The knife fell next, the blade embedding into the ground. She looked to be frozen in shock.

Tabitha looked to her left and saw Joey on the ground. He could have passed for sleeping if there wasn't a trail of blood sliding down from underneath his beanie.

It all clicked. The fog in her mind from the gunshot cleared.

This woman had saved her life.

And she was also the boy's mother.

"Juh-Jackie?"

Jackie's eyes glanced in her direction, then back to Joey. Her lip started to quiver. "My God...in Heaven...what is *this*?"

Tabitha couldn't craft a delicate way of telling this poor woman her son had been trying to kill her, had already killed at least one person that she knew of.

I don't have to tell her anything.

The disgusted grief was vivid on Jackie's face.

She already knows.

As if to solidify this thought, Jackie dropped to her knees and started to sob. Not soft blubbering sounds of betrayed disbelief a parent might let loose if she learned her child had been stealing money from her wallet. These were awful, agonized bellows that ripped through the night like the wails of sirens.

CHAPTER 15

(1)

"Where'd you learn how to do this?" Ben asked, leaning against the car door as he kept watch. The shotgun was pumped and ready, the barrel extended in front of him. So far, nobody had come along, but he knew this deceitful calmness wouldn't last.

Albright was crouched on the pavement, reaching into the van's floorboard. Her hands were buried up to the wrist underneath the steering console. "I wasn't always a cop."

Ben shook his head. "You stole cars? No way."

"You're right. I didn't. But I learned how to do it just in case I ever got the balls to try."

"Wish you would have learned how to get it done quicker."

"Hey, easy. I'm working in the dark here. Give me some slack."

"The amount of slack I'm willing to give is about thirty seconds' worth, then we have to get moving, with or without the van."

"I won't need thirty seconds."

Ben hoped not. Though he hated the idea of leaving the van behind, they couldn't keep this going. Eventually someone would come along and catch them. Ben thought their grim luck had changed when they'd found the van parked by the barber shop barely two blocks from the station. It was a service van for the school system, and was left behind, raided and ransacked.

234

But the tires were still in one piece.

The keys were missing, though, and if Albright couldn't get it started, the van was no use to them.

Wasting time doing this. We should just keep going. Find another vehicle, one with keys.

Where?

He looked around. What other cars he saw sat on rubber the density of ribbons. Not much to choose from. He should stop being an ass and start being grateful.

The engine clicked and *vroomed* once. Ben's head whipped around, a smile starting to form on his face. Albright had leaned back, holding two wires above the carpeting, and tapped them together. Each time there was a spark, the engine burped.

After four tries, the motor turned over. Albright quickly twisted the metal hairs together and let the tangled wires drop. The engine remained idling. To Ben, it was the most glorious sound he'd ever heard.

"Let's get moving!" said Albright, jumping into the van.

"I'll drive."

"Really? You're going to go that route?"

"What route?"

"Not letting me drive. I never get to drive."

"Albright, this is hardly the time or place…"

"Get in. You navigate, I'll steer."

Ben wanted to argue, but he also didn't know why it should matter so much to either of them. So to save some much-needed time, he moved around the front. The headlights clicked on, momentarily washing him in their bright glow. He pulled open the passenger door and climbed in. He hadn't even closed the door before Albright was driving away.

"Where am I taking us?" she asked.

Ben pulled the safety harness across him, snapping it in. "Probably wouldn't be a bad idea to go through town."

"Why? Shouldn't we head for the state police? If we take the back roads, it'll save us a couple minutes."

"Yes. We'll make our way there. Might be people who need our help along the way."

Albright nodded. "You're right. Sorry."

He turned to his deputy. A look of distress seemed to age her ten years. Bottom lip clamped between her teeth, her eyes were strained and on the verge of tears. She glanced at him quickly, then aimed her eyes at the road without speaking.

"You did good in there," he said. He patted her gently on the shoulder.

"Like hell…"

"Stop it. I won't stand for that. You did good, though you went against my instructions and came back."

Albright smirked. "Good thing I did."

"Yeah…"

(11)

Darryl Tucker drove a truck for Goodman's Auto Service, an establishment that sold refurbished and used parts, a junkyard basically, and it was his job to drive all over the state of North Carolina to pick up old cars, then handover a small wad of cash to whoever the previous owner was. Joe Goodman was the owner, and with Darryl being one of three employees, the pay was decent. The only downside were the long hours he endured on the road and away from his girlfriend, Sherry.

And this was what he was doing now. Driving back from Clemmons, with an '88 Trans Am hitched to the back of his truck. It wasn't a tow-truck. What they used was a 4x4 Chevy and a chain hitched to the front bumper of the car in tow. It was all they had, but it got the job done just the same, and saved them a smidgeon in fuel costs.

He had a couple hours until he reached Fairfax County. He'd

decided to stick to Highway 801 which led straight through Webster County. Being after suppertime, traffic should be light, if there was any at all. Webster County was farmland mostly, and supposedly a manufacturing plant was located somewhere nearby, though he'd never seen it. What small fractions of population the county had were made up of simple folk, so he doubted anybody would protest if he kept the dial on his speedometer hovering at sixty.

Darryl chewed on the end of a cigar that he would never light. He hated the smell of cigar smoke but *loved* how they tasted. He'd chew them until they resembled wet cardboard. Using his sagging gut to steady the steering wheel, he took the cigar out of his mouth to see how much he had left on it.

Not much on this side.

He turned it around and plopped it back in his mouth. He bit down, smiling.

Good stuff.

Darryl checked his cell phone again for a signal. He still didn't have one. He'd been on the phone with Sherry, enjoying a good bout of dirty talk while she pleasured herself in the earpiece. She'd been close to squirting her juice, her moans rising in pitch and speed when he'd lost his signal as he neared Webster County's border. It was weird considering he'd never lost signal on this route before.

Through the windshield he spotted the wooden marker for Webster County. The road curved around a large boulder just before an intersection on the county line. He applied pressure to the brake pedal as he neared it. Scratching his grizzled beard, he eased the truck around the boulder.

And felt his heart jump into his throat.

"Shit!"

Stamping the pedal with both feet, he locked the brakes. He saw the two cars sitting in a line ahead of him, headlights to bumper, getting larger as the truck skidded forward. Their lights were on, doors hanging open. Darryl steered the truck around the rear car as his tires bounced and screeched. Smoke from the burning rubber wafted up from under the truck.

Finally, he succeeded in stopping, luckily without damaging anything. Joe would have his ass if he got into a wreck. Then Darryl would be put out of a job. After being laid off from the paper mill two years ago, his choice of jobs was limited from the amount of education and experience he had—or lack thereof. He *needed* this job, especially since his unemployment was nothing but a faded memory.

Darryl sat there, his heart drumming, trying to catch his breath. The heavy odor from his tires ponged from the vents. He'd lost his cigar sometime during the near collision.

Now that he could take a moment to observe the situation, he did so.

What the hell is this?

The cars looked as if they'd been heading into Webster County, and for whatever reason had stopped short of the county line. Red and blue lights swished across the trees on both sides of the road, swirling colors inside the cab.

He flung his door open, heaving his mass out of the truck. The burnt rubber smell was really bad outside. He checked the tires to make sure he hadn't popped any, and to his surprise none had, though the driver's side looked a little low on air. He kicked it a couple of times to check its resilience. It seemed fine. Probably just needed to be topped off.

Darryl walked around to the front of his truck. The car ahead of him was a Honda, the engine still idling. Its front door was open, the seatbelt dangling. Darryl frowned. "Hello?" He approached the car, bent over, and peeked inside. There was a cup of coffee in the console holder, the radio playing low from the speakers. All the seats were void of passengers. He stood up straight. "Where is everyone?"

He waited, but got nothing, so he moved to the minivan in front of the smaller sedan. Both of its front doors hung open, but the interior light was off. So, it had been sitting long enough for the timer to run out and dim.

"Does anyone need any assistance?"

How could he assist them?

Can't call anyone.

Darryl continued walking, crossing the front of the van. Parked at angles so they blocked both lanes were a police car and a dark colored beater. Looked like an old Chevy Capris that had come straight from automobile hell. Blue and red cherries rolled this way and that, bowling light over its rusted shell. He dallied closer. The Chevy's windows had been smashed, and Daryl could tell no one was inside. His stomach felt as if tiny grenades were exploding inside. He kept going, looking through the driver's window of the cruiser.

No officer inside. The light coming from the laptop monitor filtered the interior in blue tinges. Darryl could see a bottle of Dr. Pepper, and a half empty bag of beef jerky on the passenger seat. He stood upright, gazing at the smudged-black woods across from him.

Putting his hands around his mouth for amplification, he shouted, "Is anyone around here?" He waited a minute before giving up. "All right. I'm heading out. If anyone needs any help, speak now or forever hold your peace!"

There was a faint noise to his right.

A whimper?

He turned around. Facing the boulder from the direction he'd come from, Daryl located the missing passengers. He counted five of them, all hanging from nooses snaring their necks. Two of them were already dead. Two women. But he couldn't tell what their ages were. The third was a man, his arms hung limply by his sides, but his legs still kicked. No doubt that he was dead, too, the movement and noises coming from him were just spasms. The others were shielded by the shadows. All he could see of them were dim frames.

Darryl's words were garroted in his throat. A scream was stuck in there somewhere.

He looked at his truck, engine rumbling, its headlights shining like a beacon signaling his safety. Darryl tried to run, but his jellified legs caused him to only wobble towards the truck. Then his legs felt as if the strength had been drained from them and he dropped. His chest pummeled the blacktop. His chin grated across the abrasive surface. The impact dazed him, but he forced himself to keep moving. Pushing up on his hands, he started crawling. It was all his legs could muster.

Then he felt hands all over, intercepting him on his way to the truck. He didn't have a chance to look at them, and could only feel their grips on him, clasping and squeezing, pushing him back down on the road.

Then he was on his back. He swatted, trying to clobber their hands. He saw a flash of the red moon above him before it was blocked out by four heads. They were misshapen, inhuman in appearance.

Something cold and sharp punched into his midsection, burning as it perforated him all the way through. He felt blood in the back of his throat drowning him. As he was being carved up to his gullet, he realized that he was wrong about their appearances. They weren't mutants, nor were they inhuman oddities at all.

Costumes. Hideous costumes.

Then he was being dragged to the boulder, to be added to the others.

(‡‡‡)

Allen stood with Jack as he used the belt from his robe to secure his daughter's hands. She was still out cold, jaw swollen. A four-knuckled bruise had darkened her chin and the chubby part of her right cheek. Faith was on her knees, still sobbing. She'd managed to tone it down a smidge, but she still shivered in nothing but her nightgown. The straps had slipped down her shoulders, nearly exposing her breasts. Allen offered her his jacket.

"No, thank you," she answered. "I-I'm not cold."

He had no doubt that she wasn't cold from the heat of all the fires, but he also didn't know how to tell her that he wasn't concerned about that. He'd only offered because she was so close to falling out of her gown.

He decided not to push it.

Averting his eyes away from Faith's breasts, he turned to Jack. "Can you tell me what happened?"

Jack closed his eyes as if tentative. "I'm really not sure."

"What do you mean?"

"It just happened so fast…"

"Nicole wanted to go to bed because her head hurt," said Faith.

"Yeah, she told us she didn't want to go trick-or-treating tonight because her head was hurting. We figured that since she was so willing to go to bed that she was telling the truth about her head. So we gave her some Tylenol and told her goodnight."

Faith took the next part. "Then we watched a little TV and decided…we'd go to bed ourselves." By what she was wearing it was easy to guess what they had intended on doing. Take advantage of the kid going to bed at a decent hour and enjoy some quality time together.

It was Jack's turn. "Then we heard something shatter outside, and when I looked out the window, I saw the cars were on fire. I told Faith to stay inside with Nicole and call the police while I came out here to check. That was when they nabbed me."

Faith wiped her eyes. "I tried the phone on my way to Nicole's room, but it was dead. The cell phones weren't working either. And when I went into Nicole's room she wasn't in bed. When I found her, she was at the back door letting the others inside. At first, I thought maybe she'd mistaken them for trick-or-treaters or something, but then she started to telling them to throw gasoline all over the walls. One of them held me while the others lit everything on fire. Before long, the whole house was burning. They took Nicole outside, then dragged me out."

That was when I came into the story.

"And our daughter's...involved," said Jack.

"I'm sorry to say it," Allen said.

Jack and Faith hugged, both of them in tears.

Faith leaned her head back to look at her husband, heavy torrents of tears streaking her face. "Why Jack? Why did she do this?"

"I don't know."

"We're good parents!"

Jack nodded, then gently patted Faith's hair to get her to lay her head upon his shoulder. She cried even harder.

"Good parents!" Faith repeated.

"Yes, honey. Good parents." The look on his face suggested otherwise. There was heavy doubt furrowing his brow, clouding his eyes.

Allen guessed Jack was searching his mind, highlighting every incident where he thought they'd gone wrong in their parental routines. He'd be doing the same.

Jack raised his head, looked at Allen. "What were you doing out this way, Allen, if you don't mind my asking?"

"I was actually coming up here to see if I could use your phone, or maybe bum a ride to the police station. Someone vandalized the church and slashed my tires. Killed the power, the phones. Only thing I knew to do was walk."

Jack nodded.

Allen sighed. "I should get moving again. Can't reach Jackie at home, so I need to find either a working phone or car, whichever comes first." He had an idea. "Maybe I can take *their* car." He nodded toward the unconscious attackers. "Did they drive up here?"

"I didn't notice..."

"And I didn't pass a car on the way up here, so that means they must have hidden it. We could spend all night looking for it."

"Can you handle a motorcycle?" asked Jack.

Allen used to own one when he was in his twenties, but after a friend had been hit and killed by an unobservant driver, he'd sold it. "Yes, as a matter of fact, I can."

"I don't think they noticed the trailer." He pointed to a white trailer. It looked like the sort used for hauling storage. The door at the back was closed and padlocked. "Or, if they did, they just hadn't gotten to it yet."

"Got the keys?"

"There's a hide-a-key container under the gas cap."

"Praise God for that," said Allen.

"Take the bike, Allen, and go get help."

Allen frowned, looking at the guys on the ground. Even with Jack and Faith watching them, and using their weapons for protection, he didn't feel right about leaving the poor couple with them, and Nicole. He figured that if Nicole tried, she could probably manipulate them pretty easily, keeping them distracted until the other guys detained them. "When we get the bike out of the trailer, let's lock those guys up in it."

Jack nodded. "Good idea."

At once, they all looked at Nicole. She lay on the ground, deep insentient breaths making her chest rise and fall. She looked like a girl dreaming of candy lands and butterscotch trees. No one spoke right away.

"What about Nicole?" Faith asked, putting everyone's thoughts into words.

"That's not my decision to make," said Allen.

Jack and Faith shared a look, a silent conversation was being shared between the two of them that only the husband and wife could hear. Eventually, Jack nodded. Faith turned back to Allen. "Would you lock her up in there as well? It's probably the smartest thing to do, but I don't know if either one of us can."

Allen nodded. "Sure."

But when he looked at the precious little girl with the bloated cheek, he wondered if he could bring himself to do it.

CHAPTER 16

(I)

On Goodhill Road, Albright operated the van with Ben sitting in the bucket seat beside her. She gave him a glance from the corner of her eyes.

Wow.

He looked weak, drained, and even in the darkness she could see the pallor of his skin. He didn't look to be in any kind of good shape.

How could he be?

He'd been put through hell. And so had she, for that matter. But she couldn't ignore how much more athletic she was than her superior. He wasn't fat by any means, but he was definitely a tad swollen in areas. Another few years at this rate, he'd be sagging in the front.

Still a good-looking guy in every aspect, though.

What the hell's wrong with me?

Here she was analyzing her superior while the city was being destroyed around them. What right did she have?

It was a distraction mechanism, and she knew this. Something she'd always done, even when she was little. If she got into trouble, she tried to take the tension off herself by focusing on something else nowhere near relevant. Even now, she was trying to keep her mind off the severe danger they were up against.

And the silence of the ride wasn't helping. Except for Ben's instructions early on, neither of them had spoken. Which had given Albright time to ruminate what she'd seen. She didn't want to think about it but couldn't stop the images from forming.

The shops and local businesses had been defaced, the insides torched. Orange and black graffiti had been spray-painted on the buildings.

"Prank Night," she'd heard Ben mutter under his breath.

Display windows were shattered. Flames lapped through the perforations of some and only smoke swelled from others. The Bakery had been obliterated. Aunt Betty's head was impaled on a stake in front of it, dismally carved to resemble a jack-o'-lantern. A guttering candle was in each of her hollowed eye sockets like a dancing yellow pupil. Albright had choked back her reaction. She'd lowered her head, squeezed her eyes shut, and pushed the image far back in her mind.

Even now, several minutes later, those same tears still leaked through her pinched lids, and she took heavy breaths through her slightly parted mouth. Cracking her eyes, she gazed through the windshield as if looking through flooded goggles. She wiped her eyes, hoping Ben wouldn't notice she was crying.

Autumn Creek's downtown looked like the aftermath of a zombie apocalypse.

Jack-o'-lanterns left in front of the other wrecked buildings, in other places more decapitated heads were impaled on rods, candles flickering inside them like gruesome streetlights. Litter and debris swathed the sidewalks and street. Toilet paper fluttered along with orange and black streamers like slithering paper snakes. Leaves chased after them, sprinkling over the sidewalks, making rustling sounds against the cement.

What few cars that weren't deserted in spaces or alongside curbs had been abandoned in the street, and Albright had to maneuver the van around them. Some had their doors open, others were closed with smashed windows.

Occupants probably yanked out of them.

The mail truck was parked alongside the road, one wheel up on the curb. The back door hung open. Thick red stains painted the walls inside the truck and the pile of mail spilling onto the street. Mr. Chambers's hat with the fluffy ear flaps was pressed to the tire, as if the wind had pushed it against the black rubber. The ear padding was clumpy from blood.

There was a giant bonfire burning at the town square. Albright drove the van up on the sidewalk to avoid its lapping flames. Instead of wood used as kindling, the fire swarmed around cell phones and tablets. The blocky shapes were glowing red embers in the bluish tint of the fire. Plastic melted around screens in glops, conforming the technological devices into one molten hill like mineral deposits in caves.

"Why would they do that?" Though she'd spoken the question aloud, it was meant to be a thought.

"I have no idea. It's a statement, I'm sure."

"For what?"

"Maybe to show us there's no sign of hope."

A cold chill shrouded Albright. It was a dreadful sight, the way Albright imagined the end of times to be.

Maybe it is.

The van moved past, and she was happy to leave the ghastly testimonial behind. Soon they were on the outskirts of downtown, heading toward the farms, then to the county line.

Where are they?

Since escaping the station, she'd seen nobody. Only the repercussions of what they'd done. It looked as if they'd move on, but to where she had no idea. They had to be somewhere.

Probably moved on to another area like a traveling storm.

In many ways, that was exactly what they were: a deadly unstoppable storm. How *many* were there? Judging the remnants of downtown, she would guess too many to count.

Albright drove to the intersection at Hill Top Road, where Cedar Drive led to Amity Hill Road. She never considered decelerating or looking in either direction for oncoming cars. The main reason being she had the right of way with no stop sign. And another reason was there was no worry from how forlorn the roads had been so far.

"Look out!" called Ben from beside her.

When she saw the truck in her peripheral vision her heart tweaked as the old truck zipped in from the right. The van's bright beams bounced off what looked like duct tape running along the truck's door a moment before the front of the van smashed into it.

(11)

Tabitha struggled with the clutch. It was heavy and she felt as if she had to strain with all her might to hold it down so she could change gears. Now that it was in overdrive, she wasn't going to bother anymore. Just keeping the pedal to the floor would resolve the problem of fighting with it.

She looked at Jackie in the passenger seat. Joey was in her lap, her arms hugged tightly around his unconscious body. The seatbelt had fed around Joey, so it held both of them. Her chin rested on top of his head. Eyes closed, her face was a scrunched up frown.

Poor woman.

Tabitha couldn't imagine how Jackie must feel right now. Jackie hadn't said much since conking Joey's head with the rock, but through the sporadic bursts of dialogue, Tabitha gathered the same ordeal had happened to Jackie and she was running. She'd come across Tabitha's house looking for help and instead of a sanctuary, she'd stumbled upon...

Her ten-year-old son about to kill me.

Talk about being in the wrong place at the wrong time. But when Tabitha put some serious thought to it, she couldn't help thinking she'd been in the exact place she needed to be. If she wouldn't have come along, Joey would have *killed* Tabitha. No qualms about that. Tabitha hadn't forgotten Jackie was a pastor's wife. Though Tabitha wasn't a churchgoer, she still believed there was something beyond this world. What it was, she hadn't decided. She was open to anything if it meant there was peace on the other side. Maybe there was more to this God stuff than she wanted to admit.

Giving Jackie another glance, her chest tightened again.

Holding onto him so tight.

As if he might fly away. Joey looked to be sleeping, like a kid who'd tuckered himself out after an all-day adventure at the park and had dozed off in Jackie's lap on the ride home.

Tabitha tried to picture herself in the same position. She couldn't. It was too heart-wrenching trying to envision herself in Jackie's place. How she still embraced her son, as if nothing had happened, though knowing on the inside nothing will ever be the same again.

Tears dotted the corners of Tabitha's eyes. She needed to drive as if they weren't in the truck with her. Pretend she was alone. She focused her attention on the road and what lay on either side of it. The other houses on Amity Hill had been torched, nothing but perched smoke over charred-black twisting planks. Jack-o'-lanterns sat impaled on dole rods in the front yards, gap-toothed and grinning like fiendish markers. On other rods were heads of the once living proprietors. Their necks were jagged flaps of skin dangling from underneath chins like tattered, fleshy beards. Eyes wide and vacant yellow orbs, glowing like tiny lights.

Tabitha realized they *were* lights. Tea lights. Tiny little candles inside the empty sockets, flickering and dancing.

Tabitha forced herself to stop looking. She passed another house on the right, or what was left of it—a brick chimney, and a door that hung loosely on its frame, opening to nothing behind it except ash and rubble.

Another impaled jack-o'-lantern flashed its bright yellow grin from the front yard. She looked forward before her eyes locked on the severed head jabbed on a pole next to it, and continued driving. She could see the lights of town ahead, flushing off the heavy smoke that now coated the dark sky above them like a cupola.

Nearing an intersection, where Hill Top Road sketched through Cedar Drive, she passed a row of houses on her left. Four of them, spread through a small cul-de-sac all burned together in a horseshoe of fire. Jack-o'-lanterns had been left by the plank of mailboxes at the front of the picket fence that surrounded the small area.

Their calling card.

Every house they hit, they must leave behind the jack-o'-lanterns as a message, but what the message was, Tabitha had no clue.

Again, with no worry of there being other cars out, she didn't care to take caution at the stop sign. When the cab filled with light like a train was barreling down on her, she wished she had.

The impact came with the sound of twisting metal. Glass exploded all over her. She felt piercing shards slicing across her face. Jackie's screams tore through her ears.

Her body crumpled with intense pain only for a moment. Then everything smashed to black.

Clint was waiting for her.

CHAPTER 17

(1)

Allen ached with cold. His face felt as if it was being pricked with daggers of ice. His lips had chapped, dehydrated and crackly. He assumed he was shivering, would guess that his teeth were also chattering, but it was too hard to tell from being on the motorcycle. He was almost to the Webster County line, and believed that once he got to Fairfax, he'd be able to find some kind of help. Any help would do.

The town had been...eradicated, was the only way he knew how to describe it. They looked as if a hard battle had been fought, but a battle that was lost. There had been bodies left behind, plenty of them, and other than the ravaged aftereffects, things seemed to have quieted down. Allen prayed there were people left to save. He hadn't stopped *praying* since mounting the motorcycle and left Jack and his poor family back at their house. Whenever he said *Amen,* he would think of more reasons to pray and start right up again.

Being a man devoted solely to God and to no one else above Him, not even himself, he always had to answer a lot of questions from those that felt as if God had shunned them. Usually, he didn't have an exact answer to every question, but he summed up their grief with encouraging words every time. Sometimes it helped, mostly it did not. Whether they believed what he told them was irrelevant because Allen believed every bit.

But seeing so many buildings and homes either in flames or pieces, he understood nothing he could say would be of any comfort to anyone. Nothing would be any comfort to himself. This time, Allen had questions of his own.

Where's Jackie? Where's Joey? Are they alive? Please, God, let them be all right.

Approaching a curve in the road, he eased off the throttle. The road was slick with dewdrops, and he wasn't taking any chances. Pine trees ran alongside the road, reaching over the white line with their fiber tips. He kept his weight shifted away from the turn, trying to pull away from the direction the bike was tilting to prevent a tumble. It was a long curve, but finally the road straightened out so he could get the bike upright.

And saw the police car blocking his way.

Allen cried out. His heart flipped in his chest, tugging his stomach up into his throat. It was too late to apply the brakes, not unless he wanted to be launched off the bike. He could try steering the bike off the road, but more than likely the wheel would get lodged in a gulley and the result would see Allen launched through the air.

His only option was to lay the bike down and hope for the best. He jerked the handles sideways, throwing the back wheel out to the side, and leaned the bike to the road. This time he didn't counteract gravity's natural pull and allowed his weight to carry the bike over. The sound of metal scraping blacktop was accompanied by a shower of sparks. He felt heat on his leg as the asphalt tore his pants open and peeled the skin back. The belt looped around his waist snapped as the road ripped through the seams of his pants and ate the skin over his thigh and hip.

Finally, he stopped sliding, but the bike kept going ahead of him. It smacked the side of the police car with the awful sound of impacting metal that came with a collision. Hot tendrils of pain lashed Allen's body. His leg throbbed. His shoulder felt like hot ice had been stuffed under his armpit. The hurting made his stomach queasy. Fresh tears welled in his eyes as he rolled onto his back. He'd hoped to be on his feet by now but moving felt impossible.

He moved his arm, first extending it, then bending it back. Didn't feel broken, but it was definitely sprung. He could feel the bones grating together like two sharp stones through the swollen lump forming at the bend. His hip continued to dully throb as he checked his leg. Didn't appear broken either, but it was awfully bloody where his pants had been torn up.

Could've been worse, he realized, and was grateful it wasn't.

He laid his head back on the road, eyes screwed shut, and breathed like a woman in labor to pass the pain. The asphalt felt rough and gritty under the back of his skull. Little shards of rock dug into his hair. He ignored these annoying pings easily enough thanks to the drumming sharp jabs of pain everywhere else.

He was about to attempt sitting up once more when something cold and wet dripped on his forehead, a single dot that ruptured with a light splat. Another one quickly followed, then another, and another. It felt like the early drips of rain, a light drizzle that was slowly growing in speed. He reached up, wiped his forehead, and brought back his fingers. They were dabbed in red. He quickly wiped again, finding more red fluid had coated his fingernails like polish.

"What in the world?"

Looking up, he saw multiple pairs of shoes suspended several feet above him, lightly swaying. Attached to the shoes were legs, tapering down from mutilated bodies. The one in the middle belonged to a big burly man who'd been slit up the middle. Ropes of intestines draped from the opening in his stomach, hanging far down near the road.

"God in Heaven!"

Allen quickly scurried away from the suspended corpses, his body screaming with fresh jags of pain as he moved. He didn't stop skittering until he was several feet away. On his buttocks, he gaped at the bodies hanging from rope bound around their necks.

Allen looked around. His eyes focused on the roadblock once more. Obviously, they'd done this to keep people from coming in, and to keep anyone else from going out. He noticed the big truck with another car being towed behind it at the back of a three-car line.

Where are they?

He looked to the shrubs that ran alongside the road.

Probably out there somewhere. But doing what?

Then, as if to answer his question, three emerged from the bushes on the other side of the roadblock. The trio was involved in their own conversation, ignorantly unaware of Allen. They were outfitted a lot like the bunch at the Henderson's, crude garments that came from the bags hidden in the attic, discarded clothing stitched and patterned into new threads. These suits matched like hideously assembled uniforms, with hoods either from burlap or a similar fabric. Jagged holes had been cut for the eyes.

Allen felt cold and shaky in his bowels. Unsteadily, he got to all fours, keeping low to the road in hopes the shadows would conceal him from the swirling cherries of the police cruiser. It felt as if a frosty pressure was being spread from his hip into his groin. He ignored the pain and moved in a limping crawl to the fallen motorcycle.

The machete was still strapped to the gas tank. The bungee cables Jack had found in the trailer had done a great job securing the weapon he'd taken from one of the attackers to the bike. Allen had preferred the ax, but the machete was the smallest weapon, not too big for him to take along. It was Faith's idea for him to bring it. She'd noticed it strapped to Alex Bolden's thigh when they were dumping the bodies in the trailer. He was grateful she saw it.

He gripped the hilt and carefully slid the machete out from behind the cables. It came free with a *Shinck!* that slit the tranquil sounds of the night.

Three heads whipped towards him.

"What was that?" asked the one on the left.

No one replied. They remained where they were, heads tilting in unison.

Allen pressed himself as close to the police car as he could. He bit down on his bottom lip. It felt dry and crackly from the cold, like the skin on a marshmallow after being roasted. He kept the machete close. It was strange holding the large knife, and his fingers didn't know how to properly form around the handle. Allen assumed the reason it felt so awkward to him was because in all probability he'd be defending himself with it.

Allen glimpsed his reflection in the blade's polished surface. It was slanted, distorted in streaks that made him look inhuman, like looking at an alternate reality version of himself. Pale skin, gelid sweat coating his face, and the mussed, damp hair showed a man who looked as if he'd just come from the nuthouse. Not the frivolous Pastor Allen Farrell Autumn Creek had come to know. Not the husband of the lovely Jacqueline Farrell, father of Joseph.

Please be okay…please.

As he scuttled to the point where the two cars met at the yellow line, trying to keep his movements hushed, the others started in his direction. Hopefully their footsteps would cover his. His plan was to get around to the other side of the cars, maybe approach them from behind, and subdue them if he could. They probably had the keys to all these vehicles. If he could get a set, then he could drive it right into the next town.

Allen reached the cruiser's bumper.

"Who's over there?" one of them called, not who'd spoken first. Allen couldn't see which one it was without standing up, and he had no intentions of doing that.

"Do you really think they're going to say who they are? *Idiot.*"

"I don't know, never hurts to try."

The voices were intentionally being lowered in pitch to make them sound tougher and probably older as well. He would guess they were most likely teenagers.

He studied the gap between the two cars. It was tight, but he thought he should be able to squeeze his way through. If he kept going until he reached the end of the other car, they might spot him.

Turning around, so he could enter the tight space left shoulder first, he faced the way he'd come from. The scuffles of their footsteps were getting louder. They would be coming around the rear of the police cruiser any moment on his right.

Allen slipped into the opening. The cruiser's bumper pushed down on his thighs, making him go flat on his behind with his legs fully extended under the car. He kept skimming sideways until he was completely shielded between the two vehicles. The grille was inches from his face, his chin lightly grazing the cold tip of the bumper. The chrome grid was spackled in splattered bugs and dirt.

Just as his right shoulder was swallowed, the three hoods appeared at the back of the cruiser. Allen saw them stepping around the rear bumper as he sandwiched himself.

Please God, let them be blind to my movements.

Apparently they were. They didn't act as if they'd seen him.

"Who the fuck's motorcycle is that?" asked the first voice.

"How the shit am I supposed to know?" snapped back the only reasonable sounding one. "They crashed, though, so let's spread out and find the rider. Couldn't have gotten far."

"I can't believe we didn't hear it."

"Well, we didn't. So, get looking."

Allen went stiff, too scared to move. Red and blue lights continued to twirl, briefly hitting him. Suddenly it felt as if this hiding place was no good. He knew without a doubt they would check here and find him between the two vehicles. Then what would he do? Smile and tell them hello?

Squirming, he worked his torso down between the bumpers, and when it came time for his head, he turned it, and sunk down.

One of them appeared at the space right after his head dipped into the shadows and stopped. He seemed to stare straight at him. Allen was on his side, his head craned back so he could see their heavy boots.

They stayed that way for what felt like hours. Allen would swear he could feel their eyes all over him, slithering across him like snakes. Finally, the guy moved on.

Allen allowed himself to breathe, slowly letting the air out through his mouth. He was under both cars now, lying at an angle with his legs bent at the knees so they weren't poking out the other side. The machete was gripped in his right hand, with his body lying on the arm and cutting off all circulation to his hand. If he stayed like this much longer, he wouldn't be able to use this hand if he needed to.

Need to get turned over.

If he were on his stomach, that would be a little more comfortable, and he'd have both hands free. How could he do it in such a tight spot, though?

(11)

The scratches of shoes drifted from all sides of Allen.

"See anything?" asked one.

"No!"

"Nope!" another replied.

"Where in the fuck are they?"

"Keep looking. Even if they're walking around, they couldn't be far away. We were only gone five minutes."

"I'll head up the road a ways and check for them."

"Which way?"

"This way."

Allen wasn't sure which direction he was indicating.

"Then I'll go this way, and Kurt can stay here and keep looking."

Kurt? Kurt Halloran?

Had to be. Kurt wasn't a common name in these parts, especially for someone the age Allen suspected this guy was. The line-backer for the high school football team. Kurt Halloran, whose dad owned Halloran and Son Plumbing.

Allen wondered if Kurt had executed his own parents the way Nicole Henderson had attempted with hers.

If I wouldn't have gotten there.

He didn't want to think about it. He was supposed to have been there and that was why he had been.

He'd had enough of being in this position. He couldn't handle it anymore. His back was really starting to hurt, which aggravated the lacerations and scrapes all over his right side from the wreck. He had to move.

Keeping his right arm flat on the asphalt, he gently adjusted his hips to match the position of his upper torso. Then he stopped, listened. He could hear the distant chatter of conversation. The three hoods were no longer close enough for Allen to understand them. He should be safe to move without worry.

He straightened his legs, bringing them out in front of him as if lounging at the beach, laying on his side and bent into an L. Next, he rolled onto his stomach, biting back the shout of pain that had nearly escaped him. His eyes filled with tears as his hip stabbed him with agony. Giving himself a moment before continuing, he laid flat, pulling himself upward on the asphalt, while straightening his body in the correct coordination it should be.

Now he was horizontal under the front and rear bumpers of both cars, hidden just to the right of the gap between them. He took several breaths. His heart rate was out of control and his eyes burned as sweat trickled down from his hairline.

He started moving again, intending to shimmy his way entirely under the cruiser.

Then he felt hands grip his ankles and pull.

His shirt slipped up his chest. The abrasive road scraped him as he moved backward. He pawed at the blacktop with his left hand, keeping a tight grip on the machete in the other. The tip of the blade yelped as it struck the asphalt, shooting out tiny sparks.

When Allen was clear of the cars, his feet were released. He quickly rolled onto his back, finding a hooded gargantuan reaching for him.

Kurt.

Allen glanced at the machete, saw he was in a position to use it, and quickly swung.

The hood kicked his arm away.

His hand hit the road, causing his fingers to release the machete. It scampered a couple feet away. Beefy hands clenched his shirt and hoisted him off the ground. His feet kicked air before he was dropped.

Allen hit the unyielding asphalt and called out, stunned. His body locked up from the pain that felt like it was walloping him all over.

The big guy kicked, planting the toe of his boot low on Allen's abdomen. Air blasted out of him in a dry gush. His vision burst into a shatter of bright colors, then slowly splotched back together, much dimmer. He couldn't breathe. No matter how much he tried, he couldn't get his lungs to accept air. There was a bitter taste at the back of his throat.

"Pastor Allen?"

Allen answered with a haggard sounding moan.

Kurt laughed. "I'll be damned. You're still alive? Thought for sure you were torched with the church."

They burned down the church?

Allen felt like crying, and not just from how badly he was hurting.

"You should have seen it go," laughed Kurt. He put his fingers together then quickly spread them apart with a "Poof!"

Rolling onto his side, Allen no longer felt like crying. The pain nearly subsided, his anger invading it like savages conquering a village.

He got to his knees.

His lungs opened. Fresh air wafted into him. It tasted clean and wonderful.

He could see.

Then he revved back his fist and swung for what was closest to him.

A crotch.

The punch was blocked.

"You dirty bastard!" shouted Kurt with evident surprise in his voice.

The football player brought his fist down, meaning to bash Allen on the top of his head. He fell back, feeling the big fist cut the air in front of him with a faint whistle. It might have caught the tips of his hair because he felt them rustle.

Missing the first punch seemed to anger Kurt even more than Allen's attempt at a low blow. He quickly shot his other fist out. Allen did a roll, a full summersault just like a kid showing off in gymnastics class. The top of his head scratched jagged pebbles as he went over. His back struck next, but his momentum carried him up to a sitting position. Glancing back, he saw Kurt looking at him from over his shoulder. Even behind the mask he could see there was astonishment at his dainty action.

But it couldn't compare to Allen's own surprise.

He didn't allow himself the time to feel pride. He was already moving, and so was Kurt, both rushing for the machete lying diagonally from them.

Bent at the waist, Allen made a lunge for the handle. His fingers bumped it, pushing the weapon further away. He tried again, only succeeding in spinning it around.

Then he felt thick arms hug him from behind.

They both went down. Right before they landed, Allen shifted, making them both go down on their sides. If he wouldn't have, Kurt would have come down on Allen's back, no doubt crushing him.

The road hit them so hard they were both dazed.

Allen recovered first. He sat up, shook the static out of his head. Kurt was coming around, getting up to a stance where he might leap. Allen dove for the machete, his hand slapping down on the handle. Fingers twisted around.

He shouldn't have, but he stole a glance over his shoulder. Kurt was right at his heels, climbing onto Allen as he tried to retrieve his weapon.

"What do you think *you're* doing, huh?"

Huffing breaths were in his ear, the rough stitching of the burlap hood scratching his cheek. Then an arm slipped around his neck and pulled back, cutting off Allen's air entirely.

Kurt struggled to his feet, pulling Allen up with him. He slapped uselessly at the big arms constricting around his throat. But the grip only became even firmer.

"Stop fighting, Pastor. Just stop."

Allen didn't stop. He struggled and wriggled as much as he could, and this only seemed to annoy the kid slowly killing him.

"Just quit fighting me and it'll be done in a minute. You'll feel no pain and just think, if you're right in your beliefs, you'll wake up in Heaven."

It was tempting to just let go, let Kurt finish him off because the kid was right. It would be easier than fighting, less painful, and he would also be with God for breakfast. But letting himself go would do nothing to help his family. For all he knew, they needed him, were waiting for him to come and save them. And he couldn't let them down.

His vision was darkening as if someone was turning a dimming switch in his brain. All thoughts were slowing down, running together into one low timbre.

Then he realized the machete was still gripped in his one hand while the other still slapped at forearms hugging his neck. He'd been so disarrayed by the strength in this young man that he'd completely forgotten he'd brought the machete up with him from the road.

He twisted the machete around in his hand, positioning the sharp edge of the blade up. Allen knew he only had once chance at this. If he missed, he'd be dead before the thought of another try even registered. He wanted to pray, but there was no time. Hopefully his aim would be right on the mark.

"You've really got some fight left, don't y—"

Allen swung upward with what strength he had left. He felt the machete strike Kurt behind him, killing the teenager's words. The arms released their hold of him. He only knew this because he felt the force holding him up go away, but it still felt like he was being choked as he dropped to the ground.

The road came up to meet him. He didn't feel anything when he landed.

Allen wasn't sure how long he was out, or if he ever was, but when he rolled onto his back, he saw Kurt towering above him, swaying forward, then catching himself and swaying back like someone who'd had too much to drink.

With a machete lodged into his forehead.

Before Allen could comprehend that his aim had been dead on, the kid was plummeting forward, stiff and gigantic like a tree sawed down. He rolled just before the kid's head struck where Allen's had just been, butting the blade even deeper into his skull.

Allen lay on his side and stared at the stationary body. He checked Kurt's back. It was just as still as the rest of him. He wasn't breathing. He'd killed the kid with a blind hit.

Allen exhaled a heavy, remorseful breath. His throat was tender and raw. His larynx felt as if it had been wrenched back into his windpipe.

The crunching a foot might make on gravel resounded through the calm ambience.

A tremor of fear tickled his spine.

(↓↓↓)

Allen looked to his right and found one of the others approaching. There was no point in trying to hide. By the way the guy was confidently strutting, a bat swinging by his side, Allen knew he'd already been spotted.

More footsteps behind Allen. He glanced over his opposite shoulder. The third one was drawing nearer from the other way. With the cars in front of him, and nowhere to go but dark woods behind him, he was surrounded.

"Pastor Allen?" said the one with the ball bat.

Allen didn't respond. He was too busy racking his brain for a plan. He didn't want to fight these kids, and even if he had no ethical qualms for doing so, he doubted he'd be much of a threat. He'd killed one already out of providential instinct and felt awful about it. Going against two more seemed like suicide.

The one coming from behind spoke. "Looks like he got Kurt. Got him good."

"Oh well," said the other. "Kurt was douche anyway."

"Yeah, he was," agreed the other one.

"Please guys..." began Allen, "...don't do what you're thinking. Just stop where you are and think about this for a minute."

The batter pitched back his head and offered a single laugh. Then he said, "I just thought about it and I'm having such a *good* time. It's like what you preach. 'Take a moment to enjoy the moment.' And I am." As he neared, the cruiser's flashing lights glinted off the bat. Giant nails had been hammered through the top, crossing in a pattern of piercing tips.

Allen looked away from the ball bat. His eyes landed on Kurt's back. He could see the tip of the machete poking up from the top of his head. He would never get it in time. Turning to face Slugger once more, Allen found the disguised teenager was nearly on top of him. He could also feel the third just inches behind him. It was the same feeling Allen would get if he were working in his office and someone had come up behind him to glance over his shoulder.

"What do you want to do, Lucas?" asked the third behind Allen.

Lucas Bowers. Allen knew exactly who the batter was: quarterback for the high school football team. Most likely, the third one was a teammate as well, and Allen probably knew him too. Being the quarterback, Lucas wasn't just the leader of the football team, but their leader out here.

This only made Allen hurt even more. He knew these kids from the youth ministry, seen them hanging around the youth pastor every Wednesday night. It made him feel as if his chest had been hit with a sledgehammer, nearly causing him to give up.

Nearly.

He turned toward Lucas once more and found himself eye-level with his crotch. It hadn't worked on Kurt, but maybe…

Allen swung his arm in an upward arc, planting his fist in the bend under Lucas's testicles. The giant linebacker sucked in a groaning breath. The bat slipped through his fingers, clamoring when it hit the road. It bounced out of reach.

Lucas staggered back, bumped against the police car, then slipped down the side of it. He hit the asphalt hard enough to gust what remained of his air right out of his lungs.

Allen decided to try for the bat. As he started to stand, he felt a clobbering blow at the back of his head. The impact threw him forward. His chest slammed against the car, recoiling him back. He was punched again, this time in the kidney. The force of the blow caused Allen to wet himself. He couldn't stop the urine from spraying out of him.

Allen fell onto his knees. He reached behind his back, putting his hand on the screaming kidney. Felt like he'd guzzled fire from how bad his lower back was sweltering.

The third guy stepped around the front of Allen and kicked. The toe of a boot caught Allen in the side. He hurled over, landing hard on his arm, all his weight coming down. He rolled onto his back. The sky was a flat span of black with swirls of smoke whisking across.

Two heads appeared above him, staring down at him. Lucas had already recovered from Allen's cheap shot.

"Let's kick the shit out of him," grunted Lucas, his voice a little higher than it had been previously.

"I already have," said the third. "Let's just finish him off and get out of here."

"We can't leave. Not until it's over."

"I don't want to hang out here with Kurt's dead-fucking-body."

"Toss him in the woods."

"Oh, that's perfect," the third said with sarcasm in his voice. "Genius."

"Don't start your bullshit."

"Let's kill Pastor Allen, hang him up with the others, and get it over with."

Allen remembered those poor people hanging from the tree like it was the gallows. He hated to think he might be joining them.

"Good idea," said Lucas. "After I get to kick his ass some."

"Waste of time, but whatever."

"The asshole hit me in the balls!"

"So hit him in the balls and call it even!"

This would have been the perfect time for Allen to try and make an escape, but he hurt too bad to move. Instead, he prayed. Then Lucas hit him in the balls as his friend had suggested.

Allen brought his knees up, hurled out a puff of air, and rolled onto his side. It felt as if his testicles were now at the bottom of his ribcage.

Lucas wasn't ready to call it even yet. He got down on one knee, his other leg stretched over Allen's midsection. Taking a handful of Allen's shirt, Lucas raised him up only to punch him back down. The beefy fist felt like a ball of concrete against Allen's face. His brain rattled.

Allen was lifted and punched again and again.

And again.

It seemed the hits just kept coming.

Finally, Lucas let him lay there. Allen hadn't quite lost consciousness, but he was heavily dazed. Some teeth were loose, and when he ran his tongue across his gums, he found an empty space where a molar should be. His lips were swollen and rubbery, enlarged, numb. The back of Allen's throat was coated in slobbery blood and all he tasted was copper.

"Are you done?" the third asked.

Lucas was panting. "Yeah."

"Can we finish this? I'm tired of messing around."

Lucas snorted a laugh. He stepped away from Allen, leaving him retracting into a ball on the road. The large teenager found his bat at the front of the cruiser and picked it up. Red and blue lights washed over him in a continuous cycle. "Think you should hold him?"

"For what?"

"So I can bash his skull in with these nails."

The third one was quiet a moment. "Nah. I don't think he's going anywhere."

And he was right. Allen was not in any shape to resist. This was the end for him. He thought back to the family he'd left behind, so full of hope that he was going to find help and come back to save them. He also couldn't forget all the other families he didn't even know about, probably hiding somewhere, praying for rescue.

He'd let them all down. He was going to die, and now, others probably would, too.

Please forgive me, Jackie. Please don't hate me, Joey.

Lucas stepped in front of him. "Hold him up," he said to his partner.

"Fine. But don't hit *me* with that shit."

"I'll do my best."

Allen felt hands slip under his arms and hoist him to his knees.

"Ready?" asked Lucas.

"I...wish you wouldn't...," said Allen.

"I bet you do." He sighed. "I'm sorry for this, but not too much."

He revved the bat back over his shoulder, readying to swing. As he started to lean into it, bringing the bat around, the night lit up in a tumult of explosions. Holes tore through Lucas's chest, his stomach. His shoulders jerked as bullets punched through him.

Allen threw himself forward, covering his head with his arms. He planted his hands flat against his ears. On his side, he glanced back and forth from Lucas and his partner as they did the gunshot dance.

After several seconds, the third one keeled over, a moment later Lucas dropped. The blasts halted, and the silence that waved across seemed just as thunderously loud through the ringing in Allen's ears. The air was heavy with the rotten-egg odor of gun smoke. He rolled over, looking around. At first it was hard to see from the tarp of grayish smoke eddying around him. But it started to dissipate, thin out. Then he noticed figures emerging, two of them. Behind the men was a pair of brightly lit headlights, a bar of swirling lights above it.

As they stepped away from the front of the beams, moving closer with their guns drawn and extended, Allen could make out their uniforms. The dark grays of their shirts, even darker pants. The twinkling badges pinned to their chests and the Stratton hats capping their heads all looked familiar. It was a sight that brought a smile to Allen's swollen face.

State Troopers.

The officer to the right saw Allen. "Are you okay, sir?"

Allen wanted to tell him no but when he tried to speak, he could only moan.

CHAPTER 18

(1)

The hiss of smoke surging from underneath the van's crumpled hood came from outside. Ben blinked his eyes, and for a brief agonizing moment thought he was blind. When he rubbed them, he realized they were actually just filled with blood. Feeling around his forehead, he found several lacerations, and although they were bleeding, he doubted they were very serious.

Thankfully, he'd been wearing his seatbelt.

The stench of antifreeze and oil filled the van. Ben blinked more blood out of his eyes. He saw the deployed airbag in front of him had deflated, dangling from the dashboard like a white wrinkled tongue. He looked to where Albright should be. Her seat was empty, a matching airbag dangling from the steering wheel.

"Albright...?"

Ben winced. Talking caused his head to pulsate. He reached down by his hip, fumbling until his fingers found the seatbelt stalk. He pushed the button to release the harness. Then he flung it behind him.

"Albright?"

Ben examined her seat, noting how the seatbelt dangled from beside it.

Did she already get out? Check on the other driver?

Turning to look through the windshield, he saw the hole, its jagged rim lined with piercing glass. It was large, big enough for Albright to have fit through.

No, no, no.

From the thickness of smoke pluming from the engine, he couldn't see much beyond the glass. Just swirls eddying into the cab that reeked of engine grease.

He pulled on the handle and put his shoulder against the door to open it. When the door pushed back, Ben fell out of the cab. Managing to get his feet ahead of him, he didn't fall. He reached inside the truck, found the shotgun, and grabbed it. He had trouble getting it out of the van from the barrel knocking against the door frame. Angling the shotgun to where it was almost aimed at his head, Ben got it out, and staggered around the van.

The front end was now imbedded into the side of an old truck that was bowed like a horseshoe around the van's crumpled nose. It looked as if the two vehicles had morphed together, just as trees he'd seen in the mountains sometimes.

"Albright?"

Ben turned around. The smoke had thinned but hovered around like an oily mist that he could feel on his skin. Something was on the van's hood. Stepping closer, he could faintly make out the white of Albright's tank top.

"Oh no…" whispered Ben, his voice betraying him.

Albright's rump was protruding from the driver window of the truck. Her legs were bent at the knee on top of the van's hood as if she were a dog poking her head into a rabbit hole. Her hips were awkwardly twisted toward the sky.

Ben didn't need confirmation. He knew she was dead.

Most likely so was the person in the truck.

Staving a sobbing fit that threatened to buckle him to his knees, he turned away from the gruesome sight. Nothing indicated movement from within the truck, but he would proceed with caution anyway. There was no telling who might be inside.

"This is Sheriff Ben Holly. Is anyone in the truck that can speak?"

Silence.

This stirred concern in his gut. Ben's finger moved to the shotgun's trigger. Nearing the truck, he stepped around the bed to the other side. He began to make out a pale shape through the rear windshield.

Albright.

The gorgeous deputy's head was twisted on her neck, looking at her back. Her shoulders were stuffed into the window frame, snugly lodged in the compressed opening like laundry that had clogged the chute. Ben quickly averted his eyes, but it was too late to erase the vision. There was no doubt whoever had been driving the truck was dead too. Albright had collided with the driver hard enough to ring her neck.

And the driver was a slouching form, darker than the darkness inside the cab. Ben made out enough to tell that the head was canted way too far to the right to not have been broken.

Damn.

He neared the passenger door and spotted the slouching form of a passenger. A blonde woman. Her head had been knocked against the glass, but it was hard to see her facial features hidden behind the lemony locks. There was a ridge in the window where her head rested, with a dark smudge of blood inside of it. Cracks snaked in all directions.

Ben raced over to the door, opening it. The lady tipped out of the cab, but he was quick to catch her.

And the boy she clutched like a floating plank in the middle of the sea.

Her body felt warm. He could feel the heat of her skin on his arms. Sitting the gun down, he leaned the barrel against the door so he could have both hands to support her. He found her wrist, pressing a finger to it. After a moment, he felt a steady thump against his fingertip. She was alive. He checked the boy's pulse next and found a slow but steady beat in his wrist as well.

That was a plus. Both were alive.

(11)

Jackie heard a voice, ghostly reverberations stirring in her head as if trying to settle on a pitch. She tried to open her eyes. The lids felt crusty, and her forehead felt as it was being slowly crushed with a rock. She was surprised she could move her arms. Rubbing her lids, she felt the brittle flakes of what she imagined to be dried blood clinging to her fingers. She tried opening her eyes again, and this time she could.

The cold air hit her eyes like ice water. She flinched, rapidly blinking against the chilly breeze. She tried sitting up, but felt hands gently push her back down.

"Whoa, whoa, I don't think you need to be moving right now. Just lie back for a minute."

Jackie focused her eyes on where the voice had been coming from. A blurry man's shape stood before her. He was tall, dark hair smudging the top of his head. "Allen?"

"No, ma'am. I'm Sheriff Ben Holly. Can you tell me *your* name?"

My name?

It was right there, like a fragment of a dream she couldn't quite grasp. "Um…"

"Is this boy your son?"

"Boy?" She turned her head, seeing the small body covering her like a blanket. "Joey…?" Then it all came back in a rush of flickering images. Jackie sat up with a gasp.

"Easy," said Sheriff Holly. His hands were on her shoulders, delicately applying pressure. "Don't move too fast. Your name?"

"Jackie Farrell."

"Farrell? As in Allen Farrell?"

"Yes."

"I didn't recognize you, sorry."

"It's okay…" Jackie started to check on Tabitha, but the sheriff quickly put his hand on her cheek.

"Don't look…she's gone."

"Gone?"

Sheriff Holly nodded. "She didn't make it."

Jackie's mouth dropped open. Didn't make it? She was…dead?

"Is this boy your son?"

The question pulled Jackie back to the truck. She held Joey tighter. "Yes."

Frowning, Sheriff Holly seemed to study every aspect of Joey. "Was he…involved?"

The memory of finding Joey about to bash Tabitha with the crowbar projected in her head. "Yes…but I…"

"Holy Mary, mother of God…"

"He didn't do it, I stopped him before he could…" She stopped talking. The sheriff was no longer looking at her. His attention was devoted elsewhere, beyond the truck. It looked as if his eyes were looking at something in the distance.

He stepped away from the truck, looking past the wrecked automobiles. Through the black grime on his face, and the abrasions that were already starting to scab, Jackie saw fear.

"What's wrong?" she asked.

"Get out of the truck."

"I don't understand…"

"Get out of the truck, now."

Jackie slapped at her side to unhook the safety harness. She threw it away from her. Holding Joey close, she carefully climbed out of the truck. Banged up and sore all over, her body protested the idea of movement. When she turned around and saw what Sheriff Holly was looking at, her body gave up the fight and let her move.

"God Almighty." Jackie gasped.

It was a parade of ragged costumes, several yards away, marching. Covering the road, they were a soundless fog of itinerant carnage. It would take them a couple minutes to reach the accident, but to Jackie that felt like a matter of seconds. Torches spiked with jack-o'-lanterns were clutched in hands and spread through the massive crowd. Pitchforks, axes, machetes, pickaxes, so many weapons. All of them seemed to have some type of tool.

"Why are there so many?" she asked.

"If it's not all of them, it's damn-near close." Sheriff Holly grabbed the shotgun leaning against the truck. He held it out in both hands, looking at the gun as if it were nothing more than a flyswatter. And it might as well have been against such a large horde of killers. The shotgun couldn't even put a dent in their numbers.

"What do they want?"

"To kill us all."

Jackie's breaths came in sharp bursts. "What are we going to do?"

"Run."

"Where?"

He took Joey and draped him over his shoulder. "Anywhere but here!"

And he was gone, running up the yellow line away from the mob. Jackie started after him. Looking over her shoulder, she saw the army break into a running pursuit.

"Oh, God!"

Pumping her arms, she ran with all her might to keep with Sheriff Holly.

CHAPTER 19

(1)

Ben adjusted the boy, so he wasn't bouncing so violently while he ran. Before, he'd allowed the kid's arms to dangle loosely behind him, and it felt as if the boy was throwing a tantrum, pounding on his back. Though the blows weren't hard, Ben was sore enough for them to hurt. So, he moved the kid's left arm around his front, hanging the wrist over Ben's right shoulder.

If he wakes up in the mood to kill...

He'd be able to get a firm grip around Ben's throat. It was a risk he was willing to take for the time being.

"Where are you going?" called Jackie from behind him. Her voice was a breathy grunt.

"I know someone who lives just a little way ahead. Hopefully he can help."

"Who? The only thing I know of up this is way is the funeral home."

"Right."

Jackie was quiet a moment. "Then *why* are we going there?"

"He lives in the house."

When he realized they were close to Cedar Drive, going to Russell Warner's place was the first idea that came to mind. It was located at the head of a small logging road off Hill Top Road. He and Albright would have passed right by the large house without a second glance if it weren't for the accident.

Before I got her killed.

Somewhere deep down, Ben knew it wasn't fair to blame himself. But for now, he couldn't find a reason not to.

I could make out a list of reasons why I am to blame.

The list would have to wait. They weren't far from Warner's house, which served multiple duties as the funeral home and pathology lab. Unless the bodies were toted off to the hospital, Russell Warner conducted most of the autopsies himself. No one argued against it, since the old man was good at his job.

Hopefully, Warner's house could offer them some shelter, maybe the old kook would even be alive. He doubted the refuge would hold up against so many, but the possibility was all they had right now. And it was more than they had moments ago.

They continued to run. Their shoes clapped the asphalt as they moved in silence. Just when Ben thought he was going to have to stop and take a short rest, the large Victorian house came into view. It was a pale shape with angular roofs jutting in the sky like a dark crown. A soft dimness was cast across the front, highlighting a swath of its stone-gray features.

"There," said Ben.

"But…it's the funeral home…"

"Only the parlor is used for viewings."

"That's supposed to make me feel better?"

"I honestly don't care if it does or not. It's shelter."

"You're right. I'm sorry."

Now Ben felt lousy. She obviously hadn't meant anything snarky by what she'd said. She was only scared, just as him. "It's okay. Let's just get there."

The house sat high on a small hill, a wrought-iron fence bordered the property's boundary and patches of woods surrounded all of it. Hopefully the gate was open. If not, Ben would use his shotgun to blast the lock apart. As they neared the driveway, he began to make out the tiny triangles atop the fence with their flesh-ripping tips.

Climbing over the fence was out. Just a simple slip would send one of those points stabbing into his ass.

Ben felt squirmy heat in his rectum from the thought.

No matter what, I'm not climbing that damn fence.

There would be no need. The gate was wide open. A Halloween-designed welcome sign was staked at the mouth of the driveway. *Trick-r-treaters are welcome here!* The message was painted on a small block with smeared black cats climbing around the edges.

Ben's feet left the asphalt and came down on gravel. The corrugated driveway made scraping sounds under his boots. More than once his boots threatened to slip out from under him and bring him down.

Trees were on either side of them as they made their way up the driveway. Finally, they began to spread out, dipping farther away from the driveway until opening on the front yard. Ben skidded to a stop where the grass began.

"What is this?" he asked.

Jackie stopped beside him, panting. Bending over, she put her hands on her knees. "I don't know. Looks like he's decorated for the holiday."

More than just decorated. Looks like he's throwing a party.

A decent bonfire burned in the center, and, around the fire, games had been set up. Ben saw a wooden tub filled to the brim with water. Apples bobbed on top of the glassy black surface. Across from that was a hay bale, a poster of a cartoon donkey tacked to the front. A feathery tale dangled from the donkey's rear. A paper skeleton was tacked to another bale of hay. Leading from the skeleton's bony toes was a short path etched into the grass, a red line crossed over the dirt.

A starting line?

Sure looked like it. Ben wondered if it was the same game he'd played as a kid at Halloween parties. *Mr. Bones.* The object of the game was much like Pin the Tail on the Donkey. But with Mr. Bones, participants were separated into teams, blindfolded, and sent to reassemble poor Mr. Bones into a complete skeleton.

There was pumpkin ring toss game a few feet away from Mr. Bones. And another section of games were on the other side of the yard, but it was too dark over there to see what kind.

"Games," said Ben, putting to words what was in his head.

"I don't like this," said Jackie.

Neither did Ben. "Come on."

Ben avoided the game area, keeping to the dew-soaked browning grass on the left. He climbed the stone steps to the front porch and found another surprise. A table had been placed outside the door. A bright orange tablecloth was draped over, its tails grazing the wooden floor. Cakes, candy and caramel apples, popcorn balls, crispy rice treats, and a giant plastic cauldron of traditional Halloween candy covered the orange surface. Ben even spotted small cookies with Hershey kisses planted in the middle sitting on a tray at the far corner.

"I don't understand," said Jackie. "He's giving them treats…"

Ben nearly shouted *Ah-ha!* He stifled his response and kept his voice down. "Right. To avoid the trick…"

Jackie's lovely but bruised face wrinkled with a mixture of confusion and frustration. She shook her head. "Then that has to mean…"

"That he knew this would happen." Ben noticed a tear leak from Jackie's eye. "Knock on the door."

"I don't think we should."

"Go on. It'll be all right."

Jackie approached the door with apprehensive uncertainty. She picked at her fingernails with her thumbs, making soft clicking sounds. Glancing back at Ben, she paused at the door. He nodded, signaling it was okay to proceed.

A brass featureless face was mounted to the front of the door, a ring hanging from under it like a curled brass beard. Jackie gripped the hoop and knocked it against the brass plate. "For the record, I'm against this."

"Noted."

"I feel like we're walking into an ambush."

"I don't think it's quite like that."

While they waited, Ben scoped out the yard from where he stood. So far, there was no sign of the mob. They would be along shortly, though. There was no way they'd want to miss what Warner had prepared for them. Ben wondered how much effort and trouble Warner went through to do all this.

The clacking sound of Jackie banging the ring against brass pulled Ben's focus to the door. She turned around, holding out her arms as if not knowing what else to do.

"Take your son," said Ben.

Nodding, Jackie hurried over and grabbed the boy. Ben lowered his shoulder so he would slide off. Jackie caught him, cradling the kid like he was an infant.

Ben walked to the door and pounded his fist against it. "Warner? It's Ben Holly. Open the damn door!" Trying to see into the glass panes on either side of the door was futile. It looked as if the old bastard had blacked them out with either a tarp or blanket. "Russell Warner! It's *Sheriff* Ben Holly. Last chance. You've got to the count of three to open the door before I blow it off its hinges."

Ben glanced at Jackie. She wrinkled her nose, baring her teeth.

"One!" Ben waited. He heard no movements from inside. Nothing that sounded like the popping a house makes when someone comes to the door. "Two!"

"Won't the gunshot bring them here?" asked Jackie, her voice thin and high.

"They're already coming, which is why we need to be on the other side of the door." Groaning, he raised the gun, barrel pointing at the door. "Three…"

His finger tickled the trigger, slightly applying pressure. He paused when heard the clacking of the locks rolling back into the door. Stepping in front of Jackie, Ben kept the gun aimed at the door, holding his breath.

The door cracked open. Two eyes appeared in the tightly allotted gap. Ben recognized the sagging lids and puffy half-moons underneath to be Warner's.

"Took you long enough," said Ben. "I was about to blow a hole in the door."

"You shouldn't have come here."

"I guess you weren't expecting us, judging by all the goodies you've left out."

The door opened some more, revealing Warner behind it. He was dressed in pajamas, a silky robe tied taut on top. Instead of shoes, he wore fuzzy slippers. Warner glanced past Ben, then focused his eyes on him, frowning. "What are you doing here?"

"Looking for answers."

"I don't have them."

"You obviously know more than me."

Hoots reverberated in the distance. Not quite here yet, the tootles announced the spook parade was getting closer.

Warner let out an exasperated sigh. "You might as well come in."

"Thanks for the invite."

Stepping away from the doorway, Warner gave them room to enter. Ben went in first with Jackie close to his heels.

At the sight of her, Warner's eyes widened. "What the hell is *she* doing here?"

"Watch your mouth. She's a pastor's wife."

"I know who she is." As if noticing the boy enfolded in her arms for the first time, he brought his hand to his mouth and bumped the door shut. When he put his hands on the locks, they were trembling. "She brought one of them into my *house?*"

"Calm down," said Ben.

"I see blood on his clothes. Look, it's right there."

"Warner, knock it off."

"I'm not going to let one of those wicked little shits into my home. Put him outside."

Jackie buried her head into her son's chest. In the quick instant he saw her face, Ben spotted tears smearing down her blood-stained face.

Enraged, he turned to Warner, gripped the old man by his flimsy robe, and slammed his back against the door.

"I'm going to throw *you* out if you don't shut up. Can't you see you're upsetting her?"

"I don't care, Ben. This is my house. I have the right to throw both of you out of here."

"My duty outranks your right."

"The kid has blood on his clothes. Didn't you see it?"

"It's *his* blood!" shrieked Jackie.

Her announcement shut both the men up.

Sniffling, Jackie shook her head to get fallen strands of hair out of her eyes. "And I caused it. He was about to strike a woman with a crowbar, and I just happened to show up in time to stop it. I had to bludgeon my own son with a damned rock. Thankfully I was there, or it would be Tabitha Stoner's blood on his clothes. I was chased through the woods for hours by two of those…those…whatever they are…and now I'm here. Begging for your help. Please…"

Ben pressed his lips together, huffing through his nose. Turning to Warner, he saw that the panic had subsided and in his eyes were regret.

Warner nodded.

"Thank you," she said.

"Take him upstairs to the guest room. First door on your right at the top of the stairs. He can rest in the bed."

"I'll do it," said Ben.

"Thank you," she said. "Thank you, both."

"Don't thank me," said Warner. "You might have had better luck out there."

Ben wanted to punch Warner in the gut for such a comment, but instead he let it go and took the boy from Jackie's arms. When the kid was cradled in the bends of his arms, Jackie let hers drop and sighed.

"I'll be up there with him in a minute," she said.

"Take your time. I'll be right back down."

Ben hurried up the stairs. Without the hallway light on, finding the room was still easy. The bed was old and big with hideous fuzzy green blankets and matching pillowcases, feebly lit by a single fat candle on the dresser at the front of the room. Ben's skin started to itch just seeing the hairy fabric. Using one hand, he pulled the blankets down. The mattress cover had probably once been white but was now yellowed with time.

He laid the boy on his back, tucking his legs under the blankets, and pulled them up to his chin. Ben stood there a moment, staring down at the kid. He looked so...normal. Not at all like the crowbar-wielding maniac Jackie stumbled upon. All of them probably looked like this underneath the costumes.

Then he remembered the hollowed gaze of Annette's eyes and realized how untrue his last thought was.

Leaving the room, he left the candle burning, but shut the door.

(11)

Warner poured hot tea into a tiny cup with shaky hands, spilling some in the saucer plate. He made no effort to wipe up the small mess, so Ben decided not to say anything about it.

"Thanks," said Ben.

Warner nodded once, poured another cup, and sat the vessel on the platter he'd placed on the coffee table. He lifted the saucer, cup on top, and carried it over to the bright yellow padded chair Jackie was sitting in. The upholstery nearly matched the color of her hair. "It'll warm those cold bones," he said, offering her the cup. It made soft rattling sounds in Warner's grip.

"That sounds nice," said Jackie, taking the saucer.

Warner shuffled to the fireplace, grabbed the poker, and stabbed the glowing embers. The punching motions stoked flames to rise around the burnt logs. Quickly, he added two more, and the fire hungrily swarmed over the fresh wood. Right away, Ben could feel heat spreading through the room.

The atmosphere was almost cozy. *False security.* Still felt nice, though. Made it almost possible to forget about the evil outside.

"I feel like I should be doing something," said Ben.

"There's nothing for you to do. You gave a valiant effort. You should be proud."

"I lost every one of my deputies, Warner. I'm far from *proud.*"

"It was a battle you couldn't win, but I'm sure you definitely put a damper in their cause."

"Their cause?" asked Jackie. "What is their cause?"

"Destruction. Nothing more, nothing less. Tricks. Pranks."

Jackie's cup started to clink again, and this time it was her hand trembling.

"I think you should tell us what you know," said Ben.

"Drink your tea. And please hurry, we don't have much time."

"Then maybe we should skip teatime and get down to business."

"If that's what you want."

"It is."

Jackie frowned, leaned forward. She set the saucer on the coffee table, sliding it away from her. "I'm done."

Ben added his cup next to hers.

Warner looked at the cups, nodding. "Well then. Follow me." His slouched stride carried him to a set of closed double doors, his slippers scuffling across the old carpet. "Step into my parlor, said the spider to the fly." He put a hand on each of the two knobs and flung the doors back. They slid into the walls on their rollers. Then he stepped into the unlit room, his pale skin looking as if it was being eaten by the darkness.

"Should we follow him?" Jackie asked.

Ben was hesitant. They could be walking into a trap.

No...this is Warner. Besides, they're all out there.

But Ben was acutely aware of how little he truly knew this guy. He grabbed the shotgun from the floor at his feet. Feeling the cold steal reaffirmed his courage. "We'll be okay."

Jackie didn't seem convinced, but still rose when he did. Keeping close to his side, she walked with him to the room. They paused at the doorway.

"Warner?"

"Hang on," he said. A moment later a match was struck. The small flame threw an orange mask over Warner's face. "Power's been out for a couple hours now." He lowered the match, and his face was black once again. Ben followed the guttering flame down to a lantern. The match ignited the wick. Warner adjusted the dial, slathering the room in a murky, piss-colored smolder.

And dimly illuminating a roomful of bookcases, each shelf packed full of books. More books were stacked in front of the rows stocked like short chimneys. A table was located in the room's center and on top were even more books. These were very old, with dehydrated leather spines, crinkled and creased with little fissures running from top to bottom. The title was stamped in gold, faded and hard to interpret.

"What room is this?" asked Ben.

"My study."

Ben looked around. On the left side of the room were file boxes with lids and small wooden crates, towers of them that hid the wall. He couldn't tell what was inside each compartment, but whatever the contents were spilled over the rim.

"It's everything I've been able to compile over the years on Prank Night," said Warner, settling the wondering thoughts in Ben's head.

Ben scanned the room again, taking in all the material at Warner's disposal. "You've read all of this?"

"Yes. Most of it multiple times."

"So, you know how to stop it then?"

Warner laughed in a self-aggrandizing way. "There is no stopping once it's started. Like an illness, it just has to…run its course."

"Bullshit," said Ben. He cringed inside when he remembered Jackie was in the room. "You were stopped."

"I…what?"

"Cobblestone told me about the Halloween of forty-eight. You and a few of your buddies celebrated Prank Night yourselves."

"Ah, that. Yes. Well, that's hardly similar, is it?"

"Seven people were murdered."

"I had nothing to do with any killing."

"But you were there."

"We were all there. Every kid in town, just like tonight. We rallied together, planned it out all summer long."

"Why?"

"That's what I've been trying to understand for almost seventy years. I was just a tyke then, didn't know much other than eating and shitting." Warner stepped over to some hanging curtains, lifting one of the edges to peer through. "Something just took us over."

"What do you mean by that?"

"None of us had any idea why we were doing it, and we didn't care. It started off as tricks. A few of us getting together on Halloween Eve and running all over the town, painting funny faces on the sides of barns, taking wheels off wagons, and stacking them up in the fields, throwing some jack-o'-lanterns at houses, some eggs. Then rocks. Then bricks. But we always got really rambunctious on Halloween, though. Saved the best pranks for that night." Warner closed his eyes. "Forty-seven was my first year participating, but I'd heard about the other years prior. The year we got Halloween banned, we started three nights before Halloween."

"And you have no idea why you did these things?"

"For the hell of it…at first." Warner held out his hand with a shrug. "We were kids, Ben. Back then, we worked our asses off on the farms, and we just needed to blow off some steam."

"By vandalizing?"

"It wasn't vandalizing to us, it was tricks. *Pranks.* It was the one time of the year we could put on a costume, become something else, and not follow the rules. You get it?"

Ben did, and he used to raise a little hell himself when he was a kid. Not to the extent Warner and his pals did, though. "I understand what you're saying. But how did it escalate to murder?"

"Things just got out of hand. In forty-seven we accidentally set fire to half the town. The next morning, we realized it had gone too far, but while we were doing it—we had no comprehension of what was right, or wrong. It was after that when they took it all away from us."

"When they banned Halloween."

"Right. I don't know what happened then, we were angry. They took our Prank Night and didn't let us have our fun. So...,"

"So you lashed out."

"Yes."

"You said you weren't involved in the murders."

"I wasn't. But I knew about them. I told the authorities all I knew. Spent some time in a loony bin, you know. But they let me out in a couple months. I was cured of Prank Night fever. Until the end of the summer in forty-nine."

"And those old feelings came calling again."

"Exactly. All of us could feel the need to for some tomfoolery deep inside us. And our plans were to make it the biggest Prank Night yet. Something large scale."

"Like tonight?"

Warner shrugged. "Not like this."

"So what happened?"

"Mayor Cobblestone's daddy saved the day. He started the carnival. You know how some towns celebrate the Fourth of July with a parade, a carnival, and activities for the kids? Cobblestone did that with Halloween. And he did it for us, giving us plenty of games and activities to distract us."

"Obviously, it worked."

Warner nodded. "It worked well. Each year was better than the one before it. Pumpkin carving contests, costume contests, trick-or-treating for three days. It was such a fun time." He put his hands in his pockets. They made bulging shapes through the silky fabric below his hips. "Oh, how I miss it."

"So why did the mayor cancel the carnival this year?"

"Said it was budget cuts. Said we couldn't afford it."

"Then he sold the factory. It's being moved out of state."

"That's true?"

Ben nodded. "Afraid so."

"I'd heard the rumors but had hoped it was just people being paranoid." Warner sighed. "Dumb bastard."

"That *dumb bastard's* dead."

Warner's head jerked toward Ben. "Is that a fact?"

"Killed in front of me."

"He wanted to get as far away from this night as possible."

Ben recalled the story Cobblestone had told him. How his father's mind was frozen in that night back in forty-eight. He could understand why Cobblestone would feel that way.

"And now without the carnival and with the factory being taken away, it's back."

"So, you think tonight was because a carnival was canceled?"

"I think it's a great theory as any." Warner waved his hand around. "But not entirely accurate. I've read all I could get my hands on about Halloween. We aren't the only town to ever suffer from Prank Night. It's worldwide, spread across cultures for centuries under different names. Doesn't matter what it's called, the theme is the same."

"And that is?"

"The children rising against the parents."

Ben's cheek tickled. He rubbed it with his hand.

Warner continued, "And once it's given life, it needs to feed."

"What needs to feed?"

"Prank Night."

Ben shook his head. "You're saying Prank Night is…is a force?"

"An entity of its own, yes. And back in forty-eight we gave it the life it needed, spoiled it to want nothing else. And all these years since, it's been neglected, ignored, and in most cases, forgotten."

"Starved," said Jackie, her voice a throaty croak.

Warner nodded. "Now that the carnival wasn't here to distract the kids of its influence, it took them over. And like the lady said, it's starving."

Ben held up his hand. "I see where you're going with this. Just like someone who hasn't eaten in days, the first thing they do when they find food is binge. Eating whatever they can get their hands on."

Smiling, Warner held out his hands. "Fits, doesn't it?"

Ben wanted to tell Warner he was crazy for even considering a fraction of this lunacy. He couldn't. Deep down, he agreed. The kids couldn't be addled, so they were tricked into feeding Prank Night's hunger.

In a way, they're the ones who've been pranked.

And Ben said so.

Warner's lips curled. "I never thought of it like that. You may have a point. What better prank to a child than to trick them into killing their parents?"

Jackie closed her eyes, sniffled. Her lips trembled.

"Enough of these kids *killing* business," said Ben. He pointed at Jackie. "It's upsetting her."

"I'm sure it's been *upsetting* to all the parents."

Ben looked to the window. His eyes seemed to see beyond the heavy curtains, to what Warner had organized outside. Noticing Ben's gaze, Warner approached him. He stood next to Ben.

Ben turned. "So, you set up the games for them in hopes it would keep them busy long enough to save your life."

"Can't blame a guy for trying."

"Why didn't you let anyone know? This morning at Cali Fortner's house, you acted as if you knew this would happen, but you kept it to yourself."

"Yes, I had an idea this morning, so I rushed back here with her body and instead of getting started on the autopsy, I went to my books." He pointed at the table, the decrepit book sitting on top. "By the time I had put together what I've already told you, it was too late. The phone lines were down, cell phones weren't working, the power was out. And I wasn't about to go out there, especially if it was as bad as I imagined it would be."

Ben felt his hand ball into a fist, but he kept it by his side. There was nothing to benefit from punching the old fool, other than making Ben feel better for a few seconds. Then he'd have to apologize to both Warner and Jackie. And Warner might throw them out. With what was on its way, Ben did *not* want to be out there with only a shotgun and a few extra rounds in his pockets to defend himself, a woman, and unconscious child.

"You left us all to die," said Ben. "That's what you did."

Warner closed his eyes. "Who would have believed me? Even now you're battling with skepticism. I was scared, Ben. Still am."

Warner was right. If Ben would allow it, he could believe everything Warner had told him. "We're all scared."

"Does this still work?"

Warner and Ben turned to find Jackie standing beside a desk buried under a muddle of papers. She grabbed a rectangular object, holding it up by a handle.

It was a radio.

CHAPTER 20

(1)

The radio was an old model, like something from the eighties: small body, but bulky and outrageous in its design. Warner assured the batteries were fine. If not, there was a hand crank on the side that felt too small and thin for Ben's fingers to reel. *Might break the damn thing off.* And that wouldn't help them at all.

Warner, Jackie, and Ben sat in a circle on the floor around the radio. Warner started twisting the dials.

"What are you looking for?" asked Ben.

"Channel Nine broadcasts on the A.M. frequency. Trying to find it."

The only sound Ben could hear were the soft clicks of Warner messing with the controls. Ben would have thought the portable device was shut off had it not been for the tiny orange dot of light on the front. A hiss of static appeared, startling Ben. His heart lurched and he felt a hollow drop in his gun. The static crackled and faded, followed by a ghostly fermata bleep. Warner continued to twist, a line furrowing the center of his forehead as he concentrated.

"*...Autumn Creek...*"

Static.

"There!" snapped Jackie.

"Heard it," said Warner.

And so had Ben, a crackly muffled voice. Female. "Can you find it again?"

Frowning, Warner extended the antenna at an angle while proficiently rolling the dial with the other. After some careful precision, the voice returned.

"We are still awaiting word from Captain Bill Kurtzman of the state police to either confirm or deny a terrorist attack on the quiet town of Autumn Creek, a community known for its farming and traditional Halloween Festival since nineteen forty-nine."

"Not this year," said Warner, coldly.

"Here's what we know, so far. Sherry Peoples was on the phone with her boyfriend, Darryl Tucker, who drives a truck for Goodman's Auto out of Cleveland. Her report states that she was talking with Mr. Tucker as he neared the Autumn Creek town line when the call was suddenly dropped. After trying to reach him for over an hour, she phoned the local police to see if she could find out if there were any accidents near or in Autumn Creek. Worried that her boyfriend might have been hurt or in danger, she pleaded with the dispatcher to contact Autumn Creek Police—Oh! Here comes Captain Kurtzman right now!"

Ben sighed. If only he'd listened to Duggins and Marge's pleads. If he had called Bill hours ago, this might have been avoided.

No. It was already in motion by then.

Some of it might have been prevented. Lives might have been saved. Ben felt sick thinking that he was responsible for this. He looked at Jackie. Her swollen red eyes, the welt on her forehead and bruises like tiny purple islands around the distended wound, made him shrivel inside. Maybe her son could have been stopped before he'd gone too far.

"Quickly," said Captain Kurtzman.

Ben recognized the gruffly man's voice even through the static and bad signal. They'd never gotten along. Probably because Kurtzman reminded Ben too much of his father. Strict and stern, no nonsense and so standoffish that Ben tried to avoid the retired drill sergeant no matter what.

Even tonight.

"*Thank you so much for taking a moment out of the chaos you must be wrapped up in to talk with us.*"

"*I have very little time, so make it quick.*"

Ben snorted. Same old Kurtzman.

"*Yes, sir. We just want any kind of update you can share with us on the current situation in Autumn Creek.*"

"*The current situation is still unknown at the moment, but from what we can tell so far, the town is under siege. We have a survivor in our protection, and the story he's sharing with us is unbelievable. Scary. Something you'd expect to find in a horror movie or read about it in a bad book. But, so far, everything we've gathered only supports his claims and that makes it terrifying and very real.*"

"*Can you tell us who the survivor is?*"

"*He's the local pastor, but I will not reveal his name.*"

Jackie gasped. "Allen!"

"Good news for you, dear," said Warner.

"I knew he'd make it. I *knew* he'd save us."

Ben smiled. Maybe Jackie would be all right after all. He hoped she could reunite with her husband and that things weren't already too far gone for them to mend with Joey. Maybe he was like Warner. He'd participated but hadn't actually killed anyone.

For Jackie's sake, he hoped it to be true.

"*Are there any details you can share of the story he's told you?*"

"*I will share what little we've confirmed. As I've stated, the town is under siege. Multiple attacks ranging in severity. Destruction and demolition, even murder. The cell phone tower has been damaged. We were unable to get any kind of cell reception in there. And after investigation, we discovered obvious tampering of the tower.*"

"*What kind of tampering?*"

"*It was sabotaged. How, I do not know at the moment.*"

"No wonder my phone stopped working," muttered Jackie.

Ben nodded, though she wasn't looking at him to have seen it.

"*So that confirms why Sherry Peoples was unable to reach her boyfriend,*" the reporter pointlessly stated.

"*Correct. We have discovered multiple bodies in the town put in morbid displays. Whoever did this wanted them to be seen, kind of like an artist proud of his work.*"

"*Is it true barricades prevented access into the town?*"

"*Yes. At each access point of the town barricades were set up and guarded. That was where we found the pastor. At a barricade on the west side. He was in the middle of a struggle with a trio of the offenders. He'd managed to kill one of them in self-defense.*"

"Oh, Allen…" Jackie cupped a hand over her mouth. Fresh tears made her eyes shimmer in the dim lantern light.

"*Two of my officers arrived on the scene just as he was about to be eliminated by the two remaining attackers. My men shot and killed them both before more harm was done to the pastor.*"

"*Thank goodness for that.*"

"*Yes, indeed.*"

"*Any word on who the attackers are?*"

"*These three have already been identified, but information is being withheld due to their age and pending investigation.*"

"*Age? They're minors?*"

"*Yes. So far, all of the assailants have been eighteen or under.*"

"*Dear God…*" She cleared her throat. "*My apologies for my reaction. Minors?*"

"*Yes. That is all I will divulge about that for now. A press conference will be held once the intense situation has been resolved.*"

Resolved.

My ass, thought Ben.

"*Is there anything else you can tell us?*"

"*Yes. Steer clear of Autumn Creek at all cost. We have cordoned the entire area and may soon declare martial law. No one can get in and no one can get out. To the surrounding towns I must ask that if you see anyone strange, anyone who doesn't belong lurking about or trespassing around your property, call the local authorities right away. Do not attempt to apprehend them yourself. They are heavily armed and very—I repeat—very dangerous."*

"Are there any other survivors that you've encountered so far?"

"None."

There was a pregnant pause as if the female reporter were digesting the bluntness of Kurtzman's answer.

"I also want to add," began Kurtzman. *"To the survivors of Autumn Creek, if you can hear my voice, please, stay where you are. Remain indoors, avoid leaving unless absolutely necessary. Board yourselves up inside your homes. We will find you. We're coming."*

Warner shut off the radio.

"Hey," said Ben. "Cut that back on."

Warner held his finger in front of his mouth, making a shushing gesture without the sound. Ben listened. At first, he heard nothing but the rapid drum of his heartbeat in his ears. After a few dragging moments, he began to decipher laughter.

Child's laughter.

"They're outside," whispered Warner.

"Look at them," said Jackie. "They're acting like kids."

"They are kids," said Warner.

"You know what I mean."

Jackie, on her knees in front of the bay window in Warner's living room, peeked through the slit in the curtains. The yard was crowded with costumed kids partaking in all the games and treats Warner had set out for them. It looked like any ordinary Halloween party, kids having a good time. Hearing so much laughter was strange coming from kids with blood soaking their cheaply made costumes.

"They're all getting along," she said. "As if they're all the same age, you know?"

Warner nodded. "Yes. They are one force for now, a pack. A family."

Chills prickled her aching scalp.

Ben entered the room, the shotgun in his right hand by his leg. "What are they doing?"

"Just...playing," said Jackie.

The disbelief on Ben's face mimicked Jackie's own as he crossed the room and stood beside Warner so he could peer out. She turned back to the window and observed a group of teenagers and tweens taking turns bobbing for apples. Her eyes roamed the yard. She spotted a pack of younger kids chasing each other through the gathering, stuffing their giggling mouths with popcorn balls and pastries.

Masks came off. Innocent albeit exhausted faces were exposed underneath. Jackie recognized quite a few of them from Kid's Club at church. Many of them she taught every Sunday morning the fundamentals of a Christian lifestyle.

How could they do it? How could they hurt so many?

She'd never understand. What Warner had said made sense only if she was willing to push all rationality aside. And she wasn't prepared to do that. There was *not* an invisible Prank Night force prowling the town like a fog, influencing the kids to rise and kill. No, it was deeper than that.

Evil.

But she wouldn't be able to convince anyone that the kids outside, having such a good time, had done anything wrong. Other than the blood stains on their clothes and hands, nothing about them seemed sinister. The herd had swarmed the yard with an excited eagerness, like kids finding presents under the tree on Christmas morning, filling the night of mayhem with sweet jubilant laughter.

Jackie started to cry. Tears rolled down her cheeks, clinging to her jawline a moment before dropping to the floor with soft taps. She used her arm to wipe her eyes.

"It's working," declared Warner.

"You can't be so sure," said Ben. "Just because they're celebrating now doesn't mean they won't try to kill us later."

"That's why we have to keep the party going," said Warner. "Together, we can host their celebration until the sun comes up in a few hours, or until the cavalry arrives. If we keep things going, they'll have no choice but to enjoy the merriments."

"How are you going to do that, Warner? You have no power. We can't keep baking them sweet little cakes without electricity."

"I can. My stove runs on gas."

Ben seemed to consider it a moment longer.

But Jackie was already convinced. She might not agree with Warner's reasoning for why it had happened, but she couldn't dispute his results. The kids actually appeared to be normal once again. Whatever had possessed them was gone. "I'm going to get Joey."

Warner smiled. "Yes. The ultimate test."

Ben held his hand out. "No. We have no way of knowing what will happen."

But Jackie was already standing. The tendons in her knees pulled taut as she stretched her legs. She was sore all over, and her joints ached as if she was running a high fever. For all she knew, she might be. "If it's working on them, I have to take Joey out there so it can work on him, too."

Ben held her stare. A stressful frown pinched his face as if he'd licked a lemon. "I don't think it's a good idea. Doesn't it bother anyone else that this just seems too easy?"

It bothered Jackie more than she was willing to admit to either of them. She kept it to herself, saying nothing.

Warner turned around. "Ben. The only way we'll know for sure is to try it. As of now, it appears to be working."

"Ever heard of a ruse?"

"Yes. I'm well aware that they may just be putting us on. But they haven't come after us yet, and they probably won't as long as they have something keeping them busy."

"They might not even know we're in here," said Jackie, hopeful.

Warner shook his head. "They know. Most likely we're all that's left. And I'm certain they know that as well."

Ben held out his hand. "Which is even more reason *not* to go out there. They might not be in a hurry to come after us because they know we don't stand much of a threat to them."

Jackie hadn't considered that. "You're saying they might just be taking a break?"

"Wiping out a whole town in less than a day can really wear somebody out, you know. Just wait until the state police shows up."

"We don't know how long it'll take them to get here." Her voice went thick and whiny. Another sobbing fit threatened to strike. She fought it back. "I have to try, Ben. He's my son."

Ben lowered his head, sighed. He finally realized all his arguments were invalid right now. She wouldn't be persuaded otherwise.

Warner put his hand on Ben's shoulder. "She'll have us for backup if she needs it."

"What kind of backup can we honestly provide?"

Warner had no response to that. He only squeezed Ben's shoulder, then lowered his arm. He returned to the window, slightly raising the curtain so he could look out.

Ben shrugged. "I can't stop you."

"Thank you."

She started for the stairs.

Behind her, she heard Ben mutter under his breath, "Don't thank me."

Ignoring his remark, she climbed. Slowly. Each step groaned and creaked under her feet. She reached the top.

It felt colder up here since the fireplace's heat couldn't quite reach this far. Hugging herself, she rubbed the bare patches on her arms. They felt bumpy and hard from goose flesh. She wasn't sure if it was the cold causing them, or if somewhere inside she feared she was making a mistake.

Probably a little of both.

What if she was wrong about Joey? What if she took him out there and he turned on her?

He won't. This will work. It worked on the others.

Still, she wasn't as confident up here as she had been downstairs.

Jackie approached the door. It was closed. She curled her fingers around the knob. The small iron ball was cold and slick in her grip. It felt flimsy and loose, as if it might break if she turned it. Lowering her head, she took deep, calming breaths. They didn't help. Her heart pounded, making her throat cluck with each beat.

Here goes.

She twisted the knob.

The door was thin and started to open without her putting pressure to it. She gave it a gentle shove, opening it wide. Inside, the room was dark, only a dim sheen of light coming from a candle on the dresser at the head of the room. It threw a murky spill onto the bed. She could see the lump of Joey's body under the blankets.

That was nice of Sheriff Holly to cover him up.

The silence in the room was heavy on her ears. All she could hear were the faint chortles of the kids outside. Sounded as if they were down the street, not in the front yard. Blocking out the merriment, she slowly approached the bed.

Pressure on her throat froze her. Fingers were squeezing.

No!

Then she realized it was her own hand, fearfully gripping. Taking her wrist, she forced her arm down by her side. Why was she so scared? If she honestly thought there was any risk of danger, she shouldn't be doing this at all. She'd proved her point downstairs. So why was she so hesitant now?

Jackie had no clue. But the sudden urge to turn around and leave flowed through her. She had to force her legs to carry her to the bed. Had to demand her knees to fold so she could crouch beside it. Reaching out to the Joey-sized lump in the bed took every nuance of gallantry that she had.

Her fingers bent over the top of the blanket. It shook slightly. She thought it might be Joey stirring in his sleep, but she realized it was her own jitters causing the coverlet to quiver.

Knock it off. If you're this worried, don't do it.

Jackie took another deep breath, held it in a moment, and released. Her chest tingled as the heavy breath was expelled through her nose.

She pulled the blanket down.

And saw the pillow where she'd expected her son's body to be.

"Oh…no…"

A soft bump behind her, then a prolonged creaky moan of the door closing. It bumped with a squeaky click when it shut.

Ben was right.

"Joey?" she whispered. Her voice unable to register.

Though she hadn't turned around yet, she knew Joey was standing at the door. He must have been behind it, waiting for her to come. He *knew* she would. Like a patient predator, he'd waited for the prey to enter his den.

"It's Mommy…" Her voice was still gone, abandoning her when she needed it the most.

The hiss of heavy breaths carried across the room.

Cautiously, Jackie turned her body to see behind her. Joey's dark shape looked slightly paler than the solid darkness behind him. Something twinkled down by his thigh. *A knife.* Even from this distance in such shadows, she recognized it as the chef's knife from Tabitha's, held upside down with the sharp end facing up. He must have had it hidden on him this whole time.

With each heavy exhale, Joey's slim shoulders rose and dropped. He breathed like a pervert peeping through the window of the girl's locker room.

"Baby?" she strained to say.

The knife rose by Joey's face. The candlelight gleamed off its splotchy surface.

"No…"

Joey ran, snarling. His mouth wide, lips curled back, and teeth flashing. When he slammed against her, knocking her into the bed, Jackie found her voice.

CHAPTER 21

(1)

A scream ripped through the house. Ben lowered his head, bunching his shoulders as if an explosion had been detonated close by. He spun around, raising the gun to his shoulder.

Jackie!

"Shit," he gasped.

Warner stepped away from the window. Walking backward, he bumped against the chair closest to the fireplace and dropped into it. His legs dangled over the chair's arm. "Oh no…"

"Jackie's in trouble."

"And they heard her scream. They started putting their masks back on."

"What?"

Warner turned to Ben. His face was so pale now he looked like a sculpture of hardened glue. "They're coming after us."

"Stay here. I'll be right back."

"Where are you going?"

"To check on Jackie." He ran for the stairs.

"Don't go. It's too late for her."

"If that's true, then we still have one of them loose in the house."

Warner lowered his head. "I'm sorry, Ben. I shouldn't have…,"

"Save it for later. If there is a later."

Ben hurried up the stairs, taking two at a time until he reached the top. Turning right, he saw the closed door. Not bothering with being discreet, he raised his leg and kicked. His foot hit close to the doorknob. Wood cracked, splintering the door frame and throwing the door wide.

His eyes searched the murky darkness a moment before finding a struggle of shapes on the floor. A knife was in the air, blade down, suspended as if stuck in the dark. His eyes focused and he could make out the boy straddling an even darker shape.

Jackie.

Ben ran into the room.

The boy's mouth was wide as he snarled and growled. Foamy spit bubbled in the corners of his mouth. Strings of thick drool stretched down from his chin. Tempted to fire at the kid's head, he thought better of it and turned the gun around, so the wooden stock faced out. He slammed it against the back of Joey's head. The boy slumped sideways, falling against the bed. Jackie squirmed out from under him. Once she was free, Ben helped her up.

"Are you all right?" he asked.

Crying, Jackie fell against him. "He didn't stab me…"

But you're not all right. How could you be?

"We have to get downstairs," he said.

He felt her head nod against his chest.

Then something banged against the house. Hard. Jackie let out a squeal.

"Let's go."

"Please," she said, stepping away. "Let me get Joey."

Ben wanted to tell her to leave him, but he knew she would stay behind with the kid if he protested her bringing him along. "No. I'll get him. You take this." He handed her the shotgun. She held it before her like a dead snake, grimacing. "You *do* know how to shoot, don't you?"

"Of course. I'm not a damsel."

"My apologies." He leaned over and scooped up the limp kid.

"It's just been a while since I've had a gun in my hand."

"Just like riding a bike. Are you sure you can handle it?"

Jackie brought the gun around in a smooth motion of flashing silver. "I've missed it."

Ben felt a smile tug at his mouth. "Good. I'm happy to hear you're not gun-shy. Let's get downstairs."

(11)

Warner had both chairs pushed against the front door when Ben and Jackie came back. He saw the kid in Ben's arms and shook his head. Ben understood his apprehensions because he felt them too.

The laughter had gone away, replaced by growls and shouts as blunt objects pounded the door.

"I have nothing to block the window," informed Warner. "I'm sure they'll try that way soon."

"We have to get out of here."

Warner nodded. "Already thought of that. I have a plan B."

"And that is?"

"My garage is in back. Take the tunnel that connects it to the house and get the hell out of here."

The tunnel.

Ben had forgotten all about it.

"However," added Warner, "it can only be accessed through the mortuary."

Jackie grimaced. "Is that how you…bring the bodies in?"

"Yes."

Nodding, Ben said, "Okay, let's go."

The window shattered. Jackie raised the shotgun, pointing it at the bodies hurling themselves in. They hit the floor, rolling, fighting to stand.

Warner held out his hand. "Don't shoot!"

Jackie's face scrunched up. "What?"

"You might trigger something!"

Ben smelled the rotten egg tang of gas. "Damn it, Warner! You were going to kill us all?"

"I was going to get the state police's attention! I'd planned for us to be in the tunnel by now."

An ax split the wood of the door, the gleaming wedge twisting before it was yanked back out.

A kid dressed in sheets with a paper bag mask stood up behind Warner. He held a saber in his small, gloved hands. More kids piled in through the window. They seemed to keep coming, swarming like ants after their hill has been knocked down. In a matter of moments, they'd assembled around Warner.

Ben stepped back, wanting to help Warner, but knowing it was suicide. The gas smell was growing stronger with each inhale of air. It brought tears to his eyes. In less than a minute it would reach the fireplace.

"Go!" screamed Warner. Then the saber ripped through his chest, blood sluicing the shiny blade in dark red.

The door imploded as more kids tore it down. Armed with axes and pickaxes, they rushed in.

Before he could tell Jackie to run, she was already rushing away from the invasion.

Ben doubted she knew which way to go, but he knew. He was familiar with the mortuary's location. He'd been down there many times with Warner to hear his proclamation on causes of death. "Take a left, go past the stairs to the rear hallway!"

Jackie did as instructed, bypassing the stairs. The darkness swallowed her. Ben followed her. The light vanished as if someone had just closed the door to a tomb. His night vision was awful right now.

But he could *hear* the rush of footfalls behind him.

Don't look back.

If he did, he'd fall. Already, his balance felt off, as if it kept shifting from side to side. The kid slowed him down, but he wasn't about to drop him. He owed this to Jackie. If anyone was going to make it out of here alive, he wanted it to be her. And Joey if he could arrange it.

"I'm at the wall!" shouted Jackie. "Can't find the door!" Her voice shrieked with panic.

"It's in the center! Keep searching." He was just steps away from her. Eyes adjusting, he could make out the pale shape of her bright hair.

"I can't find it!"

Ben was right on top of her. He could smell the sweet scent of her shampoo.

"Got it!" she yelled with wild glee.

A dim rectangle appeared in the blackness like a portal opening. Jackie rushed through. Ben hurried inside, kicking the door closed behind him. He turned around, threw her kid over his shoulder, and felt around for the sliding bolt. He found it and slid its metal tongue through the hoop.

The door shook in its frame. There was a whistle of metal cutting air, and the door bounced. Wood cracked.

Thank God for old sturdy doors.

It would hold for a few seconds before they tore it down.

"Keep going! Don't stop!"

He followed Jackie down the tightly cramped hallway. The darkness and pressing walls reminded him of being inside a funhouse. It was too hard to see anything, and the claustrophobia strangled his equilibrium, discombobulating him.

"Stairs!" cried Jackie.

"Can you see them okay?"

"Not really."

"Just make it work."

Ben stood behind her as she started down. He kept close to her. The boy's hands slapped his lower back as he cautiously descended. Jackie got ahead of him again, becoming a dimmer smudge as the shadows thickened.

The crash of the door being knocked open behind them reverberated off the walls.

"Shit!" he heard Jackie shout.

Even in their situation, Ben felt the urge to laugh at a pastor's wife cussing.

"Made it!" He heard her feet slapping concrete. A groan of a door. "We're here!"

"You sure?"

"Yes. It's freezing in there."

"Okay."

Ben could hear the frantic stampede of pursuit behind him. They were just above them, about to start down the stairs.

Expecting another step, his foot slapped flat on concrete. The sudden jolt nearly tripped him.

"Come on," Jackie barked.

"On my way."

Regaining his bearings, he ran forward. Jackie held the door open for him. Light seemed to seep out from the mortuary, giving him a hint of dull orange smolder to see by. Inside, he turned around to find a body rolling down the stairs. Its broken form came to an awkward halt at the bottom. His first thought was one of the kids had tripped and fallen, but just as he was about to laugh, he realized the body was too frail looking to be a kid's. He recognized the clothes as belonging to Warner.

Bastards.

They were teasing them.

Then he realized something else. The house hadn't exploded yet.

Jackie slammed the door, locking it. "Come on."

Confused, Ben turned away from the door. Jackie started to run, but realizing Ben wasn't doing the same, she stopped.

"What's wrong?" she asked.

"The house."

"Yeah?"

"It didn't blow up."

Jackie paused. Considering. "Maybe the gas…"

"They shut it off."

"How could they have known?"

"They just knew."

"But the gas we smelled—"

"—Filtered out when the window and door were broken."

The dark spaces of her eyes widened. "Then…"

"All of them are coming after us."

What bit of courage Jackie had recovered fled her. Ben watched as her posture sagged, shoulders dropping. Her head looked too heavy for her neck as it bopped.

Ben looked around. He saw the pale light was coming from a lantern hanging from the ceiling. Below the minimal spread of radiance was a metal table, and on the table was a body.

Cali Fortner's dissected body.

The jack-o'-lantern head, hollowed eyes and mouth, seemed to grin wickedly in the guttering glow. Supine on the table, the dark of the body bag held her like a sleeping bag. He shivered. The back of his neck felt like it was being squeezed with frozen hands.

"Don't look at it," said Jackie.

The door rocked behind them. Jackie screamed. Ben jumped back. Sounded like an army was outside from the multitude of growls and shouts. The door bowed inward as if pressure was building behind it. Any moment it would burst into a splintery shower.

Ben's eyes pulled away from Cali and scanned the room. He saw many flat surfaces throughout, all sleek and gleaming. Burners seemed to jump out at him. Below them were hoses that spiraled from the wall. A tiny flame from the pilot danced under the grates.

He knew what had to be done.

"Take Joey."

"What?"

"Give me the gun and take your son."

"I don't understand."

"We'll never make it."

"But the garage…"

"We might get to it, yes, but this door is all that separates us from them. And it's not going to hold."

As if to prove his point, the wood split. He felt the nick of a wood shard graze his cheek.

"What are you going to do?"

"I'm going to make sure that calling card to the state police is heard."

On his way to the stove, he stopped in front of Jackie and dumped Joey into her arms. Then he took the shotgun from her.

"Get out of here."

A hole broke through the door. Arms reached through, savagely pawing as if they might grab somebody.

Ben turned back to Jackie. She looked as if she wanted to argue, but she only nodded. Tears trickled down her cheeks. He left her standing there as he walked to the stove. Reaching under the burner's grate, he pinched the flame, extinguishing it. Then he crouched, finding the dial on the side of the hose. He began to turn it.

The hiss of gas increased. He kept twisting until the hose was fully open.

He glanced over his shoulder. "You're still here?"

"Your sacrifice will not go unnoticed…"

Ben held up his hand. "Say your prayers later. Right now, you need to run."

Nodding once, Jackie turned away and rushed for the door on the opposite side of the room. She opened it, stepped through, and looked back one more time. She smiled with disappointment before pulling the door closed.

Ben headed for the door Jackie had just exited through as the other one shattered behind him. He wanted them to come to him, to fill the room with as many as possible before he acted.

They flooded the small room in a blur of movement.

As they swarmed Ben, hands groping, sharp objects piercing his body, he pointed the barrel into the sky.

"Trick-or-treat..."

He fired.

The room ignited. A wave of fire engulfed everything inside.

(ⅲ)

Jackie was opening the door to the garage when the walls shook. The door at the rear of the hall exploded. Rolling gusts of fire soared through the tight space. In a dash, Jackie flung herself through the door, taking cover behind the wall to her left. Fire reached through the gap, flaming tongues wiggling as they tried to find something to lick.

The flames quickly diminished to thin conflagrations as its power was sucked back out.

Crying, Jackie leaned her head against the wall. She hugged Joey against her.

He did it. He actually did it.

Jackie dropped to her rump. Cold from the concrete floor leaked through her jeans. She looked down at Joey. He was out cold but frowning as if in deep thought. He looked older now, not at all like the kid she'd seen this morning wearing his Minecraft costume. Seemed like years ago now. Everything had changed in such a short span of time, and it would never be the same again.

A wet dot splatted on Joey's cheek. Then another. And another.

Tears from Jackie's eyes rained on her son as she bawled.

AFTERMATH

(1)

The helicopter's blades pounding the air increased in volume. Jackie hardly paid it any attention at first, but as the whopping intensified, she realized it was right outside and very close.

Sounds like it's landing.

Jackie opened her eyes. It wasn't as dark in here as it had been when she'd dozed off. The glare of early morning daylight trickled through the small line of windows on the garage door, pushing the darkness further into the room. A white van and black hearse were parked side by side just feet from her. Briefly, she wondered where the keys were.

She hadn't meant to fall asleep and was surprised she actually had. Her body had succumbed to exhaustion, but her mind still ran wild with frantic nightmares of her experience. She hadn't expected to wake up at all and felt relief flow through her knowing she'd made it through the night. Remembering that she'd only survived because of Ben's sacrifice transformed that relief into guilt. Why had she lived when so many had been brutally slaughtered? It wasn't fair. Didn't make sense.

Joey was a heavy burden in her lap, making it hard to straighten her legs. She looked down and saw his lids were still closed, though his eyes roamed behind them. They blinked open, fluttering against the light. He looked around, frowning at that initial confusion of consciousness in his unfamiliar surroundings. He looked at Jackie.

She held her breath, ready for him to attack.

"Mom?"

The breath gusted out of her. She laughed.

Wincing, Joey made a face as if something rancid had wiggled across his nose. "Jeez, Mom…your breath smells terrible!"

Tears streamed down her face in heavy torrents. "Joey!"

"Yuck…"

He started to sit up but groaned. "Oh…my head hurts, *really* bad. And my wrist." He looked as if he might cry. "What happened?"

"You don't remember?"

Joey pinched his eyes shut. He shook his head. "No. Where are we?"

"Don't worry about that right now. We have to get up."

"Okay…"

"Can you stand?"

"I think so…"

"All right, let's try."

She helped Joey sit up. Once he was upright, he groaned. He looked nauseous and very pale. Holding his head, he whimpered. "It really hurts, Mom."

I bet it does from all the hits it took.

Hopefully he wouldn't have permanent damage.

"We'll get you some medicine for it soon, honey."

"What's that noise?" asked Joey, talking louder so he could be heard over the *whop-whop-whop* of the helicopter.

"Let's go find out," she shouted back.

Pushing with her feet, she slid up the wall to stand. Tools dangled from pegboards attached to the walls. She could see wrenches trembling from the vibrations all around, could feel the tremors under her feet as if the foundation were shaking.

She figured it probably was.

"Let's go," she said, putting her arm around Joey's shoulders.

They started to walk.

"What am I wearing?" he asked, tugging at the dark garments covering him.

"I have no idea."

Beside the garage door was another smaller door with a latch. She unlocked the deadbolt and pulled down on the handle. The door popped open, hinges groaning as she pushed it wide.

"Come on," she said, guiding Joey outside.

The crisp air bit Jackie with artic teeth. Tensing against the harsh coldness, Jackie led Joey around the side of the garage. The sky was the color of lead, but sunlight was quickly burning it away to show a faded blue canvas underneath. Mist hovered across the grass in golden nets. Foggy fingers curled around the trees surrounding the yard.

They walked around the side of the house and were buffeted by cold lashes of wind. Jackie's hair flew back, her clothes pressing against her body so fiercely she wondered if they might rip right off. Looking down at Joey, she saw his short hair fluttering out of control around his head. The large knots from the many head hits were clearly visible along his skull. Jackie felt awful seeing their swollen juts.

Squinting, Joey looked up. "Do you see it?" There was excitement in his voice.

Jackie looked to the front yard. A black helicopter had landed where the party had taken place. Tables were overturned. Halloween decorations bounced across the brown grass.

"I see it," she said.

An orange paper streamer hopped along the grass, snagging on the arm of a dead body. It was one of the kids, a ghost. The ribbed paper clung to his bloody pale hand. She quickly looked away from the dead body, glanced over the parked police cars, to find several more slain kids around the porch. Their clothes were crispy and scorched, the skin on their hands blistered.

Her eyes locked on the front of the house. Now it was a cavernous ingress, ringed with charred-black boards. Plumes of smoke trailed out from the massive hole. She could see people moving around in there, bold yellow letters on their backs stated SWAT.

Movement to her left called her attention back to the helicopter. She saw an older man climbing out, dressed in full riot gear, except for the helmet. His hair was a closely cropped fuzz of gray. Two younger men identically outfitted hopped out behind him.

The older man noticed Jackie. He held his hand up to signal her to halt. She did as instructed. He started walking toward them.

"Mom…" said Joey, his voice changing with concern.

"It's okay, Joey. They're here to help."

"No, Mom."

Jackie looked down at her son. Tears rubbed paths through the smudges on his face. "I remember now."

"You what?"

"I remember everything. I remember what I did. I cut off…Miss Loflin's head…"

The strength left Jackie, buckling her legs. She dropped to her knees. And now she was a few inches shorter than Joey. She'd been hopeful before, thinking Joey had not killed anyone. She'd prayed he hadn't gone that far. But now she knew.

Sobbing, Jackie fell forward, catching herself with her hands. The dew was cold and wet on the brittle grass as it soaked between her fingers.

Joey's hands touched her shoulders. "I'm sorry, Mom. I couldn't stop myself…"

Jackie began to scream, pounding the ground with her fists, as the men who'd piled out of the helicopter ran to help her.

ABOUT THE AUTHOR

Kristopher Rufty lives in North Carolina with his three children and pets. He's written numerous books, including *Hell Departed*, *Anathema*, *Jagger*, *The Lurkers*, *The Skin Show*, *Pillowface*, and many more. When he's not writing, he's spending time with his kids, or obsessing over gardening and growing food.

His online presence has dwindled, but he can still be found on Facebook and Twitter.